# THE ROOT OF ALL EVIL

ALSO BY ROBERTO COSTANTINI

*The Deliverance of Evil*

# ROBERTO COSTANTINI

# THE ROOT
# OF ALL EVIL

Translated from the Italian by N. S. Thompson

Quercus

New York • London

# Quercus

New York • London

First published in the Italian language as *Alle radici del male*
by Marsilio Editori in Venice in 2012

Copyright © 2012 by Roberto Costantini
English translation copyright © 2014 by N. S. Thompson
First published in the United States by Quercus in 2015

ISBN 978-1-62365-881-6

Library of Congress Control Number: 2015954546

Distributed in the United States and Canada by
Hachette Book Group
1290 Avenue of the Americas
New York, NY 10104

Manufactured in the United States

10 9 8 7 6 5 4 3 2 1

www.quercus.com

This is a work of fiction, not a study in history. I make no claim to reconstructing the truth but simply imagining the possible.

As a result, the references to real persons, living or dead, and to actual events, as well as the description of several locations, particularly in Tripoli, have been modeled to serve the needs of that fiction. All other characters and situations connected with these references are entirely the product of literary invention.

For Wilma and Ulderico
and the free people of Libya

# TRIPOLI, AUGUST 31, 1969

## THE KILLER

*Italia was there, standing right in front of me. Her back was turned and she was looking out onto the sea, her feet only half a yard from the edge of the cliff. Half a yard that separated her life from mine. One step back or forward and everything would change.*

*I could feel the direction of her thoughts but couldn't alter them. And I wished with all my heart she could take that step forward herself, as if the moral responsibility alone could weigh less than being the material cause. But Italia wasn't that kind of person and I knew that very well. She would never do it on her own.*

*I don't know if she heard my footsteps or the beating of my heart as I came closer. I don't know if she had any idea whose hands pushed her over, but she never turned around. I don't know if she gave any thought to her favorite son, Mike, as she plunged toward the rocks below.*

*No cry came from her as she fell. And that silence changed my life.*

# TRIPOLI, AUGUST 15, 2011

## MICHELE BALISTRERI

*I've no idea if my mother thought about me as she fell toward those rocks. I hope there's no place where the dead can watch us and know everything about us. That way she could never know that while someone was pushing her over that cliff edge, I was far away in bed with her worst enemy, Marlene Hunt.*

*And that last time I was inside her, I've no idea if Laura Hunt hated me or pitied me. That's the difference between youth and age. Back then I preferred to think it was hate. Today I hope it was pity.*

*And as the pellet I fired went right through his cheek and tongue, I've no idea if Salim was aware he'd made the biggest mistake of his life when he cut the ear of his half brother Karim, because no one lays a finger on any member of the MANK organization.*

*And I've no idea if Farid remembered the promise the MANK made him all those years before, when he was thrown as live bait to the sharks, minus his penis.*

*Nor, as we faced each other on that last day of my former life, have I any idea if Ahmed asked himself which of us was the hero and which was the villain, which one was John Wayne and which was Scar, the Comanche chief.*

*If I look back now, forty years later, on the drifting boat of my life, everything disappears slowly from sight, but among the cloudy memories the one thing I can always see is La Moneta. My body survived the shipwreck and reached a shore of some kind. But my soul stayed there facing the rocks of that island, facing the coastal lights of Tripoli, which became more and more distant as I ran away from who I was.*

# SATURDAY, FEBRUARY 1, 1958

The screen door between the villa's living room and the veranda overlooking the large garden stands wide open. Although the air is warm, there are no mosquitoes in Tripoli in February.

From outside, the croaking of frogs breaks the silence of the African night.

All of us are in the living room for the finale of the Sanremo Music Festival. All three families: the Libyan, the American, and the Italian.

On the Marelli television set's black-and-white screen, Domenico Modugno is singing the festival's winning song, "Volare." I'm sitting on the three-seat sofa between the two most important women in my life. The one who gave birth to me and the one with whom I'll live. Life is very good, with everything before me. Along with the song, I'm flying up in the blue, singing:

*"That dream does not come back ever again"*

. . . .

*I'm on my feet, my tunic sticking to me because I'm sweating with fear. The soles of my naked feet are on a wooden surface, a table placed next to a cement wall. A yard below I can see the earth-and-mud floor. A beetle is climbing toward the table. My feet are free, my right arm as well, but my left wrist is held by one bracelet of a pair of handcuffs; the other bracelet is locked around a metal tube that runs vertically up the wall. The beetle is climbing up the tube again. There's a rope around my neck; I can feel the huge knot pressing against my throat. It's tight around me, but not enough to stop me from breathing. If I remain upright, that is. But if I try to kneel or sit down, the noose will strangle me. I'm trapped in here. There's nothing I can do, absolutely nothing. Except resist, not let myself bend at the knees and have the noose strangle me. I'm in his hands, and the life of others means nothing to him.*

. . . .

*The noose is at the end of a rope. I can touch the rope with my free hand, the right one, and follow it up with my fingers. I touch my head. It's bare, completely shaven. My hair, my beautiful black hair, is gone. I follow the rope with my eyes in the semidarkness. It goes up to the ceiling, passes over another metal tube, a large one that would easily take my weight. The rope goes over the tube and drops back down again. The single small window lets in only a sliver of light. I can't see where it leads, but I can manage to see the beetle that has reached the ceiling above me. Hours must have passed. Outside is the silence of the night; in the room, strange noises that I can't understand. I'm terrified. I think about the beetles and feel ill. My stomach and bladder want to burst. I can't hold out any longer—I have to go where I stand. When he comes back, he'll just laugh at me. Now I can hear some familiar sounds outside. A rooster crowing, a goat bleating. Dawn's pale light enters through the tiny window. I've been here on my feet, locked up, for twelve hours at least. I can't move. No food, no water, no sleep. My thighs are rigid. On the floor, my excrement, surrounded by beetles. The glimmer of dawn makes the outlines a little clearer. On the floor, at the foot of the table, the bastard has left a bottle of water. Temptation. Bend down, sweetheart, if you're thirsty. And hang yourself. More hours pass. Every so often, that bastard shows his face, a scornful grin on it. In the sky, the sun must be rising. Or perhaps setting. I have no idea anymore. Now there's a yellowish dust hanging in the air. The light from the tiny, dirty window streams through it. It reminds me of everything I want to have, which is my life. I can now feel the length of rope that rises from my neck, crosses over the large tube set into the ceiling then drops down again. I follow it until it comes to another very small shaven head and ends in a noose tight around another neck.*

*This neck belongs to a baby girl nearly ten months old. She weighs about twenty pounds. I weigh one hundred thirty, and she weighs twenty. If I try to bend down or sit on the table, the rope will stretch, the nooses tighten, and we'll both be strangled. The little mite's sound asleep; perhaps he put a sleeping pill in her bottle. The sounds I heard last night were those of my daughter. More hours pass. He's brought in a straw-bottomed chair and sits there opposite us, sharpening a stick with his knife. Every so often he gives my daughter and me a look of boredom. If I collapse onto the table, we'll die, my daughter and me. In his own wretched language, I ask him why. He doesn't even look at me. Now, I really feel the terror: my legs start trembling, the sweat turns cold as it runs down my spine, my urine trickles down my legs, my tears are falling and there's no stopping them. I simply have to stay awake. I stare at the strip of light under the roller shutter door, the few fractions of an inch that mark the difference between life and death. I mustn't give in. I only have to keep my eyes open. That's simple enough. I keep my eyes fixed on the light below the door, the few fractions of an inch between life and death. How many hours have passed? I no longer know; I can't tell what time it is anymore. It's over, my legs are about to give in, my eyes are about to close in sleep. But it's only now that his damnable calculation becomes clear. Only now that I see why my right hand is free. So that I can stretch it out toward the water on the table. If I make an effort, I can reach it; one hundred thirty pounds against twenty, I can do that. It's what the bastard's waiting for. That I'll sacrifice my daughter's life just to wet my lips. For him, it's entertainment. But I won't give in. My tongue's so swollen I can't breathe. If I stretch out my arm, I can reach it. I could drink that water. The urge is irresistible. I look at my daughter a last time, because after this I'll never be able to see her again. As my right arm stretches out toward that wonderful bottle, I know I'm already dead. I can feel the rope beginning to tighten around my neck. I dare not turn to look at my little one tied to the other end. I dare not think of her neck. My right hand is flat on the ground, crawling through the mud and the beetles toward the bottle. He gets up, having finished whittling a point at the end of the stick. A single thrust; the pain's excruciating. The point passes through my hand and pins it to the mud. As the knot tightens around my throat, he forces me to turn my head around. My little daughter has been raised eleven inches off the ground, the noose tight around her neck. She's wide awake now, her swollen tongue hanging out, her eyes looking at me in terror, her mouth formulating the word* Mamma *for the first time. And also for the last.*

# FRIDAY, MAY 25, 1962

We live in Sidi El Masri, just outside Tripoli, six miles from Piazza Castello at the city center. The Sidi El Masri road is a long boulevard flanked by eucalyptus, with no houses until the twin villas owned by our family.

The two villas built by my grandfather stand on one side of the boulevard, surrounded by a wall two yards high and accessed through a large wrought-iron gate leading onto the paved road. The gate is ornamented with the linked initials of my father's and mother's names, Salvatore and Italia, creating a symbol that looks strangely like the American dollar sign. My mother hates it, but my father likes it. It was his idea, and it's a reminder that a real family is always *united*.

Behind the villas there's a wicket gate in the surrounding wall that leads out into the countryside and to Granddad's olive grove. Just outside the gate there's a small pond with frogs and then a dirt path that runs for one mile through the bare fields to the Al Bakris's wooden shack, where my best friends Ahmed and Karim live, right next to a horrendous cesspit. They live there with their father, Mohammed, his two concubines, two elder stepbrothers, and their blood sister, Nadia.

After their shack the dirt road runs on for half a mile along the Bruseghin olive grove. A car can barely get down it. Herdsmen use it for their goats and have their huts beside it. It curves around and joins the boulevard after our two villas, just before the Esso gas station on the way back into Tripoli.

Although the two villas are a couple of miles from the olive grove and the herdsmen, the smell is just the same—especially from the cesspit that serves as a latrine ditch for all of Tripoli's wooden shanties, and as fertilizer for the olives.

I love the smell of earth, eucalyptus, and olives and am very proud of Granddad's olive grove. He got married at the end of the First World War and studied for his building surveyor's certificate. He arrived in Libya in 1932, six years before the mass colonization of the country that Mussolini called the Fourth Shore, bringing his wife and two children, the twelve-year-old Toni and Italia, who was only two. Thanks to his qualification, he was able to help with the construction of the new agricultural villages founded by Libya's Italian governor, Italo Balbo: Castel Benito, D'Annunzio, Mameli, Bianchi, Garibaldi, Crispi, and Breviglieri. In exchange, the INFPS—the National Fascist Institute for Social Security—together with the King's legal representative, awarded him an estate a few miles outside Tripoli, plus a thousand olive trees ready for planting.

But the land was covered in sand. Granddad employed six Libyans to work with him; they cleared the sand away and erected barriers to keep the dunes at bay, thus putting a brake on the infamous *ghibli*, the hot wind that blows in from the desert.

Then they dug the well down to the water table and created irrigation channels, and Granddad was eventually able to plant the olives. He knew it would take years for them to produce anything, so in the meantime he kept his job as building surveyor, helping to construct housing for the colonists. Thanks to those years of sacrifice, today Granddad owns Libya's largest olive grove.

My father, on the other hand, can't stand the smell of olives. It reminds him of his childhood in Palermo, two parents and five sons in a single room, the lavatory shared with three other families.

*For him, it is the smell of poverty.*

At six I have a snack of buttered bread and jam, nuts, and dates. I then get astride the veranda railing, about a yard and a half from the ground. The *mabrouka*, the Arab housekeeper, has been told not to let me, but she's supervising the cook, who's preparing the evening's couscous. The gardener pretends not to notice, and my father is away at the office in Piazza Italia, next to the castle in the city center. Jet, the boxer dog, looks at me with big soft eyes in his flat muzzle. He looks at me like that so he'll appear less ugly: that way maybe he can scrounge a date. I always give him one, even though my brother, Alberto, says they're bad for him.

This railing's my horse and I'm Kirk Douglas. I have my guns, hat, and boots with spurs that I got for Christmas. I know it was Dad and Mamma who gave them to me, not Santa Claus. Granddad likes to think I still believe and that it was Santa Claus, not him, who gave me a Zorro outfit.

I'm galloping along furiously, perhaps too fast. Dad doesn't like to see the marks of the spurs in the railing's white paint. For him, they're the mark of my idiotic dreams. He's telling me more than ever to get out of my head and my concentrate on my homework, like my elder brother does.

Fortunately, as usual, Dad's in town working. He's with a disagreeable young man named Emilio Busi, who has just come over from Italy and dined with us a few days ago.

It's very hot. My neck's dripping with sweat, an ant is running along my arm, and the sparrows are making a heck of a racket. I squash the ant. The sparrows will pay for it later with my Diana 50 air rifle.

Having come back from prayers in the mosque, Ahmed is waiting for me for our gunfight. He's in the middle of the stretch of dust and sand, dressed up as a cowboy with the costume they gave me years ago that I don't wear anymore.

As always in our gunfights, Ahmed is prepared to die. He takes the role seriously, as he does everything in life. He's tall, dark, with slightly wavy black hair and a sullen but intense look, just like his younger brother, Karim, and his little sister, Nadia. They all take after their beautiful mother, Jamila, Mohammed's second wife. Handsome Arab kids.

Ahmed's a *pezzente*, which is what the native Libyans call Italians like me, "a little grabber." I'm the son of one of Tripoli's richest and most influential families and yet I've chosen him as my closest friend. *Friend* isn't a word we use, and neither of us likes speaking of friendship, like a pair of girls. But it's obvious I prefer to spend every afternoon playing with him rather than being taken to the exclusive clubs along the coast to play with the Italian, English, and American boys there.

The plan for our games is always the same: he loses and I win. It's a pact that's taken for granted and, usually, there's no exception. But today there's a change.

Laura's standing in the shade of the eucalyptus tree, chatting with Karim, who's her age. He doesn't want to be in the film. He's very religious and says that Westerns are for nonbelievers. Laura is always telling Karim how handsome he is.

Laura offers to act in the film, just to please me, but she never shows any great enthusiasm. She is nearly two years younger than Ahmed and me, and it's obvious she likes me, but she never does what I say.

I should put Nadia in, in Laura's place, just to spite her. Nadia's always hanging around wanting to play with us and would love to act in our film. But I know Laura couldn't care less if I cast Nadia in her place or not. But then again, Arab women don't act in films—even pretend ones. Ahmed and Karim wouldn't allow it.

"Stop chattering, Laura. You have to watch the gunfight."

Karim's protective. "My fault, sorry."

He's always taking her side.

I get off the horse railing and go up to Ahmed. Jet is with him, licking his hand. In the afternoon, when he wants to run like crazy through the fields, it's the two of us who take him. But Ahmed's the one who runs around after him.

"I'm keeping an eye on him. Too many females with rabies out there," he says.

I walk up to him; he hands in my gun belt.

"You win today," I whisper in his ear and enjoy his look of amazement.

Ahmed shakes his head and stares at me. He doesn't like surprises; he prefers everything to go along as planned.

"Mike, I'd rather lose, like I always do."

"Don't worry, Ahmed, you can lose. But this time I'm going to die; you stay on your feet. Now, take ten steps back."

With our backs to each other, we start to measure the paces while Karim counts them out. That's the part I have him play. Then we turn around and look each other in the eye.

Laura isn't paying attention—her mind is on a butterfly. Or occupied with her own thoughts, which are always a little strange. She once said that she didn't like either the sun or the dark, and that she wanted *time to pass quickly but still.* Ahmed thinks she's crazy, but Karim says she's a genius.

Then we each fire a shot. A few seconds of suspense. Kirk Douglas falls to his knees. Now I'm on the ground, a hand on my chest, my eyes half closed. I see Ahmed's Rock Hudson standing still, dumbfounded, almost scared by this unexpected outcome.

Finally, Laura and Karim pay attention. Surprised. This is the first time I've been beaten in a gunfight. Ahmed is looking pale and says nothing. They all come up to me as I play the part of Kirk Douglas's dead body. Now Laura should go to Ahmed's Rock Hudson, my rival, the winner. But she doesn't. She stands there, looking down at my corpse, deep in thought.

And at this point Jet comes up and licks my cheek, probably attracted by some jam left on it. I hear Karim sniggering, and I open my eyes, furious.

"I'm sorry," says Karim, "but we don't get it—you're always the one who wins."

I explain the new twist to the plot. As Kirk Douglas, I unload the gun before the gunfight so I won't kill my very best friend, Rock Hudson.

Laura smiles at me, nodding in approval.

"*Bravo,* Mike. The winner always turns out to be hateful."

Ahmed's still confused.

"I want to be the one who dies."

Laura darts a look at him.

"You wouldn't let yourself be killed simply because your gun wasn't loaded. Not even if the killer were Mike."

Ahmed looks askance at her. He seems upset. There's no love lost between them. He's afraid that one day I'll show more regard for her than for him.

Karim steps in. "I wouldn't let myself be killed in defense of either one of you. But I would for Laura."

He's the spitting image of Ahmed. They look so much alike, but their characters are opposite. Karim is the idealist; Ahmed the realist.

Ahmed strokes the dog. He looks at me.

"Should we take Jet for a run, Mike?"

# SATURDAY, MAY 26, 1962

Every Saturday evening, people are invited to our property and the space in front of the two villas fills up with all the important people among the Italians, Americans, and Libyans: owners of estates, entrepreneurs, directors of the AGIP oil company or the Banco di Roma, diplomats, American officers from the Wheelus Field Air Base, dignitaries and ministers of Libya's King Idris.

On these evenings, we take turns with Arab, Italian, and American cuisine. Tonight's an American night: a barbecue of hamburgers and sausages prepared by Laura's father, William Hunt, followed by Coca-Cola and popcorn bought by her mother, Marlene. Laura's mother doesn't like to cook.

With a bag full of popcorn and bottles of Coca-Cola, Laura and I sneak off behind the villas, where her father has built a carport to keep the sun off the cars. We sit down underneath it to chat. It's only childish gossip. She's ten, I'm twelve.

"Your mother doesn't cook either, does she, Mike?"

"Never. My granddad says she should have never gotten married."

"But then . . ."

"When she was eighteen, she met Dad. He was already an engineer."

"And as handsome as Clark Gable."

I look at her, amazed. Sometimes this little kid *is* crazy, just like Ahmed says.

"What?"

She laughs.

"Marlene says it, but she's just joking. Your dad's Sicilian, isn't he?"

"Yes. He's the fifth son of a cobbler and a chambermaid, with four older brothers. He grew up in Palermo's poorest district and was the only one of the brothers to go to college."

"How come he went and not the other brothers?"

"He was born in 1925, so he was too young to fight in the war. His four brothers helped the American forces to land in Sicily. And they sent my father for college in New York."

"How did your father get the money for his education?"

"His brothers had money. They paid for his college. And he did very well. He completed his engineering degree quickly. The best student in his college. He also obtained an American passport. So now he is both Italian and American."

"Then he met your mother?"

"He finished college in 1948 and came to Tripoli to work for a Sicilian firm. He met my mother and they married soon after. A year later, Alberto was born, and the year after that I was born."

"Your mother's very rich, isn't she?"

*She has this way of just coming out with things. Anyone else would find a different way to say it.*

"My granddad has the money. The villas and the olive grove are his. Mamma seems unfriendly, but she's just very shy. She doesn't speak much, but she reads plenty of books. History, philosophy, that sort of thing."

"And she's a Fascist, isn't she?"

*Again, she has that way of blurting things out. Dad would be against her being my girlfriend.*

I look at her.

"Did your mother tell you that as well?"

"No, my dad said it. He says it's a shame, because your mother's like a queen."

"A queen?"

"Yes, Dad says that if your mother had been born in the sixteenth century she would have been a queen."

I don't want to talk about my parents anymore.

"Tell me about your mother and father. How did they meet?"

"Oh, it's a wonderful story, Mike. The opposite of your parents'. The poor but beautiful one was my mom. Dad comes from a very wealthy family of Texas oilmen."

"Isn't he a war hero? My mother told me he was."

Laura doesn't seem proud of it. Not like I'd have been.

"They gave him a medal when he was with the Marines in Korea. Now he's like an ambassador but he's not really. Although he works at the Wheelus Air Base, he's always traveling around on 'missions,' as he calls them. And then he leaves me and Marlene on our own."

"Your mamma's very beautiful."

I say this with genuine enthusiasm, and she smiles.

"Mom's twenty-seven, fifteen years younger than my dad. She was born in California and she was such a beautiful baby that her parents called her Marlene because they hoped she'd become famous, like Marlene Dietrich."

"My father says she's more like that American actress he likes so much, Ava Gardner. And how did they meet?"

"Marlene wasn't even sixteen when she left home to take acting lessons in Hollywood. She worked in a diner to support herself."

"A little like Dad!"

"Yes. She served my dad a steak in 1951. He was there in Hollywood for a weekend but was actually living in Virginia taking classes at Langley Air Force Base."

"And then you were born?"

"Kids don't get born immediately, you know, after just a kiss. Dad finished his classes at Langley and married her. And I was born at the end of April in 1952."

"You really take after your mother. But your complexion and eyes come from your father."

"My parents say that I take after him as well in my character."

"So you could kill an enemy?"

She looks at me a little sullenly.

"I hope my dad has never killed anyone. Or if he did, it was only to defend other people."

"Were you in America before coming here?"

"No, we've been in London, Paris, and Rome. Dad was always traveling, and Mom went to the film festivals. After three years in Rome, here we are."

"Is your mother happy about being in Libya?"

"Not at all—she says it's a sandpit. But Dad has given her a special present to help change her mind. It's a new sports car, and it's coming tomorrow. It's a Ferrari."

# SUNDAY, MAY 27, 1962

A flame-red Ferrari 250 GT Spider California is a coupe convertible. I see it the next morning outside the Hunts' villa.

On Sundays, Alberto and I are regular guests there for an American breakfast: pancakes, cornflakes, toast, eggs, and bacon. That's how I see the red Ferrari.

My parents never have breakfast with us boys on a Sunday. Dad goes to Mass at seven and then on to the Hotel Waddan to read his paper, *Il Giornale di Tripoli*. Later he drops in on Don Eugenio at his parish church, St. Anselm's, where all the Italians who count for anything in the city meet up. Mamma always keeps to herself. I think she has no time for Mrs. Hunt. I have no idea why.

Alberto only takes little bites of what's on offer. Instead, he asks Mr. Hunt how they build the skyscrapers in the United States, that vast country so far away. He also asks him about the new young president, John Fitzgerald Kennedy. William Hunt isn't very keen on him.

I listen in and grab whatever I like without bothering to ask. Cornflakes, French toast, pancakes, and syrup. Laura's mother likes me and calls me "Michelino-the-Vacuum," because I swallow everything in sight.

After a grapefruit juice and a slice of flatbread toast, Marlene Hunt goes for a jog, which she never misses. She always takes her run along

the path that starts behind the villas: one mile through the arid countryside as far as Ahmed's wooden shack and the cesspit.

She comes back, glowing and panting, covered in the sweat that
makes her running vest stick to her and puts a shine to those long legs
below her shorts. My father's right: she looks like Ava Gardner, but
even more beautiful.

Marlene aims a clip at the back of Alberto's head, offers a kiss to
Laura and a smile to me. Nothing to her husband. Then she goes off
to take a shower. When she comes back, she's wearing a pink T-shirt
with nothing underneath and a pair of cut-off jeans.

"Hey, kids, would you like to go the shore in the Ferrari?" she asks.

I rush home to get my trunks and sandals.

"We're going to the beach. Let my granddad know," I tell the
*mabrouka*.

We jump into the Ferrari. Marlene and Laura sit up front, Albert
and I are in the back. We fly down the Sidi El Masri road toward
Tripoli, overtaking a few old Fiats, Hillmans, and Morrises. The wind
slaps into our faces; we don't even see the eucalyptus trees whizzing by
at the side of the road.

"Too fast for you?" Marlene yells out.

No, I want her to go even faster.

. . . .

It takes us only a couple of minutes to get from Sidi El Masri to the
Tripoli outskirts. Marlene stops for gas at the Esso station.

The guy at the pump is Vito Gerace. He is a Sicilian of about fifty
from the same poor district in Palermo as my father and is one of
my father's minions. He's a rough sort, with a huge bush of hair and
heavy eyebrows that meet over the bridge of his nose. People say that
he gets drunk in the brothel every Saturday night.

The Gerace family came to Libya from Palermo along with my
father. Vito's wife is Santuzza, ten years his junior and a distant cousin
of my father. She's a good-looking woman, humble and cheerful, and
she works as a seamstress for the wealthy Italians and Americans.

Vito has a son, Nico, who's my age, and we share a desk in the
same class at school. His mostly resembles his mother, but his curly

hair, bushy eyebrows, and hairy arms and calves come from his father. Along with the hair, a noticeable speech impediment has given him an inferiority complex and no self-confidence.

Vito Gerace raises his black eyebrows and stares first at the Ferrari 250 GT Spider and then at Marlene Hunt, his eyes coming out on stalks. He takes an awfully long time to clean the windshield so he can ogle her suntanned legs.

Nico looks her over admiringly, too. He knows she's acted in Hollywood and he has a fixation on all actresses. He's got pictures of all the stars stuck on the underside of his desk: Rita Hayworth, Ava Gardner, Marilyn Monroe, Brigitte Bardot, Sophia Loren. All of them together, available for him in his imagination.

As we come into Tripoli through the Garden City district, Marlene is forced to slow down. We drive past the Royal Palace, with its copper domes, and come to the cathedral square, with its ugly box of a post office built by the Fascist regime. There aren't many cars, but the place is full of carriages, carts drawn by camels, bicycles, and pedestrians in the middle of the road.

We take Corso Vittorio Emanuele, otherwise known as Shara Istiklal. Shops run by Italians are closed on Sundays, while those belonging to Jews and Arabs are open, including our favorite ice cream parlor, Girus.

Marlene parks the Ferrari between a donkey and a Fiat 600, and we all get out. Everyone's looking at us, and I mean everyone. Not at us boys but the Ferrari and Marlene, who looks as beautiful as a goddess.

After an ice cream we go down Corso Vittorio to Piazza Italia with its Fascist-era arcades. We turn around by the fountain and take Corso Sicilia, the Italian name that even Libyans prefer to Shara Omar Al Mukhtar. Coming out of the center, we set off again at full speed toward the beach. We pass on the popular ones, the Lido and Bagni Sulfurei, with its smell of Wadi Megenin, and head toward the more exclusive beaches attached to private clubs with English names like "The Beach" and "The Underwater Club."

Another ten minutes and we're at the Underwater Club. We're already in our trunks and get into the seawater pool. William arrives later in his Land Rover, but he stays resolutely in his clothes, smoking a cigar in the shade of the terrace.

Tall and blond, with steel-blue eyes, he's a Texan who appreciates Libya's desert more than its sea. Also its oil, which we hear so much about. Meanwhile, Marlene does her usual fifty lengths of the pool then gets out, spreads out a towel, and lies down in the sun.

She really is a goddess. Although only twelve years old, I can see that myself, with her eyes that see right inside you, her shiny raven hair running in waves halfway down her back, her slender, tapering legs, her bikini top undone at the back for the perfect tan, and the bottoms pulled down just within the limits of decency.

Laura tells me her parents are complete opposites. Marlene's easily bored. She'd like to go to the posh parties held at the embassies, grand hotels, and out on terraces overlooking the sea, but William says they're nothing but places for *airing other people's dirty laundry in public.*

I can see all men's eyes continually turning to look at Marlene. I should think William Hunt knows, he must. Laura, as well. But I don't know if they're happy about it.

. . . .

After our morning at the beach, we go back to the villas. Ahmed and Karim come over after lunch. They go to the Libyan school on Shara Ben Ashur and have lessons on Sunday morning.

We play soccer on the spare ground in front of the two villas. Two against two, Ahmed and me against Alberto and Karim. We kick the ball among the beetles and lizards, a nice setup, except that Laura is the referee and she stops play with an old whistle just whenever she feels like it. She knows nothing at all about the game. So we take our cues from the Italian radio Sunday soccer broadcast. When the Juventus game's over, then so is ours.

Laura knows there's only a minute to go. Karim trips over the ball and she blows the whistle for a penalty. Ahmed looks furious.

"Laura, you're crazy!"

That's what he always tells me about her. Perhaps he feels one day she'll step between the two of us.

Jet's slumped in a corner by his kennel, panting with the heat and drooling a great deal. Ahmed and I have spent a whole hour with the tweezers this afternoon, pulling out the damned ticks that nest in his ears.

"Shall we go for a run, Jet?"

His two large eyes simply stare back at us. Normally, he's up and running as soon as we say the words. But this time there's no reaction. He lies there, gasping for breath and drooling.

"It's too hot," says Karim.

Ahmed shakes his head, unconvinced. "Jet would go for a run even in the *ghibli*."

He's my dog, but Ahmed considers him under his protection. Woe to anyone who touches him.

"Perhaps we can take him after sunset, Ahmed."

We exit by the back gate. The pond is almost dry, the frogs making a melancholy croaking noise. We run along the path behind the villas up to the wooden shack where Ahmed and Karim live with their extended family.

From there we pass through the Bruseghin olive grove and by the huts of the men who herd their goats there. We never pick olives up from the ground; it's hard to distinguish them from the goat droppings.

Sunset is the right time for our big-game hunting. I shoot the doves in the eucalyptus trees with my Diana 50 air rifle, while Ahmed concentrates on the scorpions with his throwing knife. Out of fairness, it's never from a distance of less than two yards away.

Karim never takes part. He reads the Koran, Arabic poetry, and the history of Libyan heroes such as Omar Al Mukhtar, who was hanged by the Italian colonial powers. Karim never kills anything, but he collects the bloody booty for us.

When we come back for Jet, Granddad's standing by the kennel. Next to him is the young local vet, wearing a rubber glove as he caresses the dog's head. Jet looks at us with his sad eyes, his nose on the ground. Granddad shakes his head. The vet turns toward him.

"I'm sorry. Jet has rabies."

. . . .

Granddad, my parents, Alberto, and the vet go inside, into the living room.

Ahmed, Karim, and I stay outside, next to the dog. Ahmed talks to him in Arabic, which I learn at school.

"Who did this to you, Jet?"

"He's got a bite mark on his side," says the vet, pointing to a dark-brown patch of skin.

"It'll be one of those mongrel bitches out there," Ahmed replies, pointing to the outside wall at the back. In fact, they've been gathering there every evening at sunset for a couple of weeks now, yelping and whining. You can hear them right now.

"They're in heat," Laura had told me a few days earlier. Seeing I'd no idea what she was talking about, she had explained the fact in that direct and easy-going way she had, as if the matter-of-fact meaning of words was enough to carry their own weight.

The vet's words are clear.

"It'll take Jet two or three days to die from rabies. We're going to put him down, so he won't suffer."

Ahmed gets up and leaves without a word.

"Unfortunately," the vet's saying, "Jet's saliva is infectious. If he's licked you, it only takes a slight cut . . ."

"We all have to be vaccinated," says Granddad, cutting him short.

Forty injections in our bellies. But that means nothing to me. I still have the Diana 50 in my hand. I leave and run behind the villas to the small back gate.

As I dash out, I hear the whining turn to snarls. Ahmed's standing next to three of the dogs with a large locust in his hand. The dogs love them. He hurls it against the outside wall. The largest and bravest of the dogs ventures near. She sniffs at it suspiciously then bends down toward the dead locust.

Ahmed's ready with his Swiss knife in his hand, open at the longest blade. He leaps astride the dog and plants the blade deep in her neck. The dog lets out a tremendous howl and tries to shake him off, but Ahmed traps her between his legs and, because he's left-handed, puts his right arm around to pull the blade out.

He must have struck an artery, because the blood gushes out. The dog bucks and pushes Ahmed off, then tries to bite him.

But Ahmed's pretty quick. He sticks the knife in the animal's right eye and cuts it out with a circular twist. At this point, the other two dogs make a move to attack him. I aim the rifle at the nose of the more aggressive one, where I know it really hurts.

And from fifty yards the pellet of a Diana 50 hurts like the devil. The dog howls and runs away. I quickly reload, but there's no need. The second dog is already running off.

The first dog is now howling desperately. She's bleeding heavily from the stab wound and her eye socket and makes no reaction when Ahmed gets astride her again and inserts the blade in her throat.

I watch him as he tugs with great strength until the throat is slit and the animal falls to the ground.

Ahmed extracts the knife, cleans it on some blades of grass, clasps it shut, and puts it in the pocket of his shorts.

"Thanks, Mike," he says.

Then he turns away and goes down the path to his wooden shack. I catch the sight of Laura and Karim staring at us from a distance. That's the distance between me and her.

# MONDAY, MAY 28, 1962

We buried Jet yesterday evening, and it's school today. Happily, we're nearly at the end of the dreadful school year. Fortunately, the school building is large and cool, with long corridors and high ceilings that help against the *ghibli's* choking heat.

Next to school there's the concrete soccer field, and the eucalyptus trees down one side to mark the touchline, so whoever's playing on that side finds themselves dribbling past the trees as well as the opposing side.

At one end of it stands the field where the old guys play bocce; at the other, the bar with foosball and bar billiards, which the adults play with a cue while the kids launch the ball from their hands.

Alberto is the school's star pupil, but he's leaving secondary school after this term. He scores the highest in all subjects but always runs the risk of someone catching up to him because he passes on his answers to the others in class and then gives private lessons for free to help the dolts.

I'm pretty weak in all subjects. I just don't like studying. And I don't like my classmates. The only friend I have in school is my classmate Nico Gerace, the kid who drools over film stars and singers. He's the son of the gas-pump attendant and the seamstress, the only poor Italians in Tripoli. If my father didn't help them, they'd starve to death.

Our religious instruction is taught by Don Eugenio, the parish priest at St. Anselm's, which is close to the school.

Don Eugenio is a young man not yet thirty, with a smooth, chubby face like a child. His light-blue eyes look kindly in his well-cared-for face; his wide, good-natured smile is framed by a head of blond hair. His manners are humble and he only ever wears a cassock and sandals.

Although he graduated in theology, Don Eugenio is excellent at math and gives private lessons to various kids, myself and Nico included. Only the richer parents have to pay, so Nico's lessons are free.

Dad says Don Eugenio is the most intelligent priest he knows and the most generous to the poor. He says he's also excellent at managing the money he collects for charity, investing it for a good return. That's the way he's able to help the poor in Sudan, Niger, and Chad.

But there's another thing about him that's important. Don Eugenio goes off to Rome every month as private confessor to the president, one of the most important men in Italian politics, the strongman in the leading Christian Democrats, which have ruled Italy since the end of the war.

Perhaps this is why all the Italians who matter in Tripoli—from the landowners to managing directors of the big firms—go to him for confession. All except my grandfather. Then they gather at St. Anselm's on Sunday afternoons, drinking coffee, playing cards, and discussing business.

I'm happy to share my desk in class with Nico, but the rest of the class treats him like a pariah. In fact, I'm the only one who ever speaks to him, the only one not to tease him, and the one who protects him from the others' sneaky tricks. They make fun of him for the thick black eyebrows that meet over his nose, the curly hair he vainly tries to straighten, his hairy arms and calves, and his ridiculous lisp that transforms any *s* into a whistle. On top of everything, he always stinks of gasoline, the smell his father brings home every day.

I have no idea why I look out for him. Perhaps only to do the opposite of what the majority does. I really hate that word, *majority*.

It makes me feel less free, obliged to say: Yes, things are fine the way they are.

Today, Don Eugenio decides to have everyone read a passage out loud from the textbook. One sentence each, around the desks in order. And every single one of the pupils makes a silent calculation about which sentence Nico will have to read, hoping that it'll be a complicated one full of *s* sounds. Today's subject's the Crusades, and Nico's sentence is: "The word *assassin* comes from the word *hashshashin*, which was used in the Christian West for the followers of Imam Hasan Al Sabbah and comes either from his name or from the word *hashish*."

Nico has also already seen his sentence. This is going to be a disaster. He gives me a look like a lamb going to the slaughter. Meanwhile, as each pupil reads his passage, excited sniggers spread around the class in anticipation of the spectacle.

Don Eugenio isn't even listening. He's reading a book entitled *Balance Sheets and Profit and Loss Accounts*.

When it's my turn, I rattle off Nico's sentence and carry on as if nothing were wrong: "The word *assassin* comes from the word *hashshashin*, which was used in the Christian West . . ."

"Don Eugenio!"

Walter is top of the class and class monitor, the one with the highest marks in every subject.

The priest lifts his head inquiringly. "Yes, Walter, what is it?"

Walter gets to his feet. In contrast to mine, his black school smock is always buttoned right to the top and the white bow doesn't look twisted and as if a rat had been chewing at it.

"This is Nico's sentence that Michele's reading; he's already read his."

He makes a face, playing to the gallery of his classmates but not daring to look me in the eye. He gets smiles and sniggers all around.

Then, as if by itself, I hear my voice saying, "Walter, you're a complete prick."

Don Eugenio abandons his book, which falls to the floor with a thud. There's no change in his rosy-colored complexion, but his light-blue eyes are a single sheet of flame. In the silence, you can hear a fly buzzing around the classroom.

He then gets up and comes over to me silently in his black cassock. With a wide sweep of his arm, so that everyone can see and remember, he grasps a tip of an ear between his thumb and forefinger.

But the ear that he slowly begins to twist is not mine. It's Nico's. A gradual movement showing no effort, which makes the ear become redder and redder, and Nico has to struggle to keep the tears of pain and humiliation from his eyes. All I get is a look of disapproval.

*You're Ingegnere Balistreri's son, and I can't lay a finger on you.*

. . . .

After class, Don Eugenio keeps the two of us back. He gives me a note that my parents have to read and sign. But that's not enough for him. He beckons us to come over to his desk. I do as he says, my instincts telling me it's better to get this over with in silence. But Nico is trembling like jelly beside me. The priest smiles at us with those blue eyes in his baby face.

"You have committed a very serious breach, Michelino, at the very moment you're about to become one of Our Lord's servants. Swear words are used only by the uneducated."

He looks at Nico, who studies more than I do but whose parents are indeed uneducated.

The thing is, although no one asked me, in about ten days I have to start serving as an altar boy at Mass. The choice was Don Eugenio's, thinking to please my father, a large donor to the cost of rebuilding his church. And Dad wants me to serve at Mass, as my brother, Alberto, has done, in order to show all those who matter in Tripoli, and also those in Rome, that the Balistreri family is based on sound Catholic values.

"I won't say them anymore, Don Eugenio."

I make this promise with no show of enthusiasm. I don't like being closed up in there with him and simply want to get out to recess. A few days before, lisping through his tears, Nico told me that, for making too many errors in his private math lesson with him, Don Eugenio had made him take his shorts down and spanked him as punishment.

"I'm sure you won't say anymore swear words, Michelino, that goes without saying."

Don Eugenio waves away a fly that's buzzing around Nico's face, then strokes his prickly mass of curls. Nico looks at me forlornly from under those two grotesque bushy eyebrows. I contain my anger by biting the white bow of the hateful black smock, chewing on the corner that's bitten and worn away by my anxieties. I'm frightened, but I have no idea what to do. After all, he's the teacher.

"In order to be an altar boy, you must be pure, Michelino. Remember that God sees everything and that in the end we have to face the Last Judgment."

I say nothing. He hesitates, his hand still on Nico's hair. He stares at me with those light-blue eyes. Who knows what he'd like to do to me? He smiles at me.

"You can go off and play soccer now, Michelino."

"And Nico?"

His light-blue eyes come to rest on my friend.

"Nico must learn not to be a nuisance in class and to read when it's his turn. I'll make this clear to him now, and tomorrow he'll come to the presbytery and make confession."

As I leave, I can feel Nico's desperate eyes drilling into my back.

*I should be there in his place.*

. . . .

"Where did you hear a word like that, Michelino?"

My father makes a grim face as he reads Don Eugenio's note. Alberto is in the room but keeping silent. Italia's reading a book and smoking. Granddad's in town, playing bocce.

I say nothing. After a while, he repeats the question.

"Where did you hear that word?"

I look him straight in the eyes.

"From you, Dad."

Alberto gives me a smile. My brother is always on my side. Sometimes openly; sometimes in a more subtle way.

Dad gives a slight start. He studies me for a long time, wondering if I'm lying. He could rest on his authority and deny it. But I know him too well. My father always gives himself a way out. And he never loses his temper. If he does, you never see it. I don't know if it's something he learned in Sicily from his elder brothers or at some negotiation course he took while he was in college in New York. Probably both.

"And when did I say this word, Michelino?"

"When you and Mamma were listening to the radio in your bedroom a few weeks ago. The door was open."

"And you were eavesdropping, Michelino?"

Alberto steps in.

"I was there with Mike, Dad. The radio said that Italy had elected a new president. You were saying to Mamma that this Antonio Segni had won because the Fascists had voted for him and those lunatic monarchists that wanted the King back."

Unbelievably, I saw a gleam of consideration for me in my father's eyes, such as when I shot my first dove with a Diana 22 before moving on to the 50.

Now that Alberto is on my side, I feel calmer. So I tell him more.

"Then you added, 'This Segni is only a prick that won't last long,' anyway.'"

Dad smiles at us. He's a little embarrassed, but in the end happy that there's a bond of understanding between his two sons, who are so different but so united. And, for him, a family must be united. Always, and no matter what happens. He says it over and over again. They'd drilled it into him since he was a little boy in Sicily. His parents, his four elder brothers, his parents' friends, the people who lent his father money when his work as a cobbler didn't bring in enough to feed the family.

*The family must be united, always.*

Dad smiles. "Did I really say that? Well, I shouldn't have, because there are certain words you shouldn't say, and also because President Segni's a good Catholic who was elected by Parliament. Thank God we now have a free democracy in Italy."

He often mentions this word *democracy* and always links it to another word, *free*, as if he wants to justify something unpleasant— like offering an excuse when none is needed.

He now adopts a calm and indulgent manner and puts on a smile that makes him look like Clark Gable.

"Michelino, your mother is also certainly not pleased that you've been talking like a street urchin."

*Like a street urchin. Spoken with the scorn of a kid who grew up in the worst gutters of Palermo.*

My mother sets her book down, puts her cigarette out, and darts a quick glance at my father.

"Michelino, leave swear words to ignorant people. Now, are you having any problems with Don Eugenio?"

*She understands everything without having to say it, just like me.*

Dad's not happy with this question.

"What problems could Michelino possibly have with Don Eugenio? He's a pillar of our community and a great help to the poor."

My mother doesn't reply. She picks up her book again, lights another cigarette, and pours out a little more of the pungent golden liquid that my father calls her poison.

In the end, Dad tells me to apologize for the swear word, make confession with Don Eugenio, and study my catechism so that I can serve at Mass.

In exchange for this, I can sign up for the martial arts class at the gym in the Arts and Crafts School and take Ahmed with me. My father will pay for him. He doesn't see what use it will be but always finds a way to keep everyone happy. He can't imagine that we'll get to be black belts and that tae kwon do will be for us much more than a hobby.

This evening, the large garden is lit only by the small lights mounted on the wall surrounding the two villas. The south wind is bringing the Sahara's sands into the city. The *ghibli* has started.

Nico, Ahmed, Karim, and I take shelter in the darkest corner, next to the back gate behind the Hunts' villa. The carport that William Hunt built to give shade for the Ferrari and the Land Rover gives only partial shelter from the gusts of wind and sand.

Alberto is studying, so he's not with us. Laura's gone to Wheelus Field with her parents to watch a baseball game. So we can talk a bit more freely.

Nico says that Don Eugenio made him take his shorts down and spanked him again as soon as I'd gone away. And that tomorrow after school he has to go to confession with him in the presbytery.

I look at Ahmed. I can see him carving that dog's eye out then slitting its throat. I know what to do.

"We have to get him to stop it, the pig. I've got a plan."

As the sand starts getting everywhere in our clothes, they all listen closely to me. Karim stares in admiration, Ahmed nods silently, but Nico has a problem with it.

"I can't do it, Mike. I'm too scared."

I try to bolster him.

"Nico, if you don't do this, you'll always be scared of him and he'll be able to keep doing those things to you. If you go along with me, you won't be frightened of him anymore, nor of anyone else."

"Can't you do it instead of me, Mike?"

In his fear he's now lisping his *s* sounds.

*No, Nico. I'm Ingegnere Salvatore Balistreri's son. Don Eugenio wouldn't dare. You're the one who is the pariah.*

"Nico is Italian, you're half Italian and half American. But we're Libyans, Mike," Karim cuts in. "What if Don Eugenio has us arrested?"

"I'll protect you. If he reports you, he'll have to report me as well, and he'll never do that."

Ahmed takes out the knife he used to kill the dog. I gave it to him as a present on his last birthday.

"If it doesn't work, I'll take care of that priest."

I look at my three friends. The *ghibli* is blowing more sand under the canopy roof, and it's now getting in our eyes.

"Let's make a pact, the four of us," I say. I get Ahmed to give me his knife.

We squeeze in between the Ferrari and the Land Rover, but the sand even gets in there.

I quietly make a cut on my left wrist. Drops of blood well up from it.

Then it's Nico's turn. He's now smiling happily. He makes a cut on his wrist and looks with satisfaction at the blood. For him, it's an honor to do as I do.

Karim's less into it. He's not happy about mixing his blood with two Christians and makes only a small cut. He looks at the tiny drops of blood uncertainly.

Then he hands the knife to Ahmed, who looks us straight in the eyes, as serious as ever. He likes the idea and shows no fear. He grips the knife in his left hand. In silence, he makes a much longer and deeper cut than ours, and the blood flows copiously from his right wrist.

The single bulb hanging under the Hunts' carport is now caked with sand and emits only a flickering, grainy light. We can smell oil and gasoline. We can hear the *ghibli* whistling, the palm leaves shaking, and the eucalyptus rustling.

The four wrists come together and our blood mingles with the sand.

*A brotherhood of sand and blood. Forever.*

# TUESDAY, MAY 29, 1962

**W**e're well prepared. Everyone has his part to play. Nico's the victim, Karim the photographer, Ahmed the enforcer, and I'm the one who can't be reported for it.

*Four little bastards against one great big one. We should be enough.*

At the end of the lesson, Nico tells Don Eugenio that he's ready to make confession.

We know that the priest will take him off to a room on the first floor of St. Anselm's presbytery nearby. It's the one he uses for his private math lessons. There's a small confessional in it.

We're already well hidden when they arrive. Don Eugenio ushers him in and locks the door. Then he slips into the confessional. Nico gets on his knees outside.

Immediately, he begins his recitation, lisping as he goes.

"We touched ourselves. Myself, Mike, Ahmed, and Karim."

"In what way, Nico? I have to know everything in order to decide on the penance."

"All four of us pulled down our underpants. Then we measured our peckers."

His *s* sounds are exaggerated. Hidden under the desk, Ahmed, Karim, and I have to wait there without bursting into laughter.

"Show me how, Nico. Stand up."

The priest comes out of the confessional. His light-blue eyes fix on Nico. Don Eugenio's good-natured smile seems like an obscene grimace.

"How far down did you pull your underpants? Let me see."

Nico is shaking. He knows we're hidden there. Why don't we make a move?

*Because it wouldn't be enough to get, Nico. We have to go further. You have to go further.*

Closing his eyes, Nico does as he's told. His shorts and underpants drop down to his knees. He looks ridiculous. He's only twelve, and yet his thighs are as hairy as his calves.

Then Karim pops out from underneath the desk behind the priest. Don Eugenio jumps at the clicks of the old Kodak. He turns around and looks, dumbfounded, at Karim and Nico.

"Nico, how dare you? I'll have you and your whole family excommunicated! As for you, you miserable little Arab . . ."

I come out from under the desk as well. Don Eugenio clams up. I'm the real problem for him. What would my father say?

But this isn't enough for this man, and we know it. Ahmed comes out and plants himself between Nico and the priest. In his hand, he has the Swiss Army knife, the one from the blood brotherhood, the one with which he kills scorpions and cuts the throats of rabid dogs.

Don Eugenio turns pale, unsure whether to give us all a slapping or to give in.

Ahmed removes any last doubt, pressing the knifepoint at the priest's Adam's apple, drawing a few drops of blood.

*The first drops of so much blood.*

Who knows why that thought comes into my mind.

"We won't say a word. But we have the photographs," I tell Don Eugenio.

But this isn't enough of a threat for Ahmed.

"If you touch my friend again, I'll slit your throat, you *gawad*. Understand?"

And now I know why the thought came to me.
*Because Ahmed would really do it.*

. . . .

Marlene's been teaching Laura how to take photographs for several months now. There's a broom closet in the villa they use as a dark room and Laura already knows how to develop the rolls of negative. We have no other choice but to go to her. We tell her about the photos of Don Eugenio but leave out the part about the knife to the throat.

As I imagined, she doesn't agree with what we're doing.

"You as well, Karim?"

*As if we three were hardened criminals and Karim some kind of saint.*

Karim looks away.

I cut things short. "We have to develop them now."

She makes an amused face.

"Really? And just where are you thinking of developing them? The photographer's opposite the Cathedral?"

"We have to protect Nico," Karim says.

She thinks for a moment. Karim's the most believable one among us. We may be right.

"Did you hit Don Eugenio?" she asks.

"No, no," Karim quickly replies.

"No, absolutely not, I swear it," Nico adds in confirmation, keeping his fingers crossed behind his back. Then he makes the sign of the cross.

The lisping of the *s* sound makes Laura smile. It makes her soften, and she is now more open to persuasion.

She looks at me. "If you hang around with Ahmed, Mike, you'll end up just like him."

She says it with sadness in her voice, showing her concern for me. I know what she means.

*An outlaw. A gangster.*

Ahmed looks at her coldly and says nothing. Then she makes her decision. I know she'll do it for Nico.

"Okay, I'll help you out. Give me the film, Mike. I'll develop the negatives."

Ahmed shakes his head.

"Don't trust her, Mike. She's only a kid. And she's crazy."

Laura moves to leave. I grab her arm and stop her. She brushes my hand away sharply. A lock of hair falls over her clear eyes: her father's eyes. She's furious.

"You're an idiot, Michele Balistreri. Listen to your dear Ahmed and you'll turn into an outlaw just like the ones in your films."

I hand over the roll of film. No one says a word, and off she goes.

# WEDNESDAY, MAY 30, 1962

'm alone in the garden when Laura comes over with an envelope she's sealed with tape.

"Have you seen them?" I ask, avoiding her look.

She makes a face to disguise the smile.

"Of course I have. You have to do that to develop them. But I looked at them as little as possible."

"We're not faggots, I swear it."

Her beautiful mouth, the same as Marlene's, curls into a snigger.

"Maybe, who knows? We'll see."

Then she breaks out into laughter and runs away to the safety of the Hunt villa.

*Ahmed's partially right. Laura is half-crazy.*

In the evening I'm alone again in the garden. Ahmed's back in his shack after the martial arts lesson, and Laura's at home in the villa.

Dad's voice can be heard through the French window. He's clearly upset.

"The American ambassador and his wife will be offended, Italia, if you don't come yet again."

"Tell them I have a headache."

"I've already used that excuse."

"Then find another. You're pretty good at inventing things."

"Listen, Italia, this idea that you're not going to anymore receptions is ridiculous. A social life is essential for business. I've just bought the Moneta island—I'm going to build a villa there to entertain people and—"

"I'll go there so that I can read in peace and quiet, Salvo, not to be mistress of the house and take care of your social life."

"You've never even invited our neighbors for dinner again!"

"Quite. I know William Hunt may be useful for you, but I don't like being around failed Hollywood actresses."

"That's unfair, Italia. People only gossip about Marlene because she's good-looking and has an extremely important husband."

"Really, Salvatore, is that so? And you know so much about her?"

"But, Italia, how can you not talk to our neighbors?"

"I'll talk to them when necessary. I'll talk to him, the few times he's here, because he's a serious man. And to Laura, who's a delightful girl, as beautiful as her mother but much more respectable, like her father. So you can do the talking to Marlene Hunt, if she matters so much to you."

Everything is spoken in hushed tones. But it's this that scares me most and stabs me in the heart. Even if he wishes I were different from what I am, my father's still my main role model. He's a handsome man, well liked by everyone, and I love him. He had to leave home and study hard and is now a great success in business.

But if he makes my mother suffer, that changes everything because I love her more than anything in the world. She is the purest thing for me. She is like my granddad and my Uncle Toni, who went off to face the enemy single-handed while the routed Fascists were taking to their heels. *And I'm just like her.*

. . . .

It's night, but I can't get to sleep. I look over to the empty bed where my brother sleeps, but he's in London, studying English and getting to know the right people.

*And learning how to steal legally, as Mom says to Dad.*

I turn over on my other side, toward the open window. I have no trouble with mosquitoes biting me; my blood is not the kind they like. But the heat is suffocating, there's too much light from the full moon and too much noise from the frogs croaking in the garden fountain. The eucalyptuses are motionless; there's not even a breath of wind to waft their scent to me.

The clock on the wall says it's eleven thirty.

. . . .

I'm nearly twelve and certainly not a mamma's boy, but I need her presence right now, just a couple of reassuring words for a minute in order to get calmly back to sleep.

I knock at the living room door before entering. She's sitting on the sofa. "Can't you sleep, Michelino?"

As usual, she's got a cigarette in one hand and in the other a glass of that dark-golden liquid Dad calls her poison.

"I'm hot, Mamma. I was thirsty, I went into the kitchen and . . ."

She smiles, happy for me to be with her.

"I think those martial arts lessons excite you too much. Come sit down here with me until you feel sleepy."

I sit next to her on the sofa, as I used to when I was little boy. Something I haven't done for three years, given it's only something little kids do. Physical contact with my parents is now only a fleeting touch or an affectionate clip.

The African night's hot air enters through the two open French windows, along with the croaking of the frogs. And swarms of mosquitoes, attracted by the light.

"Don't the mosquitoes bite you, Mamma?"

"No, Michelino, only Alberto and Dad. They have sweeter blood."

"And the two of us?"

She smiles. "Ours is sour—it's like poison to them."

"Like what you drink?"

She looks at me with a frown.

"You don't have to parrot everything you hear from grown-ups, not even if it comes from your father."

"But is it bad for you or not?"

"It's called whiskey. And it can damage your health if you drink too much of it."

I had a sudden and infinite need to embrace her. To feel reassured that everything in the Balistreri family was fine.

"I did something very serious today, Mamma. A mortal sin."

"Michelino, I just told you not to parrot things you haven't properly understood."

"But there are the Commandments, Mamma. They were written by God."

She looks at me indulgently. She knows I haven't believed in Santa Claus for some time.

"And how do you know who really wrote them, Michelino?"

I'm left speechless. If they'd heard her in Tripoli, they would have reported her to the Pope in Rome. They would have excommunicated her. If Dad had heard her, it would have been worse still.

I tell her about Don Eugenio, all in one breath. Everything, from beginning to end. About Ahmed and his knife as well. She hears me out in silence. I go to my room and get the photographs of Nico with his pants down in front of Don Eugenio and hand them over to her. I notice the faint lines in her face becoming deeper. I suddenly see her as an old woman.

I wait; she seems to be trying to catch a thought, a memory of something that Granddad told her.

"Toni was just like you at this age."

I know this is both a compliment and a concern. I also know that Dad has forbidden her to tell me about Uncle Toni. And Granddad Giuseppe never tells me about him either.

"Can you tell me about him, Mamma?"

"No, Michelino, I promised Granddad Giuseppe I wouldn't."

"But in what way am I like him?"

She thinks for a minute, then she gets up and goes over to the bookshelves on the wall, full of all the books she never stops reading. She takes one, quite a short book, and comes back to the sofa. She holds it out to me. Friedrich Nietzsche, *Ecce Homo.*

"This is one of Granddad Giuseppe's books. Toni started to read it when he was twelve. He couldn't understand a word, but he liked it.

Then, at secondary school, he picked it up again. He gave me all his books before going off to the war."

"Would he kill Don Eugenio?"

She inhales the smoke of her cigarette, takes a sip of her poison.

"Listen to me now, Michelino, we're not going to tell your father about Don Eugenio or about the photographs. It wouldn't do any good. But I'll see that you won't have to be an altar boy and he won't give you anymore trouble."

I look at her doubtfully. She gives me a smile.

"Tomorrow, Don Eugenio is going to tell your father that, because of that swear word in front of your classmates, he couldn't possibly have you serving at Mass."

# SATURDAY, JUNE 30, 1962

I f you're not Italian, you have to learn how to get along with them, and it is always better if you get along with Italians. Mohammed Al Bakri came to understand this one day in September 1931, when he was only six years old and living in the Jaghbub oasis in Cyrenaica. His father and two elder brothers had just been seized by Marshal Graziani's soldiers, accused of being members of the Libyan resistance. In less than a week they were put on trial and hanged. Italian troops surrounded the oasis with barbed wire and poisoned the wells used for drinking water. The surviving women and children escaped across the desert and, after two exhausting months, a few of them reached Tripoli. Mohammed and his mother were the only survivors in the Al Bakri family.

In Tripoli, his mother found work as a scullery maid in the house of a real gentleman, a man named Giuseppe Bruseghin, a good man who treated the mother and son very kindly. Then came the disasters in Giuseppe's life: the deaths of his son, Toni, and his wife, Margherita. Bruseghin was left on his own with his difficult daughter. Mohammed thought that Signorina Italia would never find a husband. But after the war she met and married the man from Sicily and New York,

Ingegnere Salvatore Balistreri. Mohammed Al Bakri had understood this man from the beginning, thanks to his Bedouin intuition, the same one that lets them cross the desert by following only the stars. And this Ingegnere Balistreri was a genius in business and a man who was generous to those who were his faithful and devoted followers. He taught Mohammed how to write, how to do arithmetic, and a lot more. So Mohammed became his right-hand man, feared and admired by all his employees, Libyan and Italian.

Mohammed was certain that he would work for Ingegnere Balistreri all his life. He was the shrewdest businessman in North Africa; everything he touched turned to gold. If he served him well, Mohammed knew that one day he would be able to buy a horse, then a carriage, then a Fiat 600, and, eventually, some land and perhaps a house like the Italians had. And, perhaps, if they both enjoyed good health and good fortune, a good deal more as well. *Inshallah.*

But, for the moment, what he had was a Libyan's pay, which wasn't very much. A wooden shack instead of a house and a large family. One man, two wives, four sons between the ages of ten and sixteen, and little Nadia, his eight-year-old daughter and his treasure. Ahmed, Karim, and young Nadia were the children of Jamila, Mohammed's second wife, and were tall and slim for their age, good-looking and bright. Sixteen-year-old Farid and fourteen-year-old Salim were the sons of his first wife, Fatima, and were less fortunate. Farid had taken after Fatima. He was robust and stocky, with frizzy hair, a large nose, and thick lips. Salim, on the other hand, had taken all his features from Mohammed; he was short and angular with a hollow face, an aquiline nose, and wore his straight hair in a bowl cut.

Of the two, Farid was the brains while Salim was the muscle. Farid cut a deal, where Salim tyrannized; Farid was cold as ice, and Salim was boiling hot.

Mohammed had asked the Ingegnere if he could build a brick house on the piece of land one mile from the villa, where they had the shack. It was uncultivated ground in the middle of the countryside, bordering on the cesspit used by those houses not connected to the sewers and by Bruseghin's agricultural workers for manure. The Ingegnere had agreed.

Saturday was a good day because Mohammed did not have to be in Ingegnere Balistreri's office, and his two younger sons were not at school. The elder ones had not been to school for two years, having been expelled for hitting their classmates.

For Mohammed and his four sons, Saturday began at dawn with ritual ablutions, followed by *salat al fajr*, the dawn daily prayers recited looking east toward Mecca and the rising sun. They ended this first of the five daily prayers with two genuflexions, the *rukus*.

Then, immediately, they set to work. Mohammed had calculated the number of bricks, the amount of lime, and the implements needed. With the money he had put aside over the years while working for Ingegnere Balistreri, he could afford to buy the materials but not the labor.

This Saturday was perhaps the last one possible for any physical labor before the great heat of July and August. The flies were already sucking up the sweat that soon welled up on you. Thousands of flies, what with all that manure, and thirsty more than hungry for food.

With the Jeep borrowed from the Ingegnere, they had brought the sacks of lime from Tripoli. Along the paved road to Sidi El Masri, they had stopped at the Gerace's Esso station and loaded up jerry cans with water. Half a mile later, they had taken the dirt track that ran through the herdsmen's goats, past the Bruseghin olive grove and up to the wretched cesspit.

The work was proceeding slowly. While Mohammed mixed the lime where the house was to stand, the boys emptied the sacks near the ditch. Karim, the youngest, was dragging a sack of quicklime with his two hands over the dusty ground to be mixed. He was not complaining, only moving slowly.

"Come on, Karim," Farid shouted at him, a cigarette hanging from the corner of his huge lips.

*"Jalla, gawad!"* Salim shouted at him. His mouth was a thin, cruel line. For him, the best thing about fishing was taking the fish alive out of the water and holding it firmly in his hand until it could no longer breathe.

"Back off. Can't you see he can't manage?" Ahmed protested.

He was only twelve, but he was as tall as his elder brothers.

"Oh, Professor Ahmed is coming to the defense of the little fag, is he?" said Salim mockingly.

Ahmed made no reply. He went up to his younger brother to help him.

"Leave it, Karim. Let me take the bucket."

"No, Ahmed," ordered Farid. He puffed smoke out of his wide nostrils as he had seen the real tough guys do in American movies.

"Why?" Ahmed asked.

"If Karim doesn't get used to the work, then we'll have one less builder, and we can't have that."

"I'm trying, Farid," said Karim.

Karim was standing firm, not wishing to complain. He was panting and trying to shift the heavy weight but could not move the bucket.

Salim gave him a kick on the backside that had him rolling over in the dust. Karim doubled up with the pain but did not cry out, complain, or cry. Salim picked up a frog and threw it at him. Then he went up to him.

"Get up, you little fag, right now."

Ahmed stepped between the two of them. Salim gave him a cruel look. He could not wait to get his hands on him.

"If you don't get out of the way right now, I'll kick you all the way back to the shack."

Ahmed was calm. In fact, he was happy. He was learning something about himself: how not to be frightened. He was managing to keep a clear head, like he did with Mike at the martial arts lessons.

Farid had come up as well. His frizzy hair was full of flies and, with the cigarette hanging from his full lips, he was playing the part of the tough guy with brains. Not the animal, like Salim.

"Karim has to work like us. Now get out of the way."

Ahmed looked at his father, who was mixing the lime and had no idea of the fight breaking out among his sons.

"I'll count to three, Ahmed, and if you don't get out of the way I'll make mincemeat of you," Salim threatened.

But Ahmed already had his moves planned. He had only to provoke them.

"*An-din-gahba . . .*" he hissed at his elder brother.

He then took advantage of the moment of incredulity and bewilderment. He bent down to grab a handful of lime from the bucket and when Salim lunged at him, he was ready. The lime hit the eyes of Farid and Salim, blinding them. They screamed and cursed, blindly trying to hit out at him, but he moved so that they could only hear him hissing *"An-din-gahba . . . An-din-gahba . . ."*

He was able to lead them where he wanted. When they were on the edge of the cesspit, he gave them a warning.

"Hey, brothers, have you done it in your pants? I'm picking up the smell of shit!"

Farid and Salim caught on and stopped themselves dead, paralyzed with fear. Their eyes, noses, and lips were covered in flies, which rose from the ditch full of semi-liquid shit and were buzzing loudly, as if to push them in.

Ahmed thought a moment. He could easily throw them into the ditch, but afterward they would take it out on Karim.

"Keep calm, brothers, you won't end up in the shit, but you're very close. Stay nice and steady now."

At that moment, Mohammed gave an angry shout.

"Hey, you boys, will one of you bring me that damned lime to mix? Right now!"

"Yes, Dad, I'll see to it," Ahmed replied. Then he turned to his brothers.

"I'll take the lime to him and come back and help you. Make sure you stay where you are."

He went off, walked the hundred yards, and placed the bucket down for Mohammed.

"Here's the lime, Dad."

"Thanks, Ahmed. What are those idle brothers of yours doing?"

Ahmed turned around. What he saw made his blood run cold.

Karim was running up in silence, knowing he needed every bit of his strength. He chose Salim, because he was the lighter of the two, and gave him a hard push.

Salim cried out and took a step backward, waving his arms as if trying to grab onto something, then he fell almost in slow motion into the soft, slimy pit.

He floundered, shouting and terrified, spitting out the shit that had gotten into his mouth.

Ahmed lowered himself into the manure up to his waist. He took two steps toward his brother, trying not to slip. He grasped him by the arm and dragged him to the side of the pit.

Salim's foot met a hand blocking his path. His screams reached all the way to the heavens, mingling with those of the *muezzin* calling to prayer.

# SATURDAY NIGHT AND SUNDAY, JUNE 30 TO JULY 1, 1962

I catch the confidential bit of news during the usual Saturday night gathering at the villa. General Jalloun, Tripoli's chief of police, is talking about it with Dad and Don Eugenio. Two corpses have been pulled out of the cesspit. A young woman and her young baby daughter. What little skin there was left on the skeletons was dark, so they were not Libyans from the coast but possibly from Fezzan or even the Sudan.

"People from the Sahara," says Don Eugenio.

"Poor things, coming in from the desert at night, they must have fallen in," says my father.

"They've been there for some time, although it's impossible to say how long. No one's been asking after them, and the police have no time to make any inquiries about people like that," the general concludes.

I get the message. This is the world I have to grow up in. The lives of some human beings are worth no more than a pair of monkeys'.

# FRIDAY, MAY 26, 1967

In the five years that followed, I went on with my education but dedicated much more time to martial arts, hunting, and fishing than to my textbooks. I only went to school because my mother wanted me to and because no one dared fail the son of Ingegnere Balistreri. He'd become more wealthy and more important in those five years, although I didn't quite understand the nature of the import-export business from Sicily and the US he had set up.

Apart from his right-hand man in operations, Mohammed, the two people Dad spent most of his time with were Don Eugenio and Emilio Busi.

There had been no more problems with Don Eugenio after the episode five years earlier. Not for me, nor for Nico, nor with anyone else, as far as I knew. Only once did I ask my mother if she'd spoken with him about the photographs. She responded evasively but clearly.

"Don Eugenio is a highly intelligent man and is conscious of his mistake. He won't repeat what he did."

I met Emilio Busi for the first time in our house in the spring of 1962, and then more frequently over the past two years.

Busi was born in 1935 and was now thirty-two. Tall and lean, with thick, disheveled hair, he wore horrendous square black glasses that gave him the look of a bookworm. He chain-smoked the nauseating, plain-tipped Nazionali cigarettes while his shrewd eyes behind the thick lenses studied you through the smoke. His wardrobe was completely ridiculous: short-sleeved checked shirts, high-waisted pants that were too short in the leg, white socks, and moccasins.

My father and grandfather had told me more about him.

Busi came from the mountains between Tuscany and Emilia, where I'd read everyone was a partisan during the war. His father was one of the Resistance leaders against the Fascists.

*A partisan with the Catholics' white armband. A sort of Christian Communist.*

Dad was always talking about him as if he were a good example to follow. Fighting the Fascists and the Nazis in the mountains, Busi's father had formed many friendships, especially with the right men, who wore white non-Communist armbands like himself and became important people after the war.

One of these men, Enrico Mattei, had taken control of the old AGIP oil company and created ENI, a state oil company, to fight back against the "Seven Sisters"—as he called the Western cartel—formed in 1951 after Iran had nationalized its gas production, and which had denied ENI membership. Before dying of cancer, Busi's father brought his son, then training to be a Carabiniere, to Mattei's attention.

At the beginning of 1960, Emilio Busi graduated from the Carabinieri's Officer Training School in Rome. But then ENI offered him a job. So he left the Carabinieri force and promptly joined the Italian Communist Party. ENI posted him to Syracuse in Sicily, where he worked on realizing one of Enrico Mattei's dreams: the refinery and petrochemical plants between Gela, Augusta, and Syracuse set up to exploit the deposits found in the Ragusa basin. Thanks to his excellent relations both with his ex-colleagues in the Carabinieri and with the trade unions who looked on him favorably as a Communist, his work went well. But the ENI project in Sicily was the first step toward expansion in North Africa and the Middle East, and the Seven Sisters weren't happy about this at all.

One of the firms that worked on the preparation and construction of the site was the one formed by my father's four elder brothers. It was they who told Busi about their brother in Tripoli, who could possibly lend a hand in dealing with Libya and the Americans.

Busi's first visit to my father was in the spring of 1962, when he spoke to him about ENI's projects in Sicily and North Africa and about Mattei's problems with the American oil companies. So Dad introduced him to William Hunt, who seemed to have the right kind of connections in Washington.

Then, on October 27, 1962, Mattei was killed. His private jet, a Morane-Saulnier MS.760 Paris, accidentally exploded while returning from a trip to Sicily.

From this point on, my father's version of events differs from my mother's. My father says it was an "accident," whereas my mother maintains it was nothing of the sort. According to her, the instigators were the Americans and their Italian friends and the perpetrators were "the Sicilian friends of the Americans." Dad would listen patiently, smiling and shaking his head.

In any case, Mamma maintained, ENI's industrial project in Syracuse had gone ahead anyway but with modifications that made it more acceptable to everyone. According to her, the Balistreri brothers' firm had worked actively to secure these changes.

My father strongly objected to my mother's version of events. There wasn't a scrap of evidence for any attempt on Mattei's life. ENI's new board of directors was leading the company in the direction Mattei had wanted, although perhaps in a less visionary manner but with a more realistic approach in terms of the interests of Italy and its people. Which meant cooperating with the Americans, not fighting them. As for his brothers, their company had regularly won government funds; it was one of Sicily's largest firms and enjoyed an excellent reputation.

Two years ago, however, after working in Sicily for five years, Emilio Busi had left ENI and moved permanently to Tripoli, saying that he was now a business consultant for various Italian companies that wanted to set up in Libya. But he never mentioned any names. "Professional secret," he used to say, in a serious tone of voice.

At seventeen, I had no real idea what a "business consultant" was and what exactly Busi did. Here, too, the explanations given by Dad and Mamma were similar in part but also very different.

My father said a consultant is a businessman who gives advice to his clients on how to make money in Libya and is paid for it.

My mother said he's a man who's only interested in his own ideals and, in order to pursue those, he transforms his clients' unspoken dreams into reality.

Busi's money and the money of others came into Dad's explanation; in Mamma's, it was Busi's ideals and the money of others. There was a mixture of respect and contempt in her explanation. And a hint of fear.

And it was because of my mother's hint of fear that I disliked Emilio Busi.

．．．．

The Underwater Club's restaurant was crowded, as usual. There were Italians, Americans, and a few Libyans, who were almost all members of King Idris's government. The band was playing "Ruby Tuesday." Several couples were dancing, almost all the ladies in evening gowns and the men wearing dinner jackets and bow ties. On the horizon, you could see the lights of the fishing fleet sailing out for a night on the calm, dark sea.

Dad and Mom didn't dance. She didn't like to. Dad had managed to get a secluded table out on the terrace, overlooking the sea. Sitting around it were my parents, my grandfather, Emilio Busi, Alberto, and myself.

Dad loosened the knot of his bow tie and brushed a hand through his raven hair.

Mamma was forever telling him to get it cut, as long hair wasn't becoming for a nearly forty-two-year-old man. But Dad thought he looked very handsome with it, and he was. For him, long hair was a sign of virility.

He turned to Granddad Giuseppe.

"It may be that our family and some of Signor Busi's clients will become future business partners."

"And what business would that be?" my mother asked.

She posed the question in her usual manner. Cool but polite. For a moment, my father looked at her as if she were a stranger. Then he recovered his natural charming manner: the great salesman who could sell ice to the Eskimos. He turned to Granddad again, speaking to him in the hope of convincing her.

"The future of any business links between Italy and Libya will be based on two things: gas and cars. Enrico Mattei always said so. If a country wants to produce cars, it also has to have the gas."

In the general silence, Busi was watching us through the smoke of what must have been his fiftieth plain-tipped Nazionale. He looked directly at my mother, knowing he had to tackle her suspicions in some way or another.

"Signora Italia, the AGIP oil company was created by Count Giuseppe Volpi di Misurata when he was Mussolini's finance minister, after having been Governor of Tripolitana. It was the count who began the search for oil here in Libya. And he was a friend of your family, I believe."

Granddad interrupted him. His manner was more polite than my mother's, but equally firm.

"The count was a guest for dinner, which didn't make him a friend. After July 25, 1943, we neither heard nor saw anything of him."

I knew that date. It was the day the Grand Council of Fascism expelled Mussolini. I knew very well what my mother and my grandfather thought of those men.

*They had betrayed Italy.*

Emilio Busi turned to my grandfather. He was more tractable than my mother.

"Anyway, as you know, it was thanks to the research funded by AGIP and Fiat that Ardito Desio discovered oil deposits in the Libyan Desert in 1938. Then, unfortunately, the war broke out and American interests were able to take over from the Italians."

My mother gave no time for Granddad to reply.

"Signor Busi, the Americans were able to win thanks to an Italy teeming with traitors and turncoats. Like Volpi di Misurata and the Mafiosi who helped the Americans enter Sicily."

It was very clear she included Busi and his partisan father among the list of those who had betrayed Italy.

My father was visibly embarrassed and upset. Things weren't going at all as he'd hoped. I could see it in his eyes: the charming smile on his dark, handsome face, the smile he put on for church each Sunday, was looking a little tarnished. He tried to find a way to soothe my mother.

"Italia, Libya's oil now runs the risk of ending up totally in the hands of Esso and Mobil. And the car market in those of Ford and General Motors. Isn't it about time we Italians started to claw something back? Don't you think Enrico Mattei was right in his parable of the little cat?"

He'd already told the story a thousand times. The little cat goes timidly up to an enormous bowl of broth, and a large hound attacks it and breaks its back. The broth is gas; the dog is the Seven Sisters; and Italy the little cat.

By now, I'd come to recognize my father's tactics. He was now appealing to my mother's anti-American feelings. But my mother was no fool.

"And what does our family have to do with all this?" she asked.

The question was addressed directly to Emilio Busi. He looked at her coldly from behind those bookworm's glasses, through the stink of his tobacco smoke and locks of disheveled hair.

"Olives are excellent, but the future lies under the sand, not above it. If you can understand that, your family can become a minority partner and become truly wealthy."

"And you as well, I take it, Signor Busi," said my mother.

Busi shook his head.

"Forgive me for being brutally frank, but it's simply so we can be clear among ourselves. I earn quite enough from my work. Luxury doesn't interest me. I don't need the money. But our country's only now coming out of the ruin and poverty that Fascism caused. The people of Italy need low-cost gas, and they need work."

"And where do we come in?" my mother asked.

Busi shrugged, puffing out a cloud of smoke.

"You can help speed what will only be an inevitable process. Italy will go ahead, no matter what."

For some reason, that last, whispered sentence produced the effect of an earthquake or a declaration of war. It was clear that the Bruseghin-Balistreri family was the most important Italian family in Tripoli, and it counted for something. But it wasn't irreplaceable. Emilio Busi and his clients were conferring an honor on my family by choosing it. They could always pick someone else. Especially since my grandfather and mother still had Fascist sympathies.

It was Alberto who, completely unexpectedly, intervened.

"Signor Busi, in order to become partners in big business, you need to have a great deal of money, which we don't have."

In that moment, I became certain of several things. First, I could never be like Alberto. Second, not only was he more intelligent than I was, but he was also different from my father. Third, my father wasn't pleased with what Alberto said.

I saw my father struggling between an angry gesture and admiration for his son. An eighteen-year-old with the maturity of an adult. Then he laughed, that habitual good-natured laugh of his, and turned to Busi.

"As always, my son Alberto's right. He's going to college in Rome to study engineering. One day, he'll lead an industrial empire."

Dad said nothing about me. For the first time, Busi shot me a glance. It was a mixture of condescension and sympathy, bordering on pity.

*I'm the less able son. The one who only knows how to land a punch and shoot wild animals.*

# MONDAY, MAY 29, 1967

Nico Gerace's father had died three years earlier, flattened by a truck that was reversing in front of the pumps of his Esso gas station. Nico had witnessed the whole scene.

And Dad, the ever more powerful Ingegnere Salvatore Balistreri, had come to the aid of his widowed cousin, Santuzza, and her son, Nico. He bought the gas station, and Nico received a fixed wage for working there in the afternoons and on weekends. But Dad insisted that he continue his education at secondary school, and he paid for his books and fees. Santuzza cut and tailored all Dad's made-to-measure clothes and those of his friends.

My father's explanation for such generosity was very simple.

"Santuzza's one of my second cousins. The Gerace family comes from the same district in Palermo as I do, and it was I who persuaded them to come to Tripoli. That's how we Sicilians do things. If you can help somebody out, then you do so."

Perhaps Dad was thinking that Nico's presence at school would help his surly dunce of a son, who was a self-confessed Fascist. And having a Fascist son wasn't good for Ingegnere Balistreri's business dealings with Arabs, Jews, Catholic priests, and Italian Communists.

Outside Italy, Italian secondary school lasted for four years rather than five. The first two years quickly passed, but the third year had its dramatic moments. Partly because Alberto had graduated with the highest possible marks and gone on to college in Rome and, without his help, mathematics was a real trial for Nico and myself.

Nico's lisping *s* sounds, his bushy eyebrows, his unstoppable growth of hair, and his whiff of gasoline made him the school's laughing stock. The girls in class greeted all the boys with the traditional kisses, with myself always first in line. But they never embraced Nico. And the older boys gave him a hard time. The most aggressive were five wealthy little shits who were regular members of the class's first basketball team. Five tall, gangly guys, all brawn and arrogance.

Nico cheered himself up by filling notepads and exercise books with newspaper cuttings of photos of actresses and singers. And by buying stylish clothes. That's how he spent all the money he earned at the Esso station: flowered shirts, elasticized pants, frizzy hippie hairdos.

He depended economically on my father and psychologically on me. Without help, he couldn't have lasted for long against the daily taunts inflicted on him by the five basketball players.

*Hey, Eyebrows, give us a lisp, will you?*

*Hey, Whiffy, how do you toss yourself off with those smelly hands?*

Our blood brotherhood decided it was time to make them stop. Once and for all. It was a unanimous decision that took all of two minutes.

Nico, Ahmed, Karim, and I went into the changing rooms after a game. They were standing naked in the showers and looked contemptuously at us right away.

"Hey, Mike, we don't want Whiffy and those Arabs in here," said the team's center.

I gave him a tae kick in the testicles that made him double over, and then Nico fetched him a kwon punch that laid him out flat under the shower. The other four were about to react, but Ahmed already had the knife in his hand.

We had no plan for a brawl in mind. A bunch of many bruises, perhaps even a broken bone. There would have been no trouble for me but plenty for Ahmed, Karim, and Nico. No, the method of attack had to be something else. The one Ahmed suggested.

*An invisible bruise, something that couldn't be reported. The use of terror.*

Ahmed went up to the center, who was trying to get up, and put the tip of the knife to his throat, as he had done years before with Don Eugenio. Now, the basketball players were paralyzed with fear. They looked at me, the only one on their social level, the only civilized one. So I immediately made things plain to them.

"If you say a word of this to your parents or make fun of Nico again, we'll kill you. All of you."

To make the idea clearer, Ahmed made a cut in the center's throat, from which a little blood began to flow.

"Mike didn't say we'd beat you up. He said we'd kill you. Is that clear?"

They nodded, almost theatrically. From that day on, no one dared ridicule Nico ever again. And, later, word must have filtered down, because, in the school and on the Tripoli streets, everyone gave us a wide berth. And I was the untouchable son of Ingegnere Salvatore Balistreri, and no parent could say a thing.

Nico Gerace slowly began to lose his lisp. He continued dressing ever more stylishly and continued attaching photos of Playmate nudes under his desk. And for that entire academic year, no one called him "Whiffy" or "Eyebrows" again.

# TUESDAY, MAY 30, 1967

t was the last week of school. A young history teacher fresh from Rome with his jacket and long beard was spelling out the damage done by Fascism.

"Take the colonization of Libya, for example."

He stared at us, as if expecting some objection. Then he continued.

"It was planned and carried out by a bunch of criminals."

I raised my hand, but he ignored me and sent us out into the courtyard for recess.

While the others were chattering away, I stood in a corner with Nico. I was thinking about my granddad and about the hellish work he put in over many years to establish his olive grove. I felt my anger welling up.

Then the words of that Communist, Emilio Busi, came to mind.

*Wealth lies under the soil now, not above it.*

There was no longer a place for Granddad's olive grove.

The teacher was having a cigarette in another corner, something that was absolutely forbidden to us pupils.

I went up to him, Nico a couple of steps behind me.

"My granddad was one of the colonials, *Professore*. Would you say he was a criminal?"

He barely looked at me.

"We'll talk about it in class next time, Balistreri."

"No. Tell me now."

A knot of students gathered around us. I could feel the tension mounting, but all I wanted was an answer.

"If your granddad was a Fascist, then he was a criminal, Balistreri. Perhaps he hanged some Libyans, perhaps not. But he should have stayed where he belonged—in Italy."

My anger, that old enemy of mine I'd always feared and tried to check, suddenly exploded in me. I didn't use any of my martial arts, simply pushed him to the ground with a mere shove. Then Nico and I took him by the arms and legs and flung him into the goldfish pond.

"You shit!" Nico shouted at him, lisping the *s* a little. Then he spat on him.

The headmaster tried his best not to throw me out, but the teacher immediately called the Ministry of Education in Rome. A telegram arrived the following day.

Nico and I were expelled once and for all. Except that, with Dad's money, I could always go to a cushy private school in Rome. But it was the end for Nico. He would be a gas-pump attendant for the rest of his life.

. . . .

At home that afternoon was the first time my father branded me a loser.

"Your brother Alberto's studying engineering in Rome. You, on the other hand, only know how to shoot things and lash out with your fists. You'll end up a pump attendant, like that Nico Gerace. You're a loser, that's what you are."

My mother looked at him coldly.

"Losers, as you call them, Salvatore, can be better men than the victors. You'll see what kind of a world we'll be in fifty years from now, thanks to your victors."

But the toughest on both of us—my father and me—was Granddad.

"From next week, Mike, you'll be working in my olive grove. And you, Salvatore, must show more patience with him. I don't want to hear any more talk of victors and losers under my roof. Those are things that only have to do with war."

My father turned white with rage. Giuseppe Bruseghin had reminded him that it was still his house and it didn't belong to Ingegnere Balistreri. And that he had had fought in a real war, whereas Ingegnere Balistreri had only had to combat poverty.

But my father was a man able to control himself and wait for the right moment. And this wasn't it. So he simply bowed politely to Granddad.

. . . .

I went out to the deserted patch in front of the villas then went around behind the Hunt villa. The sun was a huge ball of fire setting on that dreadful day and on that part of my life.

Laura was wandering around with her new Rolleiflex in front of the carport. Instead of strolling up and down the main street in town with her friends and winking at the boys, she was a fifteen-year-old who preferred to be there by herself, taking photographs of the ants that were coming and going out of the nest in a long, disciplined line.

I was expecting her tell me off as well; everyone already knew about my stupid act of bravado. But she said nothing. She pointed to the ants.

"They know they can only survive by helping one another. We should do as they do."

*Ahmed's absolutely right. She's crazy.*

She lifted the Rolleiflex and pointed it at me. I had the sun in my eyes and instinctively raised an arm to shade them. But she took a picture just the same. Then she gave me a serious look with those clear eyes of hers, as if she were thinking of something truly important.

"Sorry, Mike. But this snapshot will be a help to you one day."

# THURSDAY, JUNE 1, 1967

The presidential office in Rome was on the upper floor of a very beautiful seventeenth-century palace that had been restored in the early twentieth century. It stood at the end of Via del Corso, with a view of Piazza Venezia. June promised to be very hot, but at seven in the morning it was still possible to breathe.

The large windows were open on the white façade of the Altar of the Fatherland, the national monument built by Mussolini that Italians now scornfully nickname "The Typewriter."

The president had been to Mass at six, as he had done every morning since the end of the Second World War. He always went to church alone and found there only the priest and several old ladies who had known him for years and had no personal favors to demand of him. Along with lunch and supper with his wife, this was the most precious time of his day. It was the moment in which he could talk to God and share his concerns about *what would be good and just* and *what was necessary.* Not for himself, obviously, but for his voters, the millions of Italians who had placed their hopes for the future in him and his Christian Democrat Party. There was a fine line between the ethics of duty and political pragmatism. It was a line he had increasingly been forced to cross.

*Lord, I know that sometimes I sin out of presumption and sometimes power demands actions a long way from your teachings, but without that power I could do nothing for others.*

It was a healthy driving force, not that of a man who engaged in politics looking for personal financial gain. It was the power to lead, to realize the dream of a democratic and Christian Italy where no one would go hungry and everyone would have work. It was a power that was impossible to acquire and maintain without the ferocity of a man who knows he is right.

At seven precisely, the president arrived back on foot from the nearby church of St. Ignatius Loyola, his bodyguard following him discreetly at a distance. Discretion was the hallmark of this indefatigable and highly intelligent man.

Don Eugenio and Emilio Busi were waiting for him in his private office under the vigilant eye of his ancient secretary.

The priest was wearing his usual frayed black cassock and sandals, Busi a large, shapeless suit that made him look as if he were wearing pajamas.

The president lost no time in preambles or opening chitchat. He could have well done without Don Eugenio Pizza and Emilio Busi, but they were useful to him.

They were intelligent, unscrupulous, and ambitious. Each of them in his own way was even an idealist: Don Eugenio was fixated on helping the world's poor; Busi on driving poverty from Italy. Their idealism rendered them both fairly easy to manipulate, the kind of men who allowed him to lead without appearing to have a heavy hand in doing so.

He had chosen Don Eugenio as his private confessor in order to keep up to date on that patch of sand that was now proving to be full of oil. And he had to have a confessor, at least in formal terms. Better to have a young man who had need of him and would never dare ask him difficult questions.

As for Emilio Busi, he really was a necessary evil. He was a contradiction in terms, a hybrid, a dangerous genetic experiment: son of a Catholic partisan, trained as an officer in the Carabiniere, and now a member of the Communist Party.

An eye had to be kept on Busi. Thanks to his military training, he had the right connections with the Secret Service, and, thanks to the Communist Party, he also had the right connections with the trade unions. And he had been there in Catania next to the airplane when Enrico Mattei left on his last flight. A detail that could indeed be a simple coincidence but disconcerting nevertheless, given the outcome of the flight.

And what about Enrico Mattei? May he rest in peace. A truly exceptional man. A man with vision. Honest and intelligent. But so stubborn, *so rarely inclined to compromise*, and so ambitious he could not understand that no single man alone could decide Italy's future. The country had already had one man like that, and he had led it into a disastrous war and economic ruin. Mattei wanted take on the Americans. A lose-lose idea.

For all these reasons, the president listened attentively to Busi.

"This is a dangerous plan, gentlemen," he said in the end. "It isn't easy to manipulate a war. Things can easily get out of hand."

Busi was ready for this objection.

"The plan is safe, Mr. President. The Arabs want this war. Through my channels of communication with the Russians, we've managed to sell arms and MiG jet fighters to the Egyptians."

The president raised a hand.

"I know nothing of this and don't want to know anything. And what about the Americans and their ally Israel? What are we going to do with them?"

Busi calmed him down.

"We're going to warn them beforehand. We have the right man to do that in our team. The Egyptian air force will be destroyed on the ground, not a single MiG fighter will take off. The Israelis will inflict a few losses, the absolute minimum necessary."

The president sighed. He did not like the idea of losses. But perhaps Busi was right. This way, there would be fewer deaths.

"And where is Nasser going to find the money for this war?" the president asked.

Don Eugenio smiled reassuringly.

"Humanitarian organizations favorable to the Palestinians and charitable donations. The IOR, the Vatican Bank, finances some of them indirectly. I'm taking care of this aspect."

The president closed his eyes for a moment. Hearing the Vatican Bank mentioned reminded him of the promise he had made to Don Eugenio.

*One day I'll recommend your name to the IOR, the Institute for Religious Works.*

The president hoped he would never have to make such a recommendation to the Institute, the Vatican Bank's official name, and expressed a final concern.

"Nasser won't attack unless he thinks he can win."

Busi's thick lenses hid the smile in his eyes.

"But he'll be certain of winning. It's what his generals will tell him. There are those among them who want to see him defeated, Mr. President."

The president knew that the channel of communication with Nasser's traitorous advisers had been opened by Mohammed Al Bakri on the orders of Ingegnere Salvatore Balistreri. Balistreri was the part he liked least. He had the right contacts with the Americans and that was fine. But the president suspected he had also other contacts, in Sicily. The price to be paid for such collaboration could prove very high. Balistreri was an indispensable partner in the future affairs of Libya and Egypt. A very inconvenient partner: politically useful, morally dubious, and even dangerous, perhaps.

"Be careful with this Balistreri, gentlemen. His brothers—"

"All vote for our party, Mr. President!" said Don Eugenio, interrupting him.

"They're excellent men, work hard, and are devout Catholics," said Busi, wrapping it up with a faint trace of sarcasm.

The president closed his eyes so that his visitors could not see his contempt for them. He thought again about his morning conversation with the Lord.

*The fine line between what is right and what is indispensable for Italy.*

He rose up and looked out of the window at the balcony overlooking Piazza Venezia, where Mussolini had declared war on Britain and France.

*A naïve and presumptuous man. He thought he could fight a war and win it, instead of letting others fight it. We will not make the same mistake.*

# MONDAY, JUNE 5, 1967

I t was the first day I was to work in Granddad's olive grove after being expelled from secondary school, and I was up early. The traffic along the Sidi El Masri road in front of the villas was unusually chaotic.

Trucks, vans, carriages, carts, pedestrians, all flying the Libyan and Egyptian flags. A huge crowd of vehicles and people was heading into Tripoli, transistors blazing.

Ahmed and Karim came running up.

"Mike, a war's broken out!"

We dashed into Tripoli on our bicycles and stopped at the Esso gas station before we entered the city proper. Nico was standing in his overalls in the middle of the empty lot around his two pumps, looking in amazement at the crowds traveling past.

"What's happening, guys?"

Karim looked at him in exasperation.

"Don't you even know there's a war on? We've invaded Israel!"

Nico broke into laughter.

"Look, this isn't *Lawrence of Arabia* and you aren't Omar Sharif. The Israelis will kick the shit out of you."

Karim was about to get off his bicycle, but I stopped him.

"Leave it, Karim. Nico, close up shop and let's go."

We entered Tripoli through Garden City and came into the Cathedral Square and Corso Vittorio, where all the Jewish shops already had their shutters down.

Piazza Italia, or Maydan as-Suhada, was overflowing with crowds that extended as far as the castle and the Adrian Pelt promenade. Loudspeakers were broadcasting Radio Cairo. People were shouting with joy and coming in throngs from the twin columns on the promenade, Corso Vittorio, Via Roma, Via Lazio, Via Piemonte, and Corso Sicilia.

Swarms of kids had climbed up over the archway of the Souk el Mushir. Ahmed, Karim, Nico, and I were tossed about by the thousands of people. The square was full of police and military, many of them extremely young and carrying pistols in their hands. Some of them were shooting up in the air in celebration.

The speech of the Egyptian president, Gamal Abdel Nasser, was broadcast live from all the Arab stations, inciting the crowds.

*O most merciful Lord and my brothers, we have been attacked by the Zionist empire. All the Arab armies are marching to the front, where the Zionists will be destroyed. Israel will be wiped off the map and Palestine restored to our Arab brothers.*

"We have to go, right now," said Karim, while the crowd was pushing us in all directions.

Nico burst out laughing. "You're only fifteen, Karim, where do you think they'll let you go?"

But Karim ignored him and turned to his elder brother.

"Didn't you hear the president, Ahmed? Even boys can fight against the Zionists. We really must go to fight. Allah wishes it, not only Nasser."

They were so alike in appearance but so different in character. One an idealist, the other a pragmatist. And Ahmed was the elder brother.

"Our father won't let us go, Karim."

"Our father can't stand against the wishes of Allah. Didn't you hear? The Libyan army is setting off tomorrow for the front. They're enrolling all volunteers from the age of fifteen up. I'm going, brother, with or without you. I'll be smoking a *shisha* in Jerusalem by the end of the week."

Ahmed looked at the poorly armed young soldiers around us. They'd never trained for war. He shot a glance at me.

*Nico's right. The Israelis will massacre us.*

Ahmed was my best friend and the one who was most like me. He was my companion in games, martial arts, fishing, and hunting. We were united in everything, divided in nothing.

*Apart from his hatred for Laura Hunt.*

*But for once I was with Karim. I wanted to get as far as possible from my father.*

"Libya's our homeland, Ahmed," Karim insisted. "I'm going."

I looked at the faint white scar on my left wrist. Our blood brotherhood of five years ago.

I turned to Ahmed and Nico.

"Five years ago, we made a pact. And Libya's my homeland, too."

Ahmed had too much respect or respectful fear of me to reply.

*Don't be stupid, Mike, this isn't your homeland. Your home is way across the sea.*

I heard Nico mouthing curses under his breath.

In the end, Ahmed gave in.

"All right, Karim. Let's go and talk to Father."

• • • •

During the bicycle journey back we passed trucks, pickup trucks, carts, and motorcycles with sidecars, all full of young men singing out in praise of the war. As I was pedaling, I read the word "Jew" already daubed over the rolling shutters of the Jewish shops. The Italians were pulling their shutters down as well.

Ahmed and Karim continued on home, while Nico and I went to mine. My mother was in the living room with Granddad. Laura and her father were with them. William Hunt was in the middle of speaking as we came in.

"Israel made a surprise air attack at dawn, just like the Japanese at Pearl Harbor. They destroyed the Egyptian air force on the ground before a single aircraft could take off. It was a preventative strike, as if the Israelis had been warned."

"But, combined, the Arabs outnumber them ten to one," objected Granddad.

William Hunt looked at him.

"This isn't the First or Second World War, signor Bruseghin. In military terms, the number of troops doesn't count for anything. Sinai's open country; it's not remotely like Vietnam, with its jungles and tunnels. Out there in the desert, it's the air force that's in control. The Arabs have already lost; they'll be butchered."

It was that word, *butchered.* The inescapability of it. The certainty.

*No, I wasn't going to leave my friends to die in that shithole of Sinai.*

I took Nico out of the living room.

"I'm going with them, Nico. Are you coming?"

He smiled. He looked at the scar on his wrist.

"Without you guys, I'm nothing, Mike. I'll go home, tell my mother, then be back here in half an hour."

As I was going to my room, Laura came after me. We went in. She closed the door and stood in front of it.

"Aren't you scared, Mike?"

It was a stupid question. I was about to give her a surly reply, when she rephrased it.

"I mean, scared for your friends, Mike."

*Yes, she understands everything about me, even things I don't understand about myself.*

There was a tenderness in her eyes that I'd never seen before. She moved away from the door.

"Don't get yourselves killed, Mike. And don't kill anyone, either. And the best of luck."

She came up close, while I stood as still as a post. I felt the light touch of her lips on mine.

*Have faith, Mike. Have faith in those who know you and care about you.*

In some way, our painful feelings met like the electric arc the physics teacher once tried to explain to us. Those lips that brushed against mine signified the contact between two souls, not two bodies. Laura Hunt had won me with the lightness of a wordless understanding.

. . . .

I took less than ten minutes to prepare a backpack with my things. I wrote a note to my mother and Granddad. They would be eaten up with worry but would understand what I was doing. I wrote nothing to my father.

I crept out of the house and waited for Nico, Ahmed, and Karim by the side of the Hunts' carport. As we dashed into Tripoli on our bikes, I saw young Libyans painting signs on the Jewish shops and houses.

We crossed the overexcited city and went down Corso Sicilia, Shara Omar Al Mukhtar, and came to the crossroads for Bab Azizia, the recruitment post.

We paused, but only for a moment. We wanted that crossroads in our lives to be clearly printed in our memory.

Our blood brotherhood would take us away to meet with our destiny.

# THURSDAY, JUNE 8, 1967

Three days of a hellish journey in the back of a tumbledown truck full of young Libyans with no real weapons and no uniforms. Some were wearing gym shoes, others babouches. Three days with only brief stops for bodily functions, and no space but that for our backsides on a bench. We traveled along the coastal road through Marsa Matruh, El Hamam, El Alamein, Alexandria, and from there another one hundred and twenty-five miles to Cairo. The closer we came, the greater the journey seemed to become in both reality and absurdity.

*We're going to a place where bombs rain from the sky, bullets fly in your face, and mines explode under your feet. We're going off to get ourselves killed. Or perhaps William Hunt will be right and it will all be over when we get there and this trip will turn out to be merely a long and useless excursion.*

The heat was suffocating when we arrived at Cairo's outskirts. Most of the Libyans had gone to pieces, dehydrated and suffering from dysentery from drinking water in the wells of Bedouin camps. The stink and the heat were unbearable.

Karim was asleep, slumped against his brother. Nico was snoring, propped up against me. It was sunset by the time we entered the city proper. Everything said this wasn't in the least like a festive city celebrating a great victory.

Ahmed whispered to me in Italian, so as not to be overheard or understood.

*It's over, Mike. The war's over.*

William Hunt's prediction had proved to be all too true. The war had been lost before we ever arrived. The farther we got into Cairo, the greater the scale of the tragedy became apparent, from the slowly growing crowd of refugees fleeing from the Israeli air-force bombs in Sinai, even leaving their shoes behind so they could run more quickly over the desert sand. We woke Nico and Karim up from their heavy sleep as we drove through the hellish sight of destitute people.

Whole families were out in the Cairo streets to help the refugees, offering them whatever they had in the house: from bread, flour, and rice to vegetables and meat. And yet the radios turned up full blast in the bars continued broadcasting the now scarcely credible hymns of Arab glory, which the Egyptian people were finding out were pitiful lies. Old people were crowding the windows and balconies, looking in fear toward the horizon in the east, in fear of seeing the Star of David on the oncoming armored cars.

Evil-smelling rubbish littered the streets: plastic sacks, broken washing machines, piles of rotting fruit and vegetables picked over by beggars and ravaged by huge rats. Barefoot children kicked balls of rags among the dung of horses and asses. The *muezzin's* plaintive cry calling for evening prayers was the only sound in a city that in three days had plummeted from euphoria to desperation.

We arrived at the barracks in an ugly square on the edge of the Christian quarter of Muqattam. The head of the Libyans, whose rank I could never make out, got down and went up to an Egyptian soldier, who had every intention of keeping the entrance barrier firmly lowered. He told the Libyan in no uncertain terms that we should get back to Tripoli. The Sinai front had been routed, the Golan Heights and Gaza Strip already lost.

When our officer asked for food and lodging for us before undertaking the long return trip, the Egyptian sentry simply laughed in his face.

"You don't understand, brother. There's no food or place to sleep in Cairo. Refugees are arriving in tens of thousands from everywhere, fleeing from the Israelis. Go back to Libya right now."

There seemed nothing else to do. But Ahmed and Karim had relatives in Cairo, cousins of their father, Mohammed.

"Let's go to them," Karim suggested. "There's so much help needed here!"

"If they can let us sleep on the floor and give us a bowl of soup, we can all go back tomorrow," said Nico.

"And how can we go back?" Ahmed asked.

*He was right: How could we get back? And go back where?*

. . . .

We became lost in the unbelievable labyrinthine confusion of the old part of the city. Only after a mass of signs did we get to the square behind the Al Azhar Mosque where the Islamic University stood.

By now it was getting dark. The square was full of young and poorly clad Egyptian soldiers, many barefoot after losing their boots in Sinai during the retreat. There was rage in the Muslim quarter, the refugees shouting at the fruit and vegetable sellers to give them something to eat for free.

"Our uncle's house must be on the other side of the square," Ahmed said.

It would be an inconvenience if I suddenly appeared in a Muslim household where there were women and little girls who would have to cover themselves on my arrival.

"You and Karim go; Nico and I'll wait for you here. Then you can give us a shout."

"Okay, Mike," said Ahmed as they set off. "We'll be back soon."

Even in the middle of that hubbub Nico was drawn to the cinema posters, which were more numerous than in Tripoli. He went wandering around the square, gazing up just like a tourist would. Meanwhile, I was starving hungry. My stomach finally relaxed at the thought of not having to go and fight at the front, but it was still empty. I went

up to a stall and bought two pounds of apples. Then I walked slowly
over to the other side of the square to where Nico was wandering
among the piles of filth in front of a billboard for *Lawrence of Arabia*.

All of a sudden, three Egyptian soldiers surrounded me. One of
them, the only one armed with an old Russian pistol, stuck the barrel
in my ribs and pushed me into a dark alley. The most they could have
been was two or three years older than I was. The only one with boots
was the one with the pistol. The second was wearing flip-flops, and the
third leather babouches of two different colors.

They pushed me down to the back of the alley, which ended in a
two-yard-high wall. The feeble light from the few houses and shops
gave barely any illumination.

They took away my bag of apples. Then the one with the pistol
barked out, *"Filuss, dollars!"* while the other two each held me by an arm.

I knew they intended to take my money and then kill me. It was
the simplest way for them. There were no witnesses and, in Cairo at
that time, no one would have gone looking for my killers.

I slowly began to close up the distance from the one with the gun, but
I was too far away to kick it away with a tae. Then, at the other end of
the alley, where it met the square, I saw the familiar outline of Ahmed.
He was coming toward us alone, shuffling along like a disheveled and
unshaven Omar Sharif.

One of the two holding my arms let go and went up to him.

*"Dhahab, walad!"* he ordered.

Ahmed put on a seventeen-year-old's innocuous air and idiotic
grin. He took a couple more steps forward then said in Italian, "Take
the one with the gun!" As he let go a tae kick to the chin of the soldier
who had gone up to meet him, I simultaneously launched a tae kick
at the chest of the soldier with the weapon.

There was a sound of breaking teeth, jaw, and ribs, accompanied
by cries of pain. While the other two were moaning on the ground,
clutching broken bones, the third terrified Egyptian tried to move
toward the square.

But he found Nico and Karim blocking his path. It was Nico who
landed him among the refuse with a kwon to the temple.

Karim looked on, appalled at a sight he never wanted to witness. As a fervent supporter of Egypt's troops, he now saw them lying in front of him, laid out flat by the others in the blood brotherhood.

Ahmed went up to the soldier on the ground and pulled the knife out of his pocket. It was no longer the Swiss Army Knife he had used to scare Don Eugenio but a beautiful one with a saw blade about four inches long used for filleting fish.

"No, brother!" Karim blurted out.

"Quiet," Ahmed ordered. Then he looked me in the eye. He needed my approval.

"If we let them go, they'll only report us, Mike. And here, they'll shoot us as soon as look at us."

Perhaps this had always been written in our destinies, in our genes, in our endless solitary afternoons skewering scorpions, shooting doves, spearing grouper, and learning martial arts.

*I won't become an engineer like Alberto and my father, not even a gas-pump attendant like Nico. Laura was right: I'll end up a gangster with Ahmed.*

I had no wish to be shot or to die by the hands of those three desperadoes in a filthy back alley in a city that was not ours.

Ahmed grabbed the soldier from behind by his hair, just as he had held the dog that had bitten Jet.

I tried to say no, but the word wouldn't come out. It stayed locked in my brain while Ahmed calmly slit the man's carotid artery.

One of the others was trying to recover the gun. Nico picked it up and pointed it at him.

"No, Nico," said Ahmed. "It'll make too much noise."

So Nico gave him another fearful kwon on the point of his chin, and the Egyptian fell like a sack of potatoes.

Ahmed went up to the two now on the ground.

No witnesses.

He slit their throats. First one, then the other, without a moment's hesitation.

We quickly left the alley. Now we knew where our brotherhood of blood and sand was leading us.

# FRIDAY, JUNE 9, 1967

Next morning, Ahmed and Karim's aunt prepared a breakfast for us of dry bread, tea, and nuts. Then we went out into the teeming square. It was full of all kinds of traffic: men, soldiers, women wrapped in their barracans, donkey carts, goats. Many carts were full of trunks, battered suitcases, furniture, and piles of clothes, as refugees were coming into Cairo by the thousands from the Israeli-occupied territories.

But, despite the Arabs' defeat, Karim was optimistic.

"We had to try. Nasser's still a hero. We'll get to Tel Aviv next time."

I turned to Ahmed. He was looking affectionately at his younger brother, who was so like him physically and yet so different in his ideas.

Karim was his brother related by blood, while I was his blood brother by pact and the one with the same ideas and rage inside.

"We have to go back to Tripoli, Karim. Our mother will be worried," Ahmed said to him.

Karim looked at me, unhappy at the thought of asking me a favor.

"Mike, can you tell my father?"

"Tell him what, Karim?"

"I want to stay here and help these poor people. I want to go to the Muslim Brotherhood's Islamic school."

"Don't even think about it," Ahmed cut in. "You're coming back to Tripoli with us today."

Karim looked at his brother.

"I'm not going back, Ahmed. You can kill me if you want and take my dead body back home instead."

Ahmed remained calm.

"Go and take a walk with Nico, Karim. I'm going to have a word with Mike. Come back in half an hour."

Nico put a muscular arm around Karim and led him away.

Ahmed and I set off on a tour through the back alleys. The defeated city was swarming around us with an indescribable human chaos of life, a flotsam and jetsam of carts, donkeys, goats, bicycles, filth, and noise.

Neither of us spoke. Between the two of us there was no need. We knew we had killed three people and had done it solely to protect ourselves. Or was there anything more to it than that?

"Do you want my parents to persuade your father?" I asked him.

I already knew what Ahmed's reply would be.

"I'll never leave Karim here by himself."

I smiled at him. I showed him the scar on my left wrist. It was whiter and less deep than the one on his right. But it was from these marks that the blood had flowed and mingled together.

I remembered Laura Hunt's light kiss when she was saying good-bye to me.

*That was only a promise; if she really wants me she will wait for me. I have a pact with my friends that can't be broken.*

# MONDAY, JUNE 26, 1967

I phoned my grandfather. He spoke to Mohammed and my parents. They all came to Egypt as soon as the authorities opened the borders and the airport: my mother, my grandfather, Mohammed, and Nico's mother, Santuzza. Even Alberto came over from Rome. Everyone but Ingegnere Balistreri. It appeared Dad did not wish to speak to his crazy younger son.

Since it was practically impossible to find a bed for the night in Cairo, they came on the first morning flight from Tripoli, intending to return that same evening. A cousin of Mohammed's—a close relative whom Ahmed and Karim referred to as their uncle—had an old bus, and we went to pick them up because there were no taxis. During the trip from the airport to his house we drove through a city as alive as it ever was but devastated by poverty.

Drawing near the Egyptian uncle's house, we saw that the Al Azhar park, the Islamic University, and its mosque were one entire encampment teeming with refugees: ragged barefoot people with rickety handcarts full of household goods and furnishings.

My mother touched the Egyptian uncle's shoulder.

"I'd like to do the last part on foot, by myself with Mike."

He was worried. "Signora, it's dangerous. It's full of desperate, destitute people . . ."

My mother had never been afraid of destitute people.

If anything, the people she feared were the rich.

"With Mike for protection, nothing will happen to me."

After taking out all the money she had, she left her bag on the bus and we stepped off into the crowd. Before even a minute had passed we were surrounded by people begging.

"*Baksheesh, filuss!*"

Italia handed out coins to the children and bills to the women. When the money was all gone, she went into a goldsmith's and, speaking in Arabic, made a deal for the necklace and bracelet she was wearing, everything except her wedding ring. She gave out that money as well, besieged and followed by an ever-growing swarm of people begging.

Only when it became clear that the money really was finished did they all disperse.

I watched the scene in the way, as a child, I had imagined Jesus performed the miracle of feeding the five thousand. When it was over, this elegant woman—her features prematurely aged, a kaftan covering her painfully white skin, her eyes hidden by large sunglasses—broke into tears.

"There's nothing you can do, Mamma. There's too many of them."

She pretended not to hear me. She had made her decision.

"You can stay here, Mike, but I want you to continue your education. There's an Italian state school, and here your expulsion has no validity. If you work, you can finish your education in two years."

*So it had already been decided. We could stay in Cairo, but on certain conditions.*

We gave each other a hug.

"I promise, Mamma. I'll finish secondary school here, and the other three will as well."

Italia smiled.

"You'll become inseparable, the four of you!"

*We already are, Mamma. We've made a brotherhood of sand and blood. It can't be dissolved now.*

# INTERMEZZO

# JULY 1967–JULY 1969

Thanks to the money my mother regularly sent, Nico and I were able to find a small room to rent in Al Azhar. Ahmed and Karim were living with their uncle and went to the Islamic school, while Nico and I went to the Italian one. We had promised our parents that we would study, and we did it seriously, going to school every morning.

But for the rest of the time Cairo was all ours: twenty times larger than Tripoli, teeming with life, drama. And opportunities for recreational activities—and there were plenty to cater to all tastes.

Karim devoted himself body and soul to Muslim Brotherhood meetings for helping the refugees. The cemetery became a residential quarter, with families occupying the funeral chapels. Gradually, the gas rings and cylinders arrived and electric cables hung down from the lampposts and the chapels with do-it-yourself connections.

Every afternoon, Nico went to the cinema, a different film each day. Then he went to the barber to have his wretched curls straightened and his black bristly beard shaved, and then he was off to visit Cairo's many bordellos. He went there to look, and no more, because he had no money to purchase the goods.

*One day, Mike, I'll buy them all.*

Ahmed and I hung out together a lot. Each afternoon, we went to a gym for three hours of martial arts and then we explored the defeated city's endless districts. It was a special time and place, a world to reconstruct, full of opportunity—particularly for the likes of us, who had never worked in an office or a shop.

"We can't just keep on being schoolkids and looking after Karim and Nico," we said.

It was my idea to start a business, but it was Ahmed who was able to develop it. We began with what we knew best. Ahmed was the organizer, Nico was an excellent driver, and Karim had the right contacts in the Alexandria fish market, through the Muslim Brotherhood. Ahmed and myself were aces at underwater fishing, either free diving or scuba, and, among the things my mother had sent us, were our underwater spear guns.

We left for Alexandria on a Friday night in the bus borrowed from the Egyptian uncle, fished all day Saturday, sold the catch at the Sunday-morning fish market, and were back in Cairo on Sunday evening.

And then the money started coming in. It was only a little, but enough for our needs. I didn't need it at all, really, but I wanted to show my father that I could get by without him.

Then a second idea arose from Karim's complaints.

"These refugees need jobs, some future prospects," he was always declaring.

"You're right," we said to him, "but Egypt's on its knees and there's no work here. All they can do is go begging or die of starvation."

Then, one day, I came up with a different answer.

"We'll take them to where there's work. Only those who can work, mind you. We can help their families to stay and survive here by taking the young men off to work."

"But where?" asked Nico.

"In Libya, where there *is* work and we know the area," I answered.

Karim protested.

"But that's illegal, Mike. And it's immoral to exploit those poor guys."

"We won't ask the refugees to pay us, but the employers in Libya can," I said. I looked at Ahmed and, after a moment, he smiled.

*Illegal? Immoral? We've killed three people. We've gone well beyond those words.*

His mind started racing. He would take on the task of finding the first work for the refugees in Tobruk, just over the border with Egypt.

The project went extremely well. In those two years after the Egyptian defeat of June 1967, the four of us set about work seriously and without the need of setting up a business with invoices and bookkeeping. It was strictly cash only, which we kept in the Egyptian uncle's house.

With the first cash we bought a red Fiat 850T: a seven-seater camper van nearly four yards long with sliding doors and a tailgate on the back. Nico adapted it for our purposes. He brought forward the second row of seats and, immediately behind it, inserted a partition wall, leaving only the first of the three side windows with glass and covering the other windows and rear doors with metal sheeting. We could fit five passengers in the seats and up to six clandestine workers crammed in the rear.

On one side of the van he painted the letters MANK, the name of our organization, formed from our four initials, and he put up a Barbra Streisand poster in the back.

"When I'm older, I'll manage a star like her and then marry her."

We laughed at such an idiotic idea, but it wasn't long until Nico began to spend his money on the girls in the bordellos. The opportunities for girls had grown in Cairo, but he'd decided that paying for it was the best way of avoiding having to speak to them. So his lisp was kept a secret, and no whore would dare laugh at his eyebrows and hairiness. Nico had formed his own idea of women, and it would never change.

"They're all alike, Mike. They're all whores. You buy them a cinema ticket and a Coca-Cola; I buy their services up front."

My sex life in those two years was very occasional and unsatisfying. The girls were boring and all the same. I found them small-minded, but I knew this was not the case with all of them. In those two years, Mohammed, my parents, and Nico's mother made occasional visits to Cairo. Everyone came except my father, whom I spoke to on the phone only at Easter and Christmas, and even then only about my studies and never about our MANK organization. It was better to be cautious with him.

In May 1969, a new business opportunity came up. Karim suggested buying a small restaurant on the Nile. The price was excellent, thanks to the good offices of his friends, the Muslim Brotherhood. We thought it over for a while, then the unanimous decision was taken in favor and we stopped with the refugees and the fishing.

So, by June 1969, after two years spent in Cairo, MANK became a legal enterprise. We were four young entrepreneurs in the restaurant business. Nothing that important but enough to get by on.

*Enough not to have to depend on Salvatore Balistreri for money.*

# SUNDAY, JULY 20, 1969

t came as a complete surprise when all four of us passed our final-year exams, Nico and I even getting our national *maturità* diploma from Cairo's Italian high school without Dad having to do any behind-the-scenes manipulation.

Everyone came over from Tripoli to celebrate: Mamma, Granddad, Alberto, Santuzza, Mohammed, and even my father.

Unexpectedly, Ingegnere Balistreri was actually getting a hard time on my behalf.

*Perhaps his son isn't a failure. Perhaps he can still make up for lost time.*

That evening, we went to our restaurant on the Nile, the Balistreri and Al Bakri families, together with Nico and his mother. We had a meal of fish fresh from Alexandria and the typical dish of greens, *molokhiyyah*, followed by dates. The atmosphere was so upbeat and happy I thought everything would finally be settled for the future.

Mamma would stop her excessive drinking and smoking. Dad would be proud when I told him that I had not only passed my exams but also started a business.

"So," my father asked, "what exactly is this MANK organization?"

*Of course, he'd seen the letters Nico painted on the van. Or did he know already?*

Everyone turned to look at me.

"We'll tell you after supper," I replied.

Dad changed tactics and direction. He turned to Nico.

"Now that you've finished high school and are coming back to Tripoli, I'm going to give you the Esso station and help you build a large workshop that will be all yours."

I was not happy with this. What he was offering Nico was simply bait to draw us away from Cairo.

*Dad hasn't given up. He wants me back in Tripoli. And then at a university in Rome.*

When it came time to pay the bill, my father took out his wallet.

I placed my hand over his. "You don't need to, Dad. This restaurant belongs to us."

As usual, I had underestimated Ingegnere Salvatore Balistreri.

"I'm well aware of it, Mike. It's owned by this MANK organization. That's why I want to pay."

All the others—with the exception of Mohammed—were taken aback. Of course, Mohammed was my father's Egyptian antenna, getting his information through the cousin in Cairo who had put us up. Everyone was now looking at us with different eyes, a mixture of amazement and admiration. Everyone except Dad and Mohammed, that is.

*They know about everything, including the less legitimate side of MANK's activities.*

"Aren't you happy, Dad?" I asked him as we left the restaurant.

He took me by the arm.

"Of course, Mike. Happy and proud. Now that you've graduated from high school, you can go to a university in Rome, just like Alberto."

I felt my feet beginning to sink in quicksand. I was almost nineteen, and my father didn't give a damn about what I really wanted to do.

"Dad, business is going well here in Cairo. I like the city and I want to stay in Africa."

*And I detest Italy. A country governed by the priesthood, with the workers always taking to the streets and students daubing their university walls with the hammer and sickle. That's not for me at all.*

Ingegnere Balistreri brushed it all away with a gesture and a few words. All of it. MANK's small business operation, my dreams, everything I really was.

He pointed to Ahmed, Karim, and Nico, who were sharing a joke near the camper van.

"Leave that kind of thing to them, Mike. You and Alberto are destined for much more important things."

And, looking at the van, I realized how pathetic we must have seemed to him. Two years of work to open a little restaurant on the Nile, in a city still recovering from disaster.

But there were things about me that Dad did not know. Like the murder of three Egyptian soldiers.

I had done everything in order to find myself, get a life, and create a space for myself. And a point of contact with my father. But it was hopeless. I could have—and should have—told him to go to hell. But then there was my mother, Granddad, Alberto. And there was Laura Hunt. The way her lips had brushed mine the day I left.

# END OF JULY, 1969

When our families had gone back to Tripoli, the four members of the MANK organization talked things over at length as we smoked a *shisha*. Karim would not hear of going back. He had the war refugees to help—in particular those living in the cemetery, that city of both the living and the dead. Nico did not want to give up his cinema and his whores, and he had found a hairdresser in Cairo he could trust to straighten out his bushy head of curls.

We came up with a compromise solution. As far as our restaurant was concerned, August was a dead month, so we might as well spend it with our families in Tripoli. We could then come back to Egypt in September. Or not.

# FRIDAY, AUGUST 1, 1969

We were now back in Tripoli. The Hunt family was due to arrive from the United States, where they had spent the month of July. I had taken a few days to reflect and to reacquaint myself with Tripoli's tranquil rhythms.

That Friday, with the air conditioning on maximum, I was having breakfast alone in the living room. A wind from the desert was bringing in the first signs of sand that heralded the *ghibli* forecast for the weekend. In the forecourt before the two villas, the frogs, grasshoppers, and scorpions had taken refuge under the shade of the eucalyptus and palms.

Nadia, the younger sister of Ahmed and Karim, was pouring caffè latte into my cup. Now that she was fifteen, we employed her as a maid. Each morning, she walked the one mile of dirt path through the bare countryside from Mohammed's wooden shack to the Balistreri villa and arrived at exactly half past eight. She first made coffee for my mother, then breakfast for everyone else.

She was always hovering around me, as she had done since she was little. She was obliged by her religion and her father to wear a costume that covered her entire body and wear a veil on her head that left only one eye uncovered. But you could feel that underneath the veil was a beautiful face and under the costume was a body as slim and graceful as those of her brothers.

"Would you like more nuts, Signor Mike?"

Even when she was little and came over to play, hoping for a role in one of my films, she used to call me "Signor." Mohammed must have instructed her to do so. She served me the best toasted peanuts, knowing how much I loved them.

"No thanks, Nadia. Do you like working here?"

"Of course, Signor Mike. The only thing I don't like is walking along the path by the cesspit."

"Are you still frightened because they found that young black woman and her baby there all those years ago?"

She was taken aback for a moment.

"Were they black, Signor Mike?"

It had slipped out like that, without my thinking. So many years had passed. The information was old and pretty useless. I told her to prove that we were friends, even if we did employ her as a servant.

"It's supposed to be a secret, Nadia. Can you keep a secret?"

"Yes, Signor Mike. So they were black?"

"They were. They weren't sure if the baby was a girl or boy, the bodies were too decayed. But they were black."

"I think the little one was a baby girl," she added, inexplicably.

# SATURDAY, AUGUST 2, 1969

At nine o'clock on its second day, the *ghibli* was blowing strongly. I headed for the Hunt's house, attracted by the smells of French toast and bacon. I was hoping to see Laura, but there was only her father, sitting alone in the large kitchen.

William had come back from the United States with Laura and Marlene the day before, but I had not seen him since I left for Cairo.

"Hi, Mike, come on in. Marlene's out for a run, despite the *ghibli*. Laura has an upset tummy. One of those girl things. So it's just me here, all on my own."

"Okay, I'll go back home, Mr. Hunt. Sorry to bother you."

"Won't you have breakfast with me? I'm having it in the kitchen because there's too much damned sand outside, but we have corn-flakes, French toast, bacon, pancakes."

The invitation took me by surprise. I had never been alone with Mr. Hunt, and he had never shown any particular liking for me. His preference was obviously for Alberto. But breakfast was difficult to refuse.

"Oh, well, thank you, Mr. Hunt. I'd like that."

We began eating in silence. It seemed impossible to think of any subject we had in common that we could chat about, as he and Alberto did about international politics and the Vietnam War. But William Hunt had something on his mind.

"You like Laura, don't you?" he suddenly asked me.

Now I knew where Laura's habit of asking direct questions came from. But it was difficult to know how to reply.

"Laura takes beautiful pictures. She'll become a real professional one day."

"Isn't there anything else you like about her?"

Again, I was at a loss for words. I stared at the bowl of cornflakes.

*Here was a man who'd never stand for any "bullshit," as the Americans said.*

"She's very beautiful, Mr. Hunt."

He laughed.

"Of course, she takes after Marlene, who's also a beautiful woman. Don't you think?"

This was too much for me. In fact, I was reeling from the shock of it.

"Laura's very serious, as well."

William Hunt seemed not to notice the implications about Marlene and took up the compliment about Laura.

"She got that from me, Mike. She has the qualities of both her parents."

"And the defects?"

I had given it some thought, I believed. But the question just slipped out.

He did not bat an eyelash. Rather, for the first time since I had known him, William Hunt deigned to look at me with real interest. He thought about it for some time, as if the question needed a well-considered reply. Then he said something surprising.

"Marlene has no defects at all. As for mine, I really do hope Laura hasn't inherited those."

Not to see any defect in Marlene meant either being blind or deluded. But William Hunt seemed to be neither. As for his defects, I had no idea what he meant.

"Your Uncle Toni died in the war, didn't he, Mike?"

Now I could follow him.

*His defects. The pointless sacrifice of heroes like Toni, like his friends who'd died in Korea and Vietnam.*

"Yes, sir. And you fought against the Communists in Korea, didn't you?"

I knew what I had been told: a little from my mother, a little from Laura. A desperate battle against 300,000 Chinese, a human avalanche that swept down upon the South Koreans and the Americans, including the X Corps of Marines. The Yalu River was frozen, there was a single wretched bridge, dead bodies everywhere and endless prisoners and civilians. At Chosin Reservoir, the Marines were surrounded. A few men parachuted in to help, William Hunt among them.

*A war hero. A man ready to die for his principles.*

William Hunt nodded. He was tracing memories that could not have been pleasant.

"War is ugly, Mike. It leads you to do things you'd never, ever want to do. It changes you, forever."

At that moment, Marlene came back from jogging, dripping with sweat. She popped her head into the kitchen, waved a hand at us, and went upstairs, while I avoided following her exceptional body with my eyes.

William Hunt got up. His assistant had arrived in a jeep to take him to Wheelus.

"I know you read Nietzsche, Mike. So you'll know that there are no essentially *moral* things, only moral *interpretations* of things."

He went out and climbed into the jeep, leaving me alone in the kitchen, half speechless in front of my French toast and eggs and bacon.

• • • •

Ten minutes later, I was still in the Hunts' kitchen when Marlene came in. She had changed out of her shorts and running vest and was now in a bikini, ready to sunbathe on the veranda. I tried not to look at her.

"Thank goodness you're here, Mike. Laura's asleep. I could use a hand."

She handed me the sunblock and I stared at it in the middle of a bite of French toast. She turned away, went out of the kitchen, and stopped in front of a mirror. With one hand, she lifted her hair off the nape of her neck and held it there. With the other she lit a cigarette, her green eyes watching me in the mirror.

"Come on, Mike, let's be quick."

I tried to protest.

"But on the veranda there's the *ghibli*. You'll be covered in sand."

She laughed with that extraordinary mouth.

"So I'll become a beautiful breaded cutlet, won't I? Do you like cutlets, Mike?"

I felt my forehead in flames and my legs turn to jelly. I spread a little cream around her neck then stopped. She looked at me in the mirror, the cigarette hanging from the corner of those fulsome lips.

"And the rest? Do you want me to get sunburn all down my back?"

I spread cream on her shoulders, avoiding her gaze in the mirror. When I reached the strap of the bikini top I stopped again.

"You'll have to undo it, otherwise it'll leave a stripe."

She said it just like that, absolutely casually. Naturally, the two damned hook and eye closures were impossible to undo with my nervous hands. She stared at me in the mirror.

"You're almost nineteen, Mike. You must have undone a bra or two. Is it me who's making you feel uncomfortable?"

*You don't make me feel uncomfortable. You shake me to the very roots, day and night, when I wake up in a sweat imagining you naked on the veranda.*

She put out the cigarette, threw her long hair forward over her shoulder, brought her arms behind her back, and her hands guided mine to the hooks and eyes. I felt my hands trembling as I undid them. She took her hands away so that she could hold the top of the bikini over her magnificent breasts.

I closed my eyes, praying that she would not turn around and see the large bulge in my jeans. I began spreading the cream with both hands, up and then down, getting ever closer to the elastic of the bikini bottom.

*An uncrossable border, the entrance to a forbidden paradise.*

Perhaps it was my imagination, but she let out a tiny groan of pleasure.

. . . .

"It should be my husband doing this, but he's always at work or traveling. And here am I alone, in the middle of all this sand."

Her voice wavered between joking and bitterness, as if she were walking along a narrow plank, not knowing on which side she might fall.

"I'm sorry," I said stupidly.

"What are you sorry about, Michelino?" Now there was a scornful tone to her voice.

I had arrived at the edge of the bikini bottom. I felt the elastic under my fingertips. I tried to lower it in my mind, but failed.

"I'm sorry, but I have to go now."

I had no idea what I was saying. In horror, I heard my adolescent voice turn raucous and guttural, wavering in pitch in my excitement.

She fastened the bikini top and suddenly turned around, facing me. I was five foot nine and taller than she was by several inches, and yet I felt like a child caught in a lie, red-faced, and dumbstruck. I was terrified by the thought of the erection pressing against my jeans and prayed she would not notice it.

Marlene stared straight into me for a moment with those eyes that made you feel as if you were the only man in the world. And the most stupid.

"You have beautiful hands, Mike. You use them well. Perhaps we can do this again."

She gave me a little pat on the chest with two fingers and, as I felt the electric shock waves running through my body, she turned away and went off up the stairs.

*I stopped at the edge of that bikini bottom as if on the edge of an abyss.*

When I came out, despite the *ghibli*, my father was chatting in the garden with Don Eugenio, Emilio Busi, and Mohammed. Four pairs of eyes followed me with curiosity while I waved a hand at them and—pretending there was nothing wrong—went off in the opposite direction.

That Saturday evening, we celebrated our return from Cairo and the Hunts' from the United States. At dinner, the fish had been caught by Salim the night before and cooked by Farid, who extolled its freshness as if he were selling it on the market.

· · · ·

Inside the villa, the windows were firmly shut and the air conditioners on maximum. Outside, the *ghibli* was slowing in intensity before its climax on the third and final day.

It was a notable gathering. The entire Bruseghin-Balistreri, Hunt, and Al Bakri families; Nico and his mother, Santuzza; Emilio Busi and Don Eugenio. Happy people.

Everyone, that is, except my mother. She had aged a great deal in the two years I had spent in Cairo. It was as if an illness were slowly eating away at her. Thin lines had appeared in her pale complexion and also many white strands in her short blond hair. She was now as thin as Marlene Hunt, except that Marlene was all tone and curve while Italia was only skin and bone.

At the end of dinner my father asked for a moment of silence. He had an announcement to make.

"Tomorrow, boys, we're going fishing. There's a bank of shallows around La Moneta that's good for both underwater fishing and inshore trolling. It was Salim who suggested the place."

Even Alberto was concerned.

"Dad, there'll be a hell of a heat. The *ghibli*'s blowing at twenty knots."

"Precisely. It'll be an inferno in these villas with all this sand around. It'll be a little better in Tripoli, but it'll be a lot less hot out at sea on that stretch of water."

It was clear my father was keen on it. That island was the new jewel in his crown. But Nico pointed out a problem as well.

"Tomorrow they're going to close the Sidi El Masri road into Shara Ben Ashur and Garden City from ten till one, and you won't be able to get into Tripoli. There's a folk festival with a camel parade from the Cathedral to Piazza Italia. Italian television will be there."

Nico was always well informed about these things, but my father was not to be discouraged.

"Then we'll have to get into the city before ten. I'll go with Alberto and Granddad to Don Eugenio's for Mass tomorrow instead of to the cathedral, then I'll go to the barber next to the market in Shara Mizran. You'll remember my paper, won't you, Nico?"

Among the new duties my father had Nico perform was bringing him the *Giornale di Tripoli* hot off the press to the barber's at eight o'clock every Sunday morning. That was his usual opening time, but for Ingegnere Balistreri he opened fifteen minutes earlier in order to trim his beard and mustache straight after Mass. Then Dad went to sit on the terrace of the Waddan Hotel with his newspaper to have breakfast and chat with the important Italians for a couple of hours.

"Of course, Ingegnere, not to worry."

"On the dot, Nico, if you please."

"We'll have to refill the tanks, though," said Salim. "You can fish really well on the bottom of the shallows there."

I was not enthusiastic, either about going fishing during the *ghibli* or getting up at an ungodly hour for the tanks.

"It's already half past midnight. I'm not getting up before nine. We can do without the tanks."

As usual, my father thought me a slacker. He turned to Ahmed as if I had not said a word.

"Will you see to them, Ahmed?"

"All right. If Nico leaves them at the gas station, I'll pick them up tomorrow morning."

"Okay," said Nico. "I'll put them in the van tonight and drop by the station toward eight fifteen. You can take over, then I can come to the villa to collect Alberto and Mike."

All this activity was getting on my nerves.

"Not too early, Nico. I said I wanted to sleep."

My father gave me a dirty look, but Alberto came to my defense.

"There's no hurry. Nico and I'll have breakfast together and, as soon as Mike's ready, we'll set off for Tripoli before they close the road."

Now my father was happy. He turned to Busi. "We'll see each other at the barber's?"

"No, this time I'm with Mike, I want some sleep. I'll meet you at the Waddan at ten."

Dad looked at the Americans.

"William?"

Hunt shook his head.

"Thanks, but we can't. Tomorrow at Wheelus there's the final of the baseball championship, and a brunch. Laura, Marlene, and I never miss it. We'll be back in the afternoon after the brunch."

Dad was a little disappointed.

*He wants to show off his new island to Marlene.*

"You'll see to the office, won't you, Mohammed?"

Sunday was a work day for the Arabs.

"Of course, Ingegnere. I'll be in the office as usual at eight thirty."

"And you boys?" Dad asked Farid and Salim.

Farid brushed a hand through his frizzy hair and shook his head.

"Thanks, but we're going out fishing tonight and if Salim's on form I hope to be selling a good catch at the market tomorrow."

Dad did not even ask my mother and Granddad. He knew that neither of them liked fishing. The Bruseghin were people of the earth and olives. She would stay at home in the villa with the air conditioning. After Mass, my grandfather would stroll around the market as usual and then go to the Italian Club for a game of bocce.

So that endless night finally came to an end, while the *ghibli* was gearing up for its third and final day.

# SUNDAY, AUGUST 3, 1969

## MORNING

Born in the Sirtica coastal desert, Mohammed Al Bakri was fond of telling everyone about the wind. *The* ghibli *starts in the Sahara, from the dunes of the Calanshio Sand Sea. It blows softly at first then more strongly. The third day is usually the worst.*

The four Al Bakri sons had done their best to seal the shack with thirty square yards of metal sheeting and some plasticine, an old gift from the Balistreri sons. Their shack had one advantage over true houses. Their floor was already made of sand, covered with mats. All the *ghibli* did was add a good deal more.

It was the sense of smell that confirmed Mohammed's prediction. By the middle of the night, the south wind had risen even earlier than usual and was picking up the smell from the cesspit that lay a few hundred yards from the shack.

Under normal conditions, Cuckoo the cockerel waited for dawn's first light to announce to his four hens and the world in general that he was up and about. And that this was his territory. On this morning, however, he crowed his cock-a-doodle-doo while the stars could still be seen in the sky and dawn was a milky glow on the horizon.

Nadia turned over on her bed base, covered in sweat. She had not slept a wink, what with the fetid smell and the whine of the *nnamus*, the large mosquitoes that came in with the *ghibli*. She was also thinking a lot about Michele Balistreri.

*We share a secret together. We're friends.*

She was careful not to disturb Ahmed and Karim, who were sleeping next to her on the other side of the old sheet that served as a curtain. Her two other brothers, Farid and Salim, were out night fishing and at that hour were bringing their boat into port. They could then exchange places with Ahmed and Karim on the traditional wooden beds.

The bed base Nadia slept on was placed directly on the floor matting. It was old, but the springs were still in good shape. Father had been given it by his employer, Ingegnere Balistreri.

There were no clocks in the house, only her father's wristwatch, an old Omega also given to him by Balistreri to be sure that he would get to work on time. Nadia wondered when it would be dawn. It usually came at half past six this time of year. Being the daughter, she was the first to rise, at seven sharp. She had to milk the goat and make tea for the men. Then she had to get ready herself and wake her father's two wives.

Nadia placed a hand on the shack's metal sheeting. It was hot. She guessed it was over 100 degrees. It would be 120 by midday. She got up and took a peep at the time on the Omega her father placed by the bed at night. Cuckoo had started crowing early. It was not yet six thirty. But in any case she would not be able to get back to sleep.

. . . .

It had been a hell of a sleepless night, what with the *ghibli* whistling, the heat that came in even through the walls, and dreams of Marlene Hunt and the elastic of her bikini bottoms.

*I touched it with these fingers. The edge of the abyss.*

I had survived the two years in Cairo on a poetic memory of my lips brushed by Laura Hunt's. But, underneath that, deep in my gut, it was Marlene's sensuality that set me on fire and kept me awake at night.

I was feeling groggy when the sound of my father's jeep woke me up completely. I looked out of the window toward the sandy forecourt whipped up by the wind. Dad was in the driver's seat, Granddad next to him, Alberto in the rear. I looked at the time. It was six thirty.

*The good side of the family was off to church.*

. . . .

At seven sharp Nadia dragged herself off the bed base and found she was covered in *feshfesh*, the very fine dust the *ghibli* carried in, so fine it obscured your vision and choked your breathing.

First thing she did was roll her nightgown down to her ankles. On this point, Father was unbending. Since the time she had reached puberty, she had to keep her arms and legs covered, even in the home, out of respect for her father, brothers, and half-brothers. Outside, she had to wear the barracan that covered her body down to the wrists and ankles. And now, at fifteen, she also had to wear the veil, with only one eye uncovered. How she would have liked to show Mike her long hair dyed with henna. But she could not. Only the eye.

But she was very happy that he had come back to Tripoli. And that he had spoken to her, even confided a secret in her.

*The young woman and the baby girl were black.*

Of course, she had to be very careful not to appear a flirt. But Mike would certainly show her respect, not like all the other Italian boys. Today, she would serve him breakfast before he went off fishing. She had some special toasted peanuts for him.

She had to hurry with the tea and the goat. She had to leave at eight in order to arrive on time for eight thirty at the Balistreri villa. In the shack, it was like being in a hot oven. She went barefoot across the single living space, divided by the sheet hanging from clothes pegs. On one side were the three women; on the other, three wooden beds for the men. There was no space for more beds.

When she went outside, a sliver of pale-yellow sun was beginning to show in the washed-out sky to the east. The *ghibli* caught her with its hot breath, the sand immediately hit her face and the flies, excited by the smell of dung, were buzzing around her.

Nadia slipped quickly into the wooden closet her father had built for the needs of his wives and daughter. It was an old toilet bowl from the Balistreri home but, without a soil pipe, the urine ran along a descending channel that ended up under the nearest olive tree. There was the chamber pot for feces, which had to be taken immediately to the cesspit, otherwise the hungry flies arrived in hundreds. Nevertheless, the women of the Al Bakri household were privileged in having an outside toilet, whereas the men had to see to their needs out in the open.

She urinated then went over to the large, rusty tank. It was a yard square and held the water everyone washed in, protected by a tarpaulin. They changed the water every ten days, and only five days had elapsed since the last time, so it was still sufficiently clean. She rinsed her face and filled an enamel cup to wash her hands after milking the goat.

Barbetta was ready and waiting. She was the only goat they had and the chief source of sustenance, along with the wages her father received from Ingegnere Balistreri. Nadia milked the goat twice a day, at dawn and dusk. She placed herself behind it, and Barbetta gave her an affectionate bleat when she thought she had delivered enough milk. Nadia would then stroke her. Afterward, she would rinse her hands in the enamel cup and see the goat was watered. She never wasted a drop of water. Conserving water was a real concern for her father, who almost died of thirst as a child when crossing the Sirtica desert to get to Tripoli.

The fresh milk had to be drunk right away. In that heat, and with no refrigerator, it would not even last until the afternoon. From one milking came five portions for the five men. Nadia and the two wives had to make do with tea.

Nadia went to the old two-ring gas stove under the little canopy, another generous cast-off from the Balistreri household. She turned on the gas cylinder and used the lighter her father lit his *shisha* with in the evening. She took a pan of water from a second, smaller tank, which held the drinking water. She put the pan on to boil and went back inside.

Making no noise, she took off her nightgown and placed it on the bed. They had no mirrors, so she always brushed her hands quickly over chest and hips to check them, careful that no one should see her. She had a slim and graceful body, and she wondered if Michele Balistreri imagined how it looked under the barracan. Then she became embarrassed at the thought and asked Allah's forgiveness. She decided to wear the midnight-blue barracan her father had given her for her fifteenth birthday, which suited her best, she thought.

The family had an old metal chest of drawers from the Ingegnere's offices. Seven drawers on either side; one side for the men and the other for the women. She took out the summer barracan and a pair of large linen underwear, along with the band that went around her chest. When she heard the water boiling for the tea she went and shook her mother awake.

She would then wake the others according to the strict order laid down by her father, so that the women could have all their things done and be dressed by the time the men got up.

· · · ·

I had tried to put away the thought of Marlene Hunt's naked back and had fallen into a troubled half-sleep. In my half-sleep, Laura and Marlene's faces had become superimposed, one blending into the other. But the part of me that was awake was desperately trying to tell me something.

*That's not how it is, Mike. You have to choose, or you'll lose both.*

The noise of a car woke me. I looked out of the window and glimpsed William, Marlene, and Laura getting into the jeep driven by Mr. Hunt's assistant. They set off toward Tripoli. The last thing I saw in the whirlwind of sand was Marlene's glossy black hair, which fell down that glorious back of hers.

· · · ·

Nico Gerace said good-bye to his mother Santuzza, giving her a kiss and a hug. He did this every morning and, as ever, asked her if she needed anything before he left the apartment in Via Lazio, Shara Mizran, near the market, which they had courtesy of Ingegnere Balistreri.

Santuzza straightened her son's shirt collar and smelled the expensive cologne he splashed on his cheeks. She was proud of him. He was so elegant and clean when he could get out of his pump attendant's overalls and get rid of the smell of gasoline.

He was still too hairy, but now he no longer lisped and was much more self-confident. Those two years in Cairo had built up his self-esteem, too much, perhaps. But Santuzza liked her son like that, even if he was cocky.

Nico left the apartment around seven thirty. Down on the street, it was a boiling inferno. But, despite the *ghibli*, there was sufficient visibility.

There was also a lot of traffic, both pedestrian and vehicles, because of the Bedouin camel parade. Nico looked enthusiastically at the outside-broadcast van with the letters RAI, *Radio televisione italiana*, Italy's national television, which was on its way toward Piazza Italia, threading a route through the carriages, bicycles, and carts.

He drove the MANK van and in less than five minutes parked it on Shara Mizran, opposite the market that had just opened for business. He went in and found Farid and Salim's stall among the general confusion. There was a huge crowd of people, everyone speaking loudly in Arabic or Italian.

Salim was telling Giuseppe Bruseghin and Alberto Balistreri about the enormous greater amberjack he had caught that night. Small and slender as he was, he had hooked it, let it tire itself out, then pulled it onboard. As usual, Farid was busy selling and haggling prices with the customers and other fishermen. He was smoking a cigarette that hung between his fleshy lips, blowing the smoke out through his nostrils.

"I'm going to take the newspaper to your father," Nico said to Alberto.

"I'll come with you," said Alberto.

They said good-bye to Giuseppe, Farid, and Salim and went out into the baking, sand-filled heat. Nico thought that Italian television would be happy with all this sand to have around the Bedouin and their camels. There was barely enough visibility, but this sand gave a taste of the real Africa.

. . . .

Don Eugenio scrutinized the sky with distaste. In church, it was fine: you were cool and there was no sand. But the *ghibli* was blowing outside, and he had to drive to Sidi El Masri. He was wearing his usual worn cassock.

He had to go. He had made a commitment and a promise, both important. And Don Eugenio always kept his promises.

Despite his intentions of the night before, Emilio Busi woke up early and in an ugly mood because of the heat, the noise of the *ghibli*, and the thoughts that would not leave him alone. He left his house behind the cathedral and went on foot toward the market, trying to protect his eyes and mouth from the sand. His long hair flapped around in the wind, and his large horn-rimmed glasses acted as a screen.

He was dressed in his usual getup of checked shirt, striped pants, white socks, battered brown moccasins. He didn't like fishing—he was a mountain peasant—but he had to humor that show-off Balistreri and remove any last obstacles to their plans.

. . . .

Alberto and Nico walked to the newsstand then to the barber's next door. They delivered the newspaper to Ingegnere Balistreri at eight on the dot and then went back to the market without exchanging a single word along Shara Mizran. If you opened your mouth, it would be full of sand. They saw one of the RAI's outside-broadcast vans turning around toward the cathedral in Corso Italia.

. . . .

At eight, Nadia and Mohammed were ready to go out. Ahmed and Karim were up and almost ready as well. They had to meet Nico at the Esso station at eight fifteen to fill the air tanks for the scuba diving.

Nadia saw Karim talking earnestly with Ahmed but could not gather what it was about and went out with Mohammed. The sun was very pale in the chalk-white sky, the temperature 113 degrees and visibility in the sand cloud down to five yards. In order to conserve energy, no one wasted any words. They said good-bye with a wave of the hand.

Mohammed got into his pickup truck and left via the dirt track that ran along the olive grove and through the goat pastures to the paved road for Shara Ben Ashur and Tripoli.

Nadia set off in the opposite direction through the one mile of bush and bare earth that led to the Balistreri villa. The one mile that she walked down sedately in half an hour and Marlene Hunt ran up and down four times in less than an hour.

. . . .

At five past eight Alberto and Nico were back in the market. Giuseppe Bruseghin was still chatting with Salim, while Farid was in loud and earnest conversation with a bunch of customers. The two brothers really did complement each other and were indefatigable workers: Salim fished by night and Farid sold by day. They both worked with a violent passion, as if success would somehow redeem them from being poor in the eyes of the world.

Alberto went up to his grandfather.

"Granddad, Nico and I are going back to Sidi El Masri. Do you want a lift?"

His grandfather said good-bye to Farid and Salim and left the market with them. The traffic on Shara Mizran was still passable.

"Don't you want to stay here?" Nico asked Giuseppe. "It'll be much worse out in the countryside."

"Aren't you boys going fishing?" Giuseppe asked.

"Yes, Granddad. Dad's set his heart on it."

"Salvatore's right. It'll be much better out at sea. I'll get a coffee at the Italian Club and then perhaps watch the camel parade. I'll get someone to give me a lift. You go and wake up Mike."

Alberto and Nico got into the MANK van and set off along Shara Ben Ashur, toward Sidi El Masri, in order to avoid Corso Vittorio and the cathedral square, into which the crowds were pouring for the camel parade.

Away from the sea, visibility became worse. The two golden domes of the royal palace could barely be seen and, as they were traveling through Garden City, the downpour of red-hot sand struck the windshield and sides of the van like tiny hailstones.

It took them ten minutes to get to Shara Mizran, twice the normal time, but, at the Esso gas station at the start of the Sidi El Masri road, there was still no sign of the younger Al Bakri brothers.

"I'll leave the tanks here. No one's going to steal them," Nico decided. He got out, took the tanks out of the back of the van, placed them by the two gas pumps, and off they went to the villas.

When they entered the gate off the avenue, the two houses could barely be seen due to the clouds of sand. The eucalyptus and palm trees were shaking like crazy under the *ghibli*'s intensity.

"I'll put the van under the Hunts' carport," Nico said.

"Yes," said Alberto approvingly. "We'll find it under a sand dune if we don't."

Nico parked in front of William's Land Rover and Marlene's Ferrari. Then they quickly took shelter in the Balistreris' living room, with its shutters closed, the lights on and the air conditioning cranked up.

• • • •

The hot wind whipped Nadia's back as it pushed her along the path she knew like the back of her hand. Beside the wind, it was now filled with the deafening noise of cicadas.

Flies continually landed on her face, but she let them be. She would have had to lift her hands to brush them off, which would have made her sweat more and force even more flies to land on her. All around her, the *ghibli* had raised a yellowish cloud of dust that rendered outlines a blur and anything beyond thirty yards invisible.

She focused on the pleasant thought of Mike Balistreri and wondered if she would see him today. Mike was guarded with her, and she knew why. Ahmed and Karim. They would certainly have begged him not to look at their sister. If he so much as touched her and it became known, she would be ruined; no Libyan boy would ever marry her. But a part of her hoped that Mike would not listen to her brothers. She could not understand what she liked so much about him. He was certainly not handsome; there were many better-looking boys. It had to do with something inside him, not his outward appearance. He was different from all the other Italian boys, who were so cocksure. And there was something she knew for a fact: Michele Balistreri looked calm, but he could flatten anyone if he wanted to.

The *ghibli* was blowing burning sand in her face, making breathing difficult. She held the veil tightly over her half-closed eyes in order to avoid the red-hot grains and berserk flies as she walked down the dirt path on automatic pilot. She went down it every morning, and her bare feet knew every single stone.

In the howling wind, she heard the frogs croaking and knew she was almost there. She was on the large curve near the small pond, the last one before the Balistreri villa.

All of a sudden, she felt his presence more than saw him. About thirty yards from her, there was a hazy figure, motionless below a eucalyptus in the dusty sand cloud. There was no reason for him to be there and, for a moment, Nadia was confused. Then she smiled at him and shyly took another step forward. In the thick mist of sand blocking out the sunlight, she missed the gleam of his knife.

· · · ·

Jamaal the goatherd was a little addle-pated and confused as to his whereabouts. He had seen one of Mohammed's younger sons go past, either Ahmed or Karim. They looked so alike, and he had this damned glaucoma. And with all that sand swirling in the wind you could barely see a thing.

*I'm lost. I need help.*

Trusting his nose more than his eyes, he found the cesspit and walked slowly back toward the olive grove. He hated the *ghibli*, even more so now that he was over seventy. He could hear his three goats bleating frantically and, behind him, could feel the panting of the little mongrel that was supposed to be guarding them. He had no idea where he was.

Then, all of a sudden, he saw her. There was only one olive tree between him and the young girl. His eyes were poor and the *ghibli* was buffeting sand in his face, as if blown by a propeller. But he recognized her by the midnight-blue barracan.

*That's Nadia, Mohammed's young daughter, the one who works for the wealthy Italians.*

She was coming closer. His mongrel dog growled at that moment and Jamaal turned around, startled, because that dog never growled without a reason, even less in the heat. The mongrel was pointing at the girl in the yellow whirl of sand while Jamaal tried to get to the old olive-pressing shed.

It seemed to him the girl was making signs for him to come over, perhaps to ask him for help because she was lost as well. Jamaal brushed a hand over his eyes, trying to drive off the swarms of flies. Then the dog barked and he turned around to calm it down. When he turned back to Nadia, she had disappeared.

*It was impossible: five seconds earlier the girl was there.*

And around him there was only empty space, nowhere anyone could hide.

"Allah, my great Allah . . . The desert's swallowed her up! Or have I gone mad?"

The dog was growling again. Frightened, Jamaal took from his knapsack the long, serrated knife he used for filleting frogs before boiling them.

In the distance the *muezzin* called out his sorrowful prayer. It was nine o'clock.

. . . .

I went into the living room. The *muezzin's* cry from the mosque had stopped. Alberto was having breakfast with Nico.

"What terrible weather to go fishing in," I said as I flopped down in a chair.

Nico was eating toast and jam, dunking it in his caffè latte.

"Sorry, Mike. Did the van wake you?"

"It's nine twenty—we need to get a move on," Alberto cut in.

"Don't worry. Have Ahmed and Karim been to the Esso station for the tanks?" I asked while I poured myself some coffee. I drank it black with no sugar.

"They weren't there at eight fifteen, so we left the tanks there for them," Nico replied.

At that moment, my mother appeared in her bathrobe, her face full of sleep. She turned to the older housemaid.

"Isn't Nadia here?"

"I'm sorry, Signora, Nadia's not come in. She's probably not well. I'll make you some coffee."

My mother looked at the tempest of sand swirling outside the windows.

"And you're going fishing in this?" she asked.

"Yeah . . ." I grumbled, sipping my black coffee.

"It'll certainly be better out on the water than in here," Alberto explained, trying, as ever, to justify my father's demanding nature.

Breakfast over, Nico, Alberto, and I went out onto the forecourt. The heat was dreadful and the sand engulfed us. You could not even see the front gate onto the main road. There was no sound now from the doves, frogs, or cicadas. Even these creatures had to keep their beaks and mouths closed to avoid the sand.

*Damned* ghibli. *But perhaps Dad's right. It'll be better out on the water.*

Blown by the red-hot wind, we reached the van under the Hunts' carport, in front of William's Land Rover and Marlene's Ferrari. On the seat was the tube of sunblock I had spread on her back.

*Don't think about that anymore, Mike. That's enough now!*

Alberto got in front beside Nico; I stretched out on the backseat. Behind my back, the metal sheet dividing the back of the van was scorching hot. I had to be careful not to burn myself.

*You've already burned your hands, Mike, on Marlene Hunt's back.*

Nico drove carefully in the middle of the mist of sand, but the road was empty. After a few minutes we were at the Esso station. Ahmed was waiting for us on the tiny sand-swept forecourt.

"Put the tanks on the seat. Let's hurry or we won't get through," Nico said.

Ahmed seemed upset about something. I helped him load the tanks onto the backseat between the two of us, and off we went.

Behind us, we heard the noise of a vehicle coming from Sidi El Masri, but it was impossible to see it in that sand and I had no interest at all in knowing who it was.

"Isn't Karim coming?" Nico asked Ahmed.

"He says he's got a stomachache. I think he didn't want to come fishing," replied Ahmed, a look of disgust on his face.

"Isn't Nadia feeling well either?" Alberto asked.

Ahmed looked confused for a moment.

"Nadia? No, she went out at the same time as our father to come to the villa. Isn't she there?"

"No," I said. "I think, with the *ghibli*, she must have turned around and gone back home."

We entered Tripoli down Shara Ben Ashur at five to ten, a few minutes before the police blocked the road. Behind us, I could still hear the rumbling of the other vehicle's motor. Then, in the city, the visibility was decidedly better; it was farther away from the sand and more sheltered by its houses and apartment complexes.

Over by the cathedral square, Corso Vittorio, leading into Piazza Castello, was already blocked for the Bedouin's camel parade by the edge of the crowd and the RAI's outside-broadcast vans. So we took Via Roma, Shara December 24, then turned onto Shara Mizran. Outside the market entrance there was also a large crowd, and Nico had to stop to allow the pedestrians across and to let donkeys, bicycles, and carts go by. Then he managed to park between a donkey cart and a horse carriage.

"I'll go," I said.

I got out and ventured in among the market stalls. A mass of people stood in front of Farid and Salim's stall, buying fish. While Farid was serving the customers, Salim handed me the bucket of bait for the inshore trolling.

"Absolutely fresh garfish, Mike. The amberjack should love them."

I thanked him and went back to the van.

We turned down Corso Sicilia—Shara Omar Al Mukhtar—and set off toward the shore. We passed by the International Fair Grounds, the Lido, the Bagni Sulfurei, and the Beach Club. We got to the Underwater Club at half past ten.

As usual, Dad was right. You felt the heat and the sand far less. Out on the water, it would probably be fine.

. . . .

My father, Emilio Busi, and Don Eugenio arrived ten minutes later. Busi looked a sight, as usual, ridiculously and totally inappropriately dressed for fishing.

"My fault, boys," he said, excusing himself. "I was late."

In a few minutes we had unloaded the tanks and backpacks from the MANK van and stowed them on the motorboat, then we set off with Dad at the wheel. The farther we went out to sea, the less heat and sand there were.

La Moneta lay half a mile off the coast, a little beyond the Giorgim-popoli suburb and twenty from the Underwater Club. It had the shape of a jagged coin and was about two miles across. The side of the island facing the coast was low-lying and covered in sand, then the land rose slowly over to the opposite side, looking out to Sicily and the open sea, reaching its highest point in a rocky cliff rising vertically from the sea where my mother went to read and paint. Twenty yards below the cliff were jagged spikes of rock that could not be seen from above because of an overhang of a couple of yards and, depending on the tide, were either underwater or totally uncovered. Crossing the island was a single sandy track that ran from behind the large villa and provided a brisk thirty minutes' walk up to the top of the cliff.

At eleven, we reached the sandy shoreline. Dad had built a small jetty and created a beach with little gazebos in front of the large white villa, built in the Moorish style.

Then we drew around to the rocky side, the one looking onto the open sea, where there were more fish. We were more comfortable there, sheltered from the wind and sand, and came to the shallows Salim had recommended.

While the others prepared the rods and bait for trolling, we boys put on wetsuits and got the spear guns ready. Alberto and I had two new pneumatic Medisten guns, while Ahmed and Nico would use our two old spring-powered Cernias.

Don Eugenio took hold of a Medisten. "New guns, boys?"

Seven years had passed since the business of the photographs and, since then, Don Eugenio's behavior had been above reproach. To all appearances, at least. I really had the impression that he might have recovered from that "illness." Perhaps it was by force of will, or perhaps he had received help. Nevertheless, for me, he remained a dangerous man.

And, despite continuing to show the placid and humble air of a country priest, Don Eugenio had become an important man. Alberto told me he was the bridge between Tripoli's influential Italians and the Christian Democrat Party in Italy. And Don Eugenio had added a degree in economics to the one in theology and celebrated Mass less and less in favor of managing a large number of funds, the proceeds of which he used to help Africa's sub-Saharan poor. At least, that is what my father maintained, and everyone else in Tripoli confirmed it.

*A saint, a protector of the desperately poor. But also a priest with wandering hands.*

We had not spoken of the photographs again. But my mother still had them. I was not concerned whether Don Eugenio knew or not. But Nico's lisp came back every time he saw the priest, and Ahmed and I had certainly not forgotten.

In fact, it was only Alberto who spoke to him.

"Mike chose the guns, easier to handle."

Don Eugenio looked at me. No, he had not forgotten either.

"To get in where the fish hide, Mike? You like sneaking into their abodes, then?"

As a boy, when I still went to him for confession, I had told him that I had sinned in thought about Laura's mother. I had dreamed of her in a bikini. And Don Eugenio had seen me coming out of Marlene Hunt's house the day I had put the sunblock on her. Had he picked up on anything?

I made no reply. I had nothing to say to him. I would happily have done away with him, like the three soldiers in Cairo. But I couldn't.

We put on our Cressi masks and flippers. We chucked in the float with its homemade line made of corks, and Alberto, Nico, Ahmed, and I dove in and spread out so we wouldn't get in one another's way.

The water was warm. I went down to a depth of twelve yards but had no desire to fish. All I could think of was Marlene Hunt's naked back and her bikini bottom's line of elastic that my fingers had brushed against. And my voice hoarse with desire and the stupid things I said.

It had been more humiliating than arousing.

It was by instinct that I saw the grouper as it swam around the algae on the bottom. It must have weighed between thirteen and eighteen pounds. I calmly took aim and fired. The spear pierced it exactly where I wanted, right in the eye. Then I swam silently up to the motorboat's stern to hand over the catch. On board, they did not hear me emerge, but I could hear their voices.

"Everything's okay in Rome. The president's been informed," said Don Eugenio.

"My connections have been kept up to date as well," Busi added.

"Mohammed's been to Sirte with them. They're almost ready."

This was my father speaking.

Unfortunately, Alberto came up noisily beside me. Everyone on the motorboat suddenly went silent.

## AFTERNOON

At one thirty, we were eating some fruit under the canopy in the boat when we saw the Underwater Club's lifeguard approaching at high speed in his motorboat. I could see my mother in the prow with Karim. Despite the *ghibli*, she was wearing one of her usual long kaftans, a scarf, and dark glasses to protect herself against the sun. As soon as the two motorboats were side by side, she called to my father.

"We can't find Nadia."

Her eyes were hidden behind the dark glasses, but I could clearly see the lines were etched more deeply on her face.

My father said nothing. The boats were bobbing on the waves under the baking sun and I felt a pain spreading through my stomach and getting worse. And yet I never suffered from seasickness. I looked at Ahmed and Karim, but they were waiting without a word while my father decided what to do. Ahmed was coolly intent; Karim tense and worried.

"She's not ill?" Alberto asked.

"No. I wanted to see how she was and I went to visit her."

My father was speechless. In his view, his wife was not the sort of person to go off and visit a wooden shack near a cesspit. He knew very little about certain aspects of my mother.

"I went there at midday. There was only Karim and Mohammed's two wives. Mohammed was at work in town, and Farid and Salim were at the market. I tried to phone Mohammed in the office but he wasn't there, and I couldn't get here any earlier. Entry into Tripoli was closed because of the parade. They only opened it half an hour ago."

There was a prolonged silence while the *ghibli*'s noise suddenly increased. I shut my eyes to protect them from the sand. I could hear everyone breathing around me.

"We have to go back and find Nadia," my mother said. No one objected.

We boys went back with Mamma in the lifeguard's boat, following Dad's wake. She smoked in the prow in silence behind the impenetrable wall of her large sunglasses and scarf. I was thinking about Nadia. Only Alberto was sitting close to Mamma, speaking quietly to her while she listened. But it was clear that she did not agree with what Alberto was saying.

. . . .

When we came to the Underwater's pier we delegated the tasks and separated. Dad took Busi in the jeep back to his house behind the cathedral and Don Eugenio to his presbytery. Italia went in her Volkswagen to fetch Mohammed from the office. We went into town in the MANK van, Nico at the wheel. We went to pick up Farid and Salim, but the market on Shara Mizran had already closed.

Then, with the vehicles in single file, we all set off toward Sidi El Masri. *A funeral procession.*

The *ghibli*'s intensity increased gradually as we left the seaside. It was a gloomy, slow and silent journey: the jeep, the van, the Volkswagen, Mohammed's pickup.

Enveloped by sand and that oppressive humidity, each person kept to their own thoughts.

We arrived at the villas just before three and all parked on the dirt forecourt. Farid and Salim's pickup was already there and they were talking agitatedly with William Hunt, Marlene, and Laura.

"Have you found her?" my father asked.

William Hunt shook his head.

"No, we only came back from Wheelus an hour ago. We couldn't any earlier, because of the camel parade."

Farid was very agitated and ran a hand through his frizzy hair.

"When we came home, our mother told us that Nadia was missing and that Signora Italia and Karim had gone to tell you."

"We've looked a bit for her here, around the cabin, but found nothing," Salim added.

Naturally, William Hunt and my father organized a search. The men and boys only. Italia took shelter in our villa, Marlene and Laura in theirs.

We began to sweep the countryside around the one-mile path between our villa and Mohammed's shack, the route that Nadia walked every morning.

The *ghibli* was raising sand devils and, at Sidi El Masri, the visibility was poor. We looked like a bunch of phantoms, with sweat in our eyes, flies on our faces, and sand sticking to our lips. We searched under every bush, behind every tree, and in every dip in the ground.

At five, after two hours of searching, we reached the Al Bakris' wooden shack. Visibility there was even worse and the smell of dung was much stronger.

*How can they live like this?*

We found no trace of Nadia. William Hunt said that, at this point, we should call the police. We all went back to my family's villa and my father phoned the head of the police in person, one General Jalloun, who arrived in record time with no fewer than ten policemen. This was not efficiency but the influence of the powerful Bruseghin-Balistreri family.

"Does Nadia have any friends in the city, Ingegnere?" the general asked, studiously ignoring Mohammed and addressing only my father, in an obsequious manner.

My mother cut in immediately. "Shouldn't you ask her father or brothers, General Jalloun?"

But the general was a friend of my grandfather and held him in high esteem; they had known each other for twenty years and smoked a *shisha* together at one of the outside tables in a Piazza Castello bar. Granddad broke in, to conciliate.

"Let's hear Mohammed first, General, if you don't mind."

Jalloun looked at Granddad and nodded. Giuseppe Bruseghin was his friend, but his daughter was an arrogant Fascist and married to this Salvatore Balistreri, the most important of the Italians in Tripoli.

"Very well," the general conceded. "Let's hear Mohammed."

At that moment, Laura came in. I felt her eyes on me but avoided them. Since I had put sunblock on her mother's back and shoulders, stopping at the edge of those bikini bottoms, I could no longer look her in the eye. My mind was only on that body. Even in that tense moment, all I could think of was Marlene Hunt alone in the villa next door.

Hoping not to be noticed, I slipped out into the garden. After three days of hell, the damned *ghibli* was finally calming down and the sun's rays were now filtering through the curtain of sand.

*You're crazy, Mike. At a time like this?*

But I was drawn by an irresistible magnetic force. I went over to the Hunts' house and peered in through the half-open door. In silence, I crossed over the threshold and began to climb the stairs.

Marlene appeared at the top of them, walking to the terrace door, completely naked. She stopped to look at me, and it was like receiving a tae blow to the chest. I staggered and fell back, rolling down to the bottom of the stairs.

As I was laboriously getting up, bruised in body and pride, I heard her laugh and the terrace door closing.

*A young boy filled with desire, scorned and shut out of the Paradise Garden.*

I was in flames as I ran toward the back gate and then on toward Granddad's olive grove.

. . . .

The *ghibli*'s last howls hit me in the face as I ran. My mouth and eyes were caked with sand and the sweat was pouring down my spine. I got to the Al Bakris' shack in less than twenty minutes. I went quickly past the cesspit and on toward the olives. The sun was starting to set but looked like a ball of fire on the horizon now that it was able to penetrate the *ghibli*. Every so often, along the path I could see the goatherds' tin sheds. I could hear the goats bleating, tended only by the dog that kept an eye on them.

But the dog was barking too much. It was agitated, sniffing at the door of the brick shed that used to house the old olive press. It was six-sided and was where the olives had been pressed for years, thanks to a mule that trotted around, turning the two enormous millstones that crushed them. One day, it had caught fire, but the charred ruin had been left standing, although it had been unused for years.

The dog was barking at the brick shed and flies were buzzing around it—too many to have been caught up in the wind that was still blowing. There was a small lock on the door that bore no sign of rust. I glanced through the window, its glass left opaque with years of dirt. The sunlight barely penetrated, and all I could see was the sinister outline of the two enormous millstones.

The goatherd's dog was still barking furiously at the door. In front of it, the ground had been disturbed, and caught in a bush was a paper handkerchief stained red.

I picked it up and put it in my pocket. I didn't know what to do. Both my mind and my body were paralyzed. I refused even to think about it. I could have broken the glass and looked in. But it was as if some kind of fever was making my legs weak.

As I was rushing back to the villa, I already knew what was in the shed. *Nadia's body.*

I stopped and heaved up everything I could.

. . . .

Led by General Jalloun and the other grown-ups, the police raced around to the charred brick shed. Women and boys were forbidden to follow but, after a while, we heard the sirens. More police cars and an ambulance.

By now, dusk had fallen and it promised to be a sleepless night. Ahmed, Karim, and Nico stayed with us, sleeping in the guest room. This was my mother's decision. Naturally, no one was in any mood for supper.

Before going back to her house, Laura came up to me. She pointed to Karim, who was trembling silently in a corner.

"Please, Mike, stay close to him."

*Stay close to him? Me? I couldn't even keep my own emotions in check.*

I put the bloodstained paper handkerchief in my Latin book, the one I never opened. I wanted to hold on to it but not have it in my sight all the time. I knew that Nadia Al Bakri's blood would change the course of our lives.

# MONDAY, AUGUST 4, 1969

slam asks its believers to accept death as the will of Allah. Therefore, its funerals are simple and humble. The afternoon after she was found, Nadia's body was washed and wrapped in a white sheet. Immediately after the midafternoon Asr prayer, the funeral began in the Arab cemetery behind Corso Sicilia, near the old station for the diesel train to Sabratha.

The ceremony was conducted without anyone kneeling. The body was placed between two stone slabs, the head pointing to Mecca then covered with earth. Mohammed had chosen a headstone without a name, simply the dates of birth and death according to the Muslim calendar. His four sons watched in silence at his side.

From the gossip in undertones, but still audible, between General Jalloun and Don Eugenio and Busi, I caught those terrible words: *raped, sodomized.*

Laura and Marlene were away in a corner, separate, faces hidden by large sunglasses. They came forward only to offer condolences to Mohammed and his wife.

Before leaving, Laura came up close to me.

"My mom and I are leaving tomorrow. Dad has to go to Vietnam and Marlene doesn't want to stay here alone. It's impossible not to think of Nadia, but it's even worse for Mom here."

I was surprised, but, in some way, happy they were going. The sight of Marlene was unbearable, because it reminded me of where I really was: all at sea and hopelessly adrift.

"Where will you go?"

"Marlene decided everything at the last minute this morning. We'll go on a trip around Europe. Rome, Paris, and London."

I said nothing, and she repeated her request.

"We'll only be away ten days, Mike. Stay close to Karim."

"Ahmed lost a sister as well. Or have you forgotten?"

"He doesn't need you, Mike. It's you who needs him."

. . . .

That evening, Italia was sitting in the swing seat out on the veranda, smoking a cigarette and drinking whiskey. The light was on, and she was reading. I was sitting beside her.

"Mom, I have to ask you something."

She turned to look at me. She was almost forty and the lines in her face were getting deeper. But her aging went beyond the lines and white strands in her hair; it was as if something or someone had taken away her will to live.

I instinctively thought of Marlene Hunt. She was only five years younger than my mother but still looked like a student, with her golden skin, her rigid diets, her swimming, daily jogging, and beauty creams.

"Go ahead, Mike."

"It's about Nadia."

She didn't seem surprised in the least. "I know. I think I know you a little, wouldn't you say?"

I summoned my courage. I had to put the question to someone.

"I heard Don Eugenio and Emilio Busi at the funeral today. They were talking to the general and he was saying that Nadia had been raped before being killed . . ."

Italia's tired eyes stared at the large garden in the dark where the crickets and frogs were making their noise. Yes, Mamma was tired, very tired.

"And then the general said something else as well, Mamma, he said she'd been—"

She raised a hand to stop me at the word. A tear fell from her eyes. I got up and left her in peace.

# TUESDAY, AUGUST 5, 1969

Normally, the fishing boats came into port at six in the morning. At six thirty, the men went to the market to sell the catch to the fishmongers at the stalls before the market opened at seven thirty.

Farid and Salim were privileged. They had both a fishing vessel and a stall at the market. So they had to arrive only twenty minutes or so before the market opened to set the catch out on the stall.

I got up at dawn and was ready in five minutes. I went out by the usual exit through the gate at the back of the villa. I got on my bicycle and went over the fields so that my father would not see me from the car as he went to the office.

Pedaling along the path that Nadia used to walk down and that Marlene Hunt jogged along, I hurried past the cesspit and came to the olive-pressing shed.

Had she been killed there? Not possible. There was no room there to do those terrible things: *rape, sodomy.* Not even inside the building, which—from dawn until ten o'clock—was surrounded by herdsmen, dogs, and goats.

They must have seized her there and taken her into Tripoli, or God knows where. Then, after the traffic stoppage, they'd dragged her back to the olive-pressing shed.

*Had she gone willingly into the car with her killer? Or was she forced? Did she know him?*

At that hour, Shara Ben Ashur was almost deserted. Opposite the Royal Palace, I turned off toward Shara Mizran. A few donkey carts were transporting foodstuffs to the market. I got there in twenty minutes, arriving at six thirty.

The weighing counter had just opened for business. In a furious round of negotiations shouted in Arabic, the fishermen were selling their fish to the fishmongers.

At the weighing machine, I looked for old Mansur, one of Granddad's old hands, who had the fish stall next to Farid and Salim. When Mansur had become too old for work in the olive grove, Granddad had given him a lump sum to buy a market stall and then taken on his son in his place.

"Signor Michele, how good to see you!" said Mansur.

His eyes would light up with gratitude to Granddad whenever he saw me or Alberto.

"Ciao, Mansur, how's business?"

"All good, Allah willing. And what brings you here, Signor?"

I could trust him. I immediately told him the truth. I wanted to know at what time Farid and Salim had arrived the Sunday before. Mansur didn't follow me and looked bewildered.

"The day of the camel parade," I specified.

His yellow teeth showed a smile. I was under no illusions that Mansur would remember exactly. Two days had passed, and he'd had no reason in all that hubbub to notice when Farid and Salim arrived. But this was my lucky day.

"They were here well before seven thirty," he said immediately.

"How can you be so sure?"

"They came to the weighing counter very early. Usually, they don't come at all. But, on Sunday, they had to bring the pickup close to it because Salim had caught an enormous greater amberjack. A monster it was, over one hundred and ten pounds. Too big for a single stall."

"And you bought it?"

"Farid and I haggled for quite a while. Then we fixed on a price and I bought half of it."

"And you're sure it was this Sunday morning?"

"Yes, because it's only on a Sunday I would buy a monster that big. All the Italians come to buy fresh fish for Sunday lunch with their families."

"And both of them were here, Mansur?"

"Yes, both of them. Farid and Salim. Farid was doing the negotiating; Salim was cutting the fish."

"I saw them at ten, Mansur, when I came to pick up the bait. But, before and after, were they always here?"

The old man scratched the few white hairs on his head.

"I think so. They opened the stall at seven thirty; it's next to mine. And both of them were there. And there was the huge Sunday crowd. Toward eight o'clock, your grandfather, your brother, and your friend Nico came by."

"And they never closed the stall; they never went away?"

"I would have noticed if they'd closed the stall, Signor Michele. The pickup was just outside. Every so often one of them would go to cut a piece off the amberjack, which was being kept there on ice. After ten, the Bedouin camel parade began and the market emptied. Farid and Salim were still here, both of them. We talked a lot about the amberjack and joked about how lucky they'd been. They stayed here right up to the market closing at one o'clock."

I looked at my watch. I had to get away before the two brothers arrived.

"Thanks, Mansur, it was just a thought. You mustn't say a word, understand?"

He gave me a complicit smile.

# WEDNESDAY, AUGUST 6, 1969

D ad went to Rome on business for a few days. Before leaving, he insisted I go with him to see the new house he'd bought in Piazza di Spagna.

*More bait to get me to move.*

But there was nothing to attract me in Italy. I'd declined the offer, citing the stress from Nadia's death as my excuse. And this wasn't really a lie. Strangely enough, Dad didn't seem too upset.

*Perhaps he doesn't want me under his feet.*

When I went into the living room for breakfast, there was only my brother there, his head buried in a mathematical analysis textbook. As soon as he saw me, he shut the book.

"You don't want to go to Rome with Dad, Mike?"

"Thanks, Alberto, but I'd rather stay here. I don't like Italy. How can you live in a country where the students occupy the universities and sing the praises of China's Red Guards? I'd like to see them try it in Moscow or Peking!"

"That's democracy for you, Mike. It's what distinguishes us from both Fascist and Communist regimes. With us, everyone has the right to free speech."

"Bullshit, Alberto! Do you know what the Italians really want? A new Fiat, cheaper gas, a job for life and, if possible, a not-too-demanding one at that."

My brother looked at me understandingly. Like my father, he wasn't absolutely in agreement with my ideas and choices. But, unlike my father, his dissent brought him closer to me rather than distancing him from me.

"Okay, Mike, nevertheless, I'm here at all times for advice, anything you want. But don't argue with Dad, and keep an eye on Mamma."

The last words took me by surprise. I thought he meant her health.

"She's aged so much, Alberto. She seems worn out."

He nodded thoughtfully.

"Mike, Mamma listens to you more than anyone else. And she does things and says things that could seriously damage Dad's business concerns and the family."

I didn't like hearing that, especially coming from my brother.

"Alberto, don't you think they should just sort out whatever's between them?"

"No, Mike, not if the final consequence means separation. There's no divorce under Italian law, even less in the Church."

I was speechless and, for once, thought my highly intelligent brother was mistaken.

"Alberto, Mamma loves Dad, I'm sure of it. She doesn't always agree with his ideas, but she loves him."

"Dad was born into poverty, Mike. He wants to be sure that we don't experience what he's lived through."

"If I'm not going with Dad, it's because I can't stand Rome, not because I don't want to be with him."

My brother nodded.

"Very well. But let's stop Mamma from doing anything too compromising, anything that could seriously damage Dad."

"Just what do you mean, Alberto? What could Mamma do?"

He looked uncertain, unable to make up his mind. Then he decided not to say any more, perhaps so it wouldn't weigh on me.

And Marlene Hunt came back into my mind. My hands on her golden skin. Her naked body at the top of the stairs.

# SATURDAY, AUGUST 9, 1969

R ome was veiled under a summer heat haze, its ocher walls and red roof tiles spreading out from the banks of the Tiber as the river lazily flowed through it.

Mariano Rumor's new premiership was yet another Christian Democrat government, the same as all the others since the Republic's founding in 1946.

The air conditioning kept the temperature pleasant, but the air inside the private lounge in the hotel next to the Parliament building was fouled by the cigarette smoke of Emilio Busi, who was wearing a horrendous short-sleeved gray-check shirt. His white socks left a hand's breadth of hairy calf visible.

"So everything's ready?" Emilio Busi asked Salvatore Balistreri, who was sharply dressed in a made-to-measure pinstripe suit.

"Yes. Mohammed's friends in Sirte have given word back. All the junior officers in the Qadhadhfa tribe are united in agreement. And the same goes for those in the Warfalla tribe, who control the south and west. Cyrenaica will have to bow to the evidence and follow suit."

"Aren't these men rather young?" Don Eugenio asked.

"A little young, perhaps, but all the more enthusiastic for it."

"And easy to manipulate, I hope?" Don Eugenio added.

Emilio Busi was worried. "Wouldn't it have been better to make contact with Omar and Abdulaziz Al Shalhi? They control the police and senior officers in the army."

"I've spoken to them," Balistreri replied, "but I gather they're loyal to the Crown and closely tied to English interests—while the junior officers we're supporting will be easier to manipulate. And grateful for our help."

"Who's their leader?" Busi asked, inhaling his foul cigarette.

"They don't want to say. It's being kept secret," Balistreri replied.

"A secret?" Busi laughed. "Is this all a joke? We come up with a coup d'état, organize it and finance it, and we don't know who'll be in charge afterward?"

Busi sometimes went back to being a Carabinieri officer. Information, checks, sureties. Balistreri answered him with his calming smile.

"Mohammed knows his name; he's from a family close to his. They've asked to keep it a secret for security reasons. It's better that Mohammed doesn't even tell us, but you needn't worry. Let's call him X for the moment. Anyway, Mohammed and myself are the guarantors. We're backing the coup."

But Busi was not interested in possibilities. He dealt only in certainties.

"What assurances do we have that this X won't do the same with Italy? We Italians are the ex-Fascist colonialists, the sons of those who massacred their women and children. Perhaps X hates Italians?"

"Mohammed and I are meeting the junior officers at Abano Terme here in Italy," replied Balistreri, completely unruffled.

Busi looked at him, surprised.

"Isn't that unwise?"

Balistreri shrugged.

"The only people who know are we three, X himself, and Mohammed, who's organized everything. I also want some guarantees from X, gentlemen."

Balistreri was well aware that the meeting in Italy was a gamble. But his brothers in Sicily and their friends did not want to risk all that money on an unknown Bedouin.

He brushed a hand through his thick, black hair. His dark eyes were calm. He had to go along with these two partners and put up with their doubts and hypocrisy, even if it meant he had to do it for the next fifty years.

"Tell your connections their interests are in good hands. After all, I'm risking everything here, putting all my family's money in. We're selling the Bruseghin olive grove for it. My brothers and their friends are also backing it."

Busi was immediately worried by Balistreri's frankness.

"My connections know only that we're working to bring about a political situation that will be more favorable to Italian interests."

Don Eugenio also wanted to maintain a certain distance.

"Furthermore, my dear Salvatore, let's be clear that, as far as our connections are concerned, the financing is yours alone. With the greatest respect, your brothers and their friends will not be holding any shares in any future businesses in Libya."

Salvatore Balistreri smiled. The hypocrisy of Italians was phenomenal, as was their Machiavellian ability in plotting. The Americans were much more straightforward in taking what they wanted. In the end, his eldest brother, Gaetano, was right about his compatriots on the mainland.

*These guys will only understand two things: hard cash and high explosives.*

But he preferred to work with these men rather than spurn them or even oppose them, as his wife or son Michele would have done.

In the silence beyond the hotel windows, a few cars were slowly scuttling between the corridors of power: the president's Quirinale Palace, the premier's Chigi Palace, and parliament in Montecitorio. Salvatore Balistreri decided there and then that he would one day have an office in one of those buildings.

# SUNDAY, AUGUST 10, 1969

It was one week after Nadia's death and silence still reigned in the two villas.

Dad was in Rome, William Hunt in Vietnam, Laura and Marlene touring Europe. Italia read, smoked, and drank her whiskey, lost in her own thoughts. My granddad was unusually distant and preoccupied, while Alberto spent his days in his room, studying.

Nico, on the other hand, had bought an plane ticket for New York.

*There's this really cool festival in a place called Woodstock, Mike. All the biggest rock stars together in one place. Really very cool. Then I'm going to tour the States for the rest of August.*

It seemed a ridiculous thing to do after Nadia's death. Especially as, on that one trip, he'd be blowing all the money he'd made in the two years in Cairo, if not more. But perhaps there was a reason behind it. Nico wasn't happy with just me around. I was even gloomier than ever. And, after all, it was the States, a music festival, and singers were his passion. What's more, I thought he might find girls there he wouldn't have to pay for.

Ahmed and Karim were still in mourning, shut in at home with their mother. We hadn't managed to see one another after the funeral.

Nadia's death had thrown everyone off-balance. It was as if each one of us were locked inside ourselves, trying to make sense of what had happened.

I no longer went outside. I spent whole days in my room with the shutters and windows closed. It was stiflingly hot outside and very quiet. Even the flies were taking it easy, resting on the fly screen. All you could hear was the occasional frog croaking in the fountain's warm water.

I tried not to think of anything. Not about Nadia, Marlene, nor Laura. But solitude was no help in emptying my mind and clearing my conscience. So I stole my mother's sleeping pills from her cupboard.

I was sleeping that afternoon when I heard the telephone ringing in the hall. After a few minutes, Granddad knocked and put his head around the door.

"Michele, run over to Mohammed's house, quickly."

Behind him, I saw my mother's face drained of color.

"Why, what's up?" I asked.

"They've arrested the killer. Go on, Mike, please."

. . . .

I took my time, without really knowing what I was going to say. When I got to Mohammed's place, he, Ahmed, and Karim were kneeling in prayer on the ground outside, facing the Qibla, Mecca.

"They've found the killer!" I blurted.

Ahmed jumped straight up.

"*Haya al salat!*" his father ordered. "Signor Michele, if you could be patient and wait, we will have finished the *ruku* in five minutes."

After the fourth genuflection, Mohammed sat on his heels, followed by his sons, for the part of prayer known as the *Tashahhud* then gave the ritual salutation: *Al-salamu alaykum.*

"Who is it?" Ahmed asked me.

Mohammed looked at him, and Ahmed lowered his gaze.

"Ahmed, you and Karim stay here and look after the women. I'll go with Signor Michele."

"Can I come with you, Granddad?"

Mohammed and my grandfather were getting into the jeep.

If it had been my father, he would have packed me off into the house without even replying. But Granddad was a different man from my father.

"Very well, Mike, get in. But when we're there, you're not to say a word."

The city was semi-deserted. In that heat, everyone was waiting for sunset to leave the house.

As soon as we arrived at the large barracks of Bab Azizia, we were greeted by General Jalloun, who looked at me with concern. My grandfather smiled at his old friend.

"Don't worry, General, Michele's very discreet."

The general nodded uncomfortably. Then he explained succinctly that, thanks to days of tireless work, they had solved the case.

"It was the goatherd, Jamaal. We've arrested him. And after a little taste of prison, he'll confess to everything, you'll see."

"Is there any proof, General?" my grandfather asked politely.

The general was beaming at us with satisfaction, his chest puffed up in conceit.

"Overwhelming proof."

Granddad was taken aback and conveyed this with the greatest respect.

"But, General, I've known Jamaal for over thirty years. He's an odd and solitary old man who talks only to his goats. He's never been violent."

General Jalloun's eyes shone with pride.

"After careful investigation, I found a witness. One of the other goatherds saw him with Nadia near the pressing shed toward nine o'clock. The time fits; the place as well."

"And this witness is sure of the time?"

The question slipped out without me realizing it. All three looked at me in surprise.

The general gave me a scornful smile then continued addressing my granddad.

"The goatherd's sure of the time because he saw Nadia and Jamaal immediately after he'd heard the *muezzin*, who starts punctually at nine."

*The* muezzin's *cry. Just before I went down for breakfast with Alberto and Nico.*

And the general had yet more proof.

"We also found a knife with a saw blade in the pressing shed. The other goatherds say it's Jamaal's knife. It was covered in blood. And it matches the wounds on Nadia's body."

I just couldn't hold back.

"Jamaal's seventy and half blind. How could he manage to drag Nadia all the way there?"

The general gave me a withering look and turned to my grandfather.

"Would your grandson like to take my place in this investigation?"

My grandfather smoothed things with his more conciliatory manner.

"I'm sure there's a perfectly good explanation, Mike."

The general glanced in embarrassment at Mohammed.

"The explanation's in the knife. I won't say what was done with it to Nadia, not in front of her father and this young man here, but it was an atrocity and it took some time. You could only perform such butchery inside, not out in the open, that's for sure."

I was beside myself. This was all a pack of lies.

"In that pressing shed, under its lock and key? By a half-blind goatherd?"

General Jalloun was clearly upset.

"And how would you know, Signor Michele?"

"I saw the lock on the door. It was brand-new and very small. Jamaal would have had neither the money to buy it nor the sight to lock and unlock it."

The general wavered. His expression darkened and he muttered something in Arabic. I looked at Mohammed, who was standing silently in a corner. Here we were, talking about his daughter. About her presumed but unlikely killer. And yet he had nothing to say.

"Mohammed, Jamaal's known Nadia since she was born! He's known you and your family for years! Come on, you know this isn't true!" I burst out.

Mohammed hesitated. I saw the uncertainty in his eyes, the effort he was making in having to choose between humiliation and fear.

The humiliation of having to accept an unlikely killer of his precious daughter and the fear that Nadia had been killed by a descendant of the Italians, who had massacred his family.

*If he accepts Jamaal as guilty, the case is closed. If he protests, it could damage his boss. And he'd lose everything.*

Finally, with his eyes to the floor, he chose humiliation.

"Signor Michele, Jamaal was a very odd man. Sometimes he would give Nadia some milk from his goats. Sometimes cheese. Too many times."

• • • •

During the journey back to Sidi El Masri in the jeep, no one spoke a word. As soon as we arrived, Mohammed and Granddad went into the house to report the news to my mother. I went out by the back gate. It took me less than half an hour to get down the dirt track to Ahmed and Karim's shack.

*I want to tell them before Mohammed does. I want to know what they think.*

Ahmed and Karim were waiting for me.

"They've arrested Jamaal for it," I said.

Ahmed stared at me and said nothing, as if he were waiting for my view. But Karim immediately said what he thought.

"They could be right. Jamaal was a very odd man."

"My granddad knows him and says he wouldn't hurt a fly," I protested.

"And what do you think, Mike?" Ahmed asked.

"Jamaal's seventy, and shows it. How could he manage to drag her to the pressing shed, right past your house? Nadia would have screamed out. You were here, Karim, you would have seen or heard something."

Karim shook his head. He was embarrassed for some reason.

"I was in the toilet, Mike. I didn't feel well, and the *ghibli* was howling a gale."

I pointed to the thin white scar on my left wrist. Our blood brotherhood.

"You have to help me find the truth. For your sister's sake!"

Ahmed looked at me. "What do we have to do?"

"Let's write down everything we know. And note what we don't know."

Karim was totally against it.

"What should we write then?" Ahmed asked.

It must have been the influence of all those Agatha Christie books I'd read over the years. Or perhaps a deeper intuition. That breathing on the boat out at sea when Mamma told us that Nadia had disappeared.

*Someone there was panting rather than breathing.*

I fixed Ahmed and Karim with a look.

"Nadia knew her killer."

"Of course," Karim replied. "She knew Jamaal."

"No. He was too old. Even with a knife he couldn't have managed to take her to the pressing shed. Or buy a new lock."

Ahmed's eyes looked serious, lost in thought. Karim's were burning with rage.

"You think it was one of us?" Ahmed said at last.

I said nothing. My reply was silence. That was enough for Ahmed. In the shack he found a math exercise book with large-squared paper, the kind he and Karim had used in nursery school. He tore out the last page and handed it to me with a stub of pencil.

Karim made a last attempt to stop us.

"Ahmed, it's sacrilege. What about Nadia's memory . . . ?"

"Shut it," Ahmed ordered. It was the order of an older brother.

I started things off. After a moment, Ahmed picked up on the procedure and gave a hand. Karim kept quiet and listened. It was his way of expressing disapproval of what we were doing.

We took two hours and, in the end, I had filled almost a whole side of the squared notepaper:

*Salvatore Balistreri, Alberto, and Granddad Giuseppe went out at six thirty, seen by Mike. They were at Don Eugenio's Mass in Tripoli by seven and at seven forty-five Salvatore was at the barber's, Alberto and Granddad at the market with Farid and Salim, who had been there since dawn.*

*Nico was at the market just before eight and together with Alberto took the* Giornale di Tripoli *to Salvatore Balistreri at the barber's. He then went to read the paper on the Waddan terrace (CHECK) until Don Eugenio arrived at ten, and then Busi, who was a little late (CHECK BOTH).*

*Alberto and Nico came back with the van. At eight fifteen they left the air tanks at the Esso station to be filled and were back at the villas just before eight thirty. They parked the van in the Hunts' carport and were together in the villa having breakfast. Mike Balistreri joined them at nine twenty.*

*Nadia left at eight with Mohammed, and they immediately went their separate ways. She went on foot to the villa; he took the pickup past the olive grove and off to the office, where he remained until Italia came by to pick him up at two. When Italia called him at noon he wasn't there (CHECK).*

*Farid and Salim went fishing at two in the morning, as always. They were in the boat until dawn then at their market stall. They were both there at eight, seen by Granddad, Alberto, and Nico. At ten, they gave Mike the bait for the trolling. Mansur is almost certain they never left the stall.*

*Mike saw the three Hunts as they left together to go to the baseball game at Wheelus, and they returned about two, after the road was open again (CHECK).*

*Mike woke up early. He hung around for a bit, then went down and had breakfast with Nico and Alberto at nine twenty. The three then went to pick up Ahmed at the Esso station and went into Tripoli just before the road was closed.*

*Ahmed went out after Nadia and her father and walked through the olive grove to the gas station, where he arrived, a little late. Nico and Alberto had left him the tanks and he waited there for them until a quarter to ten.*

*Karim felt ill and stayed in the toilet at home.*

*At nine, a goatherd saw old Jamaal with Nadia near the oil-pressing shed. The* muezzin *was calling. Mike heard him just before going down for breakfast with Nico and Alberto.*

I was surprised, and Ahmed was even more surprised.

*This was like Hercule Poirot and Miss Marple.*

The thought served to make another point clear.

"We have to include ourselves in the investigation," I said to Ahmed and Karim.

Karim was strongly opposed.

"Our religion says that the dead should be left in peace, Mike. And we're Nadia's brothers."

Ahmed, on the other hand, agreed with me.

"There's no one above suspicion in an investigation, Karim."

Karim was scornful and incredulous.

"Except this isn't a serious investigation. You aren't the police and they've already arrested the guilty man. And there are witnesses. You'll have Nadia's name on everyone's lips."

I looked at Ahmed. He was gloomy and silently chewing something over.

"All right, Mike," he said finally. "I can check your alibi and you can check mine and Karim's. But how can we check the alibis of the grown-ups?"

I had a ready answer. I folded the squared page and put it in my pocket.

"I'll check up on Farid and Salim. As for the grown-ups, I'll speak to my mother."

Ahmed signaled his approval. Karim ruled himself out.

"I'm not going to help in this. So don't count on me."

I stared at him coldly. "Then we'll do without you. But don't say anything to Laura."

I said it in the tone of an order, not a request.

"Laura's away touring Europe anyway," he answered rudely.

Ahmed intervened.

"Mike's right, Karim. When Laura comes back, you mustn't breathe a word of our investigation."

And this was a peremptory order from an older brother. One who had cut the throats of three soldiers in a back alley in Cairo.

· · · ·

In the late afternoon I joined my mother on the swing seat out on the veranda. She now spent most of her time either there or up on the solitary cliff on La Moneta. The sadness in her eyes couldn't have been caused by Nadia's death alone. It had already been there at the beginning of August, when we came back from Cairo. During the time I was away something must have been slowly eating away at this woman made of steel and soft butter.

*Steel for everyone else. Soft butter for Alberto and me.*

She was drinking whiskey, smoking, and reading Nietzsche's *Beyond Good and Evil*. I sat down next to her.

"How are you feeling, Mamma?"

She raised her eyes from the book and smiled. There may have been many lines around her eyes, but her smile was the same. The same one she had when I was two and she sang lullabies and recited nursery rhymes to help me get to sleep.

"I'm tired, Mike. I still can't believe Nadia's dead."

I pulled the crumpled sheet of squared paper from my jeans and handed it to her without a word.

She contemplated the penciled notes in silence. For a moment, I was afraid she might refuse to read it. I saw her expression turn into a frown while she weighed up the points.

"I need your help, Mamma. Where it says 'CHECK.'"

*I need you to check the alibis of the adults, your husband included.*

She did not say, as my father would have done, that I was still a kid and these were serious things, for grown-ups and the police.

I saw her smile sadly, torn between pride and concern. She went over the page with my notes several times. She then folded it and placed it in the Nietzsche book.

"Very well, Mike, I'll check. But you're not to do a thing."

It was as if she were following a train of thought, as if there was an obvious solution on that page that I could not see.

# MONDAY, AUGUST 11, 1969

I was alone having breakfast in the living room when Ahmed rushed in.

"Radio Tripoli's announced that Jamaal slit his veins in his cell last night."

"Does your father know?"

"I've no idea. He left early this morning to pick your father up from the airport."

"Then let's pay them a visit in the office. The plane from Rome landed an hour ago."

"I can't go, Mike, I'm not allowed."

"Please come along, Ahmed. We have to speak to our fathers."

"I have to stay with my mother and Karim. I can't disobey my father." He meant, *Like you do, Mike.*

"Don't worry. I'll speak to him."

So the two of us took the jeep and headed for Tripoli. Corso Vittorio was quiet. Carriages, donkey carts, a few cars and bicycles. The bars on the street were empty; it was too hot outside.

We parked outside the austere white Fascist-era building in Piazza Italia, or Maydan as Suhada, where Dad had his offices, and walked slowly up the three flights of stairs. My father's private secretary rose to his feet when we entered.

"Signor Michele," he said respectfully, but with a disapproving glance at Ahmed.

He led us into a meeting room. After a while, my father entered the room, followed by Mohammed, who looked severely at his disobedient son.

"Go home, Ahmed," he ordered immediately.

"Mohammed, I asked Ahmed to come here with me."

I had the authority of his Italian boss's son, which counted for more than a Libyan father.

My father dragged a hand through his thick, black hair. His forehead was sweating slightly, the bags under his eyes darker than usual. His good looks were a little jaded. Perhaps he had drank too much and slept too little in Rome.

"Mohammed's right, Mike. What are you and Ahmed doing here?"

"Did you know about Jamaal's death?" I asked them.

"Of course," my father replied. "He committed suicide."

"Committed suicide? And who says? The police? General Jalloun?"

My father was a prudent and patient man; if not by nature then from experience.

"Michele, he killed himself using the shards of a broken bottle. There were five other detainees in his cell, who all gave evidence. It was the weight of his guilt."

I had had about enough of my father's omniscience.

"Dad, you're an engineer, not a psychologist. Do you always think you know everything?"

I saw both Mohammed and Ahmed give a start. But my father gave an understanding smile. Perhaps he still had hopes for me. Certainly, he still had patience.

"Whatever you say, Michele. But he committed suicide; that much is certain. General Jalloun told me he's closing the case today."

I looked at Mohammed, but he was avoiding my eyes.

"Mohammed, how can you go along with this?" I said.

Ahmed placed a hand on my shoulder, took me by the arm, and pulled me gently outside.

"It's no use, Mike. Let's go, please."

My best friend was trying to protect me from myself. And those words "It's no use" were the most that his Islamic education allowed him to say about his father.

They were also a clear message from Ahmed to Mohammed. He was sacrificing the truth about his daughter's death on the altar of economic interest and a quiet life.

*But I know that you don't forgive, Ahmed. Not today, not ever. Your sister's killer will come to a worse end than the dog that bit Jet.*

Dad came home for lunch, something he never did on workdays. He had important news to tell us, much more important than Nadia's death and the old goatherd's suicide.

"I think we'll soon be able to move forward on the business with Busi and Don Eugenio's friends in Italy," he announced to Granddad and Alberto, while Mamma was reading in her armchair.

Granddad didn't seem particularly enthusiastic.

"Salvatore, I've already asked you this. Where are we going to find the money to go into this business with them? They want significant amount."

My father had a ready reply.

"I paid my brothers a visit in Palermo. They and their friends will loan half the amount. But they want to be sure that we're putting in the other half."

"You're not to sell Father's olive grove," said Italia icily.

*Granddad's olive grove up for sale!*

It was unthinkable. My mother's anguish explained the lines and sadness in her face.

*Or perhaps only partly.*

My father ignored her. He fixed his eyes on Granddad, speaking directly to him.

"Dad, the olive grove's the only thing we have to sell in order to embark on an enterprise this big."

I hated my father when he addressed Granddad Giuseppe as "Dad." Granddad's real son, Toni, had been killed in the war.

And now he was asking my grandfather to hand over his life's work.

"I agree with Mamma!" I said, on an impulse.

My father didn't so much as glance at me, but I carried on.

"And as far as your partners go, Dad, Don Eugenio's a revolting priest and Busi's only a wheeler-dealer Communist."

"Michele," warned my grandfather.

Naturally, my father took it all with a smile.

*This man who could sell ice to the Eskimos can change tack immediately when things don't seem to be working out.*

"In the end, it's Granddad's decision. After all, it's his olive grove," he said in his accommodating tone.

He then changed the subject, as if the previous conversation had never taken place. He turned to Alberto and me.

"As for you boys, seeing your excellent grades, I have a present for you."

*My excellent academic results! Could Dad now tell fortunes? The grades weren't out yet.*

"Alberto, I've booked a language course in Oxford in September, the one you were wanting to take."

Alberto looked concerned.

"But Dad, that course costs an arm and a leg! You could have waited. Perhaps with my grades I could get a grant."

"Please don't worry, Alberto. The money spent on your education is an investment."

My father then looked at me.

*And for me, Dad? Perhaps a vacation with the Foreign Legion?*

"For you, it's a surprise. And we leave today."

I was more incredulous than angry. I pressed the point again.

"I am *not* going to Rome!"

He slipped a brochure over to me. Three days on a lion hunt in a Tanzanian game reserve. A night flight that very evening. It was a childhood dream. I'd devoured books, films, and photos on the subject.

*He's able to engineer anything. He can read your soul and buy it, without giving you any time to think.*

It was a shameless attempt to seduce me by his usual methods: a mouth-watering surprise with no time for me to consider the matter.

I was about to tell him to go to hell when a thought crossed my mind. Was it a thought, or simply a regret from a lost childhood?

*Perhaps it's a last opportunity to understand each other, Dad.*

I forced myself to smile, trying to be something of the son he wanted me to be. Not the one who, after peppering sparrows, lizards, and frogs with pellets, had turned to killing human beings.

"Thanks, Dad. That's great. I'll go and get ready."

I exchanged glances with my mother, just for a second. Then she looked at my father and asked him that damned question.

"Did you see Marlene and Laura in Rome, Salvo?"

The great salesman hesitated a second, made a vague gesture of assent, and gave me a beaming smile.

"We'll have some great fun, Mike! Go and get your bags ready."

# TUESDAY, AUGUST 12, 1969

We took the night flight to Nairobi and then on to Dar es Salaam. From there, we went by light aircraft and were in Southern Tanzania's Selous region in less than two hours. It was both the best place and the best season for hunting lion. And for not thinking about Nadia, Marlene, and Laura.

During the flight, Dad and I discussed rifles, calibers, tracking, and bait. I wanted to use a 12-gauge smooth-bore shotgun, which is what I was used to, but Dad had already been on a few safaris and advised against it.

"You need a hunting rifle, Mike, with .375 ammunition and a good telescopic sight for shooting at dusk or dawn. With the target lined up, you need rapid fire."

"You don't need any rapid fire, Dad."

"You're not used to a rifle, Mike. Once we get to camp you'll have only a couple of days to learn how to use it. There's always the possibility of only wounding one, and a wounded lion is truly an ugly beast."

"How could I not kill it with a .375 bullet that travels at over seven hundred yards a second?"

"Believe me, Mike, you need to hit it in the chest between the ribs, and it's not that easy. Even a badly wounded lion can still run at you at fifteen yards a second, and for ten seconds. They can easily cover a hundred and fifty yards; the stronger ones even more."

My father had little faith in my math. But that hypothetical lion charging toward me ready to claw my brains out held no fear for me.

*What frightens me more is the life you want me to lead, Dad.*

From the airplane window I could see the Africa I'd always dreamed about: first, a mass of vegetation, then the brick-red rough terrain with its low, dense bushes. As we flew over the Kilombero River, the pilot descended, and now I could see hippos flocking to drink there, along with buffalo, antelope, and impala.

"Happy, Mike?"

With this unexpected gift, was Dad trying to make me forget that everything wasn't right between him and me and in my life? In part, he was succeeding. But it was only temporary. We both knew this. And yet neither of us wanted to face the fact.

*I can never be the son you want me to be.*

We arrived at the base camp on the Kilombero River in the afternoon. The temperature was agreeable, about seventy degrees. In charge of the camp was Ian, a professional hunter from South Africa who Dad already knew. His French wife was in charge of the kitchen. The others were native Tanzanians, all smiling and extremely polite. We had only two and a half days' hunting and had to use the time well. So, for the rest of the afternoon, I practiced with the hunting rifle.

Ian looked incredulously at my father.

*"Your son's a real champion, sir."*

*Yes, this son knows only how to shoot and land a punch.*

· · · ·

We ate out in the open that evening, cocooned in large pullovers by the fire. It was under fifty degrees and dead quiet, the African night illuminated by stars I had never seen before.

When Ian and his wife retired for the night, Dad and I were left alone. He had a whiskey and was smoking a cigar. He offered the same to me.

"No, thanks, Dad. I don't to the smoke or the taste of alcohol. I'll never touch either."

Dad laughed aloud, patting his thick locks of hair and showing his gleaming white teeth. It was true: he did look like Clark Gable.

"Always so cocksure and assertive! So you like it here? Would you like to live like Ian?"

I could have said that this wasn't the point. It wasn't a matter of starry skies, nature, hunting rifles, lions, Africa.

*It's about freedom, Dad. The freedom to be as I am and not to be like you.*

"Do you think a man's happiness depends on how wealthy he is, Dad?"

He took his time to ponder the question.

"That's not how it is, Mike. Wealth doesn't bring happiness. But poverty's a sure-fire way of being unhappy, even if you and your mother can't see it."

*Because we didn't grow up in a family of five kids in a poky hole with no bathroom.*

"Then why did you marry Mamma, if she doesn't understand you?"

There was only a moment's pause. But it was a pause too long.

*Because she was rolling in it, Mike. And I need that olive grove. What I'm doing is for you and your brother as well, you know.*

# WEDNESDAY, AUGUST 13, 1969

I practiced with the rifle all day. Calibration of the sights, magnification, position, target points. We shot buffalo, gnu, and impala. But I wanted the king of the beasts. During supper around the fire, Ian gave us the good news.

"We've found the tracks of a lion of over four hundred and forty pounds, an adult male. It's very, very big. We can have a go tomorrow before sundown."

After supper, Dad took me aside, away from the fire.

"The plane I've booked to take us to Nairobi can wait a couple of hours. What do you say, Mike?"

"I'm all for it, Dad."

"I know you're all for it. That's what worries me. You work on instinct, not by reason. That lion is very big."

"Do you mean I'm not wise? Are you always so wise, Dad?"

"I try to be rational, which doesn't always mean wise. When you desire something that's dangerous, you have to decide if the risk is acceptable."

*Such as fucking Marlene in Rome, far away from Mamma and William Hunt?*

"I'm not like you, Dad. If I really want something, then I go for it. No matter what the cost, and I'm ready to accept the consequences."

Dad didn't agree.

"A lion isn't a dove or a hare, Mike. You weigh up the possible benefits and make your decision, just as in business."

"Business." This word was the obstacle to any attempt to find a meeting point. I wanted to find that point. But in order to do so I had to be clear with him.

"I don't like business, Dad. And I don't like Italy. I'll never live there."

My father immediately frowned.

"Why not?"

"Because it's a country where everyone's ready to go behind everyone else's back if they think there's some advantage to be gained."

Clark Gable, the great salesman, gave me an understanding smile. He knew perfectly well when to let things drop.

"Very well, point taken. We'll have the plane wait a couple of hours. Now, off to bed, it's going to be a tough day tomorrow."

# THURSDAY, AUGUST 14, 1969

I t needed more than ten men to set the trap: a large piece of buffalo tied by a rope over a branch at a height other animals couldn't reach.

*But not this beast. Not the king of the jungle.*

Ian and my father looked on with satisfaction as the men hoisted up the rope with its one hundred and ten pounds of carcass. They tied another thirty-six pounds of blood-soaked meat to the Land Rover and dragged it from the tree to where the lion tracks had been spotted.

We placed ourselves downwind on a mound two hundred yards from the bait. The waiting lasted all afternoon and, as the sun was beginning to set, I dozed off.

I dreamed of Marlene sunbathing naked on the terrace. I was spreading sunblock on her shoulders, then lower down, toward her buttocks.

"Mike."

I woke up suddenly, terrified. Had I been speaking in my sleep? Dad's voice was soft as I roused myself.

"Quiet," whispered Ian, ready with his rifle. "Damn, it's so big!"

Ian's gun was much more wieldy than mine, with a single-point sight that would allow him to keep both eyes open and fire a backup shot as quickly as possible.

*In case I make an error and only wound it.*

I looked at the bait in the tree. There was no lion. I let my eyes run between the trees and thorn bushes. And then I saw it. Huge, majestic, and very close. Too close: about a hundred yards.

"Too close, Mike. Too risky," Ian hissed.

Yes, it really was too close.

*If I only wound it, it'll be right on top of us, even if Ian fires a backup shot.*

I met my father's look. He was signaling no.

"Wait till it gets to the bait, Mike."

I had to get him to see what I'd said last night. He didn't want to understand this son who was so different from his ideal version. He didn't want to accept that I wasn't Salvatore Balistreri. Nor was I Alberto.

I started to set up the rifle. I fixed the lion in my sights. It only needed a six magnification. It was like having it there, two steps away from me.

"No, Mike," Ian warned. "Don't shoot yet."

I took the safety off and calculated.

*At seven hundred yards per second a .375 projectile will hit the target in little over a tenth of a second. But it's not a question of velocity or power. It's precision that counts. I have to hit it in the center of its chest and the shot has to penetrate between the ribs.*

But the lion had its flank to us. I waited. I couldn't even feel my heartbeat. Then a slight noise. The lion turned around and, for a second, its eyes met mine in the sight.

*The king of the jungle. Magnificent, strong, invincible.*

The shot resounded like cannon fire in the wide-open space, followed by a very long second when we all stopped breathing.

Then the lion dropped to the ground. Ian looked at me, speechless. My father was shaking his head.

There was no need for a backup shot. The bullet had gone in between the ribs, passed through the heart, and the entire length of its body and had come to a stop in a back paw.

Everyone was full of praise. Everyone except my father.

*He's looking beyond the lion. Now he knows who his son is.*

# FRIDAY, AUGUST 15, 1969

Dad and I arrived back in Tripoli at dawn on the night flight from Nairobi. It was the day of my nineteenth birthday.

Outside the airport, it was already well over 100 degrees. Mohammed was waiting for us in the jeep with Ahmed and Karim and took us to the Balistreri villa through a deserted city, in which everyone was holed up inside against the heat.

"Mr. Hunt came back from Vietnam yesterday," Mohammed announced. "Signora Hunt and Laura are coming in from London late this afternoon."

*Did you see Marlene and Laura in Rome, Salvo?*

Over a lunch of fish, Dad related the story of our Tanzanian trip in his own way to Granddad, Mamma, and Alberto. He magnified the shot with which I killed the lion, skipping over the risk we ran, as if he and I had become the greatest of friends.

In the afternoon, I walked in the garden surrounding the villas. Although I didn't want to admit it, I was waiting for Laura and Marlene to arrive.

*And which of the two, Mike?*

Consumed with anger, I went and shut myself in my room and listened to Leonard Cohen until it was suppertime. And then the surprises began.

Dad had made a Sicilian dish of pasta and sardines, which he cooked very well on the rare occasions he ventured into the kitchen. Granddad had made *baccalà alla veneziana*, with help from Alberto. But the amazing thing was that Italia had made my favorite pudding, a Sicilian cassata, from an old recipe book. I hadn't seen my mother cook since I was a child.

But the surprises didn't end there. A few minutes before we sat down to eat, Laura arrived on her own, without William or Marlene Hunt.

"Laura's our guest tonight. Her parents have gone to a reception that'll end very late. She's dining with us and will stay the night here," Italia announced.

I looked at my mother, who was against scheming of any kind. And yet she'd arranged all this, even down to inviting Laura. And all for me.

*For this son of yours who has the same sour blood as you, who kills lions but still needs your affection.*

But during supper the thought of Nadia still hung over us. We talked and smiled, but there was no real happiness. Laura explained the intricacies of the Rolleiflex, from which she was by now inseparable, and went on to the development of her art, from landscapes to portraits, and the contrasts seen in faces.

*Good and evil.*

In the end, Laura sang "Happy Birthday" with my family and took pictures while I blew out the nineteen candles on my cake. It was Dad who asked me to make a speech, but I declined.

"Not even a few words, Mike?"

I looked at him.

"'Better to be crazy on one's own account than be wise according to the wishes of others, Dad.'"

They all looked at me, dumbfounded, but they were used to my strange behavior, and the sentence wasn't offensive. I exchanged looks with Mamma. She knew very well what I meant; she recognized the quote from Nietzsche. But there was no smile. She was tired. Or frightened. Or both.

After supper, Laura and I strolled alone in the large garden around the villas.

"So you're going to be a photographer?"

"Yes, of real people, if I can. Like in the city of the living and the dead in Cairo, where Karim worked."

"Ahmed helped the refugees as well."

"No, Mike, he doesn't care about the poor. Karim isn't anything like him. Nor are you, I hope."

"How do you know what I'm like?"

The question was a little aggressive, and I knew it. But I was jealous and upset.

Laura didn't react. For her, arguing was pure folly.

"Do you remember Kirk Douglas, when he went to the gunfight with his pistol unloaded?"

"Yes, and so?"

"Winning isn't your thing, Mike."

"Don't start talking weird; I'm not Karim."

"I know you're not Karim. You've got many things he hasn't, but he's got one advantage over you. He was born poor."

"And Ahmed? He was born as poor as Karim!"

Laura paused for a moment, as if thinking about it.

"The poor have no middle way in life. For them, it's either ideas or strength."

"Why do you hate Ahmed, Laura?"

Now she decided to be serious.

"I don't hate him, Mike. But over ten years ago I met a young boy. I liked him a lot, and you know why?"

I said nothing. What was I expecting?

*A declaration of love or a good-bye?*

Laura pointed to the precise spot where Kirk Douglas fell all those years ago with his unloaded pistol.

"That boy didn't need to win. He preferred to be a loser, a beautiful one."

*And Ahmed takes me away from being that young boy.*

Laura took a white envelope from the back pocket of her jeans.

"Two photos, Mike. My birthday present for you."

I took hold of the envelope gingerly, as if it held a bomb.

The first photograph was in color and must have been taken by Marlene during the recent trip to Rome. Laura was wearing a low-cut black evening dress that went down to her ankles, with thin shoulder straps that left her arms bare. She was going down the Spanish Steps in Piazza di Spagna with the elegant, slow gait of an eighteen-year-old model. That was her age, but she had the knowing look of a woman of thirty.

"I look just like my mother, don't I?"

I was a little vacant, having no idea what to say. I didn't want to think that Laura resembled Marlene. Or perhaps I did, in part. I wanted both of them, but completely differently and separately.

*One is an angel, the other is a devil.*

"Your father invited us to an important party, in Rome, and Mom had to buy me a dress."

*Did you see Marlene Hunt in Rome, Salvo?*

"So I asked Marlene to take a picture of me."

"You look just like your mother."

"What do you like about it?" she asked.

The usual too-direct question. Serious, but with no malice or irony. A question that took part of the reply as a given. It was that "what" that made it impossible answer.

*I like that look that makes you feel like you're the only one in the world but in two completely different ways.*

She seemed to read my thoughts, as had happened since we were kids.

"It's the photo of how I'll never be, Mike."

*And now you know, Mike. You can make your choice in life.*

To change the subject, I slipped the second photo out of the envelope. It was in black and white, taken by surprise more than two years ago in this very garden: me, with the sun in my eyes, when I'd been expelled from school. A well-built boy, just seventeen, who had grown too quickly, muscular and awkward, with an insecure and belligerent manner, holding up an arm to protect himself from the setting sun.

Because of that arm, a sharp shadow cut almost diagonally across my face, leaving half in the sun and half in the shade.

*Good and evil.*

I was afraid that Laura could see into the depths of my soul, but I also wanted her to.

I drew close to her in the garden shadows.

"Give me what's missing, Laura. Please give it to me."

She smiled at me and turned the photo over. There was an inscription.

*To my beautiful loser.*

She brought her face an inch from mine.

"There's nothing to give, Mike," she whispered, "because, for me, there's nothing missing."

It was our first real kiss. A kiss between two faces, each divided in half.

# SATURDAY, AUGUST 30, 1969

I n the following two weeks no one spoke anymore of Nadia's death. The only sign of that tragedy was the hours that Ahmed and Karim spent locked in their wooden shack on Mohammed's orders. Although Ahmed was nearly twenty and Karim nearly eighteen, their Muslim upbringing bound them to obligations that were incomprehensible to me. I saw nothing of them for two weeks.

Nico sent me several postcards from various American cities. After Woodstock he went to New York City, then Florida, then California, and yet all the postcards were the same. Buxom blondes in bikinis.

Dad went to Italy again for several days with Mohammed. They came back on the evening of August 28, two days before his forty-fourth birthday. All these trips meant that his activities now extended beyond the Mediterranean Sea, and his range of business even wider.

Mohammed had told my mother not to cancel my father's usual birthday party on account of Nadia. Probably because he knew how useful these social gatherings were to my father's business affairs. And therefore to himself as well.

Although my mother was against it at first, in the end she was persuaded to go ahead but decided to cut down the celebrations by half.

There would simply be a dinner dance on La Moneta that Saturday night. The music would be light; no head-banging rock and no fireworks. Then most of the guests would go home.

I was glad the occasion meant that the four of us in the MANK organization could see each other again and decide what to do about our business in Cairo. Nico had only been back two days, and there'd been no time to meet up.

After lunch that day, I was at the helm of the motorboat. We had the three Hunts onboard. Italia had agreed to let them stay the night after the party. I knew she was doing it for Laura and me, for our hypothetical relationship, a relationship that would make her so happy.

While I was at the helm, Marlene decided she wanted to sunbathe.

"The sea's like glass. Can I stretch out on the prow?"

We were almost there; another ten minutes and Marlene could have sunned herself comfortably on the beach. But you couldn't say no to Marlene.

"Of course, Marlene," my father said. "Mike, watch the sea, and careful with the waves."

I shot a glance at my mother. As usual, she was wearing a long dress down to her ankles with long sleeves to protect her pale complexion from the burning sun. She had a scarf around her short hair, and she was wearing large sunglasses. She was standing up astern with her back to us, smoking and contemplating the coastline. Her preference was to look at the sea from dry land. She actually disliked being at sea and even more being in it. And, that day, she seemed more distant than her usual self.

Observing her, I had the clear impression that something was wrong. There was a strange tension in the air, as if everyone knew something unpleasant about which no one knew what to say.

Laura was on my left, next to her father, who was speaking in English to my brother. They were talking about Vietnam and the war that was perhaps about to end.

"Would you really withdraw from Vietnam?" Alberto asked, incredulous.

"Unfortunately, our politicians haven't understood that you have to respond to barbarity with horror," William replied.

As we drew close to La Moneta, I saw the Libyan coast guard vessels patrolling an area particularly favored by cigarette smugglers because it had lots of coves where you could dock and unload.

My father was standing behind me, like the true captain he was. I couldn't see him, but I was sure that, like me, he was looking at Marlene's splendid body as she lay flat on her stomach, sunbathing. I was studying the edges of the bathing suit, which ran over the curves of her hips and buttocks and down between her thighs.

What I felt for Laura couldn't sweep away that violent desire.

Instead of worrying about my parents' marriage, I was feeling impossible, unacceptable things. Jealousy, competition, anger.

*What does Ingegnere Balistreri have that I don't?*

It was a stupid question. The jealousy of a nineteen-year-old facing two grown-ups who were perhaps lovers, one of whom was my father and the other the mother of my theoretical girlfriend.

"Watch out, Michele, there's the skin-divers' buoy!" my father warned.

I changed course sharply, the boat swerved and a wave caught the back of Marlene, who let out a yell. Then she began to laugh.

"Damn you, Mike! *Mi hai schizzata!*"

The last three words she said in her Italian of sorts, learned in the years they were in Rome.

My father ordered me to leave the wheel and hand it to my brother. Then he spoke in Sicilian dialect, as he did only rarely, and with a smile.

"Then you can give it a bit of a rest, eh?"

So he'd seen me looking at Marlene's backside, since he had been looking in the same direction himself.

．．．．

It was two thirty when we got to La Moneta, and it was boiling hot. Preparations for the dinner had been followed to perfection by Mohammed, with the help of Ahmed, Karim, and Nico.

It had been a long time since we'd seen each other, and we weren't used to it. And, on top of everything, there was Nadia's death. None of us had any wish to talk about the MANK organization and its business. We walked away to one side and Nico told us about his trip to the US.

Exciting stories: massive concerts, massive stars, Hollywood, its villas, drugs, long limousines.

"We should move the MANK organization over there," he said in conclusion.

Karim made a face.

"I'd prefer to starve to death in Africa than live like an American. Islam will reduce it to ashes one day, anyway."

Nico looked at him askance.

"You're wrong, Karim. It'll be America that'll reduce you to ashes, whenever it wants, because it's a civilized country and you're just a bunch of savages. And I'll open a bordello in New York with only Muslim prostitutes."

It was pointless talk, and insulting to Ahmed and Karim.

"The most you'll ever do, Nico, is open a knocking shop above our restaurant in Cairo. That's what you'll do."

And my tone meant no more of this shit. Perhaps I was too hard on him. But all that excitement, with Nadia only recently dead, was out of place.

I looked at my three friends. And at Laura, the girl I was in love with. I knew what was needed. "Hey, let's go and dive off the cliff."

"It's twenty yards down, Mike. And from up there you can't tell if the water's deep enough," objected Karim.

I checked the time. Almost three. Impossible to be sure. High tide was twice a day, but during the year the times changed.

"Oh, come on, let's go!"

We went over to Alberto and Laura, who were chatting on the beach, and explained the problem.

"The only solution is for someone to go with the motorboat and check, then give the signal to those on the cliff if the water's deep enough to dive into," Alberto said.

"Laura could go," Ahmed said. "I don't think she'd jump off from up there anyway."

She ignored him. "If it's Alberto who's telling me it's okay, I'd be the first to go."

As usual, my brother took on the most demanding and least pleasant job. While the MANK organization plus Laura took the path to the other side of the island, Alberto went around the coast in the motorboat.

It took us half an hour to walk the sandy track between the rocks and scrub before we were on the clear patch above the cliff. There was a single olive tree and seat, where my mother spent time with a book. The Mediterranean was a mirror of blue, twenty yards below us.

We went to the cliff edge. I lay flat on the ground and tried to lean my head out to see if there were rocks below. Impossible to see: the rock wall went in too steeply.

After a few minutes, Alberto arrived with the motorboat. He drew near the shore and we saw him disappear below us. As usual, he was meticulous, cautious, and prudent. He'd even brought a megaphone with him that my father kept in the house.

"The tide's going out," he shouted to us. "But if you jump right now it's still good."

I looked at my friends.

"Ready?"

"How about all together?" Laura proposed.

We all joined hands. Laura was in the middle, myself and Ahmed on one side, Karim and Nico on the other. It was a unique, fantastic sensation. We gazed out into the empty space in front of us, without looking down.

"I'm counting to three!" Laura exclaimed.

One. I felt Ahmed squeezing my hand. Two. I squeezed Laura's hand. Three.

We set off at a run and leapt out, letting ourselves fall into the blueness of that welcoming sea.

. . . .

Alberto took us onboard and back to the villa's beach. The guests were starting to arrive.

Little Arab boys in waiter's uniforms were keeping the flies off the food with fans. Arab women were preparing *pasta alla Norma* and a fish couscous. A Sicilian classic of pasta and eggplant and a native

Arabic dish, just as my father wanted. They stood for union and recip-
rocal respect.

The guests were arriving in groups in the two motorboats: one
piloted by Farid, the other by Salim; both hired specially for the occasion and both handsomely rewarded. They had expanded a great deal
in the past two years. Their business had become a small industry: a
much larger fishing boat, ten employees, a thirty-foot Zodiac rubber dinghy with two 200hp outboard motors. They had bought the
motorboats to take the best fish in the shortest time to Malta's lucra-
tive restaurant market. But, that afternoon, they were ferrying several
ambassadors, dignitaries from King Idris's court, two of his ministers,
and the directors of major companies out to La Moneta.

And, naturally, Emilio Busi and Don Eugenio.

Dad was looking his best. His hair was still naturally black, combed
straight back, his slim mustache well trimmed, and he was sporting
a tan from the Tanzanian trip. Wearing a spotless white-linen suit,
dark-blue shirt, and a sky-blue tie, he looked relaxed and pleased with
himself.

He was aware of the appeal of his good looks and power. He had
succeeded in ridding himself of Palermo's unwholesome taint of poverty and was keeping well under control the slight trickle of saliva he
felt as he looked at the world. Everyone—Italians and Libyans, the
dignitaries from court, and the ministers—had come to greet him and
pay their respects.

The men then went on to pay their respects to William Hunt and,
above all, to his extremely beautiful wife, as if she were the guest of
honor. Marlene was wearing a light low-cut dress bought on Rome's
Via Condotti. The cleft between her suntanned breasts and the curve
of the dress over her buttocks attracted me as much as they did the
court dignitaries, ministers, diplomats, and company directors. William was clearly aware of the lustful glances directed at his wife, and
yet he seemed neither concerned nor upset.

*He's a man of integrity with a blind faith in his wife. He'd never think
that she would cheat on him.*

The only men not looking at Marlene were Don Eugenio and
Emilio Busi. The first came as no surprise. But why not Busi? He was

sitting by himself, smoking in the shade of one of the beach gazebos. While I was watching him I realized with a certain disquiet that the eyes behind those dreadful square horn-rims were not on Marlene but on another woman, my mother.

She was seeing to the guests with a cordial formality equal to the look of regal disdain in her eyes. She did not approve of this party, less than a month after Nadia's murder. But it was something beyond that. I could feel her deep sadness and imagined I knew the cause.

*It was my father and Marlene Hunt.*

I met her gaze.

*I hate to see you suffer, Mamma.*

Italia went off to the rear of the villa, where the sandy track that led to the other side of the island began. Without thinking about it, I followed her, keeping enough distance so that she wouldn't see me. It was the same path I had taken that afternoon with Laura and my friends.

Earlier, my spirits had been up. But now I felt oppressed, without really knowing why.

When I got to the open patch on the cliff top, Italia was looking across toward Sicily. The sun had turned red and was beginning to set on the Mediterranean sea.

I settled myself behind a rock. A quarter of an hour later, William appeared along the path. Small drops of sweat dotted his forehead and square jaw. His short blond hair was turning gray at the temples. I hid myself better and waited.

Italia skipped the preliminaries and handed him a white envelope.

"Everything's in there. There's no room for any doubt."

William took the envelope and put it in his pocket without opening it.

"How much time do I have?"

Italia thought for a moment.

"Two days, no more."

It was certainly no friendly chat between two close neighbors. It seemed more of a business transaction.

*Or an exchange of information between two people who have discovered they've been betrayed.*

Italia turned away from him and started to walk. She stopped less than a yard from the cliff edge. William studied her for a long moment with those metallic blue eyes, his look more serious and concerned than usual. Then he turned the other way and started to walk down the path back to the villa. To the west, the sun's red ball was half in the sky and half under the sea.

*Just like my face in Laura's snapshot. Divided between good and evil.*

When I got back to the villa, all the guests had arrived. Dad was chatting with William and Marlene by the telephone in the large kitchen.

"You'll have to excuse me, Salvatore, I've just heard from Wheelus Field. Urgent business. I have to go."

My father seemed strangely concerned, far too much so.

"But William, it's late. Can't you go tomorrow?"

"I'm sorry, Salvo. Marlene will have to sing 'Happy Birthday' to you for me as well."

Was there any irony in the words?

*Or a subtle threat? A last warning both to him and to Marlene?*

My father had to give in.

"Very well. I'll tell Farid to take you back to the Underwater Club."

William thanked him then turned to Marlene.

"I need to talk to you for a minute, dear. Would you excuse us, Salvo?"

"Of course, of course. I'll tell Farid."

William and Marlene went off to one side, deep in conversation. I imagined there were difficult questions between them, evasive answers, the first accusations, perhaps even a threat. I saw my father giving instructions to Farid. Busi entered the house to make a phone call, and Don Eugenio looked worriedly at my father.

At the bottom of the lawn, with a scarf around her head and wearing those huge sunglasses despite the fact the sun had set, stood my mother. She was on her own in front of the villa, smoking in silence, observing the conversation between William and Marlene Hunt.

*Whatever you decide, Mom, I'll be standing right beside you.*

. . . .

The dance floor was full of couples. My father was dancing with Marlene. They weren't holding each other too close, being careful to observe the proprieties—but their smiles, good looks, and extraordinary attractiveness said everything. And chemistry was seen by everyone looking at them.

*Or perhaps not. Perhaps I was imagining it. You know, Mike, the enemy of truth is a strongly held conviction.*

Laura took my hand and led me onto the floor. She knew very well I hated dancing, and she didn't like it too much herself. So why did she do it?

Procul Harum's Hammond organ was playing the final part of "A Whiter Shade of Pale."

Her light eyes were covered by those rebellious black curls.

"What's up, Mike?"

"I have to talk to my father. And you must talk to your mother, Laura." She hugged me a little closer.

"Trust them, Mike."

"I can't," I said brusquely, letting go of her.

*I can't and I don't want to.*

I left the dance floor and swiftly entered the house. I'd made the decision on an impulse, but I knew it was the right one.

*William Hunt's a hero and a man with loyalty. He'll know what to do.*

I went to the telephone. I knew the Wheelus Field switchboard number by heart. An operator answered.

"I'm sorry, sir. Mr. Hunt's aircraft has just taken off."

"Taken off? Where for?"

There was a moment's silence. Then the operator's polite voice.

"I can't tell you that, sir. It's a military flight."

There was another path available, in the form of one influential person who could still be afraid of me.

*Because of those nice photographs with Nico Gerace.*

Don Eugenio was discussing finance with the managers of the Banco di Roma and Banco di Sicilia. Like Busi, he was only thirty-four, but was talking away as if he ran the Banca d'Italia.

"I need to talk to you," I said, rudely interrupting a discussion on interest rates.

His light-blue eyes looked at me quizzically. With his cassock, sandals, and delicate manners, he really seemed the benefactor he claimed to be.

"Do you need to confess, Mike?"

"Not to you."

My answer convinced him of the need to detach himself from the bankers. We went over to the beach, along the pathway of Positano tiles laid into the sand. Frank Sinatra's warm tones could be heard singing his latest hit, "My Way."

"Good song, isn't it, Mike? And that's what you've wanted to be since you were a boy: the fearless knight in shining armor. Like when you wanted to save Nico by reading that sentence in his place."

By freely referring to the event, Don Eugenio was letting me know he felt quite safe. Seven years earlier, I could have destroyed him with those photographs. But I was a child then, and it had been Mamma who had resolved matters in some way and saved me from becoming an altar boy.

No other unpleasant episode had emerged in those seven years. It was as if the priest who couldn't keep his hands to himself had found a way to cure his illness. Perhaps precisely because of those photographs.

"Don't you feel ashamed about that business? You were our teacher. You should have been looking after us, rather than . . ."

Don Eugenio stared at me. He appeared to be sincere.

"It was a grave error, never again committed. I have confessed and God has forgiven me."

"And Nico Gerace? Don't you need his forgiveness as well?"

He looked far away, toward the sea between La Moneta and Giorgimpopoli, where two Libyan Coast Guard cutters were patrolling the waters, looking out for landings by cigarette smugglers.

"Nico's grown up; he's happy. Thanks also to you, Mike. You've given him the self-esteem he needed. My apologies would be no use to him; they'd only bring back bad memories. But you've not sought me out for that old business, I take it."

*No, I'm here to make my father come to his senses.*

"You must speak to my father. This business with Marlene Hunt . . ."

Don Eugenio sighed, as if he knew I was right.

"No one's perfect, Mike. Not even us priests, as you've just reminded me. As to Marlene Hunt, not even you . . ."

*He saw you, Mike. He saw you leaving the villa in a state after spreading sunblock on her back.*

"You have to tell my father . . ."

Don Eugenio interrupted me, politely but firmly.

"I am his confessor, Mike. I know what I should and shouldn't say to him. You, on the other hand, don't go to confession anymore. Perhaps it's time you did."

I would have been happy to land him into the water with a well-aimed tae. But that wasn't the way. I knew there was only one way to get to his soul. Fear. Not of me; he certainly had no fear of me.

"My mother still has those photographs, Don Eugenio. If you don't get my father to mend his ways . . ."

But he made no reply to the threat. I left him on the shore by the silence of that sea.

# NIGHT OF SATURDAY AND SUNDAY, AUGUST 30 TO 31, 1969

From midnight onward, Farid and Salim ferried the guests back in the two motorboats, then the serving staff, once they had finished cleaning up. After that, they came back to sleep at La Moneta.

My mother made it clear that guests staying the night would help themselves to breakfast the next morning and, for lunch, would go to the Underwater Club. With Nadia only recently dead, my father's party had gone on a little too long.

On the island that night were the Balistreri family, with Granddad, Marlene and Laura Hunt, Busi, and Don Eugenio. Mohammed, his four sons, and Nico would sleep in the servants' quarters.

· · · ·

Salvatore Balistreri, Don Eugenio, Emilio Busi, and Mohammed were sitting in the dark under one of the beach gazebos set up for the party. Now that the guests had departed and the others were asleep, they could talk in the silence of the humid night.

"Is everything ready?" Balistreri asked Mohammed.

"Yes. The Al-Aqsa Mosque in Jerusalem was set fire to recently by a Christian extremist and the Libyan police have been mobilized around the clock to stop any protest demonstrations by Islamic extremists here. The alert will end tomorrow in the early afternoon and, after three sleepless nights, General Jalloun will send them all home to rest. Tomorrow night, Tripoli will be without a police force."

"Is General Jalloun on our side?" Busi asked.

"No," Mohammed replied. "He's loyal to the Senussi royals. But he's scared, won't do a thing, and wants to ingratiate himself with the new regime."

"This sudden trip of William Hunt worries me. Are we agreed nevertheless for tomorrow night?" Don Eugenio asked.

Busi quickly interjected.

"I've already checked with Rome. The few in the know there assure me that all information about us is absolutely secure. Unless something leaks out here in Tripoli . . ."

Mohammed was more than ready with an answer. His role had now changed. He was no longer Balistreri's general lacky but his accomplice in a coup d'état who was representing his interests for the new regime.

"It won't. These junior officers risk being hanged for high treason. And we still haven't given the go-ahead, therefore no one officially knows a thing. William Hunt will have been called away because of the worsening situation in Vietnam."

"Are we sure about the new leader?" Busi asked in a last moment of doubt.

"We met him a few days ago in Italy. Everything's in order, isn't it, Mohammed?" Balistreri said.

Mohammed agreed.

"He's a young man with backbone who grew up in my very own tribe. I know his family and we're very good friends."

"We're not concerned with your family's friendships here, Mohammed, but with this X's future relationship with Italy."

Balistreri looked at Busi. He really was a difficult man. He gave him an ironic smile.

"Did you know that X is actually a Juventus fan? He's said that, one day, when he's in power, he'll buy some stock in it. Doesn't that set your mind at rest?"

But Busi was in no mood for jokes.

"Great, we can all go together and watch matches with him. But, for the moment, I think we should stick very close to him."

Mohammed replied in his serious manner.

"Of course. I'm leaving for Benghazi tomorrow, and tomorrow night I'll be right at his side."

Don Eugenio turned to speak to Mohammed.

"It's essential to avoid any bloodshed."

"Yes, that way the West will confine itself to figuring out who the leader is and what he's thinking," Busi explained. "I know my fellow Party members. They'll be skeptical to begin with, but they'll support the change if there's no violence."

Mohammed smiled. By now he was inured to these Italians and their base hypocrisy.

"There'll be no deaths, gentlemen. Perhaps a few old men might die of fright and a few of the powerful from a broken heart, but no Libyan would give his life for this pro-Israeli and pro-American king."

Salvatore Balistreri looked with pride at this former lacky of his, who was about to become their key man on the new Libyan power scene.

· · · ·

At the same moment, in Benghazi, William Hunt was sitting in a bare room in the airport's military zone. From the window he could see the airplane that had brought him from Wheelus Field.

He was ready for the fight. Just as in Korea, when those damned Chinese had crossed the bridge over the frozen Yalu River.

No, he was more than ready. He allowed himself to smile at a memory.

*How many Chinese temples placed next to each other can a Colt 45 penetrate?*

Unfortunately, President Truman was a politician and a coward. He had no balls to do what his chief of staff, General MacArthur, suggested.

*Those Chinese need to remember what we did to the Japanese in Hiroshima and Nagasaki.*

Now MacArthur had been reinstated. And Hunt, taking advantage of his wounds, had returned to the United States. Except, American politicians still hadn't gotten it.

*Horror can only be fought with horror.*

Vietnam was proving this. You don't win wars by discussing it with the media and with the pacifists. And you don't win them by political means.

He made his first call. It was afternoon in the United States. The person in Washington who replied listened to him carefully.

"Stay in Benghazi, Mr. Hunt. We'll give you further instructions tomorrow morning."

*Tomorrow morning, fine. As if the hours didn't count at all.*

He knew very well that, in certain cases, every minute was precious.

His mind turned to Italia Balistreri, who was, without doubt, an extraordinary woman. Regal, rock solid, and pure as ice. And she had given him proof of the orders and the ultimatum. And, to him, a Marine, a war hero, one of the victors.

*Forty-eight hours at most. You were optimistic, Italia. Everything will be decided a lot sooner than that.*

# SUNDAY, AUGUST 31, 1969

## MORNING

Dawn. I was already awake. I heard the mosquitoes buzzing around Alberto, who was fast asleep on the bed next to mine. Outside, I could see the dark becoming light on the horizon and could smell the sea as I heard the engines of the first fishing boats returning.

I got up. It must have been six o'clock. Mamma was alone on the veranda, sitting on the swing seat with an almost empty bottle of whiskey and an ashtray full of cigarette butts. She must have spent the whole night out there. I sat close by her.

We were silent for a while. The only sound was that of the tide in the early dawn, still lit by the stars. Farid and Salim's fleet of two motorboats and the Zodiac rubber dinghy were moored on the jetty.

Nietzsche's *Beyond Good and Evil* was lying next to Mamma, a sheet of squared paper sticking out of the last pages.

"Are those my notes on Nadia's death?"

Italia nodded. She had promised to look at them, but the sheet was nestling in the back of the Nietzsche book, unread. Her silence confirmed it. It was strange she hadn't kept her promise.

"Did you manage to check the alibis of the grown-ups for that morning?"

A shadow crossed her face. I couldn't interpret it. Too much sadness, too many other possible reasons.

*Too much past, too little future.*

"The matter was closed after Jamaal's suicide, Mike."

"So you think Jamaal was guilty as well? Just because he committed suicide?"

Incredibly, she smiled.

"No, not because of that. If someone takes their own life, then people think they're either mad or guilty."

"Jamaal didn't kill Nadia, Mamma."

She gazed out to sea. "Of course he didn't. He was only mad."

"Or else, he was neither mad nor guilty."

"Michele, you must promise me something."

She used my full name, not my nickname. I already knew what she was going to ask.

"Do I have to make you a promise to show you I love you, Mamma?"

She gave me a sweet smile, her hand tracing out the movement of a caress in the air, but she stopped halfway, as if she had met an invisible obstacle that separated her forever from the son for whom she had the greater love.

"No, I know you love me. But you must show more love for yourself, Michele. You're not the loser your father says you are, nor are you the crazy hero that your Uncle Toni was. And now you have Laura, and I know that you're perfect together."

"Mamma, Nadia will never get any justice . . ."

She smiled at me again. The very sweet smile she gave me when she sang me that mournful song to get me to sleep when I was young. I wanted to go back to sleep like that, on the swing seat with my head resting on Italia's shoulders, as I did when I was a child. But I was no longer a child, and the sun was rising on my last day as an adolescent.

Around eight, Marlene joined us on the veranda. She was in a running vest, shorts, and gym shoes, ready for her jog. Her tanned complexion and her black hair, swept back in a long ponytail, contrasted with my mother's pale colors. Italia received her with unaccustomed civility.

"May I give William a call?"

"Of course. Mike, show Marlene to Dad's study, where she won't be disturbed."

I showed her the way. As we entered the study, I felt her breast brush against my arm. Had she done it on purpose? She smiled at me.

"Thanks, Mike. Now, a moment of privacy, please. You know, things between husband and wife . . ."

I left her in the study and went back to the veranda. My head was in a state; I could still feel the tip of her nipple on my arm.

*You're just an oversexed little boy. She can do whatever she wants with you.*

Italia was smoking in silence, her eyes already hidden behind her large sunglasses, her body covered by a long kaftan. Her exposed arms were very thin and white, her veins showing through. Next to her cup was the bottle of anisette with which she had laced her coffee.

"What are you going to do today?" I asked. I had to distract myself from thinking about Marlene.

"I'll go up to the cliff to read for a while."

"Aren't you coming with us to lunch at the Underwater Club?"

"No, Mike. I'd rather stay here."

Laura came out soon after. Her tired eyes said she had slept badly, and with evil forebodings. She kissed Italia first, then me, and poured a coffee without saying a word. Marlene came back from the study. Her face was unusually tense, as if she had made an important decision.

"Italia, I need to talk to you."

I held my breath. It was the most surprising request I could imagine. And yet my mother seemed unsurprised. She replied in the most friendly manner I'd ever seen her use with Marlene.

"You can come with me to the cliff top, if you like."

Marlene looked at Laura, who was staring at her in silence.

"I'm going to do my hour of jogging and then I promised I'd spend the morning with Laura on the beach."

"Well, then we can speak when you've come back from lunch at the Underwater Club," my mother offered.

"William's expecting me at Wheelus at two thirty, when he's back in Tripoli."

I could see Marlene wanted to talk to my mother before she talked to William.

My mother was incredibly well disposed to this.

*An urgent matter needs clearing up.*

"Then let's do this, Marlene. I'm going up to the cliff top now, but I'll be back by half past twelve. I've already asked Farid to stay and grill some fish for me. If you like, we could eat together while the others are at the Club and, when they come back, you can go and meet your husband."

"Thank you, Italia. I really appreciate it." Marlene, too, was unusually accommodating.

*They're sharpening swords for the duel. But this isn't a movie.*

The sea was beautifully calm. Farid and Salim's motorboats and dinghy were almost motionless. Marlene went off for her jog and Laura went to the beach on her own. I went back to my father's study and saw the notepad by the phone. There was nothing written on the top sheet, but I checked the wastepaper basket. There was a single ball of paper inside. I took it out and opened it up. A line of figures was scribbled on it. I dialed the number. A voice in English answered from the switchboard of Benghazi's military airport.

*William Hunt's in Benghazi. What's he doing there?*

I replaced the receiver and went back to the veranda. Shortly afterward, Italia went off behind the villa, where the path across the island began. Her pale skin was protected by a hat, the glasses, and the long dress down to her ankles that left only her thin white arms uncovered. She was the complete opposite of Marlene Hunt, the woman now taking her place in my father's affections.

*A respectable woman well covered up to read without getting herself sunburned. And a suntanned whore who goes for a run half naked.*

Over the next hour, everyone came out together in little groups. First Alberto, Nico, Ahmed, and Karim. Then Granddad, Dad, Mohammed, Don Eugenio, and Emilio Busi. Farid and Salim appeared last, with tired red eyes that said they had only had a few hours' sleep.

The day before, they had transported the guests back and forth in the two motorboats until late, and now they had to dismantle the beach gazebos with us boys and take them to Granddad's warehouses.

As soon as breakfast was finished, the grown-ups set off for Tripoli in one of the motorboats. Granddad, Dad, and Don Eugenio were going to Mass, Mohammed to the office, and Busi to the Italian Embassy.

"Please be sure to be on time at the Underwater Club," my father told Alberto.

Marlene returned from her jog immediately after they left, as if she wanted to avoid my father. I bumped into her in the kitchen while she was heading for the shower. There was only a glance between us, but it was enough.

*This isn't going to be an ordinary day.*

We began to take the gazebos down. There were seven of us, and we wanted to finish before the sun became too strong.

Laura and Marlene were taking a walk along the water's edge. It didn't look as if the conversation was an easy one. A storm also seemed to be brewing in the Hunt household.

*You have to tell her, Laura. Tell her to leave my father alone.*

By eleven, the gazebos were all dismantled and stored aboard Farid and Salim's large rubber dinghy. There was nothing more to do until lunchtime.

"Why don't we all go fishing?" Salim suggested. "We'll show you a new place that me and Farid found."

"I have to stay and cook for Signora Italia and Signora Marlene," Farid demurred.

"I'm staying here on the beach. I have to study," Alberto said.

We four in the MANK organization looked at one another. All of a sudden, I couldn't bear the atmosphere on La Moneta any longer. That interminable conversation between Marlene and Laura Hunt could only have one possible topic.

*But you won't be able to do it, sweetheart. Your mother's a demon.*

"OK, Salim, we're up for it," I said. I was the head of the organization. Nico, Ahmed, and Karim made no objection.

After ten minutes in the motorboat we came to the place that Salim had mentioned.

"There are shallows under here that are full of fish. It's only ten yards deep; you don't need scuba equipment."

When we submerged, the heat and sunlight finally gave way to the cool and the dark. But even there in that blue water I couldn't find any peace. When we came to the bottom of the shallows, Salim was right. It was full of grouper.

But I didn't fire a single shot. If I killed any living thing that day, it wouldn't have been a grouper. My mind was full of the same series of images.

*Marlene Hunt in Rome with my father. My hands spreading sunblock on her skin. My mother's sad, tired eyes. Laura watching and listening.*

. . . .

We were a little late getting back to La Moneta, just after twelve thirty. Laura and Alberto were already waiting on the jetty, Farid beside them. Salim brought the motorboat up next to the dinghy and Laura and Alberto stepped quickly onboard.

"Has Mamma come back?" I asked Alberto.

"Yes, I saw her a few minutes ago, coming down the path to the villa."

"And she's going to stay here?"

*With that whore?*

"I haven't spoken to her, Mike. We were already out here waiting for you on the beach when she came back."

I met Laura's look. She was decidedly upset, but she gave me a silent warning to keep quiet.

*Let them have a talk between themselves. We can't do a thing.*

Alberto loosened the moorings and called me into line.

"Come on, Mike, we're late. It's better if we don't get Dad angry."

*Of course. We don't want to get Dad angry.*

Instead, I got out of the boat and took hold of Laura's hand. "Can you make do with a bit of fruit?"

Laura got out of the boat as well. Perhaps she was doing it for me. Alberto gave me a resigned look while Salim got the motor running and he, Nico, Ahmed, and Karim left to meet the grown-ups at the Underwater Club.

We went into the kitchen. I pointed to the hall that led to the lounge where Marlene Hunt was telling my mother how everything was about to change.

*Your husband doesn't love you anymore, Italia. He wants to live with me. You'd better get used to it.*

"Do you want to eat with Signora Italia and Signora Marlene?" Farid asked, looking concerned.

Laura beat me to it. Her answer was also directed at me.

"No, thanks, Farid. Mike and I'll eat some fruit on the beach."

*We should leave them in peace. We can't interfere. It's pointless.*

Laura and I went back to the beach and lay down in the sun while Farid went to sit on the veranda in the shade.

It was nearly one o'clock and there was a slight breeze that made the air more breathable but the sun was hellishly hot. Laura was wrestling with her arms behind her back to put on sunblock by herself. It was the same cream I had put on her mother's back.

*The American* gahba.

"Do you want me to do it, Laura?"

She smiled. There was no evil in it, only gratitude for an unexpected kindness.

"Thanks, Mike, just a little."

My hands and fingers repeated the same movements they had over her mother's body but, if their two bodies were similar, everything else was different. She didn't undo the bikini top, and I didn't think for a minute of going anywhere near the bikini bottom.

I looked over to the villa where the decisive battle was taking place between the woman I worshipped and the woman who had brought me into this world—one of them was about to wreck my life.

*Either you stop what you're doing or I'll make you stop.*

## AFTERNOON

Laura and I got into the water. The struggle between anger and calm, between desire and love, between Marlene and Laura Hunt was eating me up.

What I wanted to destroy was what I also wanted to have.

"What did you and Marlene talk about all morning?" I asked her.

"A lot of things, Mike. About things that unite us and things that separate us."

"What separates you two, then?"

She took my hand as we began to walk in the water, Farid watching us as he sat on the veranda a hundred yards or so away.

"Several things, Mike. One of them being you."

I looked at her in surprise and took my hand from hers.

"Me? You talked about me?"

"She talked about a lot of things, including you."

"And I'm one of the things that separates you?"

"Mike, it's anger that separates us."

"Tell me what Marlene has to say about me."

*That I dream of her body every night? That I spread sunblock on her? That I saw her naked?*

Laura stopped to stare at me, there in the water, her back to the beach, the villa, and the sun, which was directly in my eyes. I instinctively raised an arm for shade so I could see her better.

"I think the shadow part, the part that Marlene sees, is only a mask."

*But Marlene knows the opposite's true, Laura, from direct experience. And she's right. That part of me does exist. And it's inside me.*

At that moment Farid got up and went into the house. He came out again after a few seconds.

"That was Salim on the phone. They're coming back," he shouted, to make sure I heard him.

"Already?" I asked, surprised.

Farid shrugged and sat down again.

*They'll be here shortly. My mother will confront my father. And I'll confront Marlene Hunt.*

In the half an hour that followed, I said nothing. I watched the coming and going of the two Libyan coast guard cutters and thought things over. Farid was on the veranda having a smoke, Laura was in a deckchair beneath an umbrella, and I was a few yards away under the sun on the burning sand. Each one of us with our own thoughts, a few yards away from the other; silent prisoners of our emotions, waiting for what fate had in store for us.

· · · ·

It had just gone half past one when the motorboat with the grown-ups from the Underwater Club was in sight of La Moneta. Even in the water, the heat was unbearable; it turned the surrounding view into a kind of gleaming mirage. Salim was at the helm and from the beach I could see Ahmed going to the bows to help with mooring. About a hundred yards from the jetty, the motorboat slowed down further. A breeze was stirring.

"Should I go?" Farid asked us. He was on the veranda, about fifty yards from the jetty.

Laura and I were much closer.

"We'll see to it." We got up onto the jetty to get ready to receive the mooring ropes.

While the motorboat was coming close, traveling at less than two knots, I saw my father deep in conversation with Busi and Don Eugenio. He was looking drawn, and at a certain point I saw his worried face looking toward the villa.

I turned as well, shading my face with an arm. The villa door was open; Farid was talking to my mother with a cigarette between his lips.

*I wondered if my mother could see my divided face. Half light and half shade. The light and dark of my soul.*

She looked at us briefly from behind her dark glasses, her hair in the usual scarf, her body enveloped by the long linen kaftan that left only her thin white arms bare. A book was sticking out of her pocket, probably Nietzsche.

Without a smile, she raised an arm in a kind of greeting and stopped halfway, as if that was all she could do, and left the gesture unfinished. Then she turned and went quickly behind the villa to the way to the other side of the island.

There we were, about fifty yards away, left wondering. In those two or three seconds on that jetty open to the sea, wind and sun, I distinctly picked up on the general feeling of fear washing in. Not the fear of one individual, but of everyone around.

*Mamma doesn't want to talk to Dad, not with all his minions around.*

We moored the boat next to Farid and Salim's rubber dinghy and everyone began to disembark, unloading the water and food. I gave a hand for a couple of minutes, but in that half-hour of silence on the burning sand I had made up my mind. And that melancholy gesture from my mother had removed any lingering doubts.

*I'll take care of the American* gahba.

I set off slowly toward the villa. Laura saw me but said nothing.

*Don't do it, Mike.*

But I couldn't trust her blindly like that. I knew she loved me and also that anything I said to Marlene would be useless. But what was driving me was stronger than either reason or love. I turned and went toward the villa. Farid was still on the veranda next to the door through which my mother had just come out, a habitual cigarette hanging from the corner of his thick lips.

"Where's Marlene?" I asked him brusquely.

His coarse features were suddenly worried. He blocked my path.

*He can see that I'm crazy as well.*

"I think she's in the bathroom taking a shower before she goes."

"I have to speak to her. You stay here," I ordered him, physically pushing him aside and going into the villa.

I had no more than two minutes before the others arrived. The door to the guests' bathroom was closed. From outside, I could hear the noise of the shower. I gave three loud knocks.

"Yes?" came Marlene's voice.

"It's me."

*The son of your lover and the woman whose heart you're breaking.*

The key turned in the lock and the door opened a hand's breadth. Marlene's wet face stared at me, while her body was hidden by the doorjamb, and I was hit by the scents of shampoo and body lotion. Immediately, desire mingled with the anger. It was an unbearable animal desire, made even more unacceptable by the hate I felt for her in that moment.

*Her naked body was only eight inches away. The scent of her body lotion.*

"I have to speak to you, right now."

I wanted my voice to have menace, but it came out wavering and weak and this increased my anger.

She looked at me with that mocking half-smile she had.

"I'll be home at three. Now go and take a cold shower—you're far too hot."

*Full of lustful hormones, that's what she means.*

The Root of All Evil

She shut the door in my face and I made it down just in time to be back on the veranda before they all arrived to eat the now-cold hamburgers. My grandfather was not with them.

"Where's Granddad?" I asked Alberto.

My brother was uncharacteristically subdued.

"He preferred to stay at the Club. He's waiting for Farid and Salim to come with the dismantled gazebos to take to the warehouse."

I went up to my father.

"I have to talk to you."

He didn't even glance at me.

"Not today, Mike. Tomorrow."

*But tomorrow will be too late, Dad.*

I looked for Laura, but she wasn't there. She had gone into the villa to look for her mother.

. . . .

Five minutes later, suntanned and in a short white skirt and pink T-shirt, looking as beautiful as a goddess with her black hair loose, Marlene Hunt came out onto the veranda, followed by Laura and Farid, who was carrying her luggage, a large black leather bag with Marilyn Monroe's face on it.

She gestured to my father.

*Here, Salvo.* Just like a little puppy.

For a moment I had the impression that Dad was about to resist the gesture, but he looked afraid and went over, while I followed behind.

I was prepared for anything, but not the exchange I heard.

*I told her everything, Salvo.*

*You're crazy, Marlene.*

Did I hear them right? Or did I imagine it? I wasn't sure.

Marlene then kissed Laura and went off to the jetty, where Farid was stowing her bag on the boat. Salim was ready in the rubber dinghy with the dismantled gazebos to take to Granddad's warehouses.

Farid helped Marlene to get onboard. There was no more time; I had to decide. I could go to my mother on the other side of the island and try to comfort her, or I could go and face my father and threaten to cause a scandal. Or I could stay behind on the beach with Laura, my only hope for the future.

*Or I could follow Marlene Hunt, the real guilty party.*

"Give me a lift," I said to Salim, all of a sudden, getting into the dinghy.

His thin lips curled into a mocking smile.

*He knows I'm crazy as well.*

Many pairs of eyes were following me. But Laura was no longer on the beach. While Farid piloted the motorboat, with Marlene settled in the bows, Salim and I started the dinghy's motor. During the short trip, he went over the plan again: that Granddad was waiting at the Club to go together with them to the olive grove in Sidi El Masri, and that we were to leave the gazebos in the warehouse there.

"You want to give us a hand, Mike?"

I made no reply. I had something completely different in mind.

• • • •

Half an hour later we were at the Underwater Club. It was ten past two. While Farid was taking Marlene's bag to the Ferrari in the parking lot, she and I walked on the jetty in silence.

I could not see her eyes, but I heard the words whispered from the mouth I had so often dreamed about.

"Today's the day, Mike, now or never."

Granddad came up to us. Marlene said hello to him and went off to her Ferrari.

"Are you coming with us to the olive grove, Mike?" Granddad asked me.

I shook my head.

"I've got a headache, Granddad. I'm going home."

A moment later, I was in the jeep.

I followed the Ferrari at a distance of a hundred yards. Perhaps Marlene could see me in the rearview mirror, but it made no difference.

• • • •

At two fifteen, the airplane from Benghazi changed course over the sea and headed for Tripoli. William Hunt was thinking what cowards politicians were. They were all the same: fence sitters, opportunists, and manipulators. *Let's not meddle here. We'll wait and see what happens.*

He knew he would find Marlene waiting for him, as arranged. And he would learn whether he could truly count on his extraordinarily beautiful wife.

*Today's the day, now or never.*

. . . .

The red Ferrari was traveling slowly along the Adrian Pelt seafront road across the empty city. The palm trees were motionless and everyone was hidden away in the cool and shade of their houses.

Marlene was at the Wheelus Field entrance a little before two thirty. I parked the jeep at a suitable distance from the air base. While Marlene was showing her ID papers, a military aircraft was landing on the runway.

There was a pair of binoculars in the jeep that we used when we were hunting. Through the perimeter fence, I saw William Hunt exiting the plane. Marlene was waiting for him with the Ferrari directly below the air stairs. There was no hug, not even a kiss. They were immediately in deep conversation in the airplane's shade. In fact, it was Marlene who was speaking while William listened.

As I watched them through the binoculars, I tried to read Marlene's lips and imagine what she was saying.

*It's over, William. Salvo told his wife yesterday and I said the same today.*

William Hunt was a dangerous man, an ex-Marine with ice-cold eyes who, I had heard, worked for the CIA. A man who had always commanded and had never been betrayed or humiliated. A man certainly capable of killing for such a grievous wrong. He listened intently, impassively, like a soldier getting ready to act.

. . . .

After nearly half an hour's conversation, William said something to his wife, something I imagined he would.

*I'd rather kill you, Marlene, than let you go off with that slick Italian.*

Then he got into the Ferrari with her and they drove to the office building on the other side of the base. After less than five minutes, the car appeared at the entry bar, with Marlene alone at the wheel.

She waved to the guards and took off toward Tripoli at high speed, the Ferrari's tires squealing. I followed in the jeep, but the distance between us was growing. Marlene was driving along the coast at nearly one hundred and twenty miles an hour. I knew she had seen me in the rearview mirror. It was a challenge.

*Frightened, Michelino?*

At the crossroads before the city, the Ferrari turned off toward Garden City and Sidi El Masri at sixty miles an hour, and I let her go; otherwise, the jeep would have overturned. She was only going home anyway. And there we would settle matters.

· · · ·

It was half past three when I got to the iron gates with my parents' linked initials. The Ferrari was parked in front of the Hunt home. The pair of villas was wrapped in the most total silence, as if the torrid heat of that last day of August had made even the sparrows, cicadas, and frogs mute.

I tried to consider matters, thinking of my mother's sad eyes, the humiliation, the loneliness, alone on that cliff edge, thinking about the end of her marriage.

I saw that half-raised hand again, that gesture she had made just before the motorboat was docking. Suddenly, I had a revelation.

She wasn't waving at us, or anyone. She was saying good-bye. Good-bye to life.

Anger and anguish churned uncontrollably in my blood. I got out of the jeep and strode in the direction of the villa.

· · · ·

As usual, the door to the Hunt villa wasn't locked. No one locked doors in Tripoli then. I knew that by opening that door I would close many others. I stood there motionless, like a compass needle caught between two opposing forces.

*My photograph. The sunlit side and the side in shadow. Good and evil.*

I swore to myself that I wouldn't touch her, only speak to her. I would persuade her to leave my father alone.

When I entered the villa it was enveloped in shadow, but a thin strip of light was coming from under a door at the end of the hall where the bedrooms were. Our villa and theirs were exactly the same, so that door had to be to William and Marlene's bedroom.

I went up slowly in silence. I had no idea what I was going to do. On the living room carpet were scattered the few clothes Marlene had been wearing. I picked up the pink T-shirt and little white skirt and smelled her scent on them: her body lotion and her sweat.

When I opened the door Marlene was sitting on a chair, busily brushing her shiny wet hair. She was wrapped in a terry cloth bathrobe, tied at the waist.

*What was she wearing underneath?*

She looked at me in the mirror.

"What are you doing in my bedroom?"

*Today's the day, now or never.*

"You said I could find you here," I almost stammered.

"And you come in without knocking—while I'm half naked?"

I was beside myself. On the one hand, I hated her. On the other, my eyes were fixed on the knot in the terry cloth belt that was keeping me from heaven.

"The front door was open," I said, weakly trying to justify myself.

There was that sarcastic smile again.

"Perhaps I should call the police. But then you're not a dangerous thief, are you, Michelino? A thief who comes and looks, that's all, and takes nothing away. A thief who only wants to talk, talk, talk."

I was on the divide between her provocation and derision.

*She's a devil, Mike. You'll throw away everything. Laura, your mother, yourself.*

Marlene looked at me. Then she said it again, and this time I was sure of what I was hearing.

"Today's the day, it's now or never, Michelino. Gather the courage or get lost."

I grabbed her by the collar of the bathrobe. Her eyes opened wide with surprise. Then the green of her iris became dark as the winter sea.

"Are you upset, Michelino? Do you want to hit me? Is that what you want to do?"

"You're probably used to that with your Marine of a husband."

The anger and desire gave me away. I felt like a boat in a storm, and she was the storm. She was in charge; she made the decisions.

"Michelino, you don't think for a minute that William is the kind of man who would hit me, do you? It's only you Italians who do such things to women. Ask your father."

I ripped the bathrobe off her and threw it on the bed. She was wearing a bra and panties underneath. I threw my one hundred and ninety pounds of weight on top of her, while she kicked and screamed and hit me furiously in the face. She scratched at my shoulders and I felt blood trickling down my back.

But I was heavier and stronger. I slapped her and took hold of both her wrists in my left hand as she fought to free herself. Then, with my right hand, I ripped off her bra. The sound of the material tearing increased both my excitement and anger.

Marlene spat in my face. I grabbed the elastic of her panties with my free hand and pulled hard, but they did not tear.

"You're not strong enough, Michelino. Too much jerking off, thinking about me."

I could no longer see anything. I let go of her arms and tore off her briefs with both my hands while she tried to claw my face. But she was a prisoner under my weight. I got up on my knees, straddling her body so I could look at her.

She was underneath me, naked, sweating, her hair all over her face. She wrestled against me, screaming insults, her eyes now as green as a stormy sea. And I was there, tossing about on those waves, raging with hate and desire.

*It's today, now or never, Michelino. No, I won't do it.*

I paused for a second to try to calm myself down. Then she stretched a hand out to my jeans and had them undone in three seconds.

I heard her speak, her voice hoarse with passion.

"Tie my wrists to the bed, Michelino. Then it won't be my fault. So no one can blame me."

I tied her up and pulled off my jeans and briefs. I wanted to devour her, destroy her, and do to her body everything that was the most ugly, vulgar, and insulting that my lost adolescent's imagination could suggest.

She bit my lip and drew blood as I penetrated her then she spat my own blood mingled with her saliva into my eyes. Now she wrestled even more, but in a different way, so that I could enter her more deeply, with the fury of desperation.

This was hell: blood, flesh, and flames.

· · · ·

Marlene Hunt got up and put her bathrobe back on.

"Get dressed and hop to it, Mike. Now. It's already five fifteen," she said, closing the bathroom door behind her.

I did as she said in silence, before she came out.

I arrived at the Underwater Club at a quarter to six, while Farid and Salim were getting out of one of the motorboats. They had gone to pick up Mohammed on La Moneta and were taking him to the airport.

"Can I take the boat?" I asked.

Mohammed stared at me, his lean features forming into a silent query.

*Where have you been, Mike?*

"Yes," Farid replied eventually. "We have the dinghy."

It was a little less hot on the water; the wind from the land had died down and now a breeze was blowing from the sea. In the thirty minutes it took to reach La Moneta I could not get my thoughts together. I had a feeling of disaster. But it lay *ahead*, not behind me.

*You've displaced the first boulder in the avalanche.*

# EVENING

The sun was setting over the island when I moored the motorboat to the La Moneta jetty. There was a certain animation on the little beach: everyone was there, grown-ups and children.

Dad looked at me, rubbing a hand over his suntanned face. His dark eyes looked unaccustomedly worried.

"Where've you been, Mike?"

*Fucking your woman, Dad. Instead of going to look after my mother.*

I made no effort to reply.

"Where's my mother?" I asked.

They all looked in each other's faces, as if I were talking about an extraterrestrial.

"She'll be in her room, won't she?" my father replied.

I turned my back on everyone, entered the villa, and knocked on Italia's door. No reply. The door was unlocked, the room tidy and unoccupied, the windows were closed, and there was no smell of cigarettes. My mother still wasn't back.

I went back outside and said I couldn't find her. Then I shot off up the path to the other side of the island, despite knowing very well there was no reason to run. The difference of a few minutes would change nothing.

But I ran just the same. Alberto was struggling behind me and Ahmed was at my side. I was running and looking at the watch my mother had given me for my confirmation. I was saying to myself that, if I could beat my record, then I would find my mother contemplating the seas in the twilight's semidarkness.

It was almost totally dark by the time we reached the cliff, but the always provident Alberto had brought a flashlight. The area underneath the large olive tree bent by the wind was deserted. There was only the folding chair and her copy of Nietzsche's *Ecce Homo*. That book left open on the chair was a silent witness that something either out of the ordinary or untoward had happened.

I looked down over the steep crag into the impenetrable dark that ended on the rocks twenty yards below.

"I'm going down," I announced.

It was a very steep and slippery descent, even by day. To go down in the dark was almost insane.

"No, Mike," Alberto said. "Let's go back to the villa and call someone from the police or the coast guard."

"Leave me the flashlight, Alberto. You run back and call the others."

It was the first time I had given an order to my elder brother. It was as if the exceptional circumstances had reversed our roles, the emergency we both saw unfolding now making me the elder brother. Alberto assented without a word and went running off to the villa.

"I'll come with you, Mike," Ahmed said.

Telling Ahmed that it was dangerous would have been offensive and useless.

I set off, flashlight in hand, and he came along behind me. You couldn't see more than a yard ahead. We went down slowly, one step at a time, first testing the ground cautiously. When we came to the steepest part, I stopped.

"Watch out, there's loose gravel in this stretch," I warned.

Too late. The foot I was standing on lost its grip. If I tried to resist I would have tumbled off into midair. So I let myself slump on my bottom and began to slide straight down until I grasped at a twisted root with my right hand and my legs traced an arc in the air and banged against the rock face.

Perhaps I had cracked something. The pain rose piercingly from my ankle, but that was the least of my worries. I knew I could hold on to that root for a few seconds.

Lying flat on the ground, Ahmed came worming his way toward me, using both hands to stop himself from slipping down and falling on top of me; otherwise, we would both have ended up in midair. The pain in my ankle was now extending to my whole leg.

"Ahmed, stop, or you'll fall as well."

He wouldn't listen to me; he was too focused on trying to get to me. He slipped his right ankle under another root that was sticking out and pushed his heel through to the other side.

"It won't bear our weight, Ahmed."

"It doesn't have to."

He stretched horizontally against the descent and stretched his right arm out to me. Like this, only half his weight was pulling on the root.

I saw his right hand coming slowly toward mine. And saw his foot very slowly lifting up the root. Then his hand locked around my wrist like a vice.

"Leave me, Ahmed, it's impossible."

"The left one, Mike."

With a huge effort, I lifted up my left arm and stretched out my hand. I still needed a few fractions of an inch to reach his arm. My foot felt as if it was being pulled off my leg.

"One last effort, Mike. First breathe out entirely. Empty your lungs."

I gathered my strength, breathed out, and lunged upward as my left hand grasped his right arm. The pain in my leg was now so strong I felt sick.

"Keep holding on to the root with your right hand and pull yourself up with your left."

It was the right moment to thank my father for letting me have years of training in the gym, and for paying for Ahmed to do the same. Our honed muscles were as tense as violin strings. Now I could no longer fall, but we were stuck.

We stayed like that, in total silence. I saw the scar on Ahmed's right wrist, where we had made our blood brotherhood as kids. As a left-hander, he had saved my life with his weaker arm. And he held me firmly to be sure I would not fall.

*If the root gives way, we'll go together.*

When Alberto came back with the grown-ups, he had brought a rope with him. They lifted us up, one at a time. I tried to stand up, but my ankle gave way. I tried to breathe, and not to scream.

While I was doubled over being sick, I felt a cool hand holding my forehead. It was Laura. My vision began to cloud and I fainted.

# SUNDAY NIGHT, AUGUST 31 TO MONDAY, SEPTEMBER 1, 1969

I woke up in the place where my mother had given birth to me, a bed in the Villa Igea hospital.

In the dim light of the hospital's bedside lamp I glimpsed Laura sitting beside me, holding my hand. Ahmed, Karim, and Nico were in the farthest corner, listening to a transistor radio with the volume turned down. Nico was terrified, Karim excited, Ahmed tense.

I tried to fight against the sleeping pills and painkillers they had given me and ask *What the hell's going on?* but was unable to. I fell asleep again.

....

The radio station in the center of Benghazi was a bare two-story building.

The twenty-six-year-old junior officer whom the Qadhadhfa tribe had placed at the head of the Libyan revolution arrived in a dusty jeep just before two in the morning with an armed escort and Mohammed Al Bakri by his side. The small number of armored cars had been more than enough to convince any dissenter to stay at home.

In front of the microphone, Mohammed handed him a sheet with the speech he had prepared with Salvatore Balistreri. It was a very short speech, which Muammar Al Gaddafi read, a little unsure of himself. There was to be no violence; cities and frontiers were secured; everyone was to stay at home; a curfew was in place. Gaddafi did not give his name. All part of the agreement.

At that time of night, there were few Libyans awake and listening to the radio. But the message was really for the leader's supporters— who had already occupied ministries, the radio station, and airports in many parts of Libya without meeting any resistance. It was they who extended the news to the rest of the population, firing celebratory shots from their rifles and pistols during the night.

Salvatore Balistreri and his friends were in the living room in the villa on the island. On the telephone, General Jalloun was desperately trying to excuse himself. He had called his men out to start the search for Italia, but the police were being held in their quarters by the military and there were roadblocks everywhere. He was not even free to go out himself.

That night, Ingegnere Balistreri and his associates were among the few people listening to the short live broadcast in which Gaddafi announced the end of the Senussi monarchy and the birth of the Libyan Jamahiriya. They had waited so long for this moment, but not one of them dared to smile.

In a silver frame by the radio, Italia's photograph watched them mutely.

# MONDAY, SEPTEMBER 1, 1969

When I woke up, my room was empty, and so, it seemed, was the whole of Villa Igea, which was completely silent. Outside, there were a few sounds, including the noise of trucks. Then I heard isolated shots. I rang the bell and, after a while, a nursing sister came in, panting and out of breath.

"Have they found my mother?" I asked her.

She looked at me, dumbfounded.

"Your mother? I've no idea. Look, I think you should know that there's been a coup d'état during the night."

I had no idea what the hell she was talking about, and began to shout.

"My mother, you damn fool, my mother! Have they found her?"

The sister ran away. After a few minutes, Ahmed appeared, his bony features more sunken and morose than usual.

"Sorry, Mike, we were on the floor below. The military is outside. No one can leave the building—there's a curfew in place."

I started to shout like a madman again. A doctor came running in with a syringe. It took four of them to hold me down to give me the injection to make me sleep.

• • • •

When I woke up again it was late afternoon.

"Have they found my mother?"

Again, silence. Then Ahmed spoke.

"They've given us permission to leave the clinic for an hour, but only to go home. Mr. Hunt came a little while ago to pick up Laura."

"Have they found my mother?"

"Mike, there's been a coup d'état during the night. The monarchy's fallen; armed troops have taken over the city."

I looked at him. Ahmed had never lied to me. He would have considered it a betrayal.

"Have they found my mother?"

"I don't know, Mike. Your granddad called. They've been stuck on La Moneta all last night and this morning. They only managed to get back to Sidi El Masri a little while ago."

I signed my hospital discharge. A young soldier said he would escort us home, since the curfew was still in place. We drove through the deserted city in the MANK van, followed by the escort jeep. There were more soldiers than passers-by, and more military jeeps than cars. Not one of us said a single word.

The young soldiers looked at us with hostility. Outside the royal palace with its two golden domes, various military vehicles were parked, as well as two armored cars. But no one fired a shot. We passed quickly through the chic residential district of Garden City. Not a soul was in the street.

Then we set out through the eucalyptus trees toward Sidi El Masri. Nico's Esso gas station was now a parking lot for military vehicles.

When we drew up to the gates of the villas, I took my crutches and got out of the van. The military jeep stopped behind us. There were no vehicles in front of Laura's house; the blinds were all down. The Hunts must have gone to Wheelus Field to wait for the situation to become clear.

I wanted to look my father in the face.

"You go on home, guys. We'll be in touch later."

As I was hobbling off on my crutches, Ahmed got out and caught up with me.

"I'll take Karim home and then come back, Mike. I'll sleep outside this gate. I'll be here if anything happens."

We looked at each other for a moment. "You can sleep in the house—you have before."

He shook his head. "It won't ever happen again. I'll be out here. Now, off you go."

. . . .

The Italian foreign minister, the Hon. Aldo Moro, was given a short note from his secretary. He was happy to read the translation of the speech by the unknown young man who was heading the new Libya and was even more interested to read the note from SID, the Italian intelligence agency, *Servizio Informazione Difesa*.

*He is Muammar Al Gaddafi. A steady hand, not anti-Italian nor a fanatical Muslim.*

Moro let out a huge sigh of relief and shot a brief glance of gratitude at the crucifix on his desk. Italy was a peaceful nation undergoing development. The last thing it wanted was to be faced by an enemy across the sea from Sicily.

Later, he took a call from his English counterpart, who asked him if he would receive the British ambassador in Rome. He met him in his office at sunset.

"Omar Al Shelhi came to see us at the Foreign Office. He's saying that these junior officers led by Gaddafi are friends of Nasser and the Soviet Union. He's asking us and the Americans to use our Libyan and Sicilian bases to get them out and bring King Idris back."

In silence, Moro handed him the SID note.

"Are you sure, signor Foreign Minister?" the British ambassador asked in Italian.

It was not a very diplomatic question; but it was driven by British worries. Nevertheless, it gave rise to a small moment of concern in the Italian foreign minister. There were men he trusted more in SID, and those he trusted less. However, he reflected, no one could have any special interest in backing a young unknown Libyan. He decided that he could trust his information.

Moro gave the ambassador his habitual good-natured smile.

"Our SID is not at the same level as your MI6, but it works quite well."

"I'm glad to hear it," said the ambassador, taking his leave. "After the Suez debacle, it's better that we British keep a low profile in North Africa. And also the Americans would rather keep out of this. Well, let's have faith in this Gaddafi, then. For a while, at least."

. . . .

Alberto came up to me. His eyes were red and sunken, underscored by dark rings of grief.

"Where's Dad?" I asked him, coming to a breathless stop on my crutches.

"He's in his study with Granddad and the others."

"I'm going in to see him. I want to know what's happened to Mom."

Alberto tried to stop me.

"Mike, leave him alone right now—he's in pieces. He really is."

I made no reply but limped on to the study. Resigned, Alberto opened the door for me.

My father was at his desk. Sitting opposite him in the armchairs were Granddad, Emilio Busi, and Don Eugenio. They all looked terrible. But Granddad was the worst; he was deathly pale.

I studied my father. I think this must have been the first time since I was born that he had not shaved; the knot in his tie was twisted and one of his cuffs was lightly stained. All things you might see in another person, but unimaginable in my father. He did not wait for my question. His voice was sorrowful but calm, like an announcer on Italian state television when they broadcast a funeral.

"The Libyan coast guard found your mother's body out at sea this afternoon."

"What kind of bullshit is this, Dad?"

He went on as if I had said nothing.

"The police couldn't look for her before. General Jalloun and his men were confined to their barracks during the curfew."

"So?"

"Italia's body was taken out to sea by the current and the tide after sunset. She fell from the cliff near the old olive tree in the afternoon, when the water was at its lowest. There were traces of her on the rocks."

Those were his exact words. "Traces of her."

"And who pushed her off?"

I could see my grandfather shoot me a look of alarm. Busi and Don Eugenio looked out the window at the garden. I could hear Alberto draw his breath heavily behind me. Only my father remained unmoved.

"No one pushed her off, Michele. Your mother, sadly, decided she no longer wanted to live and threw herself off."

*If someone takes their own life, then people think they're either mad or guilty.*

"Do you think Mamma was mad, Dad? Or that she had something unpalatable to hide?"

My father was highly intelligent but lacking in intuition. He never would have guessed those were words his wife had uttered only a few hours before she died.

*And were they the words of a woman who was about to kill herself?*

"I don't know what you're talking about, Mike. Your mother committed suicide. Unfortunately, that's what it was."

"And why would she have done it?"

"We'll talk about that another time, Mike. Now, go and rest; you have a broken ankle."

*Because of you and that whore Marlene Hunt.*

My grandfather and Alberto made a move, intuiting what I was about to do. In order to lash out, I would have to put my weight on my left crutch and try to hit my father with the other. Alberto was quicker and threw himself at me. The crutch caught him on his head and immediately drew blood.

My brother did not cry out but held on to me tightly so I could do no more harm to myself or anyone else. The tears coursing down his face, mingling with the blood, took away my last reserves. As I crashed to the ground, I saw that last half-gesture from my mother.

*Yes, she wasn't saying hello, but good-bye.*

# FRIDAY, SEPTEMBER 5, 1969

I remained standing at the back of the cathedral, leaning on my crutches throughout the funeral service, despite the pleas from Granddad and Alberto. I had no intention of shedding tears in front of my father.

Laura came on her own from Wheelus Field, without her parents, in a jeep driven by an American soldier. She held my hand in silence at the back of the cathedral. We exchanged no words.

*It's enough that you're here.*

At the end of the service, the coffin was carried away on the shoulders of Dad, Granddad, Alberto, and the Italian ambassador. I waited until they placed her on the bier and moved away. Then I went hobbling up, supported by Laura.

*I'll make them pay for this, Mamma, sooner or later.*

Laura read my thoughts.

"She only wants you to be happy, Mike. You must get rid of certain thoughts."

*There are too many, Laura. And some of them I can never get rid of. The three dead in a Cairo alleyway. Your mother writhing underneath me.*

After the funeral, General Jalloun handed my grandfather a letter of heartfelt condolences. My father wished to read it out to all of us that evening.

The Libyan coast guard continuously patrolled the stretch of coast facing La Moneta, where the smugglers slipped in and out, and they confirmed that no boat had been near the island on the afternoon of Sunday, August 31, when Italia had died.

Therefore, Jalloun concluded, this was the case of an accident: a chance fall caused by an attack of vertigo or fainting. The general avoided using the word "suicide" out of regard for his old friend Giuseppe Bruseghin.

I knew it was true that the coast guard continuously patrolled that area because of its many hidden coves, which were indeed suitable for landing smuggled goods. I had seen the patrol boats myself that afternoon when I had gone to the Underwater Club with Salim. And also when I came back after the fiery encounter with Marlene Hunt.

There was only one possible berth on La Moneta, directly in front of the villa. Of course, a rubber dinghy could have anchored around by the rocks on the other side and someone could have reached the island by swimming, then climbed the rocks where they were only three or four yards high, run along the path, pushed my mother over the cliff, retraced their steps and swum back to the dinghy at anchor.

But it would have been risky and taken a lot of effort. An operation like that would have taken several hours. Three, at least. The coast guard would certainly have noticed a dinghy anchored for that length of time.

Someone like Marlene Hunt could have done it. She had the strength, the boldness, the cruelty, and the motive. And, inside me, I would have been delighted to see her hang. But no one knew better than me that it was impossible. I was her alibi for that particular afternoon. She would have had no time, nor any way, to return to the island and kill my mother. But she was still guilty. She and my father.

If there was a killer, though, I wanted the real one, not the moral one. Given that Marlene could not have killed her, I examined the other possibilities.

William Hunt had the physique, boldness, and intelligence to do it. But he was nowhere near; he was in Benghazi and then at Wheelus Field. And he had no motive.

Then there was Farid and Salim. But one of them had left with Marlene and the other with me. Afterward, they had gone with my grandfather to Sidi El Masri and only later had they gone back to pick up Mohammed. I would check with Granddad.

There were the MANK guys, my brother, and Laura Hunt. But that was absurd; I didn't even want to think about it.

That left the grown-ups who had stayed on the island that afternoon: Busi, Don Eugenio, Mohammed, and my father. They were capable of anything and had a very good motive. Love and business for my father; business for the others.

*It had to have been one of these four who crossed the island and threw her off.*

# SATURDAY, SEPTEMBER 6, 1969

The day after the funeral my father left for Rome. He left me a letter, which Mohammed brought to me. It was very short. It said that he understood my shock and was willing to excuse my behavior; that he would always continue to provide for my education and for me, if I wanted to start college in Rome. And that, for business reasons, he would have to undertake many journeys abroad.

He had put the two Sidi El Masri villas up for sale, not being able to live where he had been happy with my mother. The Hunts would be moving to Tripoli, to live in a beachfront town house owned by the American Embassy. For Granddad and me, he had rented a two-story apartment in Garden City. He was leaving me free to choose between staying in Tripoli or going to college in Rome.

*Perhaps my mother's death had at least gotten him to accept that I could make my own decisions. Or else he had simply decided that my choices weren't worth making a fuss about.*

Laura phoned me that evening. Now that we no longer lived next to each other, now that my mother was dead, now that I had slept with her mother, what was left for us?

Her voice betrayed regret.

"We're leaving tomorrow, Mike. Dad has to go to Washington on business, and he doesn't want to leave Mom and me alone here with this new regime hostile to Westerners."

"How long will you be away?"

There was a brief silence.

"I don't know, Mike. I'll call you."

Another silence. Neither of us knew what to say. We said good-bye without making any promises.

I was sad but relieved. I had more time.

*For what, Mike? More time for what?*

# MONDAY, SEPTEMBER 15, 1969

The traffic in and around Tripoli had returned to normal, foreigners had come back, and half the world had officially recognized the new regime and sent ambassadors to meet the young Gaddafi. The only difference was in the streets themselves. The Italian names had disappeared. Corso Vittorio Emanuele was now Shara Istiklal; Piazza Italia now Maydan as Syuhada; and so on.

The radio had announced the creation of an official organ of governance, the Revolutionary Command Council, composed entirely of the military and presided over by Colonel Gaddafi. There was only one external member of the Council to represent the civilian population, and he was excluded from meetings. He supported Gaddafi in secret, alone. His name was never disclosed.

. . . .

In Rome, a cold drizzle served as the city's farewell to summer and the beginning of autumn. The arcade and huge Bar Berardo opposite Parliament and Piazza Colonna were filled with crowds. The Roman population was out with umbrellas and raincoats, filling Via del Corso, the pavements, and the shops. A great many went into La Rinascente department store.

Salvatore Balistreri, with Don Eugenio and Emilio Busi, entered Parliament through an entrance reserved only for the Senate, and then they were accompanied by an usher to the president's office.

The room was very large and plain, but warm. A secretary offered them coffee.

The president entered by a small side door several minutes later. Salvatore Balistreri had seen him only in the newspapers and on the television. He was a colorless, reserved man of few words. And yet this man counted for a lot more than the prime minister.

Balistreri stepped forward and introduced himself. He had chosen his clothes for the day with great care.

*Don Eugenio and Busi had advised him to dress subdued; no showiness.*

Of course, that was easy to say for a priest in a threadbare cassock and a Communist who made a thing of being poorly dressed. But he was different, he was a man destined to become a highly successful entrepreneur, and a powerful one at that.

He had avoided designer clothes and limited himself to a dark-gray but tailor-cut suit, a white shirt, and a midnight-blue tie. He had placed a black button of mourning in his lapel.

The president took hold of his hands.

"My sincere condolences, signor Balistreri. I know your wife was an exceptional woman."

It seemed to Balistreri there was a warning in those words.

"Thank you, Mr. President," he replied prudently.

"Do you believe in God, signor Balistreri?"

"Of course, Mr. President."

The president let go of his hands.

"Good, then we can understand each other more easily . . ."

He turned to Busi.

"It seems that everything in the Lower Chamber is going well."

Busi nodded.

"Yes, very well. In today's session Moro said that Italy had to cooperate with Gaddafi's government. The intelligence he's received is totally reassuring."

"And the Egyptians?" the president asked Balistreri.

Balistreri was feeling a little emotional and extremely proud. This all-powerful man was his ideal, the quintessence of all his thinking since he had been a boy.

"Everything's fine. The pro-Egyptian members on the Revolutionary Council are in the majority over the pro-Palestinian. Our man's in constant communication with them, and Gaddafi has their full support."

The president took a sip of water.

"Nasser will want a great many things from Gaddafi in exchange for this. Do you have any thoughts on the matter, signor Balistreri?"

Balistreri remembered very well what Mohammed had told him after a meeting with Nasser's emissaries.

*Egyptians need houses and jobs. Right away. Not fuel for another war.*

"It's possible," he said slowly, "that certain exchanges will be necessary."

The president looked directly at him and, from the look, Balistreri understood why this colorless man could be so respected and feared. He suddenly felt naked in front of him.

"Exchanges that could be most harmful for the Italians still living in Libya?" the president went on.

"Only a matter of twenty thousand ex-Fascist Italian colonists," Busi broke in, "who also happen to be blocking the interests of fifty million Italian anti-Fascists."

The president did not even deign to glance in his direction. He knew very well that the fifty million Italian anti-Fascists were for the most part the very same people who had conveniently dumped Mussolini as soon as the war started to go badly. And, as a man who truly believed in the Lord, he had absolutely no liking for harming people. Atheists had no understanding of this kind of problem.

"I hope there are better alternative solutions," the president said to Busi coldly. "We Catholics don't like to cause anyone any harm, isn't that right, signor Balistreri?"

The Ingegnere hesitated. The president was also notoriously very slippery.

*Is he really concerned about the twenty thousand Italians in Libya? Or is he testing me?*

Busi was not satisfied with all this hesitation. For him, it was the usual song and dance of Catholics who wanted a convenient solution to be found without compromising their consciences.

"Mr. President, we're not talking about personal advantage here but the interest of the entire country."

Even Don Eugenio felt moved to come to Salvatore's aid.

"Mr. President, Italy has no other choice than Libya's gas and oil, and all the gas we do import from Libya is drilled by the Americans."

The president gave a small, disdainful smile.

"Are your friends very worried, Busi?"

But Emilio Busi was not to be intimidated.

"Many of them are your friends as well, Mr. President. And all of them the captains of industry who devotedly support your party in the elections."

"No, signor Busi, they support my party out of fear of you Communists. If, one day, the Communist Party grows any stronger, they will all find themselves on the Left. Anyway, you can reassure them all. We're not going to send in gunboats to bombard Gaddafi."

Busi wanted to be sure that he had played all his cards right.

"Mr. President, these contracts will also help management of the—"

The president stopped him with a gesture. He knew very well that a part of the gas money would become slush funds to finance the political parties and to oil the wheels of politics. But for an extremist like Busi to remind him of this was nothing but insolent. It was also rash and pointless to say it in front of Salvatore Balistreri.

The president looked out of the window. He had never forgotten the first rounds of the elections in an Italy devastated by the war. People without homes, food, or work.

Now, from that window, he could see the Roman populace entering in droves a shop like La Rinascente—the lights sparkling in its huge windows—or lining up in their Fiats along Via del Corso, or crowding into the bars along its sidewalks. This was progress, the economic boom to which the Christian Democrats had led the country thanks to American money, and it had to be sustained. Without getting the Americans too angry.

The president turned to Salvatore Balistreri. He knew he was the connecting man.

"What about the Americans?"

Salvatore Balistreri chose his words carefully.

"They knew the Monarchy couldn't last any longer and that this man is better than other alternatives, which would have been led by British or French interest."

"You have worked a great deal on this project. But you are also one of those twenty thousand and have just lost your wife. You also believe in God. So you decide—you have more right to. I'll trust in your judgment."

He got up and left the room without any gesture of good-bye.

# TUESDAY, SEPTEMBER 16, 1969

With my foot encased in plaster, I couldn't use the bicycle, the car, or my Triumph.

Forced into immobility, I stayed at home inside the new Garden City apartment. A living room and three other rooms: one for Granddad, one for me, and a storage room. For Dad or Alberto, when they came to Tripoli, there was the luxurious Waddan Hotel.

On the wall of my new room was Laura's photograph—with the bewitching look she had wearing that evening dress coming down the Spanish Steps in Piazza di Spagna.

*The person I'll never be.*

The Al Bakris had also moved when my father sold the two villas. They had a normal apartment, the same kind Italians had, rented by my father, near the office in Piazza Italia. It had running water, sanitation, electricity, a room each for the four boys, and a large room for Mohammed and his two wives.

I spent the mornings playing cards with Granddad. He had lost about twenty pounds and wasn't happy in the new place. We never spoke of my mother. In the afternoons, he would get into the old

Fiat 600 and go back to the olive grove in Sidi El Masri, which he had never wanted to sell.

Ahmed, Karim, and Nico came to my room every afternoon to keep me company.

Nico was terrified of Gaddafi and the new regime. He was afraid they would take his money and his life. Even his Guzzi motorcycle and the MANK van.

Karim, on the other hand, was all for the new regime. He thought Gaddafi and his junior officers were honest, serious men. They would help Nasser destroy Israel.

As usual, Ahmed was the most pragmatic. There was our MANK organization, our business in Cairo. We decided to tackle the question at the end of September, when my cast came off.

I was only interested in one thing, though: my mother's death.

Ahmed remained my eye on the outside world. The first day he came to see me by himself, I took advantage of this to question him closely.

"Tell me about that afternoon on La Moneta. Everything you saw and heard."

He nodded. The lines in his cheeks had become deeper; at nearly twenty, his beard was darker, his eyes even more serious. We had both lost the people we loved most. Nadia and Italia. His faith in me prevented him from asking me the crucial question.

*And where were you, Mike, on the afternoon your mother died?*

"After you went off with Farid, Salim, and Signora Hunt, we boys stayed on the beach, and Laura was reading on the veranda. The grown-ups went into the living room. From the beach we could see them through the window. Then I think they all went off to their own rooms, because at half past two there was no longer anyone in the living room."

"And the four of you?"

"We stayed on the beach. At least another hour, perhaps more. But it was too hot and, before four o'clock, we split up."

"And what did you do?"

"Nico went off for a nap and Alberto had to study. I think Karim joined Laura. I swam for a long time. I was nervous and only felt good in the water. I put on flippers and a mask and explored the rocks around the island."

"Did you get as far as the cliff?"

"No, I stopped well before that. I was going slowly, trying to relax."

"Did you see any boats at all?"

"No, Mike, nothing."

"And then?"

"I went back to the beach at about a quarter past five. After a few minutes, Farid and Salim arrived with the motorboat to take my father to the Underwater Club."

"Yes, this adds up. I met them there half an hour later, toward a quarter to six. They were taking him to the airport and they left me the motorboat to go back to La Moneta. And then?"

"At some point we all found ourselves on the beach again. I can't remember in what order. The grown-ups came out one at a time, and then Laura as well. We were all there before six."

I looked at him.

"And then I came back."

"Yes." He didn't ask me where I had been, or with whom. Perhaps he had an idea.

We exchanged looks. He was truthful; I wasn't. What should I have said?

*It couldn't have been Marlene, Ahmed. I know very well why that was impossible.*

# MONDAY, SEPTEMBER 29, 1969

Granddad took me to the clinic in the Fiat 600. Tripoli was calm and bathed in sunshine. There were fewer policemen and more soldiers, but the shops were open, carriages on the go, and the shoeshine boys were again polishing Italian men's moccasins under the arcades.

At Villa Igea they took off my cast, but I still needed the crutches.

"What do you want to do, Mike, now that you can walk?" Granddad asked me. I wanted to take my Triumph for a spin around Tripoli: Corso Vittorio, Piazza Italia, Via Lazio, and on out to the Underwater Club. But I was still hobbling. And all those names had disappeared, since the street signs were now all in Arabic.

Granddad was pale and thin as a rake. In the last few months, his shoulders had stooped, and his calm and kindly eyes were now tired and red.

"Let's go out to the Sidi El Masri olive grove, like we did when you took me there as a boy."

We went in the Fiat 600. Granddad drove slowly toward Shara Ben Ashur and Sidi El Masri, while the scents of eucalyptus and olives gradually took over from the smell of the sea. He parked in front of the two villas that were no longer ours. There were different cars, different people: the new proprietors Dad had sold them to.

We took the path that Nadia used in the mornings to come to our villa. We walked slowly, in silence. I was limping on my crutches; he was tired.

We came to the old Al Bakri shack. Sheets of metal, cardboard, and straw. An outside toilet built of old boards knocked together. A trickle of water that served as a sewer. The swing made out of a tire. And that terrible stench in the heat haze.

All through my childhood and adolescence, I had no idea of the abyss that separated my life from Ahmed and Karim's. But could I—the kid who so despised his father's money—have survived a week under those conditions?

The cesspit smelled worse than ever, as it always did in the summer months. The hungry flies buzzed around it. It was here that the young woman and her baby had been found. Both black, as I had confided to Nadia in great secrecy.

We walked in silence past the goatherds' corrugated huts, including the one where Nadia's presumed killer, Jamaal, had lived, and on to the olive-pressing shed. It was here that the dog had barked, here that I had sensed death on the other side of the dirty windows, here that I had picked up a handkerchief stained with innocent blood, and here that I had seen the lock that Jamaal would never have been able to buy, or even use.

Only eight weeks had passed since that day at the beginning of August. And everything had changed. Nadia had been murdered, my mother was dead, I had been to bed with Marlene Hunt, and Gaddafi had taken control of Libya.

After an hour's walking, Granddad was out of breath.

"Let's sit down for a moment, Michele. There, under that large olive tree."

We rested against the wrinkled trunk, our shoulders touching, and I realized how thin he had become. I could feel his shoulder bones against my muscles and could count the ribs showing through his white shirt.

"You've lost a lot of weight, Granddad."

He smiled. "I wouldn't know. I've never weighed myself."

Then he glanced around and took a deep breath.

"You know, Michele, olive trees are like women. They give birth to fruit in October and, at this time of the year, I always feel like a father-to-be."

"They're beautiful, Granddad. When I used to come here hunting with the shotgun, I always fired the first shot into the air—to roust the dove—and then would catch it with the second barrel. It's fairer and doesn't damage the olives."

He brushed a bony hand through my hair. It had the same light calmness as Italia's hand.

He let out a long sigh.

"Last week, I signed a power of attorney for your father and sent it to him in Rome so he can sell the grove, all of it."

I looked at him, dumbstruck.

"It was necessary, Michele. Your father's right. He's got big business plans in mind and needs a lot of money to accomplish them. With the sale of the grove he's got the collateral; the main sum will come as a loan from his friends in Palermo and New York and from the Banco di Sicilia."

"But, Granddad, he's already had you sell the villas. These olives are your life's work."

"They're not much use to me now, Michele. Your father knows what he's doing. Besides, this way, we can ensure a future for you and Alberto."

I wanted to tell him that Alberto had a future anyway and that I had none at all. But that would only have hurt him. It was, however, the right moment to clarify another point.

"Granddad, when I left you at the Underwater Club with Farid and Salim that terrible afternoon, were they with you the whole time after that?"

He looked at me and shook his head. I didn't want to upset him, but I had to know for sure.

"Yes, Mike. We left the Club in their pickup and came to the warehouses here to deposit the dismantled gazebos. I let them leave at four thirty. They had to collect Mohammed from La Moneta."

This excluded Farid and Salim from any suspicion. Fifteen minutes to get from the grove to the Underwater Club, thirty minutes by sea to La Moneta, where Ahmed saw them at five fifteen, another half an hour from La Moneta to the Underwater Club, where I met them with Mohammed at a quarter to six. It all checked out.

Granddad was looking at me.

"There's something else, Michele. It's about your relationship with your father. And with yourself."

I felt intuitively that he had placed a condition on my father, one that was nonnegotiable, in exchange for his signature for the sale of the olive grove. And now he was going to place the same condition on me.

"I'm not going to say I'm sorry. And I'll never forgive him for—"

"There's no reason for you to say you're sorry to him. But he wasn't the cause of your mother's death. Get that out of your head, Michele."

"Granddad, he and that woman—"

For a moment, his voice went back to the firm one of the soldier Giuseppe Bruseghin.

"That terrible afternoon, after Farid and Salim left at four thirty, I came back to the villa."

I shut my eyes. "Granddad . . ."

"Your jeep and Marlene's Ferrari were in the driveway, but there was no one at home in our house. A couple of hours later I saw you leave the Hunts' villa in a terrible state and get back into the jeep again . . ."

"Granddad . . ."

He placed a gnarled hand on mine.

"A father has the right to look after his son and the right to make mistakes in doing it. A son has the right to protect himself and a duty to understand his father, sooner or later."

He made an enormous effort to complete the sentence then his voice broke off. His eyes stared first at me, then at the trunk of the olive tree. It was the first tree he had planted. He then fell silent, his head on my shoulder. I thought he had dozed off. But he was dead.

# WEDNESDAY, OCTOBER 1, 1969

I t was the third funeral in two months: Nadia, Italia, then my grandfather.

Tripoli Cathedral was crammed with tearful Italians. After the service, when Dad, Alberto, and I carried Granddad's coffin on our shoulders, along with the Italian ambassador, out onto the cathedral steps into the grounds, we could see a vast crowd stretching as far as Corso Vittorio, or Shara Istiklal—or whatever the hell Gaddafi wanted to call it.

There were huge numbers of Libyans as well. They clapped and wept more than the Italians for the good and honest man who had helped them build their country.

I was still hobbling too much. Mohammed came up to carry the coffin in my place down the steps.

Then there were the heartfelt condolences, so many of them, everyone having some tale or other to tell about Granddad. I was watching my father as I listened, his handsome suntanned Clark Gable face lost in grief. He was good at acting the part of the bereaved son-in-law.

*Perhaps he really is overcome, Mike. You promised Granddad. This hate will destroy both of you.*

William Hunt came up among the last, with his forceful handshake and square jaw. He gave his condolences to Alberto, then to me. He handed me an envelope from Laura.

"When is she coming back?" I asked, not daring to look him in the eye.

*I screwed your wife the afternoon my mother died.*

He looked at me without expression on his face, like a judge handing out a death sentence to the guilty party.

"Marlene and Laura are in San Francisco. They'll be back at the end of October. But Laura's off to school in Cairo to study photography and communication. There are no suitable colleges here in Tripoli."

*And you're not suitable for her, Mike Balistreri. So stay away.*

Then he went over to my father. William shook his hand, offered his condolences, and whispered a single sentence to him.

"Salvo, we must talk tomorrow, you know."

Among the things that were still functioning in me were my ears. And my imagination.

*We must talk about you and my wife.*

*Dad nodded silently.*

. . . .

That evening, in my room in Garden City, I placed Laura's envelope on the table and opened it. It was a cassette of *Songs from a Room*, the latest album from Leonard Cohen, which was still not available in Tripoli. I had heard one of the songs, "Bird on a Wire," on the radio. And Laura knew how much I liked it.

There was no card. I put the cassette in the deck and sat on the bed looking at the photo on the wall. A gorgeous girl was looking at me as she came down the Spanish Steps in Piazza di Spagna. Cohen's voice was whispering the magical words about trying in his own way to be free.

I was the little bird holding on to the wire, the drunk in the midnight choir. And who was the girl in the photo? Was it Laura or Marlene? Was she in the light or in the dark?

If freedom is being able to choose between light and darkness, then I was a prisoner in a dark cell.

# MONDAY, OCTOBER 6, 1969

The MANK organization was ready to leave for Cairo, but the Muslim period of mourning for Nadia and the Catholic one for my mother and grandfather demanded respect for certain formalities and a little more time. In the end, all four of us went for a few days, spoke with our associates, and left Nico temporarily as our ambassador.

He was more than happy, seeing that the city was much more alive than Tripoli and that, two years after the war, they had reopened all the cinemas and bordellos.

On the day that Ahmed, Karim, and I came back from Cairo, I happened to meet old Mansur. I was having my first ride on the Triumph after my cast had been removed and I was parked in Piazza Italia, which Gaddafi wanted to rename Green Square. Mansur saw me and came up. First of all, he remembered to offer his condolences.

"I'm terribly sorry, Signor Michele, both for your wonderful grandfather and your beautiful mother."

"Thanks, Mansur. I didn't know you knew my mother—she never came to the market."

Mansur smiled.

"I knew her since she was a little girl. But it's true, she never came to the market. It was a great surprise to see her in front of my fish stall at seven one morning."

I was dumbfounded. Mansur was old. He was probably mistaken.

"Are you sure, Mansur? When was this?"

He didn't have to think for long. "Quite sure. She came to see me a couple of weeks after you did."

"A few days before she died, then? And what did she want?"

He hesitated a moment, as if he were worried about breaching a confidence.

"Well, the same thing you wanted to know, Signor Michele. What happened that morning two months ago when Nadia disappeared."

So Italia hadn't forgotten that page of notes I gave her.

"What did my mother ask, Mansur?"

"She wanted to know about people's movements here on the market. Not just Farid and Salim, about everyone, more or less. I told her Farid and Salim had caught that huge amberjack, had come here early, had divided the fish with me, and opened the stall to sell it."

"Just as you said to me. Anything else?"

"Then your grandfather and Alberto came by, and Nico later. Then Nico and Alberto went off and you came, Signor Michele, to collect the bait from Farid. I'm not sure I can remember everything . . ."

"And Farid and Salim never moved from here, that's what you said."

The old man scratched his head.

"When we opened, there was a great crowd of people. Their stall was open all the time, as I told your mother. I can't be exactly sure that they were *both* here all the time. But, after you came, Signor Michele, I'm sure they didn't move, because the camel parade had begun, there were only a few people and Farid and Salim were definitely here."

There was something in his account that I found unconvincing. Perhaps it was the same thing that had excited my mother's curiosity—and it wasn't people's comings and goings. It was the fish, that enormous greater amberjack.

# SATURDAY, OCTOBER 11, 1969

I spoke to Ahmed immediately. That amberjack caught the night before Nadia's disappearance was just too large. It could only have been caught a long way off the coast, and not with Farid and Salim's equipment.

Then there was the new fishing boat, the motorboats, the rubber dinghy, the employees, and the market stall. And too much cash around. Where did it come from?

Ahmed thought about it and came to a conclusion that he divulged to the rest of the MANK organization on the first weekend Nico was back from Cairo.

"Cigarette smuggling. An exchange on the borders of the territorial waters with a Maltese or Sicilian fishing boat. Farid and Salim load up with cigarettes and the giant amberjack is in payment and as an alibi in case the Libyan coast guard stops them and asks what they were doing that far out."

We stared at him in admiration. I was proud of having a friend who could think like this.

"You're right. With the two motorboats and the excuse of taking fish to Malta, it's easy for them to leave Libyan waters."

"You can make a pile of money from smuggling, Mike," said Nico excitably.

I, however, was not totally convinced.

"By smuggling cigarettes?"

Ahmed had already done a few calculations.

"If we got into it, we'd make triple what those two idiots do. And we could link the business up with what we already have in Cairo."

I was skeptical. And had no wish to go into illegal trafficking again.

"That may be, guys. But that's their business, and their money."

Ahmed looked directly at me. I had seen that look two years earlier, in a Cairo alleyway.

"And we can take over that business, Mike, and the money, everything. Or do you want to go to college in Rome and become an employee of the Banco di Sicilia?"

He made the comment lightly, but it was the first time he had ever allowed himself the liberty.

*A collateral effect of Colonel Gaddafi.*

"We'd be rich, Mike," Nico added.

And yet they knew I didn't care about money. I had never suffered hunger, never had to live under corrugated iron and cardboard with no running water, electricity, or drainage, never smelled of gasoline.

"I don't know what to do with money."

But Karim knew my real Achilles' heel.

"Do you want to keep Laura with your father's money, Mike?"

I should have ignored the challenge and understood that something was changing between us. But they were my only friends and we had our blood brotherhood. And I still wanted to prove something to my father.

I shrugged my shoulders. "Okay, guys, let's make some money."

It was Ahmed's plan, therefore meticulously thought out. That same evening, he would go to the port to take down the mileages of Farid and Salim's motorboats. At that time of day they would be drinking chai and smoking *shisha* in one of the big open-air bars below the ancient castle near the souk. To be safe, Karim, Nico, and I would keep an eye on them, so that Ahmed wouldn't run the risk of them catching him.

Then, the following morning, he would do the same while Farid and Salim were at the fish market. From the mileage, we could figure out what route they had taken and it would give us an idea what they were up to.

If Ahmed's hypothesis was correct, we would follow them in my father's motorboat, which I was still allowed to use.

"And then?" Nico asked. "We follow them, and what'll we do if it's all true?"

"Then," Ahmed replied, "we'll confront them. When we have the proof, they'll have to come to an agreement with us."

"They'll carve us into little pieces," Karim said.

I calmed him down.

"We can defend ourselves. Besides, I'm the son of Ingegnere Balistreri, aren't I?"

Nico and Karim nodded, not at all convinced. Sure, I was the son of an Italian. And the most important Italian in Tripoli. But, with Gaddaffi now on the scene, things were changing. And Farid and Salim had ten brawny fishermen at hand.

*But I have my rifle and Ahmed his knife.*

To be safe, I dug out my old Diana 50 and a box of pellets I had kept. In the afternoon, I went to the Underwater Club and hid it in the motorboat's locker. It came in handy every now and again.

• • • •

The colorful market of Souk Al Mushir had been crowded all day. When evening fell, the Italians went home or to the places that sold alcohol, like the Gazzella and Waddan hotels. The Libyans divided into two groups: women and children went home; the men to smoke *shisha* in the bars around the castle square.

Farid and Salim were drinking chai. Farid was smoking his usual cigarettes, Salim the *shisha*. Karim, Nico, and I were hiding behind a car, crouching well down so as not to be seen. Ahmed was already at the port to note the mileage of the motorboats before they went out for the night.

A bicycle stopped in front of Farid and Salim's table. It was one of their fishermen, who got off and said something to them in an agitated manner. The two jumped up immediately, got on their bicycles, and headed off along the coastal road in the direction of the port.

We looked at each other. "They've seen him," Karim said, already getting on his bicycle.

"Stay here, Karim. Nico and I will go to the Underwater Club and take Dad's motorboat, so we can follow them."

But Karim made no reply. He was already pedaling off to the port.

"Damn, Nico. Can you follow him and try to look after him? I'll get the motorboat."

. . . .

On the Triumph, I got to the Club in less than ten minutes. There was a dance in progress on the terrace with a vocalist singing "Strangers in the Night" for an audience of wealthy Americans, Italians, and Libyans.

I kept clear of the terrace, taking the path down to the beach and the jetty. A few minutes later, I was off in the motorboat toward the port with my lights off.

I had my night-vision binoculars with me. The sea was dark and flat. There were no fishing-boat lights on the open sea, so, evidently, they were still in port or at anchor. The October evening air was hot and sticky.

I came in sight of the port just as Farid and Salim's boat was coming out. I slowed down immediately and let the motor run gently. Karim and Ahmed could not be seen on the quayside, only Nico, but I had no time to go into the port and bring him onboard.

I followed the boat at a distance. I had to be sure that they neither saw nor heard me. After a short time, it was clear where they were heading: La Moneta. During the night trip the only lights visible were those of the boat in front of me and the coast guard patrol boats.

They moored on the jetty in front of the villa. I put the engine in neutral, a hundred yards away. By the dim light of the lamps on the little quay, I saw them get down onto the beach.

Salim had a knife in his hand and was pushing Karim, who had his hands tied behind his back. Then came Ahmed, also with his hands tied. They bound them each to a lamppost with ropes they had onboard.

There was no time to lose. Still trying not to make myself heard, I used the oars to bring the motorboat to seventy yards from the beach. I took my old Diana 50 from the locker in the bows, a lead pellet already loaded. The others were in the box, and I put a handful in my pocket.

I stationed myself in the bows with the binoculars and the rifle. Laughing, Farid was holding Karim's head still, while Salim held the point of the knife to his throat. A lit cigarette was dangling from Farid's thick lips while Salim's thin ones were stretched out into a sadistic line.

This was the vendetta they felt justified in pursuing against their younger brothers. Ahmed and Karim were better-looking, more studious, more intelligent than them. Karim had dared to throw Salim in the cesspit. Now, Ahmed was spying on their business.

There could be no surprise; there was no time.

"Let them go, right now!" I shouted.

There was a moment's silence on the beach, then Farid gave an oily laugh.

"Oh, well, well, Signorino Michele, as well, eh? Instead of hiding in the dark in the middle of the sea, why don't you come out and enjoy the show right here?"

I saw Salim's grin through the binoculars. His thin face was a cruel mask. In the end, it was I, as the Italian boss's son, who had protected their brothers.

"Because he doesn't have the balls, that's why!" Salim shouted.

I saw the sharp knife cut off the end of Karim's right ear, while his cries could be heard above the coarse guffaws of his two torturers.

Then Salim turned triumphantly toward me, holding his bloody trophy between two fingers.

"And now," Salim screamed, "I'm going to cut off something more important from that nosy best friend of yours."

Salim stepped forward, and I took aim, not giving him time to get anywhere near Ahmed. The Diana 50's pellet went cleanly through the hand that was holding the knife and he began to screech like an eagle.

After a moment's indecision, Farid ran toward Ahmed, while at the same time I reloaded and slipped the fisherman's knife in my belt. I put the engine in gear and set off for the jetty.

"If you shoot again, Mike, I'll cut his throat."

Farid's voice was less confident than Salim's as he pointed the knife at Ahmed. Karim and Salim, meanwhile, were groaning from their wounds.

The motorboat touched the jetty. Without bothering to moor it, I put the engine in neutral and jumped down, pointing the rifle at Farid.

"If you touch him, Farid, you won't leave here alive."

Uncertain what to do, Farid lowered the knife. Ahmed's tae caught him in the testicles, making him bend at the knees and the knife fall to the ground.

Although hurt, Salim grabbed his own knife and tried to throw himself on Ahmed, who was still tied up. This time, the Diana 50 pellet pierced his cheek and tongue, coming out on the other side.

I felt neither fear nor remorse. In a certain sense, I knew that I would have gotten to the point I was heading to sooner or later. I chucked the empty rifle down and took out the fisherman's knife with the saw-tooth blade. I freed Ahmed with it while Farid backed away toward the jetty.

Ahmed took the knife from my hands and went up to Salim, who was now lying on the ground, moaning. Farid watched him, terrified.

"Watch closely."

Our eyes locked. I knew what he was about to do.

For a moment, I thought about stopping him. Then Ahmed grabbed Salim's head by his sleek hair and pulled it back. I heard both Farid and Karim cry out as the knife sliced cleanly into Salim's carotid artery and deeper, through the whole neck. There was a terrible sound, halfway between cardboard tearing and a sink being emptied.

Ahmed let Salim fall onto the sand. But he still held the head from the hair. Then he went up to Farid, his knife dripping with blood. He put his brother's head just in front of him.

"Ahmed, for the love of Allah," Farid mumbled, terrified, dropping down on his knees.

"Do not blaspheme, my brother. Allah doesn't listen to worms."

This was going too far, even for Mike Balistreri.

"Ahmed, no. Not him."

It was an order. I had given him hundreds, since we were little boys, and he always obeyed without a word. But things were changing between us.

"If we don't kill him tonight, Mike, we'll come to regret it one day."

I was still the boss. There was no argument about that. I turned to Farid.

"We won't kill you, because you can be useful to us. Tonight, you'll take us with you to whoever supplies you with the cigarettes, and you'll reassure them about us. From today, we're taking your business. Got it?"

Farid nodded repeatedly, his mouth gaping open and his eyes staring wide. I went on.

"Tomorrow, you will tell Mohammed that you had an accident at sea and Salim drowned."

Farid signaled his assent like an automaton. He was aware that Ahmed was ready to kill him. But Ahmed wanted him to be in no doubt, and he stuck the knife at his throat. Promises like that were not sufficient for him.

"Lastly, brother, I don't want to see you in Libya ever again. Tomorrow, you pack your bags, tell Mohammed you want to try your fortune elsewhere, and leave. If I see you again, I'll cut your dick off and make you eat it. Have you got that, Farid?"

Farid was already nearly dead with fear. He nodded desperately and Ahmed dropped Salim decapitated head on the sand. We then tied up Farid and we dressed Karim's ear as best we could with alcohol and gauze from the boat. The upper quarter had been sliced cleanly off. Fortunately, it was still early enough to meet the smugglers, but we would have to get a move on.

"I'll take Karim back to Nico in the port, and he can take him to hospital. I'll be back in forty minutes. You keep guard on Farid. And keep your hands off him, all right?"

Ahmed relaxed and shed his irrational shell.

"What should we say to the hospital about his ear? And to my father?"

"We say there's been an accident."

"That's hardly believable, Mike."

"Karim and I can say we had a dare going with the knives. And that, without meaning to, I wounded him in the ear. Whether he believes it or not, Mohammed's not going to report me, is he? And Karim will back up the story."

Karim was feeling a little better. "All right, yes, I'll back up the story. Dad will have his doubts, but he'll never report Mike."

I pointed to Salim's body and head. "We still have to get rid of that."
Ahmed had morphed back into the cold and meticulous planner.

"You go off with Karim, while I clean up and put the body and
head on their boat. I'll tie two stones to his ankles and head. When you
get back, we'll dump him in the open sea then we'll go with Farid to
meet the smugglers. When we get back, we'll take the motorboat to the
rocks and send it crashing into them. Farid will escape, Salim won't."

It seemed absurd to be speaking like this. We were still not twenty
and had already killed three Egyptian soldiers and, now, Ahmed and
Karim's brother.

# SUNDAY, OCTOBER 12, 1969

Fear can work miracles. The explanation Farid gave to Mohammed about the accident and Salim's drowning was faultless. Unlike Salim, who had never wanted to learn, he knew how to swim and so had been able to save himself. The fact that Salim's body had not been found was normal; the currents in that stretch carried anything far out to sea. And, anyway, there was no reason to suspect any friction between the two brothers.

The explanation he gave him about his decision to seek his fortune in Tunisia was also indisputable. There were the tragedies to try to forget, first Nadia, now Salim, and the loss of their boat; and his ability as a fishmonger would be much more appreciated in Tunisia, where fishing was big business.

The story about Karim's ear being cut and needing stitches was more complicated. Mohammed wasn't convinced for a minute that it was an accident that had happened while we were play-acting the duel in *Cavalleria Rusticana*. Although he could believe that we were crazy enough to do it, the cut was too clean to be the result of an accidental stabbing. And he also suspected a connection with Salim's death.

In the end, I had to resort to unscrupulous means.

"So you don't believe me, Mohammed?"

I saw him turn sullen. This was open blackmail. Whatever else, I was still the son of his boss. The outcast son but the son nevertheless.

He turned to Ahmed and Karim.

"I've lost Nadia and Salim, and now Farid's leaving. You two try to stay out of trouble."

He couldn't say so explicitly, but the worst of the "trouble" was me.

# SATURDAY, NOVEMBER 15, 1969

Ahmed was right. In one month, the four of us transformed that little cottage industry of smuggling into one of industrial proportions. The MANK organization did not exist on any business register, yet its profits were real and substantial.

I was the one behind the ideas and had impunity because I was the son of Ingegnere Salvatore Balistreri.

Ahmed took care of arrangements with the Maltese traffickers and organized the fishermen we inherited from Farid and Salim. We went anywhere and everywhere in Dad's motorboat. Everyone knew who owned it—starting with the Libyan coast guard, which was still under the command of General Jalloun—and no one ever stopped us.

Nico and Karim spent most of their time in Cairo, where they looked after our Egyptian interests. Combining Nico's abilities with Karim's contacts and the money sent by Ahmed and me, they turned our old restaurant into the most talked-about place in town. It became well known for the quality both of its food and the whores available there, with the sole condition imposed by Karim that the girls were never Muslim.

The place, of course, was called "The Mank." Foreign visitors and a few wealthy Egyptians went there for lunch or dinner; as did Karim's friends, leaders in the Muslim Brotherhood, who obviously paid for nothing but guaranteed a trouble-free life for us politically. Dressed in a white dinner jacket, his hair straightened and combed back, Nico Gerace received his illustrious guests. He also chose the prostitutes, after having first tested them for quality himself.

It was his complaints about Gaddafi that gave me the idea for a new business, which I proposed to my partners during one of the weekends they were both back from Cairo.

Gaddafi had drastically limited the export of capital, and the Italian and Jewish populations were desperate. When going abroad on vacation, the most that people could take was three hundred pounds sterling per adult and one hundred and fifty for each child. The Italians tried to entrust their money to diplomatic personnel, who were exempt from searches at departure. But the Libyans checked everything and searched anyone going in or out of an embassy or a consulate. If they found money, they confiscated it. So the Italians turned to the Jews, who had their own channels of communication with the Maltese, who ran the currency-smuggling operation and charged 30 percent to act as intermediaries.

All this business, we were capable of doing. We had my father's motorboat, contacts within the Italian community, impunity derived from my father's name, and—last but not least—the necessary balls.

Currency smuggling was certainly dangerous, but much more profitable than smuggling cigarettes. Cash took up less space than cigarettes and was worth a thousand times more. All that was necessary was to get the money out of territorial waters, deposit it in the Banco di Sicilia on the Italian island of Lampedusa, west of Malta, and then transfer it from our account to whoever had entrusted us with it, minus our 30 percent.

Karim was against it initially. It was against Islamic religious principles to take a percentage. What's more, we were violating the laws of his beloved Gaddafi and robbing the Libyan people.

Then he nodded.

"All right, but the money we earn goes to the refugees."

Every so often, since Gaddafi's arrival, they forgot that I was still the boss and, if I chose, the MANK organization would fold within five minutes. And that General Jalloun and the Libyan police turned a blind eye only because I was still the son of Ingegnere Salvatore Balistreri.

I reminded them of this as brutally as I could.

"With your share, you can do what you want, Karim, and the same with us and our shares."

"I'll still persuade you," Karim persisted.

Nico looked at him scornfully.

"With my money, I'm going to buy a movie theater with huge leather seats, and then I'll marry an actress."

"It'll have to be an actress who's blind," said Karim.

Ahmed had remained silent, as he often did before expressing his opinion.

"One of you two will have to come back to Tripoli to give us a hand," he said to Karim and Nico.

"Nico can come back. I'm staying in Cairo," Karim said immediately.

I had heard nothing from Laura since meeting her father at my granddad's funeral, when he handed me the Leonard Cohen cassette. More than a month had passed and I knew only that Marlene Hunt had come back a few days ago and that Laura was at college in Cairo.

Nico was reluctant. In Egypt, there were cinemas and prostitutes.

But there was more. I smiled at him.

"The Lux, the Mignon, or the Odeon. Which one will you buy with your share?"

His eyes opened wide, and it was Karim's turn to protest.

"With the MANK organization's money?"

"The owners will give us any movie theater we want, Karim, if we help them to export their cash."

Nico's eyes were gleaming with joy.

"I want the Alhambra, Mike. The one with the sliding roof."

"That one's not on offer," Karim said. "It belongs to Zanin, head of the Maltese clan. The same guys who control the currency smuggling."

My eyes met those of Ahmed.

*Couldn't be better. We kill two birds with one stone.*

# SUNDAY, NOVEMBER 16, 1969

Zanin was a practicing Catholic. So we went to his house one Sunday after Mass dressed in our best and with some excellent Sicilian cannoli made by Nico's mother.

He had the best villa in Garden City. From the terrace, you could even see into the grounds of the King's palace. In the large garden were six Doberman Pinschers: one for Zanin, one for his wife, and one each for his four children. Zanin's dog was named Killer, and it was almost like a fifth child; it ruled over the other dogs, ate with its master, and was always at his side.

It was there when Zanin received the MANK organization in his living room, along with his two lieutenants: the manager of the Alhambra movie theater and the head of his fishing fleet, the cover for his smuggling.

Zanin was a little over forty, with the face of a sailor, which he had been for twenty years, and the look of a criminal, his most recent activity. He had agreed to see us immediately, out of respect for my surname, I thought initially.

The *mabrouka* served us chai and nuts, and I outlined our proposal, which was in no way unreasonable or in conflict with his affairs.

"You've always been able to take Jewish money out of the country," I began.

Zanin raised a brawny arm.

"We don't take out a thing. It's illegal."

"All right," I went on, "then let's say that the four of us have received a lot of requests from the Italian population here. We wouldn't offer any of our services to Jews, Maltese, or Libyans. They would remain your clients."

Zanin stroked the head of his Doberman, which was sneering at us. Zanin pointed to one of his lieutenants.

"Half of our fish is bought by Italians. We can't cede that market to you."

The MANK organization had already discussed this and, in the end, we had all agreed. The opportunity to make money out of the illegal export of currency from Tripoli wouldn't last forever and was worth a fortune. We had to go all out.

"In exchange, Signor Zanin, we can offer you the Mank in Cairo."

"Which you have already visited on several business trips," Nico Gerace added maliciously.

Zanin seemed surprised by the offer. It was difficult to weigh the economic aspects there on the spot. But Ahmed offered something to clinch the deal.

"What you have here could be over in a day, Signor Zanin. It all depends on the whim of Colonel Gaddafi."

It was the first time I had heard him speak in that way: independently, decisive, and very Libyan. Only his nationality allowed Ahmed to come out with an explicit threat like this, which affected not only the Maltese.

But it had the opposite effect. Zanin's mask of a face hardened.

"Your Gaddafi won't do a damn thing. If he does, the Americans and Israelis will wipe him out, seeing as the Italians haven't got the guts to do it."

I shot a warning glance at Karim, but he couldn't hold back.

"You're guests in this country only for a short while longer, Signor Zanin, and you've already robbed the Libyan people quite enough," he said aggressively.

His manner upset the Doberman, which bared its teeth and growled. Zanin gave it a loving caress to calm it down.

"That's a good boy, Killer. These boys are just leaving."

Then he got up.

"Your generous offer is refused, boys. That's my final answer."

# FRIDAY, NOVEMBER 21, 1969

We couldn't give up the opportunity purely out of fear of Zanin and his gang. So we decided to start operations anyway.

From five Italian families among Nico's acquaintances and mine, we gathered more than thirty thousand Libyan pounds to take to Lampedusa.

We decided to take the first trip in my motorboat on a Friday night. It was the Muslim weekly holiday and the coast guard had other things on its mind. In order to avoid the port, we would leave from La Moneta. My father had left Mohammed in charge of the sale of the island but, for the moment, it was still our family property. Having Italian documents, it was Nico and I who would make the trip.

We arrived on the island at suppertime. The mid-November night was cool but not cold, and the sea was extremely calm. Karim and Nico had prepared some couscous, and we were all sitting down to eat in the kitchen when we heard the sound of engines. Two huge inflatables were about a hundred yards from the jetty.

Nico immediately looked through the infrared binoculars.

"It's Zanin and a bunch of his men."

Ahmed took out his knife.

"Put that away," I told him. "Karim, take the money bag. You and Nico go out the back way. Ahmed and I will wait for them here."

"And then?"

"Then as soon as they come in, you get away in the motorboat. It's much faster than the inflatables. Here's the keys."

"And you two?" Karim asked.

"We'll manage, brother. You two keep the money safe."

Of course, it was possible that Zanin might leave a couple of his men on guard along the jetty. But if Nico and Karim took them by surprise they would be able to overcome them.

As soon as they left, Ahmed and I switched on all the upstairs lights in the house. They would lose a good deal of time in looking for us up there.

We went out by the back door, took the path to the cliff, and started to run. We had a ten-minute head start, and the Maltese gang had no knowledge of the path. If Nico and Karim managed to escape, they would think there was no one else to look for.

At the highest point, a third of the way along, we stopped and climbed up onto a rock. You could see the villa lit up, the jetty with its two lamps, and the two inflatables.

. . . .

"There are ten of them," said Ahmed, counting.

It wasn't the number that worried me.

"He's brought that damned Doberman."

Zanin had left two men on guard on the jetty. They were sitting listlessly on its wooden planks, letting their legs dangle and having a cigarette.

Nico and Karim were already hidden on the beach. They were perfectly positioned and waiting for Zanin, his men, and the dog to go into the villa. Then, in a flash, the two of them flung themselves into a run on the jetty. The two guards had no time even to get up and were hurled into the water.

We saw Nico jump into the motorboat and start the engine while Karim untied the moorings. Alerted by the men's cries, Zanin and the others ran out toward the jetty. But Nico and Karim were already on their way. Zanin then pulled out a pistol and aimed it at the motorboat.

Perhaps he would have hit it, perhaps not, but Ahmed had no wish to run the risk. His cry carried as far as the beach.

*"Ibn kalb almaltia!"*

Zanin was distracted for a moment. But, in that time, Nico and Karim in the motorboat were already out of range. Immediately, however, Zanin and his men took to the path at a run. And that dog was in front of them.

••••

We ran on in the dark; we knew the path like the back of our hands. We had at least a ten-minute head start on them, but there were problems: their flashlights, their number, and their pistol. And that dog would sniff us out if we tried to hide.

We reached the edge of the cliff on the other side of the island in record time, but behind us we could hear Killer's furious barking as the dog raced toward us, together with the cries of Zanin's minions.

The Doberman caught up with us, snarling. Ahmed took out his knife. But Killer was clever and in no hurry. It simply had to hold us there, penned in three yards from the cliff edge, and wait for its master to arrive with his men and his gun.

I looked at the sea and then at Ahmed. But he had already caught on.

"Think there'll be enough water, Mike?"

This time, there was no Alberto down below to tell us. The tide had to be more or less at midway. We had a one in two chance. Better than being torn to pieces by Killer or shot by Zanin.

I smiled at Ahmed.

"I'll go first and tell you. If you don't hear anything, best of luck with the dog."

I took two steps to run up and leapt into the air. This time, I didn't have the courage to look down. I kept my eyes closed during the twenty yards my body was sailing through the air, waiting for water or rocks.

When my feet touched water and my body sank several yards, I hadn't even taken a breath. I surfaced, panting and spluttering. It was a lucky break I didn't drown there, after having escaped being smashed to bits.

"Okay?" I heard Ahmed yelling above me. I had forgotten about him.

"Good luck with the dog!" I shouted back.

Three seconds later, I saw him leap and crash into the water a few yards away.

"Forgot about me, Mike?" he said as soon as he surfaced, also gasping for air.

"No, I thought maybe you wanted to play with Killer for a while! Like you did with the dog that bit Jet."

He started to laugh, and I joined in. Then a thought crossed his mind.

"Do you think that shit Zanin will start shooting at us from up there?"

"He won't be able to see with just a flashlight. Unless he has a searchlight . . ."

We swam toward the rocks and hauled ourselves out so that we were completely out of any line of fire and would not catch cold in the water.

Above us, the flashlights were lighting up the sea's surface. They shone for about ten minutes, then Zanin and his men realized they weren't going to find us and went away.

"What should we do now?" Ahmed asked.

"Wait for dawn."

We stayed there half an hour in silence.

"Are you thinking about that bastard Maltese?" Ahmed asked me.

*No, my friend, I'm thinking about my mother, who wasn't as fortunate as we were in playing Russian roulette with the sea.*

I made no reply. But he understood.

"Sorry, Mike," he said softly. "Stupid question."

In that moment, we heard the sound of an engine drawing near.

"Damn," Ahmed said, taking out his knife.

"It's okay, it's the motorboat."

Karim was at the wheel. Nico threw out the ladder and gave us one of his wonderful smiles.

"Been having fun, boys?"

# SATURDAY, NOVEMBER 29, 1969

The following morning, the four of us went to find General Jalloun in his offices in Bab Azizia. The first thing we did was give him the gift of a backpack containing ten cartons of Marlboro Reds and five bottles of Johnnie Walker Black Label.

Then I told him about our ideas for business, the difficulties with Zanin, the help we needed, and how much we would cut him in. It was a fair and generous offer.

"I want twice that," said Jalloun without hesitating.

Sure, the poor general wanted to exploit his extensive powers to the maximum while he was still able to lick the new regime's boots.

I smiled at him. After all, he was an old friend of my granddad.

"It's already a generous offer, General."

Jalloun spread his arms wide.

"I'm sorry, but I have three wives and ten children to support."

Nico handed him an envelope.

"Then we can help you save in other areas, General."

In the envelope was a card with the very personal greetings of the two Lebanese belly dancers he had gotten to know at our Cairo restaurant the weekend before. And also the very poetic photographic souvenirs that had been taken from behind a two-way mirror in the bedroom where the general had entertained the two ladies.

Jalloun burst out laughing. He looked again at the photographs Nico had brought him.

"Do you pick the girls yourself, Nico?"

"One by one, General. It's a very rigorous selection process. The next time you come to Cairo, I must introduce you to the two new Filipino girls. They can do extraordinary things with their feet."

• • • •

That evening the coast guard stopped all the fishing boats in Zanin's fleet. The police limited themselves to carrying out a search, discovering the money, taking 15 percent, and then letting them go on their way.

Before dawn broke, Ahmed and I entered the garden of Zanin's villa, after we had thrown in some poisoned meatballs. I was a little sorry to kill the dogs, but it was necessary.

Ahmed carved Killer's eyes out of their sockets and dropped them on the doormat in front of door to Zanin's house.

# SUNDAY, NOVEMBER 30, 1969

As on the previous occasion, we invited ourselves to Zanin's after Mass. This time, without dressing up and minus the cannoli.

The meeting was very brief. Our previous offer was no longer on the table and our request had changed.

We demanded absolute freedom to export Italian currency, without any kickback to him. In return, we would let Zanin and his Maltese associates have exclusive rights on all the other national currencies, but with a commission of 15 percent to be given to us, which we would then pass on to General Jalloun.

"In order to protect your business from the Libyan police," I explained.

"Okay. Offer accepted," Zanin said quickly.

But I wasn't finished.

"One more thing. As it is, the Alhambra movie theater isn't making money. So we should take it over. From today on, it'll be run by my friend Nico here. We'll give you five percent of the earnings."

Zanin was in a hurry about one thing only: that we leave as soon as possible.

"All right," he said.

Ahmed stepped forward and pushed his face right into Zanin's.

"There's one last thing, Maltese. If I see you point a gun or even just a finger at any of the four of us, I'll carve your eyes out and put them in the couscous instead of the lamb's."

Zanin bid us a courteous farewell. Killer's eyes and Ahmed's knife had persuaded him far more than the Libyan coast guard.

# SUNDAY, DECEMBER 14, 1969

Karim had come back to Tripoli after two consecutive weeks in Cairo. We were counting up the MANK organization's unbelievable earnings in my Garden City apartment. Each week, we earned a clear ten thousand Libyan pounds, which would soon rise to twenty thousand, given the Italians' growing fears.

Nico was over the moon but also a little concerned.

"Perhaps we're overdoing it. The entire Libyan police force could come down on us."

"Not as long as there's Jalloun."

"They'll replace him sooner or later, the royalist pig," Karim said. "I don't trust him anyway."

"Easy, Karim. He's taking fifteen percent from us and fifteen from Zanin. A hundred times his salary."

Ahmed came up with another problem.

"We can't keep putting our money in your cellar here, Mike. Nor at the Banco di Sicilia in Lampedusa. It would attract too much attention—even a safe-deposit box would raise too many questions."

As usual, Ahmed had the right answer, and while complicated it was touched by genius. It was approved unanimously by all four members of the MANK organization.

# SUNDAY, DECEMBER 21, 1969

Ahmed had a blacksmith friend of his build four metal strongboxes similar to the safe-deposit boxes in banks. Sturdy, spacious, and absolutely watertight, each of them had a ring welded onto them and a steel cable fitted with a lock threaded through them so they could not be separated.

The initials M A N K were engraved on each box.

Six miles out from La Moneta, a large rock surfaced from the water. No one went there, because, by a trick of the winds, the current was very strong and so it was rarely fished.

Several yards down, almost at the base of the rock, was a cave that went upward to a point where it emerged out of the water.

It was here that we decided to put the money, once a week, already divided into four waterproof plastic sacks. There had to be at least three of us: two going down in scuba gear—which would be Ahmed and myself—while the third stayed onboard as lookout.

The first time, all four of us went together on a Sunday a few days before Christmas. In the cave, we threaded the cable through the rings on the four boxes to link them then passed it around a large rock and secured them all together with the huge lock.

It was a complex operation, but our treasure was worth protecting well.

We all had the keys to our own strongbox, where we could place our share. But, in order to take the boxes away, you needed the key to the lock that secured the steel cable around the rock.

And, without any discussion, since I was the boss and always would be, I would keep that key. And not even Colonel Gaddafi could change that.

When I got back to Garden City from the port, it was almost dark. I had taken the old Corso Vittorio on my Triumph. There was no one buying ice cream at Girus's parlor; a few passers-by were walking quickly past the cathedral.

I parked the bike and was opening the door when she touched my shoulder.

We hadn't seen each other since the day of my mother's funeral. In those one hundred days, Laura had matured a good deal. Not physically—at eighteen, her body was the same as Marlene's—but in her look and her feelings for me.

There were a thousand things I wanted to tell her, but not one of them would come out.

*I've always loved you. But it was your mother I screwed.*

"Aren't you going to invite me into your new house, Mike?"

We went into the apartment in silence. She looked around a bit and saw the photo taken on the Spanish Steps in Piazza di Spagna that hung opposite my bed.

*The photo of how I'll never be.*

But she hadn't come to talk. She smiled at me, reached out her arms, placed them on my shoulders, and then drew herself close to me.

She pointed to the photograph. "Can you be happy with the reject version?"

We laughed together as we began to kiss. Then I switched off all the lights and closed the blinds so that not even the streetlights could shine in on us. I wanted the dark, because I knew that I was stealing and you steal better in the dark.

I put on the Cohen cassette she had given me. Susanne.

She took off her clothes in silence and I followed suit. We slipped under the sheets.

"Do you have some protection, Mike?"

For a moment, I was perplexed by the unusual way she put it. I shook my head.

"I've got one. I got it two months ago, thinking of you at the New York airport. I hope these things don't go out of date, like medication."

She put the condom on me. She trusted me, like Cohen's Susanne. *And you trust him because his touched your perfect body with his mind.*

She didn't see the darker side of me, which was clearly there in the snapshot she'd taken more than two years earlier. Or else she no longer wanted to think about it.

"There have been other girls, Laura."

I said it like that, all in one breath, before it was too late. But she began to laugh.

"I never had any doubts, Casanova. An ugly moron like you, all muscle and no brain . . . I'm not surprised some poor girl might have found you interesting."

It was true. I had had adventures, nothing that amounted to anything, simply to distance myself from her. But I wasn't thinking about those.

I was thinking about Marlene struggling beneath me after I had tied her wrists to the bed, spitting my blood back in my face while I was fucking her.

*Your mother.*

Laura got on top of me. Love and passion were united in her, inexperience mixed with desire, total trust united with the wish to grow together. And I clung to her like a newborn at its mother's breast, knowing that, sooner or later, this would be over.

. . . .

Afterward, Laura told me all that was happening in her life.

William's job had lasted until the summer. He was head of the team negotiating the evacuation of Wheelus Field and the protection of American economic interests. Marlene had been with him in Tripoli.

"I'm taking a communications and photography course in Cairo, and I'll stay there until the summer. Any objections you'd like to voice about this plan, Mike?"

She was joking, but I was thinking about things I could not mention.

*Do you see Karim in Cairo?*

This was not the question I asked, but something else.

"Did your mother and my father have an affair?"

She suddenly became serious. She was staring at me, her clear bright eyes focused on a memory that must have been very painful.

"That awful day on La Moneta, I thought my parents' marriage was over. I was ready to do anything to prevent it. But Marlene assured me that she and William would stay together. Then your mother died and things between my parents calmed down. Almost as if nothing had ever happened. In San Francisco, I never heard them argue or even talk about it."

I was taken aback, incredulous.

"But you haven't answered my question. Did my father and your mother have an affair?"

"Why go on about it, Mike? You'll only hurt yourself and others. Your mother . . ."

She never said *is dead.* Nor *killed herself,* or *was killed.* She said nothing more.

I held her close. We lay there, holding each other. She trusted me. I trusted her.

There was love, heat, and peace in that embrace, but no future: that was already behind us.

• • • •

That evening, Mohammed Al Bakri flew from Tripoli to Rome.

His custom-made suit was a gift from Don Eugenio, and the black leather case on the seat was a gift from Busi. Inside it were the restricted documents that the Italian ambassador in Tripoli had prepared for the president: the census of Italian properties in Libya and an analysis of the situation.

This was all Gaddafi could offer to Nasser to gain his support. Before the end of the year, the Egyptian president would go to Tripoli and a pact would be sanctioned between them.

The Italian community was decreasing day by day. Already, more than eight hundred families had left and another three thousand would leave between January and July in 1970.

And, at this point, the final push to have the rest out would meet with no resistance.

No one in this world either today, tomorrow, or whenever would be able to accuse certain politicians and industrialists of having supported the end game that was about to be played out. They had "sympathized," perhaps, but for political reasons, never out of convenience: Libya was changing from a corrupt and feudal monarchy to a true people's democracy! And as for Italy and its 50 million Italians, who could then pay a little less for gas and heating, it was absolutely fine. And, besides, this Gaddafi was a moderate and could be controlled. All was well.

He shivered and asked the taxi driver to turn up the heat. Mohammed Al Bakri closed his eyes. Not all had gone well. His unfortunate little daughter, his beloved Nadia. He had a great deal to forget, otherwise he would go mad.

As the taxi was turning into a Piazza di Spagna soaked with rain and crowded with city dwellers and tourists, Mohammed recited a short prayer. He asked Allah and Nadia for forgiveness.

# WEDNESDAY, DECEMBER 24, 1969

Dad and Alberto arrived in Tripoli from Rome on the afternoon of Christmas Eve. Dad still had the idea of the united family, even if Mom and Granddad were no longer with us. Perhaps he dreamed of going to midnight Mass with his two sons by his side. But this had not happened since we were kids. I had stopped going years ago, and I only agreed to have supper together to avoid offending my brother.

Alberto took a room and Dad a suite in the Waddan. We ate in the hotel on the terrace overlooking the seafront, as we had done so many times when we were children, but then, in those days, my grandfather and mother were there as well. So many things had changed. Only my father pretended that there was no difference between memory and reality.

There were few Italians at the tables. Unlike previous years, the atmosphere was no longer festive—no orchestra, dancing, or shows. Now it was quieter, with fewer civilians and more military.

Dad had changed. In these recent months after Italia's death, his hair had started to turn gray, along with his face and even his words. His features were less affable, as if life had now taken him into a world where the struggle was more vicious.

He talked about his new deals with various Italian industrial groups: gas, cars, foodstuffs. Every so often, he came out with terms such as "joint venture" and "put and call options." Perhaps he thought this garbage would interest me. In fact, he was speaking only to Alberto, who seemed a little embarrassed.

*My poor brother. What kind of a disgusting world has Dad dragged you into?*

Then he began a running commentary on the situation in Tripoli and the Americans, who had to give up Wheelus Field.

"But will the Americans leave Libya just like that?" Alberto asked him. Clark Gable smiled.

"Americans are businessmen. They'll find a way to make a deal."

"And what about us Italians? You've sold all the family property, Dad. La Moneta, the Sidi El Masri villas, the olive grove, the town houses. And here we are just renting in Garden City? Why?"

My question took him by surprise and was not welcome. He brushed a hand through his thick hair and smoothed his well-trimmed mustache. "The situation could change here, Michele. The shares in foreign companies are one thing but property, land, and commercial activity another."

"What do you mean?" I asked him.

"That we Italians don't own Libya. Yes, we invaded it, but one day we'll have to leave."

I looked out to the sea, dotted with the tiny lights of the fishing vessels. I looked at the carriages trotting along the beach. I looked at the palms, stirring in the cool, late-December breeze.

"Libya is our home, Dad. Thousands of good people like Granddad built it up without its oilfields, without 'joint ventures' and 'puts and calls.' I will never leave Tripoli."

Dad carefully wiped some beer froth from his mouth with his napkin. Then he stared at me with that look that I knew very well. It was the patient and good-natured look that hid his rage. But it was there, always lying in wait, even in the period of mourning when he wore the black button in his lapel. It was there in his words, spoken softly as a priest giving last rites.

"You can stay, Michele. So long as your affairs don't damage our family's good name. Or someone will force you to leave."

There was no threat here. There was no need. He had all the weapons he required. He smiled at me, as usual. Paid the bill, as usual. And went off, as usual.

Alberto and I were left alone at the table.

"Alberto, I have to ask you something."

His eyes were on the luminous dots at the end of the coast beyond the castle, toward the old fortifications, the beaches, and La Moneta.

"Do you really have to, Mike?"

His tone was always that of a caring elder brother. But, this time, there was a hint of concern I had never picked up before. He already knew what the question was. But I could not spare him. I had no other choice.

"That afternoon . . ."

I left the question hanging in the air. In fact, I had no idea how to continue. My generous brother shook his head.

"You can't let yourself have any peace, can you, Mike?"

It was more of a statement than a question.

"No, I can't, Alberto. Tell me about that afternoon."

"After you left with Marlene I was on the beach for two hours with the other guys. Before four, we split up, and I went to my room to study for the rest of the afternoon. I saw Farid and Salim docking at the jetty about five fifteen. They'd come to pick up Mohammed, and I went out to the beach to say hello."

"Was anyone else on the beach?"

He thought for a moment. "Ahmed was there, perhaps Nico and Karim came along after a while. I don't remember."

"And the grown-ups?"

He looked at me in desperation at my persistence, which he did not share.

"They came along later, in dribs and drabs. Mike, you have to accept it: Mother took her own life."

Suddenly, the night air was filled with the *muezzin*'s cry coming from the mosque. *Allah akhbar.*

# SUNDAY, JUNE 14, 1970

Winter and spring passed into summer. Dad and Alberto had not been back to Tripoli, not even for Easter. Alberto phoned often, but not Dad.

The Italians continued to leave Tripoli in sporadic numbers, closing their shops and trying to sell their property, as well as taking their money out—something that was increasingly difficult to do via legitimate means. As a result, the MANK organization's business prospered and the Libyan pounds mounted each week in the four strongboxes in the cave under the sea.

Things were also going well in Egypt. Karim was now permanently settled there, dividing his time between our business affairs and the Muslim Brotherhood. I imagined that he and Laura saw each other in Cairo. But I preferred not to ask or think about it.

Laura often came for the weekend, and we would spend Sundays together. We went to the Underwater Club's beach on the Triumph or rode around Tripoli, then came back to my place in Garden City. An ordinary young couple, a normal life in front of them. A degree, perhaps, a job, marriage, a home, and children. Or so it seemed.

I hadn't seen Marlene at all. I knew from Laura that she spent a good deal of time with her in Cairo, especially when William was in Vietnam. And when he was in Tripoli she stayed at home in their house near the Adrian Pelt coastal road. No one saw her around anymore, not in her Ferrari, not at the Underwater Club, not at parties in the embassies or out on terraces overlooking the sea.

William was finishing up negotiations with the new Libyan authorities for the American withdrawal from Wheelus Field. At the end of the summer, the Hunts would return to the United States. But what about Laura?

That Sunday, we were at my place in Garden City. We had just made love. She was lying on the bed, her head resting on my knees. The Rolleiflex was on the floor. It was always by her side. She was flicking through a series of black-and-white shots she had taken of "the city of the living and the dead" in Cairo, the cemetery where refugees from Sinai in the 1967 war were still living. It was where Karim worked. I knew the destructive pattern of my thoughts started with me, not Laura, and from what had happened with her mother. But it was easier to start discussing our relationship than tell her the truth.

"You should have someone like Karim in your life. You can share all your cultural interests, like photography, with him . . ."

Laura became serious all of a sudden. Her sense of humor was never lacking, but my tone of voice worried her.

"Karim has some things I like that you don't have. But I love you for what you are, not for what you have or don't have."

*My beautiful loser. Her dedication on the back of the photo.*

"Your parents will never approve of us as a couple, Laura."

"I'm eighteen now, Mike. Pretty much grown up. After this summer, we can go to Rome together, or wherever we like. It's all fine by me."

I wanted to scream out, *Yes!*, but there was that memory, which wasn't only a memory. It was like an impending threat, and it was always there.

"I've had other girls, Laura."

"You've already told me that, Mike. But that was before me, it's not important."

"One was a married woman."

She turned around to look at me. She was still calm, but a shadow of disquiet passed over her face.

"Was it an important relationship?"

I replied on an impulse.

"No, just sex. And it only happened once."

*Only once. Now it's over. Or is it?*

Laura immediately started to downplay it, in her way.

"Well, thank goodness. A purely physical relationship is one that Plato puts on the lowest part of the scale. The least important."

*The least important point of the scale.*

It was true. It was also a lie. I was running along the edge of an abyss.

# TUESDAY, JUNE 16, 1970

I couldn't get to sleep that night. I had too many bad thoughts.

Marlene Hunt was the cause of my mother's suicide or murder. Now, not even a year had passed, and yet it seemed like a hundred. Everyone had forgotten, including the police, who had never even investigated it.

*Italia was an obstacle to the sale of Granddad's olive grove. And she was the obstacle to my father's life with Marlene. She had gone to see Mansur; perhaps she knew who had killed Nadia.*

The last thought crossed my mind in a flash. I had been an idiot. Mom had gone to see Mansur a few days before she was killed. She was checking on those alibis, as I had asked her to after the goatherd Jamaal had committed suicide. She believed he wasn't guilty and had told me so.

*If someone takes their own life, then people think they're either mad or guilty.*

I was suddenly wide awake and knew what I was looking for. Where had my mother's things been put after we moved from Sidi El Masri? Mohammed had been in charge, and he certainly wouldn't have thrown anything away.

I went down into the cellar. There were trunks, large boxes, bags and crutches, and all the clothes in wardrobes. I rummaged through everything for two hours, sweating and overcome with heat while the mosquitoes hummed around me, unable to bite.

The book in which I had seen the sheet of notepaper wasn't there. It was Nietzsche's *Beyond Good and Evil.* A slim volume, I recalled. But that was not the one Mamma had taken to the cliffs that day. That was *Ecce Homo.*

. . . .

I threw open a wardrobe and the kaftan was there.

*The light kaftan Mamma was wearing that morning on the veranda.*

It had a large side pocket and *Beyond Good and Evil* was inside it. And also the crumpled sheet of squared notepaper with my writing on it, the one I had handed to my mother, who had promised to investigate.

But on the other side of the page, in my mother's pointed writing, there now were two short sentences.

*They knew eachother. Check m.*

It was an *m* written in lowercase.

I still hadn't seen Mohammed Al Bakri's new house in Tripoli. I went on foot from Garden City, walking under the arcades along Shara Istiklal. Almost all the Italian shops had closed, the traffic was sparse, the Libyans on bicycles or in donkey carts. Arriving at the corner that the former Piazza Italia made with Shara December 24, I went up the staircase and rang the bell beside a very middle-class door plate that said AL BAKRI. Finally, Mohammed's family was living in an apartment with rooms for everyone, with running water, electric light, sanitation, and drains.

. . . .

It was Karim who opened the door. I had thought he was in Cairo, not in Tripoli.

*You're not in control anymore, Mike. It looks like the MANK organization is over.*

Karim accompanied me to the living room, where Mohammed was drinking tea before going to the office. Ahmed was sitting next to Mohammed, and there was an Egyptian housekeeper serving them toast.

The furniture was well made, the television set one of the latest models. I declined the offer of coffee and remained standing. I addressed Mohammed directly.

"Did Nadia know anyone whose name begins with *m*?"

The question took them all by surprise. They looked at me, visibly shaken.

"Apart from me and you?" Mohammed asked.

He had changed. Now he was well shaven, less stark in the face, better groomed. And more self-confident. And, for the first time since I was born, there was no "Signor Michele."

I showed him the sheet of squared notepaper.

"Whose notes are these?"

"Mine. I was making inquiries into Nadia's death."

I saw Ahmed and Karim looking down at the floor. I absolutely had to keep quiet about them knowing anything about this, or Mohammed would punish them severely.

Then I showed him the other side.

*They knew each other. Check m.*

Mohammed recognized my mother's handwriting.

"Was Signora Italia also making inquiries into Nadia's death?"

He was indignant and could barely hide his anger.

"Mohammed, I'm asking you again. Who is this *m*? Is it one of Nadia's friends?"

I turned pale as he fought to keep himself under control.

"Nadia was still a child. She knew no one apart from her relatives and her school friends. Her killer is in hell now. The case is closed, and you know it. And I think you should leave."

· · · ·

The police barracks at Bab Azizia smelled of paint. The police themselves were giving the peeling walls a fresh coat, perhaps in anticipation of a visit from the supreme leader, Colonel Gaddafi.

General Jalloun didn't seem overly happy to see me. He received me in an office that was smaller and barer than the one he used to have. I quickly gave him the bottle of Johnnie Walker Black Label I had hidden under my jacket, and he put it in his briefcase.

I handed the sheet of paper to him. He read the part I had written, puffing out smoke. He knew he had to respond to me seriously, now that we were giving him thousands of pounds each week.

"You wrote these notes yourself?"

"I did. Could you please look on the other side, General?"

*They knew each other. Check m.*

"Whose writing is this, Mike?"

"My mother's."

He was surprised for a moment, but not more than that. He probably thought Italia was mad, like me. He drew on his Marlboro Red and exhaled the smoke through his nose. He liked a theatrical gesture. He must have seen John Wayne doing it in some Western where he's questioning a Sioux warrior.

"So? What do you want to know, Mike?"

"Who *m* is."

He blew out more smoke.

"I haven't the faintest idea. But what's all this got to do with Nadia?"

"She's referring to a person whose name starts with the letter *m*, General. And, certainly, this isn't the goatherd Jamaal."

"You watch too much Perry Mason on the television. Why don't you stick with your MANK organization?"

"Nadia was raped and sodomized. How could Jamaal have done that, General?"

He shook his head.

"There are certain things you should know nothing about. It was a long and painful business. Much more than you know. Perhaps this *m* was a friend of Jamaal. Perhaps it was him who raped her. And then strangled her."

I was taken aback.

"Strangled? But you mentioned Jamaal's knife with the saw-blade, and Nadia's blood. I thought she'd been killed with that."

"The knife was used to torture her, in many differen ways. That shepherd was a beast, he even took a trophy, he cut off the middle finger of her right hand."

"And have you found this trophy in Jamaal's barrack?" I asked.

"No, but that means nothing."

"A trophy is taken to be kept, General."

The general fumed in irritation; he was losing patience. But he enjoyed the money, the whiskey, the cigarettes, and still wanted to be helpful.

"Your mother was a very intelligent woman, Mike. Those two sentences she wrote probably mean something. But they might have more to do with something else than with Nadia . . ."

"I don't understand, General."

"You're concentrating on the second sentence, *check m.* But the first one might be more important."

*"They knew each other?"*

He nodded absently, as if thinking of something he didn't really want to think about.

"There are two other bodies, Mike. You probably don't remember, you were just a kid in 1962."

"The black woman and the baby in the cesspit?"

Jalloun moved to the door.

"I am a prudent man, Mike. And not as bad a cop as you think. So without telling anyone, I did a little investigation at the time. Just to have some cards in my hands, one day."

"And?"

"And *they knew each other,* to put it like your mother. The black woman was seen once with the Al Bakri brothers."

I was astonished.

"Ahmed and Karim were just kids, General!"

He shook his head.

"Not them. The other two, Farid and Salim. But there was not much to it, and they certainly had nothing to do with Nadia's death. Besides, Salim is dead and Farid left this country. As you know."

"The day before she died, my mother handed an envelope to William Hunt. She told him it was urgent, a matter that had to be resolved within forty-eight hours. Perhaps it was something to do with this.'"

This information struck him more. Much more. Too much more.

"How do you know this, Mike?"

"I was spying on them, General."

"Seeing that you were spying, Mike, can you remember what your mother said to William Hunt?"

I remembered very well.

"She handed it to him, saying that everything was there inside, no room for any doubt. Then he asked how much time they had and she said they had two days, no more."

Jalloun lit another cigarette. He now seemed very interested, very much so.

"Could your mother have been party to some conversation between your father and his friends Emilio Busi and Don Eugenio? Or between him and Mohammed?"

I wondered where the question was coming from. Then my eyes fell on the photo hanging on the wall behind Jalloun's desk. In the place of the aging King Idris there was the youthful Colonel Gaddafi.

The coup d'état. Forty-eight hours to foil it. Mamma had been too optimistic. Perhaps that envelope had nothing to do with either Marlene Hunt or the death of Nadia.

"I don't know, General. I need more proof. Once I'll have it, be sure I will not need the police for justice."

He nodded, as if that last sentence gave him an idea. General Jalloun rose to see me out.

"I know, Mike. I know what you and your friends can do to your enemies. Perhaps I may be able to offer you some business, Mike, in the next few days. The biggest offer of your life."

I left and wondered if I should tell Ahmed and Karim about the fact that Farid and Salim knew the black woman found in the cesspit. But Salim was dead and Farid far away somewhere. And that really meant nothing. I had to find *m*, by myself.

# WEDNESDAY, JUNE 17, 1970

Piazza Navona in June was full of tourists as well as locals. The Bar Tre Scalini had no free seats outside but was quiet enough inside.

Emilio Busi was smoking a cigarette. You could see his vest under his checked shirt. Don Eugenio was reading the *Corriere della Sera*'s financial pages.

Salvatore Balistreri was filling them in on the situation in Tripoli.

"The reports from the new ambassador are reassuring. The Italian exodus is moving forward, and the Americans should be leaving any day now."

"I know that William Hunt is finalizing the agreements for evacuating Wheelus Field," Busi said. "Is he softening, Salvo?"

"Hunt is difficult. Too much of a cowboy, old style. But the big American Seven and their little siblings are in agreement about the new division, and I spoke to William and we stroke a deal."

"They have to be happy," said Busi. "Their oilfields are going to be nationalized only in appearance. In reality, the sole difference with respect to the previous situation is that they'll have to share the pie with us. Of course, it's not what Enrico Mattei wanted, but we don't want problems

with the Americans. The Yanks are attached to money and would have
no problem bombing Tripoli to defend their interests."

Balistreri nodded. Also his brothers and their friends in Sicily had
many contacts across the Atlantic and wanted no trouble with the
Americans.

"The only ones left outside will be the old imperialist British and
those snobs, the French," Busi concluded.

"So we can plan for July?" Balistreri asked.

"Yes," said Don Eugenio. "I'll drop a word to the president. He's
not happy about this solution, but he trusts us. Unfortunately, we have
to sacrifice one or two—just a few—for the benefit of the majority."

"Is everything ready in Tripoli?" Busi asked.

Balistreri hesitated. He could keep quiet, but Busi had the secret
service behind him and Don Eugenio had the president. And therefore
the secret service again. Perhaps they knew everything already. It would
be too risky to lie.

"Mike's gone to see General Jalloun. He wants him to reopen investigations into the deaths of Nadia and Italia. Mohammed has his spies
in the police, obviously. We're keeping an eye on him."

A shadow flitted across Don Eugenio's light-blue eyes.

"He's a problem, that boy. Always has been."

Busi blew out a mouthful of smoke.

"We can't risk any trouble because of a kid."

Balistreri looked both of them in the eye. It was necessary to remind
these two who he was, where he came from, and who he really had
behind him.

"I have already given up a great deal, gentlemen." He touched his
mourning button. "I will take care of my son, if you don't mind."

Busi and Don Eugenio fell silent. The message was very clear. But
Balistreri decided to put their minds at rest.

"Mohammed will get Jalloun removed very shortly, so Mike will
no longer have anyone to turn to for support. The MANK organization will lose its protection. And, at that point, I really hope he'll leave
Libya and come finish his education in Italy."

Salvatore Balistreri looked out at the splendor of Piazza Navona. A
long summer was approaching for the Italians. Economic boom, cars,

highways, low-cost gas. And, around the fountains and open-air cafés, hundreds of carefree young people.

*Italy's growing. Our future has no limits.*

"Fine," said Busi. "So, tonight, we can enjoy the match."

Italy was playing Germany in the FIFA World Cup semifinal in Mexico.

Salvatore Balistreri hated soccer. It was a stupid and ridiculous sport that got people far too excited.

*It'll end with the Italians thinking they really have a great country.*

. . . .

It was almost night. The president was watching what was happening on Rome's streets. The party outside was going crazy. The Italy-Germany game had ended minutes ago, after extra time and a total of seven goals that had almost given heart attacks to many Italians.

The president had followed the game with the sound off, barely paying it any attention, listening instead to a beautiful concert of symphonic music while he worked on his papers. But now the spectacle outside was interesting. He had even turned up the volume to follow the festivities live in the country's various piazzas.

The Italians were celebrating in their millions. This was the good life. Millions out on the streets, millions of Fiats, Vespas, Lambrettas. Millions of gallons of gasoline and champagne consumed over a game of soccer. It was also thanks to himself and the Christian Democrats that the Italians could allow themselves to celebrate a victory over the Germans, who had once invaded their country.

Well, the president knew that was not exactly how it was, but history is written by the victors.

# SATURDAY, JUNE 20, 1970

Only a few days had passed since we had last met. General Jalloun called me at home at seven in the morning. He wanted to see me. Not in his office in Bab Azizia but at my house in Garden City. A very private meeting.

I called Ahmed, telling him to come over. Jalloun arrived punctually at lunchtime, when everyone in Tripoli shut themselves indoors to escape the heat. He was in civilian clothes, without his driver, his face hidden by his keffiyeh.

*A secret visit.*

Ahmed and I immediately sensed that the general was extremely tense. I gave him the usual envelope with his money. In addition, a carton of Marlboro Reds and a bottle of Johnnie Walker. Small tokens. A sign of respect.

For the first time ever, he didn't open the envelope and count the money.

"Shut the windows, please," he told us.

He then lit a cigarette, sank into an armchair, and asked for a whiskey instead of tea. He had never drank alcohol in our company. Let alone at lunchtime.

I had a very uncomfortable feeling about this. In fact, the news was very bad.

"Boys, they're transferring me to Ghadames. Ghadames—you understand? An oasis in the middle of the desert, more camels than human beings!"

We were done for. Without Jalloun, our business would be ruined.

"I'm sorry, General. How can we help you?"

He reacted to this question in a positive way. He was expecting recriminations, not the offer of help. But I saw him as much more than a source of revenue.

He knew things about Nadia and my mother.

"I want to speak to you alone, Mike." He pointed to Ahmed. "Without him."

Ahmed looked at me. Serious, impassive. And ready to leave if I gave the sign.

"Ahmed is more than a brother to me, General. What I feel, he feels. What I do, he does. There are no secrets between us."

Jalloun must have thought a long time about what he was going to tell me. He swallowed a sip of whiskey and addressed Ahmed.

"Word is that your father is close to Gaddafi."

The statement packed a punch, but Ahmed didn't bat an eyelash.

"I think my father looks up to him, General. But he's never spoken to me about him. It's none of my business, anyway."

I was a little surprised by his reply. Perhaps this was the first time Ahmed had kept anything from me. Certainly it was only a matter of hearsay. But the fact that Ahmed had never even mentioned anything troubled me.

Jalloun glanced nervously through the closed windows.

"A few days ago, I said I had an offer to make you, Mike."

I remembered very well.

*The biggest offer of your life.*

"I have some powerful friends, boys," Jalloun went on. "Friends who are not at all happy with Gaddafi."

Ahmed rose up immediately.

"I'm leaving," he said to me. But I was still the head of the MANK organization.

"Sit down, Ahmed. Let's hear what General Jalloun has to say first."
It was an order, in the old style.

*I'm your boss's son. I give the orders. Nothing's changed.*

Ahmed remained standing a moment. It was a moment of resistance, to make me understand that things were changing between us. Then he slowly sat down.

"What do you want from us, General?" I asked.

He studied us. It was highly risky for him but, evidently, his powerful friends must have exercised a lot of pressure. And we really must have been indispensable to him, if he was being so open.

"In a couple of months, it will be a year since Gaddafi took office. And the more time that elapses, the more difficult it will be to kick him out."

He said it all in one breath, looking Ahmed and me directly in the face. Another minute's conversation with General Jalloun would mean we were conspirators and liable to be condemned to death for high treason.

Jalloun continued.

"With my transfer, the MANK business is finished, boys. But, for this job, my friends are offering a recompense of more than you could have earned in ten years."

We kept silent, and Jalloun went on.

"One million pounds sterling, two, almost two million US dollars. To be divided among you. Enough for your entire lives and three generations to come."

It was an enormous sum, unimaginable. But small compared with what was at stake.

"And what do we have to do for this sum, General?"

I already knew the answer. But I needed Jalloun to compromise himself, once and for all, in order to tell him my real price.

The general lit another Marlboro and poured himself a generous shot of whiskey.

"Before the end of August, you have to assassinate that bastard Gaddafi."

Ahmed was up in a shot. "I'm leaving, Mike. I'll pretend I've not heard a thing."

Jalloun smiled, sipping his whiskey.

"You'll not even get out of Garden City, Ahmed Al Bakri. Or do you somehow think we'd let you live?"

Jalloun already had his pistol in his hand. I had no doubt that he would shoot us, or that he had killers waiting outside. I turned to Ahmed.

"Let's listen to all that the general has to say, Ahmed. Then we can decide freely."

"Decide freely, Mike?" Ahmed replied, gesturing harshly to the pointed gun.

"Put the pistol away, General, it's not going to help. We have a tape recorder hidden in the room. We use it all the time and give the tapes to someone we trust who will send them to the police should anything happen to me or my friends. And I mean the Egyptian police, not the Libyan."

The veins in the general's neck were standing out dangerously. And it was all true. The idea of the tape recorder had been Ahmed's, and it was proving to be a good one.

"I don't believe you!" Jalloun said.

I got up. The last tape, from the month before, was still in a desk drawer. I showed it to him.

He pointed the gun at me again. "Where's the tape recorder?"

"I don't know, General. Nico installed it and, for security, we never asked where it was. He sees to all that; he gives us the tapes and we give them to Karim, who takes them to Cairo. Now that's all clear, can we get back to business?"

The general looked at me, and I caught a glimpse of respect and satisfaction in his eyes. If we were to be killers for him we had passed a pretty difficult test.

Jalloun placed the gun on his knees.

"Gaddafi is making agreements with foreign countries, such as East Germany. He's going to pay a huge price for a select group of bodyguards who have seen service in Communist Special Forces. They'll be here in time for the celebrations of the revolution's first anniversary, September 1. From then on, he'll be beyond anyone's reach."

"And right now?" I asked.

"Right now, his personal security is guaranteed by members of his tribe, the Qadhafa. He can trust them, but they have no experience."

"So it has to be in August," I said, "but will there be a suitable occasion?"

"Yes, although Gaddafi's limiting his public appearances for fear of an attempt on his life. But, in August, several tribes, persuaded by my friends, will ask for a public audience, which the colonel can't refuse. We won't know the date until the last minute, but we do know where and how the meeting will take place."

"It's a suicide mission," Ahmed said.

For the first time, he showed he could have an open mind. He was opposed, but at least open to the possibility. The colossal fee must have made him think twice.

"If they capture you alive, you'll be forced to talk, and I'd be caught in the middle as well."

"So, how do we go about it?" asked Ahmed.

"The audience will mean that Gaddafi has to come out into the open. We'll see to that. You'll be dressed as policemen; we'll supply the uniforms and weapons. Mike is so tanned and dark-haired he can pass for a Libyan. Nico as well, with his bushy hair and eyebrows. You can mingle in with the officers charged with crowd control."

There was no mention of Karim. For obvious reasons.

"And where?" Ahmed asked.

"Piazza Castello. It's a symbolic place. Gaddafi wants to address the crowd from the top of the castle wall in order to stay out of danger. However . . ."

I caught on.

"We'll need a precision sniper rifle, General. Preferably a short-barreled carbine. And a window at the same height, less than a hundred yards away."

"We'll give you the rifle you want, Mike, and a safe and secure apartment from which to fire, and at a lot less than a hundred yards. We can buy anything and anyone. And everyone knows about that lion in Tanzania."

"I'll have to practice with the rifle, General. It's not that simple."

"We'll let you have the rifle very soon, in Ghadames. Whichever one you choose. You can stay with me and practice out in the desert for as long as you need."

"And what should Nico and I do?" Ahmed said.

Jalloun stubbed out his cigarette and picked up his pistol.

"Watch his back. You'll be dressed as policemen as well and will guard the main door down onto the street and the landing outside the apartment while Mike does the job."

Jalloun blew out smoke from his nose.

"I'll advance you twenty-five percent. You'll receive two hundred and fifty thousand pounds sterling in American dollars before the end of July. The rest when it's done."

"And who's to guarantee you'll pay?" Ahmed asked.

"My intelligence, Ahmed. This money, which may seem like such a great deal to you, is nothing but spare change to these friends of mine. Once Gaddafi's dead, the country with all its oil will be in their hands, and they'll certainly want no trouble from you. And you have the tapes, don't you?"

Ahmed got up, this time without asking my permission. I followed him into the kitchen and we shut the door.

"This is insane, Mike. Not only do you need a good aim; you'll need nerves of steel. I'm out of this."

"Ahmed, I killed a lion that, had I missed, would have made mince-meat of me. I shot right through your brother's cheeks with a Diana 50 pellet. Before you cut his throat."

He stared back at me.

"If Karim knew what we were discussing . . ."

I looked at the thin white scar on Ahmed's right wrist and the one on my left. There was no doubt that Karim would have to be kept out of this. Money or no money, he worshipped Gaddafi and would report us.

"Are you frightened of our fathers, Ahmed? Do you think they're on the other side as well?"

He shook his head violently. "You've gone crazy from sleeping with that girl!"

I lashed out before I could think. Ahmed staggered under the slap. He looked at me, surprised. A trickle of blood was running from his split lip. He fell silent, massaging his cheek. I could not fathom his thoughts at that moment. Then he relaxed and smiled at me.

"I'm sorry, Mike, you're right. I won't say anything about Laura again. But I can't agree on the other business. It's madness, and I don't want to go behind Karim's back."

"And you don't care anything about Nadia, Ahmed?"

The question threw him. "What the hell's Nadia got to do with it?"

"It's the additional thing we're going to ask Jalloun for. The truth about Nadia and Italia's death."

Ahmed looked at me for a long time.

*There're only the two of us, as always, my friend. We're inseparable. As we were as kids. As we were in Cairo. On La Moneta against Farid and Salim. Against the Maltese and his dogs. Two killers.*

"Let's hear what Jalloun has to say, okay, Ahmed? I'm not keen on being an assassin either, but I want the information and only he can give it to us."

. . . .

We went back into the living room, which was now full of clouds of smoke from Jalloun's cigarettes.

"We have a counterproposal, General," I announced.

"What, a million sterling's not enough for you, boys? You really are quite greedy, aren't you!"

"No, the money's fine. But we want information about Nadia and my mother, which I'm certain you have. And if what you tell us doesn't ring true and prove useful, then not even ten million could persuade us."

Jalloun showed no surprise. Perhaps he had been expecting this.

"We already have the truth about the deaths of Nadia and your mother. Isn't that enough? What more do you want to know?"

"Then you had better find someone else for the job."

"Mike, even supposing your mother was killed—which I don't believe—it could have been anyone."

"No, General, only someone who was already on the island. You said yourself that the coast guard didn't see any boats there that afternoon."

Perhaps he was feeling desperate about his transfer to Ghadames, besides having had a good deal of whiskey. And desperately needed us for the job.

"The coast guard spotted an inflatable."

He poured another whiskey and lit another Marlboro. Outside, you could hear the *muezzin*'s cry: *Allah akhbar.* Ahmed and I were speechless.

Jalloun went on.

"The coast guard saw it near the cliffs on the island's rocky side, at about a quarter to four. The information's secret, boys."

"Did it dock anywhere?" I asked.

The general was about to blow smoke from his nose, but it went the wrong way and he started to cough and splutter.

"They're always on the move, Mike; they don't know. Anyway, a little after four, they passed by again and the inflatable wasn't there anymore."

"Are you absolutely certain, General?"

"The only absolute certainty is death, Mike. But the coast guard's report was clear. The inflatable drew up to La Moneta under the cliffs toward a quarter to four. Just after four, when they went past that way again, it wasn't there. Is that enough for our agreement?"

Not for Ahmed. "No, not at all. What can you tell us about Nadia?"

Jalloun made a face.

"What do you want to know, Ahmed? Aren't you satisfied that Jamaal the goatherd was the killer?"

I turned to my friend. There was the look I knew. Cold and sharp as a knife. I shot him a warning glance.

"Ahmed wants the truth, General. Just like me. If you want to do business with us—"

Jalloun spat on the carpet and got up. He stared right in Ahmed's face.

"Do you want to know what they did to your sister for one whole hour, Ahmed? Do you really want to know? I don't think so. It's better you forget the matter."

*Threatened with a knife. The middle finger of her right hand taken as a trophy. Raped. Sodomized. The words that had made my mother cry.*

*I'd never told Ahmed. And this certainly wasn't the right time. But Ahmed kept his control, as usual. He spoke calmly to Jalloun.*

*"I will never forget, General. And if you have no information to offer on my sister, I will not help Mike on this."*

*Jalloun spit on the floor again. He clearly wanted to convince us. And for that he knew he had to give something to Ahmed as well.*

*"I just have irrelevant information. It regards Ingegnere Balistreri and Don Eugenio. The morning that Nadia was killed they went back to Sidi El Masri after Mass and the barber and drove back to Tripoli, probably just behind your MANK van."*

*"What were they doing there?" I asked trying to keep anger out of my voice.*

*Jalloun looked at me and shook his head.*

*"Calm down. They drove to the villa of old Countess Occhini. Don Eugenio is her confessor. They stayed there twenty minutes and drove back to meet with you for the fishing. And we know this for sure, beyond any possible doubt."*

*"And how do you know all this for sure, General?" I asked.*

*He shot smoke out of his nose.*

*"Because I am a good policeman and a prudent man Mike, as I already told you. You think I just went to that shepherd as a scapegoat. But before that I had my men do some careful investigation. And the result is very simple. Anyone closer to Nadia had an alibi. With only three exceptions. You, Mike, and your two friends Ahmed and Karim. But you were asleep in your room, were you not? Then you met up with your brother Alberto and Nico Gerace, who were having breakfast."*

*He turned slowly to Ahmed, a smile of disdain on his face.*

*"And Ahmed and Karim were in the Al Bakri barracks. We cannot question their mothers to confirm that. But I trusted your word for it, Ahmed. So I think you should trust mine. Mike's father and Don Eugenio had nothing to do with Nadia's death."*

*He stood to go and* I stopped him at the door.

"One last thing, General. If that inflatable wasn't important, why is the information secret?"

"I was a friend of your grandfather, Mike. He loved you, and you already have trouble enough."

"Why was it kept a secret, General?"

"If I tell you, will you shoot Gaddafi?"

*No, I won't. I'll leave this country in peace with Laura Hunt.*

I made no answer. Jalloun sighed. He was afraid now. But he really wanted us to do this job.

"It was a US Air Force inflatable, Mike. It came from Wheelus Field."

He opened the door and went out into the 100-degree heat.

· · · ·

Ahmed tried to calm me down.

"Think about it, Mike. Confronting William Hunt about it is as dangerous as killing Gaddafi."

But that inflatable had to be linked to the envelope my mother had handed over to William Hunt the day before she died, giving him forty-eight hours to sort out the situation with Marlene and my father. Or to stop the coup d'état. Or both.

"Go home, Ahmed. We'll talk about Gaddafi when I get back."

I set off on the Triumph. The shops were all closed; the city was deserted at the hottest time of the day. As I rode along the Adrian Pelt coastal road to Wheelus Field, rain clouds were gathering to my left and the sea was looking choppy, the waves topped with small white crests.

*They've tricked you, Mike. Marlene drew you away to clear the way for her husband. And he killed Italia.*

I approached the entrance to Wheelus Field and explained to the sentry that I was a friend of the Hunts. They made a call and, after a few minutes, the bar was raised. I left the motorcycle there, and two soldiers took me in a jeep.

We drove past the hangars that once held the F100 fighter planes. There was no trace of them now. And very few soldiers around.

*The Americans are leaving.*

William Hunt's office was in a low wood-and-metal building. His secretary showed me to a seat. After twenty minutes or so, she led me to a small meeting room with the air conditioning on maximum. I could hear thunder rumbling in the distance.

William Hunt came in and sat opposite me, without saying a word. His short blond hair was now lightly speckled with white and his intelligent blue eyes were surrounded by small lines. What with Vietnam and Libya, his life was not short on worries. To say nothing of Marlene.

He had been my neighbor for twelve years, I had had sex with his wife and made love to his daughter, but I really knew little about the man. Only that he had met Marlene when she was sixteen and taking acting lessons in Hollywood, that he had been decorated for valor in the Korean War, where he had saved the lives of many American soldiers and afterward had taken classes at Langley Air Force Base in Virginia.

*And certainly he is a very good assassin.*

"So you want to speak to me about something, Michele?"

He spoke in English, with no opening pleasantries, but using my full Italian name, to maintain a certain distance.

I decided to adopt his own direct method and spoke in English, which I had learned from Laura while I was teaching her Italian.

"What did you talk to my mother about on La Moneta?"

He looked at me and sighed.

"The day before she died, on the rocky side of the island."

"I don't recall, Michele. Certainly nothing that has anything to do with you."

I couldn't care less if he was Laura's father, a decorated war hero, and a secret agent. He was in that inflatable near La Moneta at a quarter to four that afternoon.

*He dropped anchor where the cliffs are lowest. He climbed up the rock face. He threw Mamma off before I went to look for her. Then he retraced his steps. Three hours in all, with his body of steel and his unflappable nerve.*

"My mother gave you an envelope. She said it was necessary to act within forty-eight hours."

His brow furrowed. He weighed his answer for some time. His intelligent eyes were focused as he concentrated.

"How do you know about this, Michele?"

"I was there. I saw you and heard her."

"Who else knows about this?"

If he had killed my mother, he could also kill me, right there in that room. I could have said that Ahmed and Karim knew. But then he would kill them too. I was sure of it. William Hunt would show no mercy if he thought what he was doing was necessary.

*At the cost of him shooting me. At least I'll know the truth.*

"No one else, only me."

"Not even your father?"

*So that's what really worries him. My father.*

"No, not him or anyone else. Only me."

He took a moment to consider.

"Your mother discovered a secret, Michele. She furnished me with the proof. She gave me forty-eight hours to find a solution to the situation. Her only mistake was that we didn't have that much time."

His eyes were steady and held my gaze. I knew he wasn't lying to me but, nevertheless, he was holding something back.

*Everything is true in the words. Everything except the truth.*

I looked straight into his eyes.

"It was the plans for a coup d'état. Except that Italia thought there was more time. And you did nothing to stop them."

I saw him relax. Perhaps the fact that I knew everything made it easier. Or more difficult.

"You're a very intelligent young man, Mike. One day, you'll have a better understanding of politics. It's an ugly business, and I don't like it at all; it's full of cowards and wheeler-dealers. People who prefer compromises to questions of principle."

"On Sunday afternoon, the coast guard spotted an inflatable near La Moneta. An inflatable from Wheelus Field. Was it you, Mr. Hunt?"

I had entered dangerous territory. The proof was in William Hunt's icy look. But I had no fear either of him or his power.

"It wasn't me, Mike. My plane landed at two thirty, and Marlene was waiting for me. I spent some time with her; we had things to discuss."

"Yes, you were with her until three and, at that time, Marlene went home and you stayed at Wheelus Field. So, what did you do then?"

I had committed a huge error. I could tell from his face. I had seen him with my mother when she handed him the envelope. I had seen him as he said good-bye to Marlene at Wheelus Field.

*How do you know, Mike? Are you a spy as well? And a killer?*

I couldn't care less what he thought of me. William Hunt had killed my mother that afternoon between three and six thirty. He had the brains, the balls, and the physical strength. And now I knew he had the motive as well: the CIA, his real employer, didn't want that crazy idealist, my mother, to block Gaddafi's coup d'état.

"You Americans were happy with Gaddafi. And my mom was getting in the way."

"You watch too many Bond movies, Michele. That afternoon, I went in my Land Rover to join Marlene at home."

And this was certainly not true.

"That's not true, Mr. Hunt. You're lying."

*You didn't go home to Marlene. How do I know? Because your wife was having sex with me.*

I got up and quickly left. I knew who to ask. Except that I had to do it immediately, before he tipped her off.

When I went out, I was hit by torrential rain. A genuine summer storm had broken.

I set off on the Triumph at top speed. I couldn't give him any time to agree on a story with his wife. In less than ten minutes, I arrived, soaking wet, in the residential zone off the beachfront, next to Mehari. The Hunt family's home was there. William was in his office, Laura in Cairo, therefore I should have found Marlene alone at home.

Several months had passed since the day we had sex, and I hadn't seen her once. I knew from Laura that Marlene no longer socialized when she was in Tripoli.

*It was because of that American* gahba *that Signora Italia was killed, the people were saying on the street, in the shops, at the market, in the cathedral yard, in the clubs on the beach. And she had disappeared as well.*

I rang the bell, not even knowing what I was doing anymore. I could hear footsteps on the stairs. There was still time for me to get away and save myself.

But perhaps I wasn't looking only for the truth about my mother. Without being able to admit it, I was looking for the truth about myself, and about the Hunt women, Laura and Marlene.

*She's worse than those deaths in Cairo, the death of Salim, and the smuggling. Laura could have understood those, perhaps, but not this.*

As soon as Marlene opened the door, all my intentions crumbled. She was wearing only a petticoat. Her beautiful face had no makeup, the curves of her body under the transparent material were more sensual than ever. She stared at me coldly, while I stood there soaking and silent in the rain.

"What do you want, Michele?" Her tone was sharp.

"I want the truth about that day. That afternoon at your house."

I saw her turn pale, then her eyes filled with rage.

"Leave, Michele, before I call the police."

"Where was your husband while you were letting me fuck you tied to the bed?"

The hate in her eyes was as intense as the seduction once was.

"Leave now, Michele, while you still have time."

"No, I'm not leaving. First you must tell me what time William came home."

She gave a scornful smile.

"I called him at five fifteen, as soon as you left. He was in a meeting at Wheelus."

It couldn't be true. Two hours was not enough time to kill my mother and come back.

*Filthy liar.*

"I don't believe you."

She shrugged.

"Too bad for you. William was still at Wheelus Field. I told him to come home. And, as you know, when I call, the men come running, Mike."

Had I been seduced or had I raped her? I never knew. But there was no doubt now. I was nothing more than a snot-nosed intruder she didn't want around her or her daughter.

"You're a whore and he's a murderer."

She gave me another scornful smile.

"At five fifteen, William was at Wheelus, in a meeting with the American ambassador. It's common knowledge. Half an hour later, he arrived at Sidi El Masri with the ambassador and other guests for dinner. And he never left; there are at least eight witnesses. They were all our guests for a barbecue that evening."

With witnesses of that caliber, William Hunt was absolutely in the clear. Not even Superman could have been at Wheelus at three, where I saw him myself, and then again at five fifteen, having in the meantime killed my mother on La Moneta. It would have taken at least three hours to go there, kill her, and come back.

I couldn't accept the disappointment and her scorn. I grabbed her by the wrist and dragged her outside under the pelting rain. The rain stuck the petticoat to her breasts; below it, she was wearing only panties.

I was a desperate child, hurt and screaming.

"He went there to La Moneta with an inflatable! It was him who killed her!"

She looked at me contemptuously while she tried to free her wrist from my grip.

"It's done, Michelino. And you're done, too."

Blinded by rage, I dragged her into the middle of the garden.

"Liar!" I screamed, flinging her onto the muddy ground.

The glint of fear and joy in her eyes warned me.

"Mom! Mike!"

Laura was on the doorstep, wrapped in a heavy bathrobe, her eyes bright with fever. She looked at us, refusing to accept what the scene was screaming out to her.

*It's all over, Mike. That's an end to your movies about heroes who marry the beautiful heroine and live happily ever after. You'll never be one of them.*

# SUNDAY, JUNE 21, 1970

S alvatore Balistreri took the first flight from Rome to Tripoli as soon as Mohammed Al Bakri notified him of the latest stunts pulled by his son Mike.

Having him tailed had been a good idea. Everything stemmed from that question he had asked at Christmas.

*Have you spoken with William Hunt, Dad?*

How could Michele have known about the deal with the Americans? And how his friends in New York had initially misled the CIA and therefore Hunt himself about Gaddafi? It was still a mystery.

But at least they knew about General Jalloun's visit to Mike, Mike's visit to William Hunt, and the furious argument with Marlene Hunt, during which he'd flung her into the mud in her garden.

*The poor boy's gone mad.*

Salvatore Balistreri wondered if Mike's encounters with Jalloun, Hunt, and Marlene were linked to a single thread. A line of worry creased his brow. The most dangerous of them was General Jalloun, without a doubt. They had to be sure they had the whole picture.

With William Hunt they would reach an agreement. They were both pragmatic men of the world. The interests at stake were truly colossal and, being free of the obstacles created by the late Enrico Mattei, both the interest of Americans and Italians on the oil could be dealt with.

Salvatore watched the thin line of traffic along the Adrian Pelt coastal road from the large windows of his top-floor suite in the Waddan Hotel. The Italians were trickling out of the country, selling their property to the Libyans. It was almost time for the last thrust.

*A nasty job, but—for the good of the majority—inevitable.*

He was not going back to the dirty alleyways of Palermo he had left behind as a kid.

There was only a short time to wait, very short indeed. Then he would have his just reward for the huge sacrifices he had made. It had been a hard-fought battle, in which he had lost his wife and, now, it looked like, his son as well, but it was almost over.

The following morning, he would close the complicated deals with Hunt. Then he would give Mohammed instructions on how to handle General Jalloun and the MANK organization, especially Mike.

*But he was not going to leave him to die here in Libya.*

He saw Mexico's Aztec Stadium appear on the television screen. Italy and Brazil were about to take to the field for the World Cup final. He knew none of the Italian players, only the one Brazilian called Pelé.

*Let's hope he scores a goal. Excitement's one thing, but let's not get carried away. Italians should not be thinking too much of themselves. Not these days, for sure.*

He switched to the American channel, which was showing that fabulous series from the early sixties, *The Untouchables*, about the struggle between federal agent Eliot Ness and Al Capone. Now, that really was good entertainment.

*Two truly great men.*

# MONDAY, JUNE 22, 1970

After the furious confrontation with Marlene, I went home and spent the rest of the weekend with Nietzsche, Leonard Cohen, and my tortured thoughts. I didn't answer the phone or watch the World Cup final in Mexico.

Then, early Monday morning, Ahmed and Nico came knocking on the door.

"We have to talk about the MANK organization, Mike," Ahmed said.

"Otherwise, it's all going to go to the dogs," Nico added.

I couldn't have cared less about MANK at that moment.

"Where's Karim?" I asked.

Ahmed hesitated slightly.

"He's gone back to Cairo to see to business, Mike."

"Is that his business or ours, Ahmed?"

"What do you mean?"

Ahmed's tone was harsh in a way it had never been before.

"Where's Laura?" I asked him.

"She's gone off to Cairo as well. Mike, let's not confuse business with things that don't have anything to do with it."

"I'm the one who decides what concerns the business or not, Ahmed."

Nico had been silent, unable to intervene, but then he spoke.

"Listen, guys," he offered. "They are closing the American base today. Let's see what's happening out there. Then we can discuss MANK."

I agreed to this because Ahmed and I would have otherwise come to blows. And I didn't want that to happen.

We went on our motorcycles to Wheelus Field. As we crossed the city, there was no sign of any Italians. Below the arcades of Shara Istiklal and on the walls along the Adrian Pelt coastal road, the graffiti said FUCK OFF, AMERICA! and BRAZIL 4–ITALY 1.

I had put aside Jalloun's proposal, but it came back to me. Looking at the graffiti, I became convinced. Jalloun was right.

*I have to assassinate Colonel Gaddafi. Before this gets out of hand.*

The crowd of Arabs thronging the Wheelus Field entrance had two reasons to celebrate that day: the Americans were being ousted, and Brazil had thrashed Italy the night before.

Nico was sitting gloomily on his bike, spitting date stones onto the ground. There were dark rings under his eyes, and he hadn't shaved. He was starting to be affected as well.

"You Arab cocksuckers!" Nico screamed at the crowd.

Many young Libyans knew Italian. Several of them turned around, and one shouted back at us, "Yeah, you fucking Italian Fascists!"

*"An din gahba!"* Nico hurled back.

A first stone whistled over our heads as we kick-started our engines, shooting off to pick up the Adrian Pelt highway to Piazza Castello, as Nico and I still insisted on calling it. From there, we took Shara Omar Al Mukhtar toward the Fairgrounds and the deserted beaches. No Italians went there anymore, despite the sweltering heat, and the Libyans had never gone at all.

We stopped beside the public beach at Bagni Sulfurei, covered in sweat. It was the middle of the day and incredibly hot. Along the wooden pier out to sea, there wasn't a single fisherman, only the whiff of sulfur from Wadi Megenin and the braying of a donkey getting too much sun in a courtyard.

I had heard the sound of stones whizzing past us, heard the chanted slogans, and read the graffiti celebrating Italy's defeat by Brazil. And I knew I had lost Laura.

*This country's all I have left. My grandfather's and my mother's country.*

"Ahmed, let's say yes to General Jalloun, before Gaddafi kicks the Italians out, just like they have the Americans."

Nico stared at me.

"What the hell are you talking about, Mike?"

He still hadn't been told about the idea.

Ahmed said nothing. The time of blind obedience was over. Was that the reason that had kept me from telling him what General Jalloun had told me about *they knew each other,* the involvement of his stepbrothers Farid and Salim with the black woman found in the cesspit in 1962 with her baby? Or was it the sense of guilt for having told Nadia that the woman and the baby were black? But I wasn't inclined to any kind of compromise. It had really nothing to do with Gaddafi. He could have been right in his own way, and better than the corrupt old monarchy. This was about something else.

"You're either with me or against me, Ahmed."

He was still silent. That deep, strong, and serious face had been beside me for the first twenty years of my life. I looked at the scar on my left wrist, the same as the one on Nico's and Ahmed's wrists. Ahmed looked at it as well.

The blood brotherhood looked as if it was breaking up for sure. Karim was out. Ahmed knew it was an emotional decision I was making, based on the Libyan insults against the Italians and on Laura leaving. And he didn't like anything emotional.

*But his cut is the deepest. The one that will last the longest. He's still with me.*

Ahmed gunned his Ducati. He pointed to the pier that went out fifty or so yards into the sparkling sea and smiled at me.

"Want to play chicken, Mike?"

I smiled back. Then I gunned the engine of my Marlon Brando Triumph Thunderbird.

"Okay. First one to brake is chicken."

"Are you two crazy?" Nico shouted after us, as Ahmed and I shot off side by side down the pier. Then, when neither of us had braked and we both finished up in the sea, Nico mounted his Guzzi and, at top speed, whispering, "Shit shit shit," he joined us in the water.

# WEDNESDAY, JULY 1, 1970

I n the preceding days, locked inside my house in Garden City, Ahmed, Nico, and I had gone through every detail of the plan with Jalloun before he left on his transfer to Ghadames.

That morning, Nico and Ahmed picked me up in the MANK van, the one with the Barbra Streisand poster. We had to transfer the organization's latest takings to the cave under the sea.

Nico drove calmly among the carriages and carts. Ahmed and I looked out of the windows at the half-deserted, sunlit city.

"I'm off in the jeep tomorrow. Jalloun's expecting me in Ghadames. The rifle's ready. I can practice with it for twenty days. They'll leave the police uniforms, pistols, and ID cards at my house here."

"So what shall Nico and I do while you're in Ghadames?" Ahmed asked.

"Stay here. Keep the MANK business going. Do the minimum possible, just enough so you can still be seen as active."

"Your brother could call from Rome."

"I'll call him from Ghadames. I'll say I'm in Tripoli."

"What if your father or Mohammed asks for you?"

"Dad won't call me. If it's Mohammed, you can say I'm home or out fishing, whatever you like. But be careful not to say a word to Karim."

"And the money?" Nico asked.

"The advance is in my cellar. Two hundred and fifty thousand pounds changed into four hundred thousand dollars. I'm taking it to Italy, Ahmed. No one there will exchange Libyan pounds."

Ahmed was surprised. "Italy?"

"I don't care about being here anymore. As soon as this business is over, I'm going to empty my box and take the money to Italy."

"Me too!" said Nico immediately.

At the port, we had to put the cash in waterproof bags before loading them onto the motorboat. The back of the van was boiling hot, plastered with nudes from *Playboy*. Nico's mattress for his prostitutes was rolled up in a corner.

"How are we going to divide Jalloun's money?" Ahmed asked.

"In three, aren't we?" Nico replied.

Ahmed looked at me. "What about Karim?"

"What the hell has Karim got to do with it?" Nico protested.

"My brother's in Cairo, taking care of our business there. The only business we have left, so it seems."

Nico gave him a shove and sent him banging into the metal partition.

Ahmed drew a knife from his back pocket. The throw was lightning swift and accurately aimed. The point embedded itself deeply between a Playmate's tits a few fractions of an inch from Nico's terrified face.

No one said anything for a few seconds. I knew I had to be the one to speak.

I went over to the knife, pulled it out of the van wall and, holding it by the point, handed it back to Ahmed.

"If I see that knife out among us again, Ahmed, I'll kill you."

I said it with absolute calm. We both knew I wasn't joking.

Then I addressed Nico.

"We divide it up four ways, as always."

We went out to the rock. Nico stayed at the helm so that the strong current wouldn't carry the boat away, while Ahmed and I went down in scuba gear to put the money, scrupulously divided into four parts, into the boxes underwater.

# MONDAY, JULY 20, 1970

Mohammed Al Bakri was worried. He was sitting next to Ingegnere Balistreri in his Excelsior suite, watching the flood of American and Japanese tourists walking along the Via Veneto in the sultry heat. He was leaving for Tripoli that evening. He had to make sure that, the following day, Gaddafi would proceed according to plan.

"It's good that Jalloun persuaded them, Ingegnere. Mike's been in Ghadames about twenty days now, practicing with his rifle."

Balistreri gave a bitter smile.

"My son's best talent. Shooting. From doves to lions and now human beings. How much money did Jalloun offer him?"

Mohammed shook his head.

"It's not the money that affects Mike's feelings."

*He's not taken after you, Ingegnere. Unfortunately, he's taken after that madwoman, Italia.*

Balistreri studied his trusted old handyman. He had grown up alongside him. Mohammed knew him better than anyone else in the world. In the end, they shared a common beginning.

*Poverty, hunger, filth, feeling humiliated in front of the wealthy. We know all of this.*

"You'll have to break the tie between Mike and Ahmed, Mohammed. That's the decisive link. I'll see to the rest."

Mohammed was deep in thought.

"I'll try, Ingegnere. Sons still obey their fathers in the families that follow the rules of our religion. I'll speak to Ahmed."

Balistreri nodded. Emilio Busi and Don Eugenio, his brothers, and their friends had to know nothing about this business.

*If they did, he would lose all credibility. And Mike would be dead.*

# TUESDAY, JULY 21, 1970

woke at dawn in a hut made of wood and palm leaves in the Ghadames oasis. The sun rose pale in the desert, but the temperature rapidly rose to over one hundred degrees. There were only a few white houses, a well, a lot of palm trees, Bedouins, and camels. The ideal place for target practice.

I had trained for twenty days. Running, gymnastics, shooting. The rifle was the one I had requested. The old Carcano short rifle, Model 91/38 that took 6.5 x 52mm round-nosed cartridges and had a 4x magnification scope. In a shot from high to low, and less than a hundred yards, this type of rifle had already shown it could function well: it was the weapon Lee Harvey Oswald had used to shoot John F. Kennedy from a distance of eighty-eight yards. The sixth-floor apartment that Jalloun had found for me was closer than that: Gaddafi would be on the castle walls, no farther than seventy-five yards away.

And, every day, I thought about Laura. I pictured her studying in Cairo. She was probably seeing Karim.

Jalloun came to say hello. But he looked worried.

"Are you sure about Ahmed, Mike?"

"Of course, I am, General. Everything's fine. What's up?"

"Because Ahmed's a Muslim, like me, Mike. Faithful to his family, much more than you Christians are. So watch out."

"I will. Were you able to get me that number in Cairo?"

He held out a slip of paper, which I took and put in my pocket.

"No distractions, Mike. First Gaddafi, then the rest. Can I count on you?"

"I have practiced General. Do you think I could miss him?"

"No, Mike, as long as you pull the trigger. There is news coming from Tripoli that will interest you."

He switched on the radio. The only channel here was Radio Libya, and I listened to the announcer's monotonous voice. He was reading out the text of one of Colonel Gaddafi's new decrees.

In Article 1: restitution of all Italian-owned property to the Libyan people and, given the damages of colonialism, without compensation, followed by the expulsion of the Italian community. Within thirty days, Italian nationals must present themselves to the Libyan authorities with a declaration of assets, which they will renounce in writing and then leave for Italy with no more than an exit visa. Their personal safety is guaranteed as part of these conditions.

The Bedouins started to come outdoors, getting together in small knots and then larger groups, crying out for joy and shouting in the air.

*Mamma, Granddad, here we are. This is what it's come down to. But I'll shoot him like a dog.*

Jalloun stared at me.

"Do you still have doubts, Michele?"

I said nothing. He knew money really meant nothing to me. And he knew that as much as I hated Gaddafi I was not a cold-blooded murderer. My silence to his question worried him even more. He nodded.

"I will convince you, Michele. Have a nice trip back to Tripoli."

# FRIDAY, AUGUST 14, 1970

After Ghadames, I spent twenty more days at home in Garden City, alone with my thoughts and the air conditioning, waiting for the phone to ring. General Jalloun was to pass on the date of Gaddafi's speech in Piazza Castello.

Every day, I went over and over the assassination plan. I thought about Laura, my mother, Nadia. Alberto called me nearly every day, wanting to know how I was and when I would be coming to Rome. I told him that it would take me a while to get all the right documents together.

In fact, it was Mohammed who was taking care of our final departure from Tripoli, made easy because Dad had already sold all of his property.

My only radar on the outside world were Ahmed and Nico, who came by every evening. Tripoli was both blazing in excitement and dazed and stupefied: the Libyans euphoric, the Italians depressed. The confiscation related to all personal property, real estate, financial and nonfinancial assets. It included household furniture, even down to the mattresses and sheets: everything these poor people had earned in a lifetime of work.

Nico was the first to arrive that day, precisely at lunchtime. He was alone.

"I'm worried, Mike."

"You mean scared?"

Nico shook his head.

"We haven't seen Karim for a month. Ahmed comes here, but he never says a word. Do you still trust them?"

It was a worry I shared. But, in my mind, Ahmed and Karim were two separate issues.

*Ahmed looks after his friends and would risk his life for them. As long as he considers them friends.*

But, out of prudence, I had to check it out. Meanwhile, in order to distract Nico from his dark thoughts, I agreed to go out with him.

Tripoli was a morgue. We drove around in the van with the MANK sign and the Barbra Streisand poster in a specter of a city. The temperature was over 110 degrees, and there were Italians out in the burning sun. I saw families with their cardboard suitcases and trunks at the port entrance waiting for their turn to depart, while they were jeered at and mocked by Arab teenagers.

In order to have permission to leave the country, the Italians had to camp on the pavement at night outside the Office of Alien Property on Shara Omar Al Mukhtar near the Fairgrounds in order to declare themselves of no property and obtain an inventory of the property and possessions they were leaving behind, all in the hope of getting compensation in their Italian homeland.

· · · ·

When Ahmed came over after supper, we sat down in the living room, as we usually did. I had prepared a test of his loyalty.

"Can you come up with an escape plan for Nico and me, Ahmed? If anything goes wrong, we'll need to flee to Italy."

Ahmed was smoking in silence.

"There's only two ways of escape if things go wrong, Mike. Across the desert by car or over the sea by motorboat."

"Well, can you see to it, Ahmed? Mull it over and come up with a plan."

"Of course," Nico said, "we have to get our money before any escape."

At that moment, the telephone rang. It was Alberto.

"We've just arrived at the Waddan, Mike. I didn't tell you before, but we wanted to surprise you for your birthday, and Dad had to put his signature on a few papers about what we still have in Tripoli."

I was happy to see my brother. But not my father. Not when I had to be ready to assassinate Gaddafi at any moment. I knew from Jalloun that the Colonel would be speaking after sunset. A birthday supper was completely out of the question.

"Can we see each other for lunch tomorrow, Alberto?"

"No, Mike. Tomorrow we're all leaving at dawn to see the tuna fishing at Misurata."

This annual spectacle—the *tonnara*—had been a passion of mine since childhood, just like lions had. But this was hardly the right moment.

"But this is August, Alberto. It's too late for the tuna to be leaving and too early for them to be coming back."

"The season's more staggered this year, Mike. The nets are full. And you've always loved it."

"But it's boiling hot, Alberto."

"Dad had Mohammed arranged it all for your birthday. Don't disappoint him, Mike, please."

*Don't disappoint your father, Mike. Like you always have done.*

I heard the receiver being taken from his hand, and then my father was on the line.

"Mike, the tuna have arrived a month late this year—the nets are full. We leave at dawn; bring your friends from MANK. We're going to celebrate your birthday!"

*A lovely, happy family outing, just like the good old days.*

Alberto was speaking in good faith. He had no inkling that our father might have done anything wrong. He wanted to bring us together and take me back to Rome. I didn't want to disappoint him. And, when all was said and done, it was a way of passing the time before I took Gaddafi out. And it was better to have something to do during the day rather than in the evening.

"All right, Dad. Will you come pick us up?"

"Of course, Mike. Tomorrow at four."

I put the receiver down and spelled out the program of events. Ahmed looked pale.

"What's wrong, Ahmed? Out with it."

"Nothing, Mike. It's just that it doesn't seem like the right thing to . . ."

A few minutes later, the telephone rang again. This time, it was General Jalloun. His voice was excited and hurried.

"The event is set for tomorrow evening at seven. You know the address. The tripod stand is already in place. And in order to make sure you don't change your mind, I have sent you a birthday gift. One of my men has just dropped an envelope in your mailbox."

The conversation was over. I switched on the radio. The announcer was broadcasting the news of an important public meeting on the following day, August 15, in Piazza Castello, at seven in the evening. The Supreme Leader Colonel Muammar Gaddafi was going to address the people.

I made a quick calculation. The tuna cull would last until four in the afternoon. We would be back in Tripoli at six.

It was actually better like this. Keeping away from the city during the day, reducing the tension. And keeping Ahmed and Nico with me at all times, up to the hour of assassination. This way they could have no doubts, no second thoughts. It could work out well.

Ahmed and Nico always kept a change of clothes at my place, so they decided to stay overnight. The atmosphere was calm. While I listened to Leonard Cohen in my room, Nico watched *Perry Mason* on the TV and Ahmed made notes in the kitchen.

. . . .

*We don't really look like three killers ready to spring into action.*

After a while, Ahmed came to my door.

"I've been thinking about your escape plan, should anything go wrong."

Nico and I went to join him in the kitchen.

"If things go badly, you need to escape immediately, tomorrow night, using the most powerful motorboat that MANK has."

"Where should we leave from?" asked Nico.

"Let's go out now and get everything ready. We go to the port, take the inflatable and the motorboat and anchor them near the Waddan."

"And then?" Nico asked.

"Immediately after you shoot him, whichever way it goes, we come back here. After dark Nico will go to the Esso station and get some jerry cans of gasoline, as much as you need to get to Lampedusa."

"Can't we do that now?" I asked.

Ahmed shook his head.

"Dangerous. The motorboat will be there unattended the whole day but that's not a problem. Unless someone notices too many cans of gasoline. Nico can do that tomorrow, we'll have plenty of time. We'll leave at two in the morning, when the fishing boats go out."

"But we have to get our money," Nico reminded us.

"Sure. We'll stop on our way and pick up the money from the cave. Then I'll come back to the beach in the inflatable and you'll continue on to Lampedusa in the motorboat."

We went out and, in less than an hour, we anchored the fast motorboat and the inflatable in front of the Waddan. We were back home before midnight.

It was an excellent plan, as it always was when Ahmed was involved. But I had a very different plan. Kill Gaddafi, celebrate my twentieth birthday in a Tripoli liberated from Gaddafi. With the girl I loved. I had no intention of fleeing to Italy.

. . . .

As soon as Ahmed and Nico had gone to bed, I took out General Jalloun's slip of paper. On it was a Cairo telephone number.

Although it was night, Laura answered at the first ring.

"It's me, Mike."

Silence.

"Tomorrow night, I may have to leave for Italy. But, first, I want to see you."

Another, longer silence. Then the calm voice I knew so well.

"I'll be on the afternoon flight, Mike. We'll meet up at my house."

"Your house?"

"My parents are in New York. At eight, OK?"

*No, Laura, at that time I have another appointment.*

"Too early. Would nine be okay?"

"Yes, see you then. Ciao."

I then walked out to the mailbox to get General Jalloun's gift. I found a simple brown envelope. I tore it open. There was only a black-and-white picture inside. Midnight had just passed. The day of my twentieth birthday had just started with an extraordinary gift.

. . . .

Everyone had left when General Jalloun walked out of his small office in Ghadames. It was cool and dusty in the middle of that damned desert hundreds of miles away from Tripoli. But it wouldn't be for long. The picture he had sent Michele Balistreri would make sure he would shoot down Colonel Gaddafi, his friends would take over, and he would return triumphantly to Tripoli.

He was almost at his jeep when the young man stood in front of him in the darkness.

"Ahmed, what the hell are you doing here?" he said angrily.

But then, in the dim light of the moon, he saw the cut ear and anger turned to fear.

"Karim," he murmured, terrified.

"Quiet, General. It's over."

"What the fuck is over, Karim?"

"Life, General. Your life."

The knife was already deep in his stomach, turning and turning. Karim Al Bakri left him there in the sand, vomiting and suffocating by his own blood.

# SATURDAY, AUGUST 15, 1970

Dad and Alberto came to pick us up at four in the morning in a Land Rover driven by Mohammed.

The greeting with Alberto was very warm. We had left each other on bad terms last time. And it was all because of me. Yes, I could trust Alberto.

But not my father. He had changed; he was still handsome, but he looked older. His graying temples, shorter hair and trimmed mustache, and pale complexion made him look more refined, perhaps more suited to his new social role in Italy.

"Happy birthday, Mike."

He made no move to put his arms around me or kiss me. At least he was sparing me that.

"Do we really have to go on this trip to Misurata, Dad?"

"I believe it'll be the last one for many years, Mike. Since you were a child, you always liked seeing the fish caught and killed."

"Yes, well, I'm a big boy now. Seeing a tuna's blood doesn't give me a buzz anymore. And it's August now—it's far too late."

"The tuna nets are full, Mike. We'll have a splendid time. And we'll have a good memory of the country before we leave."

*Of course we will, Dad. Who cares if it's the country where Mamma died . . .*

I slept for the whole journey as we drove through the deep silence of the night. I woke at dawn, two hours later, as we were coming into Misurata's harbor, where the fishing boats were returning. The city, with its white houses, was still asleep.

Everything was ready for the *tonnara*. Eight galleys of twenty yards in length with twenty or so people to each, then the boat of the *Rais*, the head of the *tonnara*. The line of boats set off.

I was in a boat with my father, Mohammed, Alberto, Ahmed, Nico, and a score of Libyan fishermen. I fell asleep again on the slow voyage out to the nets, partly because I hadn't slept the night before, partly owing to the tension, and partly because I didn't want to talk to anyone. No one at all.

We arrived at the nets at eight thirty. The boats dispersed around the so-called death chamber, the net where the fish were killed.

"Do you want to go into the *Rais*'s boat?" my father asked me.

It was a treat I had asked for so many times as a child, and he had always said no.

*Too dangerous, Mike. Too much blood.*

Now, though, according to my father, I was ready for it.

The *Rais* was the oldest fisherman in Misurata, an imposing aged man with a huge beard. He took me aboard his vessel without objection. Perhaps because I was the son of the man who owned everything.

. . . .

The "death chamber" net was the fullest I'd ever seen it. Dad was right again. At least three hundred tuna weighing between four and six hundred pounds were frantically swimming around and around, bouncing off the sides of the nets, blind with fear.

We took our boat into the center while the other galleys closed up around us, one next to the other along the four sides of the net, each side about thirty yards long. Everything was ready.

Then, at a sign from the *Rais*, the propitiatory songs began—the *salaams*—and the men began to haul up the nets. This was the moment that excited me most and had done so since I was a child. It was when the tuna understood their fate. Each one of those large brutes tried to stay far away from the boats and the surface by flipping their weaker brethren toward the butchery with a flick of their tail.

Then began the slow hauling up of the nets by arm and by hoist. The victims fought madly among themselves as they rose to their deaths, the water boiling from that fierce primordial struggle, while the first tuna, the ones that were most tired, were caught by the long-poled hooks, thrown onboard, hooked again by hand, taken by their two fins, and flung into the bottom of the boat in a pool of their own blood. And there the fish died, looking their murderers in the eye.

Below me, in the center of the square, the strongest was fighting to keep a safe distance.

"*Kullu quais?*" the *Rais* asked me, seeing my face suddenly turn white as a sheet. He thought that I was frightened of the beasts, these huge fish that twisted their tails, surfaced, jumped, and sank down into the blood.

But that was not what had made me lose color. It was the body I saw in the bloody water, tossed about by the fish.

When they finally managed to gaff the corpse and drag it onboard the boat where my father and friends were, I already knew who it was. I knew it even before my eyes met my father's icy gaze and the troubled ones of Ahmed and Nico, before even seeing General Jalloun's swollen and tortured face.

*Do you understand now, Mike? You'll end up the same way.*

Mohammed called the Misurata police and spoke to the young commander. He seemed very much at ease.

The police took Jalloun's body away and allowed us to set off back to Tripoli without asking a single question. As if the general were nothing more than another tuna.

The Land Rover was speeding along the asphalt ribbon in a heat that was more suffocating than that of the day before. We were sealed inside with the air conditioning on full blast. Mohammed was driving, my father sitting next to him. The four of us were sitting behind: Alberto, Ahmed, Nico, and myself. We sat in absolute silence. There was no need for words. The message had been clear.

*We know everything. This is your last chance to call it off, Mike. Otherwise, you see how we punish traitors.*

But the real traitors were the ones I had around me in the vehicle. The two adults certainly were. I could trust Alberto and Nico implicitly, but then there was Ahmed. He was my oldest friend, the one who had twice saved my life, first in a putrid Cairo alleyway and then on La Moneta's cliffs.

*But can I trust you still? Are we still blood brothers in the sand?*

As the Land Rover was hurrying toward Tripoli, I made my decision. I knew it was crazy, but there was only one way to get to the truth about Ahmed and our friendship.

*I'm not going to call off the plan, my friend. You're coming with me to Piazza Castello to assassinate Gaddafi.*

. . . .

We arrived in Garden City at around six that evening and pulled up outside the apartment.

"Okay, boys," my father said, "let's not ruin Mike's birthday. Have a good nap, and we'll see each other later at the Waddan for dinner and a celebration."

I looked at my father. He assumed that I had given up on the assassination attempt.

"No, Dad, we're too tired. Can we have dinner later, when it's less hot? Say, about ten?"

I looked at Ahmed and Nico. They both were keeping their eyes lowered.

*Fear or betrayal?*

My father stared at me for some time.

*Well, so much the worse for you, my son.*

Then he gave a shrug.

"As you like, Mike. You're old enough now to make up your mind about what to do and what not to do."

. . . .

We were now ready, having gone over the plan one last time. Nico had raised a mass of objections, all legitimate, because he was scared. The principal one was that, with Jalloun dead, there was no one to pay us.

"We're not doing it for the money, Nico. We're doing it for us, for your mother and my mother, for those twenty thousand poor people who were robbed of everything by Gaddafi."

And for that gift from General Jalloun.

Ahmed kept silent. He raised no objection. Said not a word.

All three of us dressed in the uniforms Jalloun had provided. We left at seven and headed off among the crowd for Piazza Castello. Once we got to the address Jalloun had given us, we made our last arrangements.

"Okay, Nico, you stay here in the piazza and, from now on, don't let anyone come into the building. Say it's for reasons of security. Ahmed, you come up with me and stay on the landing outside and keep watch on the stairs."

They were both extremely pale but made no objections.

• • • •

Salvatore Balistreri was with Mohammed Al Bakri in the Waddan suite.

"Are you happy with it, Mohammed?"

The Libyan nodded. Others would perhaps have preferred to take the opportunity of this lunacy to put a definitive end to the problem of Mike Balistreri, but he had known the boy from the moment of his birth. And he was different from the other Italian boys, with his sense of honor and loyalty, which were quite unusual. Certainly, he was violent, dangerous, and stubborn. But he was also generous and had taken his son Ahmed as his best friend when he could have chosen anyone in Tripoli. He did not like to break such a true and deep bond, even less to have the boy killed.

Of course, Michele Balistreri was a problem and a risk. But a manageable one. This solution was the right one. There had been enough deaths in their families.

• • • •

Ahmed and I went up the stairs. I was watching him, looking for any sign of hesitation or nerves. Nothing. Ahmed was as ice-cold as ever.

Using the keys Jalloun had given me, I went into the apartment while Ahmed stayed outside on the landing. I found the rifle and ammunition hidden in a leather bag under the sofa, as arranged. It was already fitted with the scope. The tripod rest I had asked for had been placed eleven inches from the chosen window, on a side table with a heavy marble top. Through the half-closed shutters I had a perfect view of the platform.

Gaddafi was to speak for ten minutes, starting at eight. The platform was lit by four huge floodlights and stood twenty yards lower than the window I was to shoot from and at a distance of seventy yards. Exactly what I had practiced for during those twenty days at Ghadames.

I had to hit him with the first shot. There would be no time to reload. I set the rifle firmly on the rest and began to adjust the scope without opening the window.

I opened the shutters a little more and allowed the barrel to swivel on the rest. Then, I calmly set the sights for the point nearest the microphone, where Gaddafi's head would be, and had it in the crosshairs. I was ready.

Gaddafi appeared in his uniform, surrounded by his bodyguards. I put my eye to the telescopic sight but had no time to focus. There was a whistling sound, then one of the floodlights behind Gaddafi exploded into fragments, leaving the platform in the dark.

The crowd let out an "*ohhh*" of disappointment, but I knew this was not a short circuit. It had been a shot. Gaddafi's bodyguards knew as well and immediately bundled him away to safety. And Ahmed knew, too. He was banging furiously on the door.

I left everything there, the rifle and the rest, and got out of the apartment. I locked the door and we raced down the stairs. Nico was waiting for us outside the main entrance, pale and trembling among the terrified, fleeing crowd, his dark eyebrows knitted in fear.

· · · ·

Mohammed telephoned Balistreri immediately. He was in his suite in the Waddan.

"Everything's fine. It all went ahead as planned, Ingegnere."

"And Mike?"

Mohammed wondered if the concern in his former boss's voice as he uttered his son's name was more out of fear for the boy's safety or more for their business affairs. He knew Ingegnere Balistreri like the back of his hand but, on this particular point, could never figure him out.

"He's all right, Ingegnere. Safe and sound."

"Well done, Mohammed, an excellent job. Thank you."

They ended the call.

Salvatore Balistreri was happy. Gaddafi had welcomed Mohammed's idea of arranging a bogus assassination attempt that he could attribute to the opposition, discrediting them in the eyes of the West. Naturally, the colonel did not know that a real attempt had been planned and thwarted and that its perpetrator was Michele Balistreri.

Now his "son gone wrong" had his back to the wall. All he could do now was escape.

We left Piazza Castello, quickly crossed Piazza Italia, and turned into Shara Istiklal. We walked hastily but without running, mingling with the crowd up until the cathedral square and from there to Garden City. We reached my house at eight twenty without having encountered any problems.

Nico and Ahmed threw themselves onto the armchairs in the living room. Nico was exhausted and agitated; he started to ramble, his *s* sounds lisping once again.

"*Santa Madonna*, they'll find us. We must get away immediately."

I looked at Ahmed. He was impassive, cold, and rational as usual.

"I think we should keep to the original escape plan," he said.

I knew there was now little choice. I would have to get out of Libya and convince Laura to come with me. What I was enjoying right then was the last breathing space that my enemies were allowing me.

*A birthday dinner, congratulations, and then either you get out or Gaddafi's police will arrest you.*

"We'll go to Italy by motorboat tonight, Nico. After dinner with my father. Now, get some rest, the two of you."

"I have to go to the Esso station and get the gasoline for the boat," Nico reminded us.

"It's still not dark enough," said Ahmed. "You can do that after the dinner, Nico."

I went to the bathroom upstairs. I took off the police uniform and the holster with its pistol and took a quick shower. Then I put on a sweater and jeans and went into the living room.

"I've some urgent business. We'll meet up with my father at the Waddan at ten."

I gave no explanation. It was obvious I had no intention of giving one. Nico tried to ask where I was going and pointed out the risk I was running by going out, but Ahmed asked no questions and said nothing at all.

.....

It was a warm evening, with a full moon shining in a sky dotted with stars. I passed by King Idris's old palace and took the Adrian Pelt coastal road into the inner city rather than the cathedral square route. There were plenty of police around, but none showed any sign of frenetically searching for Gaddafi's would-be assassin.

*Because Gaddafi knows there was no real attempt on his life.*

I arrived at the Hunt family's villa a quarter of an hour early for my meeting with Laura. There was an old Fiat 124 in the driveway in front of the garden and a light on in the living room.

I stayed outside, hidden around a corner. Karim came out five minutes later, got into the Fiat, and drove off. I didn't even know he was in Tripoli. To my knowledge he was in Cairo, attending our business.

*But that time is over, Mike. The MANK is dissolved. The brotherhood of blood and sand is over. And Laura has betrayed me, like many others have.*

I walked across the garden. I had flung Marlene Hunt into the mud there. And, there, Laura had started to understand who I really was. Now she would know me even better.

She opened the door as soon as I rang the bell. The last time I had seen her in that doorway, she had stood there incredulous as I dragged her mother around in the rain.

"Come in, Mike. The radio announced that there's been an attempt on Gaddafi's life."

She didn't wish me happy birthday, because she knew it couldn't be a happy birthday. She seemed neither angry nor resentful with me, just sad. And it was that resolute calm that confirmed for me that a definitive decision had already been made—without me.

"I want the truth, Laura."

*The truth about who you really are.*

There was a violence in my words, more perhaps than in the ones she had heard me say to her mother as I pushed her into the mud. Laura said nothing. I saw only sadness and compassion in her eyes. It was that compassion, after I had seen Karim leaving the house, that had made me start to lose control. And brought the memory of the worst day of my life.

"You were there on La Moneta that afternoon. Tell me it was my father, Laura. Then I can kill him, and you and I can leave here and live happily together for the rest of our lives."

I saw a tear trickle down her cheek. It was a tear for me, not for her. For that boy she had known many years ago and who had chosen to die, like Kirk Douglas, with an empty pistol in hand.

"Your father's got nothing to do with it, Mike, and your mother killed herself. Why won't you forgive yourself?"

All of a sudden, she hugged me. I was immediately aware that, in that unexpected gesture, an inevitable one for her, there was something different, because there was no longer any joy in the way that Laura was holding me.

*There's no future anymore.*

Laura was grabbing onto the boy she had stupidly believed in but with whom she had decided she couldn't live.

The thought suddenly struck me hard: this was the last time I would be seeing Laura Hunt. These were our last minutes together. Our last encounter. It could become a beautiful memory. One that would make my future easier. But that's not what I wanted. There was too much anger in me not to destroy that memory as well.

"I don't believe you. You're lying. Just as you were dishonest about us. How long have you been sleeping with Karim?"

Her arms fell by her sides in a gesture of surrender and resignation. I could now read what was in her eyes, and I knew she was saying good-bye against her own wishes. I moved toward her, and she instinctively stood back. And that step back was more than I could take.

I threw myself on her like I had done with her mother, except she hadn't provoked me. Nor did she bite me or spit as I lifted her skirt. She didn't incite me to tie her up as I ripped off her underpants. She didn't whisper to me to fuck her harder as I penetrated her.

Even in that moment Laura was still somehow with me, spread out on the floor under me, neither encouraging nor stopping me, her head buried in my shoulder so as not to look me in the eyes, her hands placed lightly on my arms without trying to scratch or push me away. She let me be, even as I was raping her.

And after it was over she remained on the floor, motionless, half naked, and silent, as I got dressed. She made no complaint, nor did she curse me. Neither of us had anything to say. It had all been said.

I didn't turn to take a last look at her as I left. That was the only image of her I wanted to take away with me.

· · · ·

The Waddan was only a few hundred yards from the Hunts' house.

They were waiting for me outside. Nico was nervous and fretting; Ahmed, absolutely calm.

"What do you want to do, Mike?" Ahmed asked me.

"Let's eat with my father, and then we'll go back to my place and change for the trip. It looks as if we have all the time in the world. There don't seem to be any police around."

Nico wasn't happy.

"Who cares about eating, Mike? Let's go right now. All we have to do is get our money from the cave and leave this country."

Ahmed pointed to the sea.

"Everything's ready. The motorboat, the inflatable; Nico just has to take the cans of gasoline to get to Lampedusa. We can leave right after, if you like."

*No, Ahmed. That's your plan, not mine. I want to look you all in the face during this dinner. Before I leave, I'll know all those who betrayed me. And settle this now and forever.*

"No, guys. My father could get angry and start suspecting things. Let's stick to the original plan. The fishing boats leave at two in the morning, and we'll slip out among them. After the dinner I'll go with Nico to the Esso station to fetch the cans of gasoline."

. . . .

Dad had ordered the usual table out on the terrace overlooking the sea. The one where, as kids, with my grandfather and mother, we used to eat *pizza napolitana* while the orchestra played "Volare" and "Magic Moments."

They were all there, friends and enemies, to celebrate my birthday: Dad, Don Eugenio, Emilio Busi, Mohammed, Alberto. Then there were Ahmed and Nico. Perhaps I could count on these two. Perhaps not. Anyway, I knew how to settle that doubt.

*There's plenty of time.*

Only Karim was missing but, officially, he was in Cairo, looking after our affairs—except for the fact I had seen him leaving Laura Hunt's house an hour earlier.

Supper was uneventful, the atmosphere absolutely normal, relaxed. A family get-together with old friends; not too happy and noisy, because it was still less than a year since my mother's death. The black mourning button on Ingegnere Balistreri's blue linen jacket was still there to remind us.

But in sixteen days' time, it would be a year, and Dad would calmly take it off.

*And, once the mourning was over, I bet that Marlene Hunt will go to live with him.*

Dad, Busi, and Don Eugenio monopolized the conversation. They talked about the Libyan situation, General Jalloun's tragic end, and the attempt on Gaddafi's life.

"Probably the two incidents are connected," said Busi, blowing out a cloud of smoke.

"I'm sure they are," Don Eugenio agreed.

"They'll be looking for Jalloun's accomplices," Mohammed added.

I looked at my father. He stared back at me.

"You know that someone tried to shoot Gaddafi, don't you?" he asked me.

He was provoking me. He wanted to be sure I was leaving.

"No," I said, looking at Ahmed and Nico, who were studying the food on their plates.

"You've not heard? But the radio's been speaking of nothing else for at least three hours!"

"I know. But they didn't shoot at Gaddafi. They shot at one of the floodlights."

The looks of my traitors were interesting.

*This kid isn't that stupid, after all.*

But it was only Ahmed and Nico who really interested me.

Sitting opposite me with his eyes lowered, Ahmed was staring at his plate as if the pieces of grouper were the most interesting things in the world, while Nico, on the other hand, was staring at me, terrified, his deep dark eyebrows knitted together and his beard as black as pitch.

*Are you crazy, Mike? Do you want to have us shot?*

I winked at him to calm him down. The cake with twenty candles was brought in at midnight. They all sang "Happy Birthday" to me and I blew out the candles. Once the cake had been passed around, along with the spumante, everyone raised his glass for the toast.

"Here's to you, Mike," Dad declared.

I looked at him. I raised my glass as well.

"To Italia and Nadia. May they find justice one day."

There was a moment's hesitation then everyone drank the toast in silence. My father stared at me.

"Something wrong Mike?"

*Yes, Dad, everything is wrong. Since the day I was borne from you.*

"We need to have a few words, Dad. Just the two of us, privately."

He didn't ask why. He led me to his private apartment, overviewing the terrace and the Mediterranean sea. We stood there, silently, watching the calm water on which I would escape from my own country to a foreign country. Thanks to this man who should have loved me. I didn't look at him when I started to speak.

"Okay, Dad. What do you want from me?"

"I want you to be safe, Mike. And that is no longer possible here in Tripoli."

"And what if I don't leave? You'll have me tossed into those tuna nets like General Jalloun? Or else you'll have me captured and shot for the attempt on the life of that criminal Gaddafi you and your friends brought to power?"

"Michele, I have never killed anyone and never would."

"Of course not, not with your own beautifully clean hands. So what about General Jalloun?"

He shrugged his shoulders.

"Jalloun was a traitor to Libya's new regime. He was plotting to get rid of Gaddafi. Anyway, I didn't kill him."

"Naturally, it was your man Mohammed Al Bakri who saw to that. But he didn't see to Nadia; he could never have done that. So tell me who did?"

My father shook his head.

"Mike, believe me, you don't know what you're talking about."

But I clearly remembered the sound of that engine behind the MANK van while we kids where driving in the thick *ghibli* to Tripoli that terrible morning. And General Jalloun had said that my father and Don Eugenio were in that van.

"You were behind our van while we were getting back to the city before they closed the road."

He feigned the effort of trying to remember. Or it really was an effort, as if he were looking for some detail that time had buried.

"That's true. After the barber, I gave Don Eugenio a lift. He had to confess Countess Occhini, not far from our villas. After Don Eugenio heard the countess's confession, we drove back to Tripoli. We found ourselves behind your van. Up until the market, when you slowed down and Farid got out of the back of the van. We turned off for the Waddan."

I could no longer contain myself. I was tired of this pack of lies.

"Farid was at the market when I went to pick up the bait, Dad. Therefore, I'm afraid you're lying."

"I'm not lying Mike. That's the truth. Your van slowed down and Farid jumped out the back."

I was outraged by his lies.

"I don't believe you. You and your friends killed Nadia. Like you did my mother."

I had no time to dodge the slap. It was so sudden it took me by surprise. I had touched his one truly exposed nerve. My father then made a decision that he should have made many years ago.

"I want you to leave Libya immediately, Michele. I don't want to see or hear from you again in Italy. You're no longer any son of mine."

I nodded.

"I never was."

I handed him the snapshot I'd just received from General Jalloun. My father took it between the tip of his thumb and forefinger, keeping it at some distance.

*But no distance can save you from this, Dad.*

It was a sharp photo, in black-and-white, taken outside the Grand Hotel in Abano Terme. Two men were smiling and shaking hands. One of them had the folded newspaper *Corriere della Sera* in his pocket, showing the date—August 28, 1969—three days before the coup d'état that would oust the Libyan monarchy.

The first man was my father. The other man was younger and, at the time, entirely unknown. Now he was known throughout the whole world as Colonel Muammar Gaddafi.

Dad stared at the photograph. In his eyes, where I had thought I would finally see a glimpse of fear, I felt there was only a hint of regret.

*How much has that photo cost you, Dad? A wife, a son? But money is no substitute for love.*

He knew that picture on any Italian newspaper would mean the end of any of his future business in Italy and perhaps even jail. He could have taken the photo or torn it to pieces. Instead he handed it back to me. He even seemed relieved. Perhaps he'd always imagined that settling accounts with his son would eventually come.

"What do you want me to do?" he asked me.

*We only had one thing in common, you and I, Dad. The inability to live together under the same roof.*

"This time, it's you who has to leave, Dad. You are expelled definitively, not from Libya but from Italy. In the name of my mother, my grandfather, and those poor twenty thousand Italian souls that Gaddafi is kicking out. Like Jesus, you can assume all the guilt of sixty million Italian traitors on your shoulders. Forever."

Then I looked at him one last time. Clark Gable, the man who could sell ice to the Eskimos.

"Such a shame, Dad," I whispered in exhaustion.

Unexpectedly, he smiled. Over the years, I'd glimpsed many things in his eyes as he watched me grow: love, hope, surprise, concern, disillusion, anger. But I'd never seen the pain that I saw now.

"It's my fault, Michele. Don't give it another thought. I'll do as you wish."

My grandfather's last words ringing in my ears.

*A father has the right to look after his son and the right to make mistakes in doing it. A son has the right to protect himself and a duty to understand his father, sooner or later.*

Now it was time to go. But I knew the reckoning was not over yet.

*I have settled with Laura and my father. But there are still my three best friends.*

# SATURDAY NIGHT–SUNDAY MORNING, AUGUST 15–16

We walked back to Garden City a little after midnight.

We had two hours before we had to make a move. I sent Ahmed and Nico upstairs to rest for a while.

I was in a state. I hadn't slept for twenty-four hours, and it hadn't been an easy day. But I had plenty to do other than sleep.

My swimming trunks, denim cut-offs, white T-shirt, and boat shoes were already in a bag. They were the only clothes I was taking with me, the ones I was going to wear for my arrival in Italy.

Also in the bag were the Nietzsche book, the handkerchief with Nadia's blood on it, the photo of me, and the Leonard Cohen cassette. The keys for the lock in the submarine cave where in the plastic box under my bed. I checked they were still there, where I had left them before going to see Laura. I would take them later.

The three uniforms and the guns in holsters were on the sofa in the living room. They would be useful for making it from the house to the beach. No one would stop us if we were dressed as policemen.

One thing was still missing, and it was the most important. I decided to do it while looking myself in the face. I took Nico and

Ahmed's pistols and went to the mirror in the bathroom. And I did what I had to do.

Finally, I gave a last look at Laura's photo opposite my bed.

*The photo of how I'll never be. Your mother killed herself. Forgive yourself.*

But Karim had left her house. My mother didn't kill herself. And she was just as she appeared in the photo.

*A whore. Just like her mother.*

I left the photograph there on the wall, along with all my dreams. I went to call Nico and we drove in the MANK van on the road to Sidi El Masri through a sleeping and deserted city. We didn't speak at all. Nico most likely out of fear, me because I was thinking about the recent conversation with my father and the conversation I had with General Jalloun.

*Farid and Salim knew the black woman found in the cesspit in 1962. When your MANK van slowed down in front of the market the morning Nadia was killed, Farid slipped out from the back of the van.*

"Why did you slow down, Nico?"

He looked at me, surprised.

"I haven't slowed down at all, Mike."

"Not now, Nico. The morning Nadia was killed. You were driving this van. Why did you slow down when we got in front of the market?"

"For Christ's sake, Mike. You wanted to get off, the place was packed, visibility down to zero because of the *ghibli*. What are you talking about?"

Sure, I didn't know what I was talking about. We arrived at the Esso station, Nico filled several five-gallon cans stamped Esso with gasloline, and we loaded them on the MANK van.

Then we quickly drove back to my apartment in Garden City. Everything was quiet. We woke up Ahmed. Silently we put on the uniforms and the belts with the holsters and guns. Nico had his bag, with a few clothes for the night crossing. I took mine and the keys for the lock in the submarine cave, and we left.

We encountered no one on the streets. In ten minutes, we were at the beach. It was two in the morning. Exactly as planned by Ahmed.

We parked the MANK van on the small beach. Ahmed's inflatable was in the water, two yards from the shore. The motorboat was anchored farther out. It took us less than fifteen minutes to transport all the gasoline cans from the van on the inflatable.

"The tank in the motorboat's full," said Ahmed. "Nico can transfer the can in the inflatable onto the motorboat while we dive for the money."

He took us with the inflatable to the motorboat anchored at the port exit. Nico and I climbed into the motorboat and waved to Ahmed.

"See you at the rock."

I switched on the navigation lights while Nico raised the anchor and started the engine. I checked the water, the gas, the wetsuits, and the compressed-air tanks. Everything was there. We departed with an easy motion, the radio playing Arabic music. But I could see that Nico was visibly stressed and worried and was singing to himself in an effort to keep calm.

We got to the rock in half an hour. Ahmed was already there and was taking off his uniform to put on the wetsuit. When we drew alongside him, he tied a rope from the inflatable to the bollard on the motorboat's bows.

Despite the calm sea, the current was always stronger at the rock, and it was pulling us out to sea. Nico let the anchor down and switched off the engine.

I got ready in silence. I took the uniform off, placed the gun and holster on top of it, put on the wetsuit and the air tanks.

Apart from the moon, the only light was the one on the bows. We all knew that these minutes would be the last ones we had together for a long time, perhaps forever. But none of us wanted to speak. We had already said everything that had to be said. What remained was what we did not want to reveal to one another.

The blood brotherhood in the sand hadn't lasted. The MANK organization was dead.

While Nico began to transfer the cans of gasoline from the inflatable to the motorboat, Ahmed and I dived into the water. We descended evenly, following the heavy chain that Nico had fixed to a bollard and dropped to the seafloor.

It was as if neither of us wanted to reach the end of that chain.

*All we have together is that money. Nothing else.*

The fish near the large rock were watching us, motionless. I let them swim in front of me as we entered the cave.

The steel cable was lying loose, the lock open. The four boxes had disappeared.

We looked each other in the eye for a single second. We both knew. *One of us won't live to see this night out.*

I swam as quickly as possible; Ahmed was a few yards behind me. I reached the chain and began the ascent. Karim had already taken the money. But that wasn't all. Nico and I were about to end up like Salim and the Egyptian soldiers. So I had no choice: either die now or die every day from here on out, tortured by bloody nightmares.

I get to the surface next to the motorboat. I tear off my mask and mouthpiece and unhitch the tanks, which sink to the bottom. I hurriedly climb the motorboat ladder.

Nico's on the inflatable, moving the last gas can. He stares at me, stupefied.

"Get out, Nico! Get into the motorboat!" I scream.

"What going on?" he replies, looking at me stupidly.

Ahmed emerges from the water. It takes him a while to climb the inflatable's ladder, as he's still wearing the tanks.

Nico looks at him, stunned. "So where are the boxes with the money?"

I yell even louder at him.

"Get in the motorboat, Nico! Right now!"

With his scuba knife, Ahmed cuts the rope tying the two vessels together.

Nico stares at him. "Where's my fucking money?"

The inflatable starts to veer away, pulled quickly by the current.

Ahmed grips his knife but Nico draws his pistol and shoots at him. One, two, three shots. But obviously nothing happens. I loaded their pistols with blanks earlier, not knowing for sure which of the two had given me away.

Ahmed moves toward Nico, clutching the knife.

The motorboat's about twenty yards from the inflatable. I start the engine.

"Jump into the water, Nico!" I shout, as Ahmed draws close with the knife.

But Nico acts as if he's paralyzed. He stares stupidly at his pistol, murmuring, *"Shit, shit,"* his lisp reappearing.

I halt the motorboat five yards from the inflatable. Ahmed has the pistol in his left hand, the knife in his right.

"Leave now, Mike! Turn that boat around and get back to your own country. Libya doesn't want you anymore."

"Or you'll kill us, right?"

Ahmed stretches out his left arm toward me and points the gun at my chest.

"That's right, Mike. First you, then Nico."

I pick up my own gun. It's too late now for words.

I meet his gaze as he starts to fire at me. One, two, three shots.

In the moon's feeble light, I see his eyes looking surprised, then scared, when he realizes the roles have been reversed. This time, he's the Kirk Douglas character with the unloaded gun. And I'm Rock Hudson with the loaded one . . .

Ahmed throws the gun away and lunges at Nico with the knife.

*The duels fought in the sun in front of the villas. The slit throats of Salim and three Egyptian soldiers. His arm that saved me on La Moneta's cliff face. And that slap when he said that I'd gone crazy because of my relationship with Laura.*

Perhaps the end had begun with that slap. It was then that I was ejected from his circle of close friends, the ones he protected. And, with him, there were no half measures.

*Either you were close friends or mortal enemies.*

The first bullet makes him twist around on himself and fall to his knees. He grips onto the inflatable's rail, trying to draw himself up.

At last, Nico jumps in the water and starts swimming to the motorboat. As he climbs the ladder, Ahmed manages to get to his feet and, staggering, starts the outboard motor.

I fire the second shot level with his heart. Ahmed puts his hands to his breast, collapses over the railing and drops into the water.

I put the engine in high gear and steer toward the inflatable at top speed. I sail straight over it, crushing it. Then I stop twenty yards away.

Nico and I watch Ahmed's body sinking down under the weight of the air tanks. In a moment, he disappears underwater.

I stay there a few minutes in silence—to contemplate the smooth, dark surface that's swallowed up my best friend and the line of lights along the Adrian Pelt coastal road where I forced myself on Laura Hunt.

Then I tossed the gun into the sea, although I knew it would take much more than that to forget. We turned our backs on Africa and pointed the bows toward Italy.

. . . .

Neither of us spoke a single word for hours, while I was driving the motorboat on the flat sea in the darkness of the night. Nico was sitting near me, just one yard away. But it was as if he was far away.

Thoughts were coming into my mind, thoughts I wanted to discard, but it wasn't possible.

*They knew each other. Farid and Salim knew the black woman whose body was found in the cesspit. I had inadvertently told Nadia about the fact they were black. That triggered some memory in her. She had seen Farid and Salim with a black woman. She was a naïve little girl, she made the big mistake of going to them and asking. Quite a sufficient reason for those two animals to kill her. But how could Farid get in the MANK van without Nico knowing? How could he get in the back of the van with Nico and my brother from the market to Sidi el Masri, kill Nadia while they were having breakfast, and get back in the van with all of us as we headed to the fish market? Unless the owner of the van knew.*

And then there was *m*.

The gasoline cans were all around us. Suddenly a wave in the sea, probably the result of a large boat somewhere in the darkness. One of the cans fell, it was no longer in vertical position, lying down horizontal on the floor of the boat. And there was *m*. The Esso *E*, rotated by 90 degrees.

My mother had taken those notes for herself. But she knew they could one day fall in my hands and didn't want me to see through them. Because she knew Mike, her younger son, was so similar to Uncle Toni.

"Why, Nico?"

Those two words in the middle of the dark night could have meant anything. But under the dim light of the moon Nico's face went terribly pale, as though he had been reading my thoughts.

"Mike . . ."

"Why, Nico?" I repeated. "Why did you help those two animals kill Nadia?"

He slowly stood up, shaken. And moved slightly away from me.

"Mike, can't we just forget about it?"

"No, Nico. Not me. You know me well enough by now, don't you?"

"Farid and Salim would have killed her anyway. She knew something terrible they had done years before."

"I know that. The two bodies in the cesspit. But why did you help them by letting Farid in the back of the van?"

"She was just a little Arab bitch, Mike. First time I put a hand on her she should have been grateful for my attention. Instead she threatened to tell Ahmed. She even showed me her middle finger and told me to fuck off. Farid knew about all this and asked me to help by taking him from the fish market to Sidi El Masri."

"So when you parked the van on the back of the villas and went for breakfast in my house with Alberto, he got off and went to take Nadia."

"Yes. He shoved her into the back of the van. The sand was kicking up and visibility was down to zero. That's where he raped and killed her. Then he dressed himself in her clothes and went back to the shepherd's barracks, where someone could see and testify that Nadia was still alive at nine and Jamaal was with her."

I listened to all the incredibly well-planned monstrosity and although I knew it was all true, I couldn't see Farid and Salim planning something so complex.

"Whose plan was this, Nico?"

He shook his head.

"I don't know. Farid and Salim presented the plan to me. It was a very good plan."

"You asked Farid to cut off that finger for you, didn't you, Nico? As a trophy for your revenge on a sixteen-year-old girl? Was that part of our brotherhood? Is that what you learned from me all these years?"

He moved away from me, toward the back of the boat. I caught a glimpse of the shine of his knife in his hand. His eyes were full fear and rage.

"What the fuck did I learn from you, Mike? That you can kill your best friends, like you just did with Ahmed? Or that you could turn your back on me that day when you left me alone with Don Eugenio after class? It's your ass he wanted to caress, Mike, not mine. Except that you were untouchable, and I was shit."

On that point only, Nico was right. I had always felt that beyond his admiration for me there was a resentment. I had betrayed him and he had now betrayed me.

So now we were equal.

*Should I leave it at that? Disembark him in Lampedusa and let him go? Forget about what he did to Nadia in exchange for the day I left him with that horrible priest in my place?*

It could have been a reasonable solution for any young man who had just turned twenty and was looking ahead to an entirely new life. But not for me. My life was over. Those final twenty-four hours in Libya were the closing of all accounts with those who betrayed me.

Nico didn't stand a chance. My knife was much faster and his throat was cut from side to side even before he could raise his knife.

I dumped his body in the middle of the Mediterranean.

*Laura, Father, Ahmed, Nico. Only one traitor is left.*

# THURSDAY, JULY 28, 2011

## ZAWIYA, LIBYA

In the preceding days, troops had arrived from Tripoli to restore order for the local tribal leader. They passed through Gargaresh and then Zanzur, with its oasis of palms by the sea, its huge electric power station hit by NATO's bombing, and its chaotic clusters of shops and workshops among the trees, interspersed with potholes and dusty squares where barefoot little boys played with a rag ball among old abandoned vehicles.

The coastal road that was usually extremely busy with trucks transporting gas from the large refinery in Zawiya to Tripoli was full of craters caused by the bombing and now used only by jeeps armed with machine guns. Two tanks stood at the city entrance, but they were now of no use because the rebels were all dead, or taken prisoner, or had escaped. But they served to remind the defenseless survivors—women, children, and the elderly—that nothing would be as it had been before and nothing would be forgiven Zawiya's inhabitants. They no longer had any civil rights, neither in the present nor the future. Their houses could be swept away at any moment on the orders of an officer of the forces loyal to Gaddafi.

Leading up to the school was a twin row of twelve poplars, a leftover from the time of the Italian colonists' agricultural estates. The school façade was now riddled with bullet holes, with not a window left intact. At the center of the courtyard in front of the school was a smoking crater, which had blackened and withered the trees with its flames. The smell of gas and burning flesh hung heavily on the air.

Tied to every poplar with a noose around his neck was a man, a Berber—or *Amazigh*, as they prefer to be called. They were the first to rise up in rebellion after February 17, the beginning of the revolution against Colonel Gaddafi. Five personnel carriers of loyalist guards armed with Kalashnikovs were pointing the weapons at the dozens of desperate women, children, and elderly, who were wives, sons, daughters, and parents of the men waiting to be hanged.

The single officer in charge was European, possibly a Bulgarian or German, and, like many in the Colonel's pay, a mercenary.

Beaten, with several fractured limbs, the Berber captives were standing with nooses around their necks, their feet on chairs taken from the school. The women were crying and weeping, but no one dared run to their son or husband to offer any comfort. Standing around them in a circle was a crowd of silent terrified city dwellers, quietly glad they had chosen not to join the Berber rebellion, even though they hated Gaddafi as much as the rebels, possibly even more.

The *ghibli* was blowing sand in from the desert. Together with the flies, it stuck to the prisoners' bloody wounds and mingled with the relatives' tears. The scene resembled an Old Master painting on a yellowish canvas, the stationary figures waiting for someone to make a decision.

A black armor-plated SUV, a Mercedes M1 with dark windows, drove up and parked in the middle of the road, effectively blocking it. As the driver switched off the engine, the Bulgarian or German officer rushed to open the rear door.

The man who got out was an Arab, about sixty years old, wellpreserved despite the deep vertical lines that furrowed his face below the prominent cheekbones. He was wearing civilian dress, a dark suit over a white shirt, but no tie; his hair was still thick, a little crinkled and gray, his eyes hidden by dark glasses. Part of one ear was missing, as if it had been cleanly sliced off.

*"Which one's the leader?"* he asked the European officer in English, pointing to the rebels strung up to the poplars.

The European mercenary had met many cold-blooded murderers in Uganda, Darfur, and Kosovo: sadists who took pleasure in killing. But the man with the severed ear was different. This man really scared him, because he showed no hate or pleasure in his killing. There was no emotion at all. It was simply a job. And it was the job of terror.

The mercenary pointed to the nearest poplar. The man strung up there was standing on one leg, the other unnaturally twisted at an angle of thirty degrees; he was covered in blood, his fingers and thumbs broken by hammer blows.

In the absolute stillness, the man with the severed ear went up to him.

"In much pain?" he asked in Arabic.

The Berber made an enormous effort to gather enough saliva to spit in the man's face. But he only succeeded in producing a thin stream of spit and blood that trickled from his broken teeth down his chin. The man with the severed ear turned to the women.

"Which if you is the wife of this poor man? Come here immediately and wipe his mouth."

"No!" the Berber managed to rasp.

But the man with the severed ear had already had time to notice the woman who had started to come forward. She was completely covered in a barracan, with only one eye showing.

"I'll give your wife to my soldiers later," he told the Berber.

He said it nonchalantly but in a loud voice, so that everyone could hear. He knew that blind obedience could only be obtained by terror.

Suddenly a boy of about thirteen emerged from behind his mother, wielding a knife, and flung himself at the man. His eyes were the same as the man strung up on the poplar.

With lightning speed, the man with the severed ear took out his pistol and shot the boy in the middle of his stomach, careful not to hit any vital organ. It was necessary for everyone to see the boy bleed and think he could still be saved as they watched him slowly die.

*"Bring him here,"* he ordered the European, pointing to the boy's body lying in the dust.

The officer hid his look of disgust. He had killed children, but only in the heat of battle. What he was feeling right now was not pleasant. However, he was being paid very handsomely and this was part of what he was being paid to do.

It took two soldiers to drag the boy's body under the tree where his horrified father was and four to hold still the mother who was screaming and gesticulating like someone possessed.

For the man with the severed ear the boy meant nothing as a human being. He would bleed to death in a few minutes and die like the thousands who perished in Africa every day through hunger and disease. He felt absolutely nothing, neither pity nor hate. It was simply the most convincing way of making his audience there understand something fundamental.

From behind his dark glasses he let his eyes run over the silent crowd, the people of Zawiya. These people were his immediate audience, the ones he had to convince. These were the imbeciles that despicable opportunists, extremists, and terrorists had persuaded they could fight for freedom. He would make no speeches to counter this and tell them they were wrong and that if Gaddafi fell they would only find themselves in worse hands. Words mattered only in a democracy, which—thanks to the Colonel—was not the case in Libya. All he had to do was to convince these idiots never to try it again, not even to think about it, independent of who was right or wrong. And he knew men well enough to know that there was only one way of doing this.

Are you willing to pay this price to try and liberate yourselves from us? Then look what happens.

He turned to the crowd. He pointed to the rebels strung up in the blackened poplars.

"These men are terrorists, friends of Bin Laden. The man Colonel Gaddafi protects you from."

The crowd hung their heads, many nodding in agreement, gripped by silent terror. The man with the severed ear took out a knife with a saw blade, four inches long.

"Take a look, rebel swine!" he said to the boy's father, whose eyes were now streaming tears. Tears wasted on the man below. Dribbling blood, he gave a desperate cry as the man with the severed ear cut the boy's throat in one swift movement, then kicked away the chair on which the rebel father was teetering on one foot.

There's not much use in killing terrorists themselves, perhaps a little more in killing the relatives. For true terror, it's the innocent you have to kill.

He turned to the European officer, speaking again in a loud voice, leveling a finger at the rebels strung up to the trees.

"Hang the lot of them! Then kill their children and rape and kill the mothers. And as for the fathers of these terrorists, cut off their hands, but leave them alive. I want everyone to know what happens to traitors and to those who do not report them."

He got into his Mercedes and ordered the driver to depart. As they were driving toward Tripoli, he gave not a second's thought to the traitors. They were of no interest to him whatsoever, merely dead meat in a war declared when other traitors, like the opportunist Americans, British, and French, had joined forces with the cowardly Italians and began a move against Gaddafi and against a regime that had bankrolled their consumerist populations for years and sometimes even their pathetic heads of government.

He leaned back in his seat and closed his eyes behind the dark glasses. He was thinking about that day in the *ghibli*'s windblown sand when four boys cut their wrists and mingled their blood. There was himself, his brother, Nico Gerace, and, naturally, Mike Balistreri. Almost fifty years had passed. But it was not long enough to forget.

Perhaps along with this war it's time to settle all accounts with old friends and old enemies. And put an end to any kind of a dream.

# FRIDAY, JULY 29, 2011

## ROME

"Rome's like a really beautiful women. Better when she's just woken up rather than for the rest of the day."

Every morning, just before six thirty, Michele Balistreri took the same route on foot from his apartment down to his office in the city's historic center. From the silent greenery of the Oppian Hill he walked down to the Coliseum and from there passed along the most beautiful three hundred yards in the world between the Imperial Forums and the remains of the greatest empire history had ever seen. Within half an hour its extraordinary beauty would be invaded, trodden over and exploited.

Things had been better until to a few years ago, but now with the economic crisis, only a part of Rome could enjoy the summer as it used to do. The people who were feeling the squeeze were staying at home and on weekends packing onto the free communal beaches of nearby Ostia. While the truly rich were already on their yachts on Capri, Elba, and Portofino, as has always been the case.

If the morning stroll gave rise to a good many grim thoughts, it also helped Balestreri exercise the knee that was growing ever more painful since it had been fractured five years earlier by a bullet.

Unless he had to, that precious hour between dawn and the incoming tide of vehicles was the only time Balistreri went out and about. He now lived his life indoors. He tried to stay within the confines of home and office. His life had gradually become devoid of all stimulus and any opportunity for conversation, socializing, and new interests.

Nothing attracted him anymore. The rare poker games with friends and the very few lovers had become duties rather than pleasures. In the office he limited his contacts to his closest colleagues and then only to discuss work, which was now based on intercepts and DNA, things that held no interest for him.

As much as he was at peace, he was also bored. He'd slowly emptied himself of everything, but for him this was no Zen exercise or effort of the will. It was the natural consequence of the scorched earth he'd created around his relations with people over the course of many years.

At a quarter to seven he went into the tiny bar under his office block, drawn there by his habitual weakness, a well-made espresso. Inside were the usual clients at that time of the day: the barista, the street cleaner, the fruit vendor, the high school teacher. Simple folk he would willingly have spoken to years ago, but now he only gave them a fleeting greeting. They knew who he was, though, the head of Rome's Homicide Squad.

Balestreri didn't enter the conversation, but listened in silence. These people were normal people, *the people*. They weren't capable of stealing, not even the sweets by the cash desk in a crowded bar. They made up the greater majority, that of the losers, the ones who only interested the powerful in that they possessed the right to vote.

Now there was the crisis: recession, stagnation, depression. Every day educated ministers, bureaucrats from European offices, banks, and treasury departments—all of them overpaid, with too many roles and even conflicts of interest—explained to these poor souls that they had to understand and accept these imposed sacrifices for the good of the country and of their children. It wasn't very clear if this meant the children of the listeners or those of the privileged speakers.

In any case, the people, ordinary folk, were able to go about complaining because no one would put them behind bars for what they said, and for that they had democracy to thank.

As he thought all these things, there was no anger in Balistreri or even resignation. The people who complained were likeable people, but he couldn't feel solidarity with them anymore. He was tired of listening to Italians complaining about the very politicians they themselves had elected.

The news on the bar radio began to talk about Libya and the war there that was now bogged down with no end in sight. Hundreds of millions of euros spent as the NATO allies attacked and Gaddafi fought back to defend his regime. And this was to say nothing of the human cost, especially among defenseless civilians. Looking at the bottom of his cup, Balistreri listened to the reports of a massacre at Zawiya, nothing less than complete extermination of the women, children, and elderly there.

He paid the bill a little more quickly than usual, nodded to everyone, and left. If there was one thing he really didn't want to hear about it, it was the war between Colonel Gaddafi, the rebels, and NATO.

The Colonel is evil, but those who decided to bomb him in order to obtain extra oil contracts are no better.

At seven Balistreri went through the grand entrance into the Flying Squad offices situated in the small square. He smiled back at the obsequious salute from the duty guard. Balistreri had glared daggers at the man until he addressed him as Commissario and not Head of Homicide or even worse, Deputy Assistant Police Chief.

Gasping a little for breath, because of too many cigarettes, the pain in his knee, and the little physical exercise he did, he went on foot up the three flights of marble staircase to the half-deserted offices of Section III. Only the switchboard operators were in the open-plan office, almost all the others would arrive between seven and eight o'clock.

Balistreri had held on to his old office, even though he was entitled to a more spacious, modern one with a little reception room attached. But he was used to this ancient, peeling space. And it wasn't for its view of the Coliseum and the Roman Forum, given that he almost always kept the shutters closed, as much as this room was a reflection of his state of mind, his ever more stooping shape, the white hair on his temples, the rest turning gray. The wood of the door and desk were made of cheap honeycomb core, the springs had gone in the old armchairs, the black leather sofa was worn and cracked, the architectural friezes on the little balcony covered in dust and grime.

In appearance, that office was a little like the myth that dogs end up looking like their owners. Had it been all modern and sparkling clean, it wouldn't have been his. For him it was something between a den and a tomb. The hunt for the Invisible Man five years earlier had been the last investigation he'd led out in the field, the last time he'd fired his gun, the last time he'd been overwhelmed by feelings.

Since then, all that remained for him was the apartment and the office—sealed against the world by double-glazing and shutters—impregnated with cigarette smoke and the smell of whiskey and where each day, as soon as signing pointless paperwork was over, he could stretch out on the old leather sofa to listen to the music of Leonard Cohen, shutting out—at least for a little while—both the infinite beauty and inescapable sleaze of his city and his country.

On that sofa he could let time pass as if he were on a boat in the sunshine, letting himself be carried by the current to the mouth of a placid river.

He wanted to change the world, but the world changed him. It was all a dream, only a dream.

# FRIDAY, JULY 29, 2011

## TRIPOLI

Linda Nardi was lying stretched out fully clothed on the bed in her room in the Hotel Rixos. She had switched off the lights and opened the windows on the blazing red sunset. Everything was warm and peaceful outside, the palms were still and the *muezzin*'s cry was soft and mournful. The war seemed very far away without the noise of the NATO fighters that passed over in the middle of the night.

She wanted to have a word with Lena, her mother in California, but had called the night before and knew from the terrible cough she had that it was tiring for her mother to stay too long on the phone. She also wanted to talk to her father, but there was no solution to that a problem, seeing as she'd never met him and never even known who he was. At the very least, she wanted to talk to a man who was pleasant and sensible. But at this moment there was none.

At this moment, Linda?

She'd turned forty a few months ago, but there'd been no close connection with men in her life, except for a brief period five years earlier. She thought she'd found that close connection—and the one man in the world *right for her*—when she'd gone to the hospital to pick up Michele Balistreri, who was convalescing from the wounds inflicted on him by the Invisible Man.

They had lived together for months, chatting, having dinner and a glass of wine together, a closeness based not on words but more on what was not said. With Balistreri she had found the right that women have lost.

The right to be ourselves, not what men expect of us.

The two of them had never even exchanged a kiss. That was a door that had remained closed on both sides and she still didn't know why. But after the calm had come the storm. She had emerged from that storm stronger in some areas, but weaker in others. Strength and weakness were the two sides of a skepticism that made her self-sufficient and totally incapable of bowing to the usual customs of courtship.

She pushed the memory of Balistreri aside and tried to concentrate on the job at hand. She was there to report on the civil war. At first it seemed the rebels were going to win, then it was Gaddafi, and now, with NATO's intervention, the war seemed never ending and the outcome still uncertain. News from the battlefronts was contradictory and, whatever the case, terrible. On both sides the war was being fought on the ground by troops that were ever more weary, with ever more scanty means, and among the terror of violence against civilians and the bombs raining down in the name of freedom. The freedom of others to have Libya's oil. She had already filed an article on reports of the mysterious death of General Younis, Gaddafi's former chief lieutenant, who was said to have defected to the rebels but was also accused of being a double agent. Now she had to write something on this dreadful business at Zawiya.

She couldn't wait to get out of Tripoli.

There were only a few hours to wait. At dawn the following day she had a flight to Nairobi, but that evening she still had to deal with the war.

She rose from the bed, ran her hands over her clothes to iron out the creases, but didn't look in the mirror or even dream of putting on lipstick or a little makeup. She knew very well that not taking care of her appearance was a leftover from what the Invisible Man had inflicted on her. But painful memories aren't wiped away by a simple act of will.

She took the elevator down to the lobby and went into the hotel bar. It was a mandatory stop each evening to catch up on the latest war news and gather material for an article. Among her journalist colleagues you could always pick up some nugget that slipped out through too much drink or wanting to brag.

"Miss Nardi?"

Bashir Yared was a Lebanese entrepreneur in construction whom she'd met in Nairobi. He was around fifty, somewhat rough and ready, but always friendly and polite, and always chasing after her.

"What are you doing here in Tripoli, Mr. Yared?"

He made a slight bow and kissed her hand. He was dressed in a smart blue blazer and red tie.

"I'm here on business. And to offer you an apéritif, if you would have one."

As always on these occasions, she immediately wanted to withdraw to her room. Solitude was a gift for her, not a burden. But she didn't want to be rude to a man who was fundamentally kind and so, because she also had to find a lead for an article, she accepted his offer.

They sat down at a table. The bar was noisy but cheerful, full of men, both Arabs and Westerners, who were talking more business than war; that is, the business they could do thanks to the war.

No one here in the Rixos will end up dying. As always, the real fighting's left to other poor souls.

Bashir ordered a nonalcoholic beer and Linda a tonic water. He lit a slim menthol, which Linda refused.

"You don't mind if I smoke, Miss Nardi?"

"No, please do. Only it's a vice I've never . . ."

"I know. It *is* a vice. That's why I promised my daughter I'd give it up. I made a . . . how do you say? . . . a . . . ."

"A vow?"

"Yes. I made it because she's my only daughter and she's turning twenty and getting married. They'll be taking her away from me, so I'm thinking of having another . . ."

He was trying to tell her two things. One was his bafflement that a beautiful forty-year-old had no husband. Also that, even in later life, his spermatozoa were strong enough to procreate.

"She's getting married in a church," he continued. "We're Christians, you see. There'll be three hundred guests."

Linda wondered if Bashir Yared's pride was over the marriage or the number of guests or in his religion, to which he probably attributed a greater level of civilization in his country than the Muslim part.

"Are you here for work, Mr. Yared?"

He looked at her through the spirals of menthol smoke. Everyone in there was smoking.

"Yes, many contracts, Miss Nardi. Wars are manna from heaven for me."

He winked at her, as if his witty remark made them partners.

"And the contract's going ahead for the new hospital in Nairobi?" she asked, as much to pass the time as anything.

He smiled with the air of a man who knows a thing or two.

"Of course, the hospital's going ahead and I have won the subcontract. You double the estimate, win the contract, and then give half the money back. In cash and, naturally, under the counter. Italian rules, Kenyan accounting, a perfect combination . . ."

"But aren't those people building the hospital Swiss Italians from across the border, not Italian nationals?" Linda objected.

Yared gave a shrug, as if the observation was irrelevant.

"Nothing is ever really Swiss, is it, Miss Nardi? Apart from the chocolate, the watches, and the banks. The Ticino consortium is only Swiss on the outside, inside it's run by Italians for Italian interests."

Linda had now been an investigative journalist for many years. She knew very well how the world worked; it was foolish to be shocked and pointless to be indignant. She had earned her living with stories like this, but every so often she still committed the error of getting emotionally involved and believing that her investigations had the power to change things. In reality, there was nothing new in what Bashir Yared was saying and nothing she could do about it either.

Besides, it was common knowledge that this was part of Italy's famous creativity, applied here to balance sheets rather than fashion or the arts. The Italians had become great experts in the art of overbilling, creating slush funds, and in false accounting.

But people aren't interested anymore in stories like these. Mere trifles depenalized in the courts and journalistically irrelevant. But Bashir Yared knows I'm a journalist and wants to make himself appear interesting.

"You don't surprise me, Mr. Yared. Unfortunately, the newspapers don't publish these things anymore. The public's become used to them."

But he was not discouraged.

"Finance for the new hospital is also coming from Italian public money. And part of this money will be quietly returned. But not to the public."

"Nor in Italy?"

The question came out without her really thinking, without any real interest, purely to give him a little satisfaction. Bashir made a face that was even more knowing.

"No, not in Italy, but almost. A state situated in the middle of Rome. And one bank in particular."

Linda showed slightly more interest.

"Would that be the IOR?"

Bashir nodded.

"Yes, the Institute for Religious Operations. 'God's Bank,' isn't that what you call it?"

"Yes, that's what we call it. And how can you be so sure that the kickbacks end up precisely there?"

"Intuition and a clue. The director of the Swiss consortium to build the hospital is an Italian, Gabriele Cascio. He goes to the building site each morning and each evening at seven goes home to his apartment in central Nairobi, then he goes to the Bluebird Club in search of female company."

Linda smiled.

"Nothing strange there, I think . . ."

"Of course, except that on Sundays he leaves two hours earlier and deals with the business of making his dirty money turn into clean money. As you know, here in Africa everyone works on Sundays.

Should we have dinner together, Miss Nardi, and talk further?" asked Bashir hopefully.

The invitation was more an act of old-fashioned gallantry than a real move on her. Some men were happier to spend on dinners, jewelry, and trips. Others preferred a prostitute.

Linda was tired. What she needed was a lead on the Libyan civil war and had no real interest in Yared's story. She decided to use the excuse she used with many men, the one that worked best in not upsetting them. In this case, it also happened to be the truth.

"I have to get my bags ready. I've got an early flight to Nairobi tomorrow."

Bashir smiled and tried to make the invitation more appetizing.

"They say that this Gabriele Cascio used to work for the IOR and was the right-hand man of that Monsignor that comes to Kenya every so often to set up charitable works, the one with that perfect Italian name, Pizza."

For a moment, Linda was taken aback. Monsignor Eugenio Pizza, who liked to be known more familiarly as Don Eugenio, was the most mysterious and talked about man in the Catholic Church. His career through the Vatican's secret chambers was a mystery that time had gradually wrapped in dense fog.

"And how come you know this, Mr. Yared?"

He smiled again.

"I keep myself well informed. I know everyone in Nairobi, as *you* know . . ."

At that moment a Western woman, surrounded by four young men who had all the appearance of the Libyan Secret Service, walked quickly through the bar and the lobby. She had blond hair, beautiful delicate features, and a slim and graceful body. She was well dressed, but not provocatively so. She and the four men were following an Arab man of about sixty, olive complexion, hollow cheeks in a deeply lined face, high cheekbones, his thick hair slightly frizzy and turning gray. A part of his ear was missing, as if it had been cut off very cleanly. They quickly entered an elevator and disappeared.

Bashir Yared was visibly pale.

"Do you know who that woman is?" Linda asked him.

The Lebanese shook his head.

"No, not her. She'll be an escort for . . ."

She stopped him short.

"That Libyan? A competitor of yours?"

"He's not a businessman."

"A friend of Gaddafi?"

Bashir Yared wanted to show off even more, being under the combined effect of several things: Linda's breasts protruding under her tight, buttoned blouse, his empty stomach, and the excitement running through Africa at the time over the revolutions in Tunisia, Egypt, and Libya.

"Have you heard about what happened in Zawiya, Miss Nardi?"

Naturally, she'd heard rumors about the massacre. Indeed, they were more than rumors. It was as if the regime itself wanted to broadcast the fact, not hide it. As always, Bashir Yared was well informed, even in Tripoli.

"Was that man involved?"

"That's what I hear. They say he was the one behind General Younis's death . . ."

Linda tried to get more, but now Yared was frightened and suddenly remembered he had some business to attend to. He gave a slight bow, kissed her hand, and left the bar.

Linda went back to her room and jotted down the notes for her article. A massacre in Zawiya, women raped, old people and children murdered, men mutilated. She was happy to leave. She had had to deal with the Invisible Man, but he was only a *single* killer in a world where life was highly valued.

Here the world's far worse, there are people here for whom life has no value at all.

## ROME

At the end of the day Balistreri was sitting with his leg with the painful knee stretched out under the desk, his foot resting on a humiliating footstool, while he smoked away and signed papers that he no longer bothered to read.

That was the way Italian bureaucracy functioned. From reports of highway infractions to the laws of state, the writer drafted a memo that was incomprehensible to his superiors, who in turn signed it without reading it. If they had bothered to read it, there was nothing in it they could understand anyway.

And Balistreri was happy with that, shuffling papers and having no serious crimes that needed his attention. Although it was less than a year until he could collect his pension, he had retired five years earlier, after the end of the Invisible Man and all that went with it. And all that went with it still came with a name, which surfaced occasionally. Linda. Memories he didn't want to have. But that's why they still persist.

There was a knock on his office door. It was Corvu. He always knocked and had done so for years. Balistreri knew that he did it for fear of embarrassing him if he had found his boss on the sofa instead of at his desk. Two taps, a pause, a third tap. He did it precisely to be recognized and with the mathematical precision that was typical of this little Sardinian, who possessed the best analytic mind in the entire police force.

Balistreri left his paperwork, lit a Gitane, and went to lie down on the black leather sofa with the air of someone who had been lying there all day without doing a stroke of work. Only then did he call out "Come in!"

Corvu entered, well groomed and shaven and even decently dressed, guided by the tastes of his girlfriend, Natalya. A red tie with the gray suit and white shirt was evidently her artistic touch. Embarrassed, Corvu tried not to look at his boss lying on the sofa.

"Nice tie, Corvu, beautiful color."

"Thanks, *dottore*. Red's Natalya's favorite color. She sends you her very best, by the way. And if you'd like to come to lunch on Sunday . . ."

Balistreri was horrified at the thought, even though Corvu was an excellent cook.

The thought of having to make conversation for two hours . . .

"I'd be happy to come. But I promised to take Antonella to the beach . . ."

"Not to worry, that's fine . . ." his deputy mumbled, looking abashed.

Balistreri was immediately sorry. Corvu worshipped him like some old saint, worrying if he lost weight, if he smoked or drank too much, and wasn't happy if he was alone too much. But Antonella was a kind of reassuring guardian spirit: lover, friend, and nurse, when necessary.

Corvu was allowed to think all these things, but never express them openly.

"Could I have a word about Giulia Piccolo, Commissario?"

Balistreri felt a burning in his esophagus, that blasted reflux he had. The name was enough to get all the acid in his stomach going.

Giulia Piccolo was a complex case. She had grown up in small town on the coast near Palermo in an all-male family with a submissive mother. She was six feet of iron muscle and a lesbian. Needing to escape from the small town in Sicily, she had come to Rome and passed the exams to enter the police force, at the same time as Corvu, to whom she was very close.

For Balistreri she had always been both a gift and a punishment. Piccolo's role had been decisive in the success of many investigations, but her physical strength and complete disregard for danger had gotten her into serious trouble. They had gone through the ups and downs together right up to the end of the Invisible Man case.

Five years earlier he'd asked both his deputies to come with him to Homicide. Corvu had accepted without a moment's hesitation, but Giulia Piccolo had declined to be transferred. He'd never asked why. He never asked women for explanations; he considered the words superfluous. From then on, whenever their paths crossed, it was a simple "Good morning" or "Good evening."

Resigned, Balistreri raised himself from the sofa.

"What have you got to say about Piccolo?"

Corvu coughed and cleared his throat.

"Yesterday there was an enormous dustup between Giulia and two of her colleagues. They'd stopped two young girls who were kissing each other in a corner of a Metro station and, according to the guys, it was on the mouth and far too passionately. The girls say the officers insulted them. So after one of the girls told them to fuck off, they started to handcuff them."

Balistreri closed his eyes. He could imagine what came next.

"And Giulia Piccolo happened to be passing by at that very moment?" he asked.

Corvu coughed to hide his embarrassment.

"Giulia maintains that she identified herself immediately, but the other two say she didn't show her ID. Result: one colleague with a broken nose, the other with a fractured rib."

"Witnesses?"

"The two girls say that Giulia was attacked verbally and physically and only acted to defend herself from the two officers."

Balistreri had no difficulty believing this was exactly what happened. But it wouldn't save Piccolo from expulsion. The police force wasn't very understanding when it came to brawling colleagues.

Corvu continued in funereal tones.

"The head of Section II has asked Colombo for Giulia to be dismissed."

Colombo was head of the Flying Squad, the job Balistreri had declined.

"And so, Corvu?"

He knew he was being wicked. He knew very well what Corvu hoped he would do. But in order to be able to do it, he had to convince his deputy that he wouldn't intervene.

"Commissario, Colombo's about to make a decision, I was hoping that . . ."

Balistreri made no effort to reply.

"All right, Corvu, off you go now. And don't bug me anymore about that woman. She's nuts."

Corvu bowed his head.

"Very well, but you might want to reconsider . . . And, anyway, I wanted to remind you that it's late, there's nothing urgent here, I'm coming in tomorrow, so if you want to go somewhere with . . ."

Balistreri's foul look dissuaded him from continuing and sent him quickly on his way.

Balistreri pressed the direct line to Colombo.

"Balistreri! Any good corpses lately?"

The sarcasm irritated him more than the jocular camaraderie. Colombo was a good policeman, but he enjoyed playing the role too much, especially with journalists.

"I'm calling about Giulia Piccolo," said Balistreri, cutting him short.

"Oh dear me, yes, the hot head who's always causing trouble."

"Inspector Piccolo is one of the few real investigators we have in here, Colombo."

"Could be," came the cautious reply. "But you know there's no excuse for what she did."

Balistreri wanted to bring the conversation down to brass tacks.

"In the same way there was no excuse for where your son was when I hauled him out of that little party full of underage kids out of their minds on cocaine."

He could hear Colombo swallow from the other end of the line.

"So what do you suggest, Balistreri?"

"Two months' suspension without pay."

"Three, at the very least," Colombo replied.

"All right. Not a word to anyone that I've said anything. You'll look better then, won't you?"

"But when she comes back on duty you can take her on in Homicide, Balistreri. She's burned her bridges in Section II. No one wants her anymore."

"We'll see," growled Balistreri and replaced the receiver without saying good-bye.

• • • •

Two hours later, Corvu came in beaming.

"Giulia's only got three months' suspension. You spoke to Colombo about her, didn't you?"

Balistreri rose from the sofa and took a step toward Corvu, who moved quickly backward.

"Corvu, if you dare spread it around that I did, I'll send you right back to those goats in Sardinia."

Corvu hid a smile. That's the way Balistreri was. An act of generosity was a sign of weakness. He excused himself and made an even quicker exit.

Alone again, Balistreri casually scanned the daily papers. It was one way to pass the time. In *Il Domani* there was an article from Tripoli by Linda Nardi about the death of General Younis. For some reason, he found the name of Linda Nardi in association with that city deeply disturbing. And it brought to mind all that had happened five years earlier, a love affair that never began, the crazy hunt for the Invisible Man led by Linda Nardi and Giulia Piccolo using any means they could, including ignoring the rules and putting their own lives at risk.

They're like those two boys of so long ago, Mike and Ahmed, who also ignored the rules and scoffed at danger.

The thought of Ahmed Al Bakri, shot and drowned by his best friend, Mike Balistreri, in the early hours of August 16, 1970, was one of the nightmares that had deadened him. He put on Cohen's music and got back to signing useless paperwork.

# SATURDAY, JULY 30, 2011

## NAIROBI

I t was cold when Linda landed at Jomo Kenyatta airport. But she immediately felt happy to be there among the smiling faces in the confusion of Arrivals. The photos of wild animals and incredible land-scapes on the walls, the stalls full of Masai handicrafts and the colorful clothing all made her feel lighter and full of energy.

She passed through the tremendous hellhole of baggage reclaim, where only Westerners raised their voices and protested about the delays. When she managed to get her bag she went out and caught a taxi that immediately slipped into the traffic chaos. As they gradually approached the city center, which was clean and modern, the traffic became less congested and more orderly and the trucks, pickups, and carts gave way to cars.

. . . .

An hour later Linda was in her room in the African Beauty and had no energy to unpack. She was very tired and ready to collapse. But the thought never entered her mind. Orphanages and hospitals in Central

Africa where her real life now. She had become dedicated to them after the Invisible Man's death and the split with Michele Balistreri.

She had neither the time nor the money to stay more than two or three days in Kenya and, besides visiting her beloved orphans, she had decided during the flight there she would investigate what Bashir Yarfed had told her in Tripoli. All things considered, it was worth it. So she took a shower, changed, and went out.

She crossed the gardens of Central Park and went straight to buy a third-hand motorcycle. It was necessary for her to get around quickly.

She then rode easily through the center, all hypermodern skyscrapers, shopping centers, elegant shops, flyovers, and gleaming hotels. But as soon as she was out of it she found herself on another planet.

Nobody bothered about lane discipline, everyone sounded their horns furiously and went through traffic lights at crossroads no matter what the color. Progress was at walking pace, surrounded by crowds of pedestrians who crossed when and where they pleased, dodging this way and that between the cars, trucks, and scooters that were held up by goats that appeared out of nowhere and holes in the road that were more like craters.

Linda crossed the vast city over to the area around the smaller Wilson Airport in Nairobi West and into the shantytowns full of *mitumba* markets. Here the average income was half a dollar a day and the number of HIV sufferers shocking. She pulled up at the orphanage.

· · · ·

As soon as she entered the building, the nuns hugged her and the children all ran up to meet her. If she hadn't found the money, hadn't persuaded the authorities and overseen the work, many of those children would be on the street now and perhaps already dead.

She stayed there for hours, playing with the little ones: she had brought Punch and Judy puppets with her and had the children rolling around with laughter at a performance that overcame all linguistic barriers. She ate supper with the nuns and children, helped to put them to bed, and kissed then one by one as she went past saying good night.

Then she got back on her motorbike and drove back across the city. Other people might have said she traveled *from the hellhole of shantytowns to the paradise of Central Park*. But for Linda it was the exact opposite. Once in her room she threw off her clothes, jumped into bed, and fell into a deep and restorative sleep.

# SUNDAY, JULY 31, 2011

## NAIROBI

Linda spent the whole morning at the orphanage, busy with questions of administration and discussing with the nuns ways to resolve all kinds of problems. She then played with the children, had lunch with them, and set off once again on the bike to Mitumba.

Only there among the *mitumba* markets in the slums and the people with no future, where to win only meant to survive and poverty wasn't a religious choice nor the result of financial collapse; only there did everyday tedium, anger, and cynicism allow for a minimal space in the balance between pointless existence and the inevitability of death.

Among the *mitumba* market slums there were no schools teaching *mors tua vita mea*, "your death means my survival." A pointless concept for people who walked close to death every day since childhood.

She followed the edge of the shantytowns as far as the offices of the Swiss consortium, ELCON, on a construction site surrounded by barbed wire and armed security guards. Beyond the wire were mounds of waste and open drains next to homes made from corrugated iron and cardboard; tangled electric cables dangled from a few wooden poles; and the inevitable goats, chickens, dogs, and skinny cats wandered in and out of the refuse.

Linda settled into a noxious-smelling bar opposite the site. She ordered a coffee every hour and never touched a drop. The cups looked as if they'd hadn't been washed in years. She had a supply of bottled water and bananas in her knapsack.

At five o'clock Gabriele Cascio came out for his customary Sunday visit to the bank, just as Bashir Yared had told her in Tripoli. He was carrying an overnight case chained to his wrist and at his side two armed guards served to keep away evildoers and beggars. They got into a black Toyota pickup and set off.

Linda put on her helmet and followed them at a distance. It was much easier for her to make her way on the bike among that confusion of men, metal, and animals as they headed further west, skirting the shanties around the National Park, then over a reinforced steel bridge covered in mud that spanned a turbid stream full of floating rubbish and excrement. Then they were onto muddy lanes bordered by ditches of stagnant water and banks of stinking rubbish. There were no more goats crossing the roads, just huge rats that Linda tried to avoid. The homes were no longer recognizable as houses, but hovels made of anything recyclable: corrugated iron, cardboard boxes, carpets, tarpaulin. All the children were barefoot. They didn't even have a ball of rags to kick around. But they all smiled at her, just like her orphans.

The pickup cleared the district and in a few minutes came to a small brick building with a neon sign outside that said International Cooperative Bank. Half the letters were unlit, but for a bank neon was held to be more dignified than a painted sign.

It was almost six in the evening and they would soon be closing. Linda decided to risk being seen and went in a couple of minutes after the man she was following. This rundown branch of the International Cooperative Bank was on the ground floor. There were two black Africans at the cash desks and several white clients. She could see Cascio through the drooping Venetian blinds of the only separate office, sitting opposite an African wearing glasses. A peeling sign on the door said MANAGER.

Between the two employees she chose the one who seemed less proficient, a very good-looking young Kenyan. She asked for information about opening an account while stealing looks at what was going on behind the Venetian blinds. She saw Cascio counting out hundred dollar bills and the Kenyan manager recounting them.

This went on for a good while and Linda had no idea what else to ask the cashier, who really was good-looking, probably about thirty. He seemed openly embarrassed, unfamiliar in dealing with white women.

*"Would you like to have a beer?"* Linda asked him in English, without even realizing what she was saying.

The cashier's eyes opened wide.

"I'm sorry?"

He was surprised and looked concerned. He turned to look at the manager's office. Linda smiled at him and pointed to the time. Five minutes to six.

"Just a beer, five minutes. My name's Linda."

He gave her a faint smile, incredulous, a little worried but also flattered.

"Okay, I'm John. John Kiptanu. There's an application form to fill out."

She was amazed at how natural and easy it had been for her to be so brazen. But it wasn't her who was suddenly another person. It was the young man in front of her.

Kiptanu handed her the form, which she pretended to complete so the other cashier wouldn't get suspicious. In the meantime she saw the manager giving Cascio the deposit slips to sign. The Italian tucked his copies into his pants and went quickly out. Linda positioned herself so he had no way of seeing her face.

When she left the bank with the young cashier the sky at sunset was now peach-colored. She had no plan in mind, nor wanted one. John had never been able to have a plan in his whole life, especially with a woman like Linda Nardi.

He looked at the motorbike with a mixture of attraction and fear.

"Is this yours?"

Linda handed him a helmet and helped him fasten it. Then she had him get on behind her and off they went to the center, the only two motorcyclists wearing helmets in the whole of Nairobi. John immediately clung onto her. Linda could feel him trembling as he pressed close to her, out of fear, not desire. So she dropped her speed to that of the cyclists and he began to relax. But that way it would have taken three hours to get back to the center. Linda pulled over, switched off the engine and turned to face him.

"Haven't you been on a motorbike before?" she asked.

John looked back at her, his irises an intense black in the white of the cornea.

"No. Only a bicycle. But I do trust you, Miss."

He looked deeply ashamed, as if this was the clear sign of his indignity on being on a motorcycle behind a beautiful, independently minded white woman.

But I do trust you, Miss.

This was the most beautiful and honest thing a man had ever said to her.

And what Michele Balistreri denied me. Trust.

Linda got back on the bike and told him to put his arms around her, even if he did feel highly embarrassed and uncomfortable, and they set off again.

"*Sorry, Miss,*" he kept saying at every pothole that thrust him against her. As he did so, she could feel his erection pressed up against her spine. With any other man she would have stopped and told him the ride was over. Instead, she simply smiled.

Once back in the center, she parked near the hotel.

"Just a beer and something to eat, okay?"

She pointed to a restaurant where she had often been on her previous trips to Nairobi. John stopped her outside the entrance. He pointed to his sandals and faded jeans.

"I can't go in here. I've no money."

He must have seen many Western television films where successful men offered a girl dinner. But with a salary of seventy dollars a month, John Kiptanu couldn't even allow himself an apéritif in there.

Linda took him inside. The elderly black waiter looked disapprovingly, but after a look from Linda he led them to a table for two with wooden chairs in the shape of giraffes. She ordered beer and roast crocodile meat for both of them.

Between mouthfuls, John stole furtive glances at her.

"How old are you?" Linda asked him.

"I'm not sure. My passport says thirty, but it could be more."

Considering the local habit of registering babies only when they had their first serious illness, it was likely that John was thirty-two or thirty-three, even though he had the body of a twenty-five-year-old and the serious face of a man of forty. He seemed tired, sleepy.

"Are you tired?"

"Yes, I'm sorry. After the bank, I have to sleep, because I have other work at night."

She looked at him in surprise.

"What work is that?"

He studied his hands. This embarrassment in a grown man was so different from the men she knew, who were always so ready to flaunt themselves and their success, that she was afraid this might be some illegal activity.

"From ten to one I sing and play guitar in a nightclub," he said, avoiding her look, as if admitting he were a drug dealer.

All of a sudden Linda was aware of an emotion she hadn't felt for many years. Everything was pulsing faster: her heart, her breathing, her life.

"Do you have a girlfriend, John?"

If a man with dark skin could have blushed, John Kiptanu would have blushed deeply.

"No, no girlfriend."

"But you sleep with girls, right?"

He looked at her in fascination. No one had ever talked to him like this. He was embarrassed, curious, but not gratified as a Western man would have been. And he replied with a sincerity that no Western man would ever have used.

"Well, for the sex, yes, not love."

"And you'd like to have love, a wife and children?" Linda asked.

He stared at her with those black irises in their stark-white corneas.

"I have no money for a wife. And I don't want children."

"Why not?"

The question hung in the air over the abyss that separated their two worlds, their desires, their expectations, even the very value of existence.

"Maybe five or ten years from now I'll be dead from AIDS, you know that? Everyone gets it here, sooner or later."

Linda tried to stop herself, struggling against the words rising in her heart. But those words of his, that smile, that unconditional trust offered in exchange for nothing was pressing on the defenses built up over the years against the hostility, unwelcome advances, and persuasive tricks—great and small—of powerful men attracted to her and her general sense of inadequacy in the face of those male expectations.

She studied the man in front of her. He was wearing the white short-sleeved shirt of a bank employee, its collar worn but clean. This was the half of him that the customers saw above the desk. Below were the torn faded jeans and sandals that were the real John Kiptanu.

He lives in a shantytown and has no future. He works in a bank, plays the guitar, and sings to get by. Anything beyond that would be an impossible dream.

John had to catch the bus to the nightclub where he performed.

"I have to go now, Miss."

"My name's Linda, not Miss."

"Yes, Miss Linda."

"And where do you sing?"

From his wallet he took out a creased business card. He held out his hand, shook hers, made a small bow and smiled.

"Good night, Miss Linda."

As Kiptanu left, Linda parked the bike in the garage of the hotel and walked over to African Heights. Inside it was full of locals and Westerners, tourist couples, businessmen, girls in miniskirts and vertiginous high heels all flocking into the Bluebird Club. Linda sat in an armchair in the lobby from where she could see people entering and exiting the club. She knew that Cascio was inside.

The Italian came out at about ten thirty with an East European blonde. She was tall and slim, elegant with little makeup, wearing black leather pants and a pair of cowboy boots, her long straight hair hanging down to her backside, her fingernails sporting matching black varnish.

Linda was satisfied. It was important to understand what type of woman he liked. With her body and features she could easily take on another woman's looks. It wouldn't be difficult to become the right type for Signor Gabriele Cascio.

Having scoped out Cascio, she took a taxi across the center of town to the hotel where John was performing. The nightclub was overflowing with Westerners, all of them tourists. On stage were not only local girls but also good-looking local men, there to attract the eye of female tourists.

Linda remained standing at the bar, half hidden by a column, sipping a mineral water. John's act came on at midnight. He walked onstage barefoot, wearing skintight black pants and a bare torso, a pirate bandana around his head.

Linda felt a surge of protest and anger as women nudged each other at the sight of his athletic body and perfect face.

It was John's job to take song requests from the women, the numbers chosen by a horrendous bidding process, the winner throwing bills onto the stage. An attendant collected the proceeds, which certainly went largely to the establishment and only a small percentage to John.

. . . .

John's jaw dropped when he found Linda waiting outside the club. They walked off together in silence, and when they arrived at her hotel, he stopped.

"I can't go in here, can I?"

Linda took him by the hand and they went up in the elevator. John looked around the tidy and well-furnished room as if he were lost. Naturally, he had had sex with local girls in the shantytowns on beat-up old mattresses among the huts and garbage. But he had never seen such an elegant bed as the one in this room.

Linda looked out of the window at Central Park. Neither of them knew what to do or say. Then John summoned his courage. From the back pocket of his jeans he pulled out a tattered wallet and handed her a piece of paper and a condom.

"I had a test last week. Still no AIDS. Here's the certificate."

So this was John Kiptanu's proposal for sex: a condom and a certificate. Well, it was worth much more than a thousand dinners.

They kissed and hurriedly undressed. Linda was relieved to find that she felt no embarrassment. She was even more relieved to realize that John was looking into her eyes far more than at her body.

The awkwardness of inexpert lovers soon turned into passionate embraces in the arms of this man who kissed her and looked into her eyes, then caressed her, still looking into her eyes.

Sex with John was different from anything else she had ever experienced. At a certain point with previous lovers, her body became a separate thing, her mind detached from it as she watched how the man tried to please her and she went along with it for the pleasure. During sex her soul seemed to leave her body and only returned when it was all over. But now she could feel her soul fully present, perhaps more excited than her body by the total absence of assumptions and expectations. She felt liberated.

As for John Kiptanu, he had nothing to offer and nothing to ask for. One day he would die from AIDS, reduced to skin and bone in his shanty on the Nairobi outskirts.

*Perhaps on that day I'll be sipping a cocktail in Piazza di Spagna with another man.*

But it was this man without a future that she guided inside her. He lifted himself up above her and gave her such a look of complete adoration it felt as if a boiling liquid were coursing through her arteries and veins and she was losing her virginity for the very first time that day. Her body and her soul were reunited and were melding together in that embrace.

Linda felt joined to this young man by something quite ordinary, but which she had never felt before, the feeling that *this was authentic.*

• • • •

Before he left to go home, John pointed to Linda's still unpacked suitcase.

"Are you leaving?"

Here was a man capable of sensing and noticing a lot.

"Tuesday morning. Tomorrow's my last day here."

There was a sad smile on his face that he lost instantly, probably so as not to upset her.

"If you want, I can come back tomorrow. I think I love you."

No Western man would have said such a thing so suddenly and so openly.

Without thinking about it too much, Linda made a decision. She knew that in some way she had to be honest with John. So she explained that she'd gone into the bank as part of her work, following the man who had come in to see the manager. Kiptanu listened to her story almost as if she were the heroine of an adventurous romance.

They agreed to meet at midnight in the hotel the following night.

# MONDAY, AUGUST 1, 2011

## NAIROBI

Linda spent the whole day at the orphanage, eating an early supper with the nuns and children, then returned to her hotel and dolled herself up to play an exotic *belle de nuit*.

At the Bluebird Club, Cascio noticed her as soon as she entered and sat down at a small table in a booth behind a screen. Tall in six-inch heels, platinum-blond hair with extensions, black leather pants and shoes, and black enameled fingernails, she was dressed for the part.

*Just the kind you like . . .*

Cascio made his appearance a few minutes later. There was some subdued chatter from the other booths and music from the bar, but it felt as if they were alone. Cascio was suntanned, his hair was tinted hair and he wore a blue Armani jacket, white shirt, gray slacks, and suede moccasins.

"Mind if I sit here?" he asked in English.

She replied in Italian, with a slight French accent.

"If you must," she said, sounding bored and almost without looking at him.

This was not the reply of a prostitute in search of a customer. Cascio was doubly surprised.

"You're Italian?"

He used the familiar "tu" form, ignoring the fact that she seemed to show no interest in his presence.

"Half Italian, half French."

"I've never seen you here before. What's your name?"

She continued to ignore him, staring instead at the dance floor, where a flabby American was gyrating with two local Kenyan girls.

"I arrived yesterday. The name's Catherine."

Cascio seemed very interested in her boobs, their generous shape protruding from her buttoned-up white blouse.

"And what are you doing in the Bluebird, Catherine?"

"I'm allowing myself to have a little adventure. I'm married to a man who's too rich to pay attention to me. And I want to stretch my wings a bit."

For a moment he was left speechless. Linda went on, almost surprised at how easily she could play the part.

*We girls all know the part. It's you men who've made us learn it.*

"Every so often I take a trip around the world and find places like this one. And then choose what I want."

The message was clear. Just as it was clear he wasn't the type that Catherine would be looking for.

But he was immediately hooked by the challenge. Cascio usually bought his women, but money wasn't enough in this case.

"And your husband isn't here, I take it?"

*He's an accountant. A prudent man.*

"He's in Paris. I'm here just for tonight. Tomorrow I'm off to the Seychelles."

A dream scenario for the Cascios of this world.

He ordered champagne and lit a cigar. Linda looked around her as if scoping the place for someone more interesting, then decided it was time to give him a helping hand.

"And what are you doing in Kenya?" she asked, as if she couldn't care less what he did.

Cascio had his own vision of the world of women. If you wanted to win them over you had to show them how important you were.

"Business, finance, property. I'm here to see if purchasing the Blue-bird would be a good deal."

She showed a first sign of interest.

"You're a banker?"

Cascio felt that he'd found the right path toward impressing her.

"I worked in a bank in Rome for many years."

She pretended to be very disappointed.

"Oh, what a shame! Bank employees are ever so boring, usually. It's different with bankers."

Cascio hesitated, then decided that it wasn't anything that private. And there was no other way of getting her interest.

"I was a manager in a very special bank, Catherine. Perhaps since you're half Italian, you'll have heard of it: the IOR."

Linda stopping studying the dance floor and turned toward him for the first time.

"Ah, God's Bank, isn't it?"

Cascio gave a satisfied smile.

He's blessing Marcinkus, Sindona, and all the others who contributed to making the name so famous . . . or notorious . . .

His foot brushed against Linda's ankle. Just a slight contact, but enough. She didn't move, but neither did she return the gesture.

"I see you know what that means, Catherine."

She smiled at him.

"What did you say your name was?"

That sudden moment of familiarity caused him to move himself a little closer to her foot under the table.

"Gabriele Cascio."

He was getting cocky now that he had gained her attention. Linda gently moved her ankle away.

"So, you were one of God's bankers, Signor Cascio. Doing business in Kenya must be very boring for you . . . ."

He was undecided. True, he could make things up, but he really had to impress her.

"I'm here for a very important project, hospitals for the poor. With Islamic and Italian funds. I'm the director of a Swiss consortium, ELCON."

She looked disappointed again.

"Oh, the poor people, they're so boring. The IOR was much more interesting!"

By now it was clear to Cascio that it was only the IOR that excited her. While what excited him was the idea of having a woman without having to pay her. Linda studied him: a grown man, who was as uncertain as a little boy, wondering whether he could steal some candy and get away with it.

But look how good the candy is, Gabrielino.

She got up and went to the bar for a cigarette, which she avoided inhaling, and came back to Cascio at the table, giving him plenty of time to appraise what was underneath those black leather pants. So he made a stronger effort.

"Well, the building site I'm looking after is linked in part to the IOR. But this is strictly confidential information."

What a lack of imagination, you're almost telling me the truth . . .

Linda was incredibly relaxed. Cascio's idiotic presumption freed her from any embarrassment; it was all too easy, like drinking a glass of water. Or perhaps it was a side effect of John Kiptanu.

She stretched out her leg under the table and placed the stiletto heel delicately on the fly of his pants. He was so surprised that he spilled champagne down his front.

"You know, Gabriele," said Linda, looking him in the eye as she started to massage the delicate part, "Confidential things excite me. They're a kind of challenge for me. I'll do anything to find out what they are. Anything."

Within five minutes he was fully aroused. When Linda realized from his breathing that he was almost ready to come, she quickly took her foot away.

"I don't want you to stain your clothes, Gabriele. Not here, at least."

He looked at her, his eyes inflamed with desire.

"We could go to my place?" he suggested.

She made a face.

"I told you I'm not a prostitute. But I want to be paid in some way, otherwise there's no fun in it."

"How much do you want?"

"Have you no imagination? I don't want money. My husband's filthy rich."

"So what do you want, then?"

"I want to play. I want to go somewhere exciting."

"All right, I'll get the best suite in the hotel."

*I have to take him to where he keeps his papers in a safe.*

She made an even more sulky face, looking very bored.

"Luxury is part of my everyday life, Gabriele. Can't you give me anything a little different? Somewhere I'd never go without an adventurous man like you?"

She saw the idea slowly making progress in Cascio's mind.

"What about the building site I run in West Nairobi? That's a dangerous place. It's in the outskirts. Ever heard of Mitumba?"

She stared at him with her glorious green eyes.

"And do you have an office there with a desk?"

Cascio had a momentary vision of what they could do on that desk. But the idea of venturing out into the shantytowns was decidedly unattractive. Linda could read it in his eyes, so she had to provoke him.

"You're not afraid, are you?"

Cascio had begun to sweat despite the air conditioning. He shook his head and forced a laugh.

"There's a loaded gun in my car."

"Good. Then buy some more champagne and let's go."

Cascio came away with a bottle and two glasses, and five minutes later they were in his Toyota SUV heading for the construction site. He drove for half an hour with the pistol beside him. The worry of an attack kept him from putting his hand between her thighs. He only relaxed when they reached the site gate, where there were armed guards on duty. They entered and drove a quarter of a mile and parked outside the motor home that served as his office.

They went in and he switched on the light.

"Do sit down, *signora mia.*"

Linda's eyes took in the desk full of papers, then the filing cabinets, lastly a small safe built into the wall. She imagined there had to be one, seeing that Cascio kept a lot of cash there.

"Is that the safe where you keep all your secrets, Gabriele?"

She took off her jacket. Then she pushed all the papers off the desk while he watched her in fascination and excitement.

"We'll need this space in a while. Now give me the bottle."

He passed it to her and she opened it, poured champagne into the two glasses, and offered one to him.

"Let's drink to our secrets!" she said.

He emptied his glass and started to move in close, but she stopped him.

"Oh, Gabriele, don't be so obvious, or I won't feel like it anymore. Let's play a little game. Just use your imagination, come on, it's fun!"

"What do I have to do?"

"We trade secrets. I'll give you one, if you give me one. If you don't have a secret for me, then I won't have one for you."

Linda put her fingers on her blouse and undid a button. Cascio finally caught on. Linda watched him as he made up his mind.

*Of course, you'll try to befuddle me, telling me anything you like, all useless information. But all I need is for you to open that safe.*

"Gabriele, you mentioned that the construction site here's linked to the IOR. But outside there's the nameplate of a Swiss consortium, this ELCON . . ."

Cascio gave a sly smile and poured out more champagne.

"The ELCON consortium's only the first protective shell."

"Protecting what, Gabriele?"

Cascio was wavering, hovering between fear and desire.

"An Islamic trust. I don't know who's behind it. It's someone in Luxembourg linked to some Italians."

Linda knew that the Valium she had slipped into his champagne would soon take effect. She had to get Cascio to open the safe before he fell asleep.

She undid the belt of her pants and the first of the five fly buttons.

"Italians? So what's the IOR got to do with it?" she asked in her most airhead manner.

He was breathing hard, his voice hoarse.

"The Luxembourg trust has an account with the IOR. Now will you take those frigging pants off?"

She smiled at him. Cascio had downed half a bottle of champagne by himself; his eyes were out on stalks and he was staggering a little. She took a step back and gave him a serious look.

"I don't believe you. Only priests are allowed accounts with the IOR. And you're nothing but some weedy little accountant who's not worth my trouble. Show me some proof or take me right back to the Bluebird now."

She saw Cascio's eyes shoot to the safe, then back again. They were bugging out even more now. He grabbed the champagne bottle and finished it off. Linda had only taken a few sips from her glass.

"My head's spinning," Cascio mumbled as he made for the safe. While he punched the code into the lock Linda took a heavy metal binder from a shelf and, as soon as the safe was open, she let it come down heavily on his head. Cascio fell to the floor like a piece of ripe fruit.

In a few minutes she found the memorandum of association signed by a notary for the Swiss consortium ELCON. Headquarters: Lugano. The investment companies forming fifty percent of the consortium were GB Investments (head office: Luxembourg) and Charity Investments (central office: Dubai). Two nuggets of information that were difficult to crack.

Unfortunately there was no trace of the bank accounts relative to the transfer of monies from the International Cooperative Bank of Nairobi. They were probably in another safe in Cascio's home. But there was his secret weapon, the one with which he had probably hoped to take off her pants: a business card with a single name printed on it: *Monsignor Eugenio Pizza*.

Below the name was a handwritten cell phone number with Switzerland's international prefix. Linda jotted it down.

She made a copy of the memorandum, put the original back in the safe and closed it. Cascio wouldn't even remember he'd opened it.

She dragged his body toward the desk. That way he'd think he'd banged his head as he fell down drunk there. She emptied his glass in the washbasin and rinsed it, together with the bottle and the other glass. She then put on her jacket and went out to get help from the guards, who called for a taxi to take her back to her hotel.

During the trip, it began to rain. She thought about that name: Monsignor Eugenio Pizza.

The same one Bashir Yared had mentioned. The gray eminence behind the Vatican's finances or a true benefactor of the world's poor?

Once back in the hotel, Linda had just enough time to take off her *belle de nuit* garb and take a shower. At midnight, John arrived. He had to call from the lobby because they wouldn't let him take the elevator unannounced. She had to explain he was her guest.

When he entered he was soaking wet from the rain, but he had brought two presents. The first was three roses, which were also soaking wet and must have cost him half a month's salary. Linda tried to find a vase to put them in, but there wasn't one. They had to make do with the glass in the bathroom where she kept her toothbrush.

*By morning they'll be dead and gone, just like our love affair.*

John had taken a great risk for the second gift. He had used his own keys to enter the bank when it was closed and had opened the manager's desk.

John handed her photocopies of the deposit and transfer slips filled in by Cascio at the bank. There was a number for an IOR account in Rome but no name for the account holder.

Perhaps Monsignor Eugenio Pizza's business card was the answer to that.

During that night, which was both very long and too short, Linda asked herself several times what was stopping her from giving everything up and staying there instead with John and the orphans.

But choosing to leave and running away aren't the same thing.

# TUESDAY, AUGUST 2, 2011

## ROME

Several different thoughts kept Linda awake during the return flight from Kenya to Rome.

Which was the more important present from John? The copies of the deposit and transfer slips or the rain-soaked roses?

Then there was the IOR account and Monsignor Eugenio Pizza's business card in Gabriele Cascio's safe. Everything could be true and then she would make the headlines with a cracking good article. But there were plenty of obstacles. There were few Italian newspapers that published real investigative journalism. Getting a piece in print depended on who was being investigated, the political climate, and how dangerous the reaction might be.

Mentioning the IOR was like entering a minefield, and Monsignor Eugenio Pizza was a man who really was untouchable. She had thought about this at length, and unfortunately the only way of moving on it was by means of Senator Emilio Busi.

The senator was as exceptional as he was questionable. Exceptional as a politician and a director on boards of directors, but questionable as a man. From the moment his star had begun to rise in the 1970s, he had steadily built up his power base, meticulously buying the public's soul, distributing floods of growing good fortune to everyone: electorate, collaborators, friends, and adversaries, especially the adversaries, so that they never became enemies. The result? People were glad to have dealings with him. They trusted him.

From 1970 onward, Busi's political and business ascent had been as unstoppable as it was exceptional, aided by an initial personal fortune of unclear provenance, created by means of a oil brokerage firm that dealt with gas securities in the Arab states, which he had sold for huge profits when first elected to Parliament.

By the beginning of the 1980s, Busi had been in Parliament for some time and it was said in the Italian Communist Party that he was the true intermediary with the Christian Democrat Party, thanks to his excellent friendships in the Vatican.

. . . .

With the fall of the Berlin Wall, Communism—even in its Italian version—had an identity crisis. And in 1992 the so-called Clean Hands investigation into the "Tangentopoli" culture of bribery and corruption in Italy practically swept away the Christian Democrat Party and the Socialist Party and destroyed the careers of many an entrepreneur and director. But there was nothing on Busi.

With the death of the Christian Democrats, the Left seemed finally destined for power in the 1994 elections and Busi on the brink of great things, a ministry at the very least, if not Speaker of the House.

But just before the election, he put on a tie that matched his shirt and jacket—something he had never done in his life before—and had gone onto the major Italian talk show, where he had never wanted to appear before. There he explained his views: that the destruction of the political parties by the judiciary in the "Clean Hands" investigations would only bring trouble to Italy; and that Communism had clearly shown itself to be a mistake; it went against reality, the claim that everyone could be equal in poverty was only made possible by the use of tanks and the Gulag.

And to be consistent with this, he said, he was withdrawing from political life and would not be running for Parliament again.

This gesture proved to be a real stroke of genius. Against all predictions, the Left lost the 1994 elections to Silvio Berlusconi's brand-new party, and in a very short time it was the Center Right that came looking for him.

From then on, as the fortunes of the Center Rights and Center Lefts rose and fell, Emilio Busi was the shadow minister for infrastructure in governments of whatever stripe.

Then, for his great merit and innumerable services to the state, he was nominated a senator for life, reentering Parliament in triumph and now, in his seventies, his word was law, even for prime ministers, particularly in the field of energy and industry.

Linda had known him personally for less than six months, since a foreign journalist friend of hers had passed on rumors about a business deal regarding contracts for military aircraft commissioned from Busi's Gruppo Italia by several foreign countries. It was hinted that they had been obtained by bribes and other unorthodox means.

When Linda had contacted Busi's personal assistant for an interview about those contracts won by mysterious means, she had expected to be refused.

Instead, he had received her in his private chamber in the Senate. After that interview, as polite as it was inconclusive, a discreet courtship had followed, subtle but insistent, which had enabled her to understand the man that much better. He was probably not looking to have sex with her, but to bring an important investigative journalist in the circle of his close friends.

Behind the fascination of Busi's intelligence, Linda was aware of a vision of the world with which she could never agree.

The slow crumbling of the conscience in favor of self-interest, resulting in the corruption of the soul.

# WEDNESDAY, AUGUST 3, 2011

## ROME

Linda woke up after a night of intense dreaming: the lascivious face of Gabriele Cascio, the sweet one of John Kiptanu, Monsignor Eugenio Pizza's business card found in Cascio's safe, together with ELCON's memorandum of association. For a while she wandered around her apartment not knowing what to do. The peace of her tiny penthouse facing St. Peter's cupola had been violated by some dreadful scenes: Michele Balistreri's slapping her and tearing off her clothes, the Invisible Man lying in a pool of blood. But it was still a place she had no desire to run away from. And the same with her memories.

She made a strong espresso from her old Moka, took a shower, then sat down on the terrace and called the number for the secretary of Gruppo Italia's chairman.

The call was answered by a young male voice that passed her on to Beatrice Armellini, Busi's personal assistant.

"Linda dear, what an unexpected pleasure to hear from you!"

She bore no antipathy for women like Beatrice, who tarted themselves up to please the men on whom they depended for life's happiness.

She understood them well enough and felt no superiority to them, merely a genetic difference.

"I've just come back from abroad and need some professional advice from the senator," she confided, politely.

"He's in the Senate for the vote on the new budget," Beatrice replied.

"Okay, I'll call back later, perhaps when he has a free moment."

Beatrice gave a little laugh.

"Actually, this really is the time when he's most free. And then he'd be angry with me if he knew I hadn't passed you on to him. Hang on."

Linda had no time to say that this didn't seem to be the right time, but after a moment Busi was there on the line.

"It's always a pleasure to hear from the country's most beautiful journalist."

In the background she could hear a senator speaking about the Italian fiscal system.

"I'm sorry to bother you, Senator. This doesn't seem to be the right moment . . ."

"It's the best moment there is, Linda. I have some real business to attend to after the sitting in this chamber, where it's nothing but pointless talk. And even if this cell phone is most certainly being tapped, you can call me Emilio. Just don't mention those nights of passion we . . ."

He laughed. Linda did not. Obviously, there had been no nights of passion. And she was certainly not happy about using his first name. But this was the way this highly influential man reminded her that she was special, although not that special, and that he could have plenty of women who were younger and more attractive. It was up to her to make a move.

"I need to speak to you in private, Emilio. Do you have a moment?"

She had used his first name, despite really not wanting to. He was obviously pleased by this first small concession.

"Are you looking for contributions for your charity work?"

"No, this isn't about orphanages, Emilio. I'd like to interview Monsignor Eugenio Pizza."

Busi was quiet for a moment, as he weighed up the pros and cons. Asking a favor of Monsignor Pizza was no problem for him, but it was

well known that questions asked by Linda Nardi could be very irri-
tating. "I've an invitation to the Italy–Middle East Economic Forum
tomorrow. A meeting of delegates that's a complete waste of time, no
one ever does any business, but as Gruppo Italia's chairman I have to
be there. There's dinner and a night onboard a cruise ship sailing from
the island of Elba to Civitavecchia."

He left the rest in the air. She hesitated, and he realized she needed
more motivation.

"Monsignor Pizza will certainly be there, so I can introduce you.
There will be separate cabins, of course."

Emilio Busi chuckled at the last detail and left the choice up to her:
refuse and have no help or play his game in return for a little favor.

Linda needed his help, so she accepted. Immediately afterward,
however, she felt the need to take another shower.

· · · ·

At Homicide everything was quiet, and, in any case, Corvu was there
on duty. Balistreri had let Antonella drag him to the beach the previous
afternoon, well after the weekend crowds, but also to avoid meeting
Giulia Piccolo. The idea that she might think he had interceded in
her favor disturbed him, and the possibility of her asking him directly
terrified him.

Antonella was the perfect companion. More friend than lover, she
had never felt betrayed years before when Balistreri interrupted their
relationship with his usual disappearing act. She had a little place in
Ostia and had assured him that in exchange for a total body massage,
she would feed him well and not insist he sit with her on the beach.
The first part of the program worked perfectly, pure pleasure.

In the morning, after a coffee without sugar, Balistreri went out to
buy his newspaper, *il Domani*, then went back and sat on the terrace
overlooking the sea. He scanned the headlines quickly, as he always did.
Only rarely did he find an article that interested him enough to read. But
there was another piece by Linda Nardi. She was writing again about the
death of General Younis and talked about agents of Gaddafi infiltrating
the rebels at Benghazi, coordinated by a man she called "the exterminator of Zawiya," where so many innocent people had been massacred.

He immediately felt he had to find an alternative to Leonard Cohen, who was starting to feel too light.

He could see there was a strong land breeze, the current flowing out to sea, but the calm surface was full of kids out kite surfing. He had never been kite surfing but had surfed as a boy in Africa and windsurfed as a young man here in Ostia.

He had to distract himself from Linda Nardi and this exterminator of Zawiya. Besides, Antonella's company was soothing him.

"I'll come with you to the beach."

Antonella was taken aback for a second, but she was happy he was coming. Balistreri put on a baseball cap and a long sleeved shirt over his swim trunks and followed her to the beach. There were still only a few people under the umbrellas and only the kite surfers out on the water. He sat in the shade in a deckchair while Antonella lay on a beach towel in the sun.

Gradually the beach filled up with children demanding ice cream, couples hitting the ball at everyone as they played beach tennis, and African peddlers sweating over the hard work that Italian women made of negotiating the price of a beach towel. Antonella glanced at Balistreri. She knew him all too well.

"Should we go back to the house, Michele?"

"No," he growled. "You can still get a little more sun."

He was concentrating on the kite surfers' maneuvers. As the strong land breeze was carrying them further out to sea, many of them were starting to pack it in.

The lifeguard's whistle cut through the air twice and Balistreri asked Antonella to lend him her distance glasses. He refused to wear his own except when driving—which meant hardly ever. Out to sea there was only one person left, but the distance between surfer and kite was too great, the line must have become detached.

The lifeguard was already racing toward the inflatable. Balistreri got up and half-ran, half-limped on his painful knee.

What am I doing?

"I'll come with you. I'll take care of the inflatable if you have to dive in."

The lifeguard made a quick calculation, gray hair but still muscular biceps, and decided he could be useful.

"Put the lifejacket on and keep an eye on the person in the water. Here's the binoculars."

They set off quickly and Balistreri struggled to keep the binoculars on the surfer. He managed to see the arms waving, and that was a good sign. But the head was going under every five seconds, then every three, then the arms were still. The inflatable was still fifty yards away.

"Get the lifejacket and throw it to them, while we carefully get alongside leeward."

When they were ten yards away Balistreri saw the face of a young girl with freckles and blond hair come bobbing to the surface. Both men knew she would never be able to get hold of the lifejacket.

Suddenly Balistreri had dived into the water, while the lifeguard shouted, "What the hell . . ."

He swam furiously, but had to stop halfway. The seawater was all up his nose, he was fighting for breath and his knee was giving him dreadful pain. The lifeguard reached him with the inflatable and threw out the ladder.

"Get back up!" he yelled.

While Balistreri climbed up, the lifeguard dived in, quickly reached the girl, grabbed her under the arms, and pulled her toward the boat. As Balistreri helped the lifeguard drag her onboard, he realized she must be younger than eighteen. She was still wearing braces on her teeth.

"Get this thing into top gear!" he ordered the lifeguard, who gave him a dirty look.

He then bent over the girl, pulled down the wet suit zip at the neck, and took out her tongue. He knew how to perform CPR, but with the inflatable hitting the water so hard it was impossible, so he held the girl in the head-tilt chin-lift position, not allowing her cranium to hit the bottom of the boat. In the meantime, on the water's edge a crowd had gathered, all ready to take photos with their cell phones, none of them thinking to offer any help.

*Keep calm, Michele. You chose to stay and live here in this country. No one made you. By now, you shouldn't let these things get to you.*

The lifeguard moored the inflatable. Balistreri took the girl in his arms and limped his way through the crowd in the water. He laid the girl on the sand and saw that she had already turned blue. Again, he tried mouth-to-mouth resuscitation.

Then he got up and shook his head. Antonella took off her pareo and covered the girl's face.

"Hey, bella!" came a cry from two suntanned young men who obviously spent a lot of time in the gym, "Get that thing off her face, will you? We want to get a shot of this."

One of the two went to lift the pareo, but Balistreri's hand gripped him around the wrist. The young man shot him a menacing look.

"Hey, Pegleg, move your ass, will you?"

Without a word, Balistreri twisted his wrist harder.

*Was I like this once, or was that someone else?*

To avoid any accusation of abuse of authority, he waited for the other young man to wade in. As soon as he motioned to land a punch, Balistreri dodged and caught him below the solar plexus with an upper cut.

The young man staggered, fell face forward in the water, and began to vomit. Balistreri then released the now bruise-colored wrist of the first young man. With all the strain his knee was screaming out in pain and acid reflux was creeping up his throat from the frustration.

"Now get lost, both of you," he barked.

The two rough young men moved off, and the crowd quickly dispersed. All that were left were the other silent kite surfers, all very young, with tears in their eyes.

Balistreri turned to Antonella, who was staring at him in amazement.

"Take these kids to the bar there and have them drink something hot to calm them down, and then get the girl's information. We'll need to inform the parents."

Not that he would do that himself. He had had to do it so many times he was no longer capable of it.

You have to be capable of loving someone in order to tell a father and a mother that their daughter has drowned.

As the girl's body was lying there, covered by Antonella's pareo, life around them had gone back to normal: children wailing for ice cream, beach tennis, women haggling with the beach sellers.

Balistreri turned to the lifeguard.

"I'm a policeman. Go get the owner of this place."

A spare gentleman came up, gasping for breath. Balistreri showed him his ID. When he read *Deputy Assistant Police Chief—Flying Squad—Head of Section III,* he turned pale. Everyone in Rome knew that Section III was Homicide.

"Sorry, *dottore,* I was just making a nice bit of ice cream up for the kiddies."

Then, mindful of the mishap, he pointed to the girl's body under the pareo.

"Not much point in an ambulance now, eh? Poor girl."

Balistreri pointed to the beach club full of people, all having a great time. He had become a man without emotion, not that he was he overbearing, he was simply a wise policeman who stuck to the rules. But there was a limit to everything.

"For today, this club is closed in mourning. Send the people away, please."

The owner opened his eyes wide.

"What the fucking hell for? Kid's dead, isn't she?"

Balistreri's look made him lose any desire for further argument.

"I'll claim damages!" he threatened.

Balistreri nodded.

"And I'll send the Guardia di Finanza around here to check your receipts for ice cream, deckchairs, and umbrellas. Each and every day. For the whole summer. Now get a move on!"

This was the most efficacious threat in Italy, unless you were a Mafioso or a Camorrista, and was instantly understood. Receipts had to be issued for every purchase, for the sales tax. Thus, the facility was shut down, the tickets refunded, and the tourists all went off cursing their rotten luck.

"Why did she have to drown here, the idiot?" a girl said to her boyfriend as they left.

As soon as the police arrived, Balistreri turned to Antonella.

"Would you take me back to Rome, please?"

During the journey they exchanged no words.

Only when she left him on the street below his office did he speak.

"I'm sorry. I don't know what came over me."

She smiled and said nothing, but quickly but gently ran her hand over the side of his face before she took off.

He went up and lay down on his sofa. His knee was throbbing from all that effort, his esophagus was burning from the anger, and his hand was painful as a result of punching that kid. His reaction stunned even himself. And yet he knew very well where the anger and the punch came from: everything stemmed from a game, a game among children who dreamed of changing the world.

But it turned out not to be a game.

# THURSDAY, AUGUST 4, 2011

## AT SEA, OFF THE ISLAND OF ELBA

Everything onboard the cruise ship spoke of wealth, power, and the future, from the business stands to the napkins on the tables laid for dinner.

Linda immediately went off to her cabin on one of the lower decks, the less luxurious ones. But it was clean and spacious nevertheless. She didn't want to go onto the bridge deck and mingle with the other journalists. In fact, she didn't want to talk to anyone until dinnertime, when Emilio Busi was to arrive and introduce her to Monsignor Eugenio Pizza. It was a matter of not giving rise to comments or questions from any of her colleagues who might wonder why she was there. Nor did she wish to be courted by some powerful man who hadn't brought his wife, lover, or an escort along. Especially now, after John Kiptanu.

She lay on the bed and thumbed distractedly through *il Domani*. On the first page she noticed the interview with Gruppo Italia's chairman, Senator Emilio Busi. The headline was both interesting and surprising.

The Olympics and a Bridge Across the Straits of Messina: Will They Really Help Italy?

These were two enormous projects that had been talked about for years. And Gruppo Italia's chairman had been a strenuous advocate who had always sought to bring them about. But there had been doubts and objections about both projects raised from all sides, both about the financing and the risk of infiltration by the criminal underworld, which in Italy was always ready to make money out of public works like these.

Linda read the interview closely. In effect, Busi wasn't denying the need to go ahead. But *Il Domani's* staff writer had highlighted the real news in the section about the world economic crisis which, Busi said, would give *the opportunity for a serious check into the financial backing.* Others had voiced the same opinion, but coming from the mouth of Gruppo Italia's chairman it meant there was a remarkable rift in the group that was pushing for the projects.

Further on, in the Rome pages, she saw a picture of Michele Balistreri coming out of the water with a young girl in his arms. She read about the young kite surfer's death, the man's desperate attempt first to save her, then resuscitate her. Also the fact that he was head of Rome's Homicide Section and without any ceremony had dispersed all the gawking bystanders and closed the beach club, sending everyone away.

Yes, this is the man I was in love with five years ago. A man capable of closing down a beach club out of respect for a fatality, but also of attacking a woman if he felt betrayed, because the compassion he feels doesn't come from love but from pain.

She put the paper down, took a long shower, and started to get ready for cocktails and dinner. She had rented an evening dress that morning in Rome before leaving. The occasion had never arisen where she would wear such a thing, and she couldn't see herself needing one in the future. The one she had chosen was high necked, long, and loose fitting. Over it, she was wearing a gray cardigan. On account of the air conditioning, she would say.

The lounge bar serving drinks was an enormous panoramic room overflowing with more than five hundred guests. The Italians almost all knew one another: politicians, entrepreneurs, managing directors, and journalists. All faces known to the newspapers. They bumped into each other, embraced, and exchanged nods and winks. Only those few who had any decent English were speaking with the guests from the Arab states.

Linda found Beatrice Armellini at a table with several journalists. She was perfectly happy playing her role in designer evening wear, chignon hairstyle, and horn-rimmed glasses, knowing very well the long skintight dress showed off her built-for-sex figure to great advantage.

Linda sat opposite her and watched as Beatrice drank a nonalcoholic sparkling wine with evident distaste. She lit up when she noticed Linda.

"Dear Linda, we're so happy to have you here."

Linda wasn't there to spend the night with Busi, as Beatrice Armellini thought, but she couldn't bring herself to explain things.

"Has Senator Busi arrived?" Linda asked.

Beatrice gave her a complicit smile.

"His helicopter's just landed on the ship with several of his friends. He's in his suite now. I'm sure he'll be down in a moment. He doesn't want to mingle too long with these people."

"Aren't they his guests?" Linda asked.

Beatrice looked around.

"Italian entrepreneurs complaining about the state of Italian politics to foreign ministers? Italian politicians complaining to Arab backers about Italian entrepreneurs' lack of competitive spirit? No, Senator Busi prefers the company of a few long-standing friends."

The man himself then entered the bar, impeccably turned out in black tie, accompanied by three people. The one with the dog collar, rosy complexion of a baby, and thin white hair, which once must have been blond, had to be Monsignor Eugenio Pizza.

Then there was an elderly Arab gentleman with a heavily lined face. Lastly, another elderly gentleman in a white dinner jacket, still very handsome despite his years, almost the double of the older Clark Gable with his white locks, still-gleaming smile, and deep dark eyes.

"Who's the Arab gentleman with him?" she asked Beatrice.

"A Libyan VIP, an old friend of the senator who's very close to Colonel Gaddafi. His name is Mohammed Al Bakri."

"And the dashing old man in the white dinner jacket?"

Again Beatrice gave her a complicit smile.

"Yes, he must have been gorgeous when he was younger. I think you were close to his son a few years ago."

For a moment Linda was speechless.

So that's where I've seen those eyes before.

She remembered that Michele had always steered clear of mentioning him. He had introduced her to his brother, Alberto, and had talked to her with sparkling eyes about his mother Italia. But when she had asked about his father, the reply had always been: *He doesn't live in Italy anymore. I haven't heard from him in twenty years.*

· · · ·

Busi introduced her to his friends, and Linda took a seat between Monsignor Eugenio Pizza and Salvatore Balistreri.

Don Eugenio struck up a conversation with her, perhaps because asked to by Busi, or perhaps so she wouldn't hear what the other three were saying, even if she had no idea what it was because they were speaking in Arabic.

"Senator Busi tells me that you travel a lot."

"I'm a journalist. I was in Libya covering the war there. And I was in Kenya a few days ago."

"And what did you do in Kenya?"

There was something in the man's politeness that Linda found annoying, like chocolate sticking to her fingers.

"I go there a lot. I have a charity there. We've opened a children's hospital." Monsignor Pizza nodded and only then pretended to recognize her.

"Of course, now I remember who you are. Excellent! God will reward you for all you do. I also have an interest in helping out the poor in that part of the world, whenever I can."

Monsignor Pizza touched the arm of the dashing old man in the white dinner jacket.

"Salvo, Signorina Nardi isn't just a distinguished journalist. She does wonderful work in Kenya!"

Salvatore Balistreri slowly turned to look at her. Linda had the impression that he was not at all happy to see her at the table.

"And what brings you onto this ship, Signorina Nardi?"

His manner was polite and his voice low, warm and gravely from smoking, his Italian tinged with a heavy American accent. Linda decided to tell him at least part of the truth.

"I have to talk to Senator Busi about an investigation I want undertake. So he invited me here. He didn't have any time in Rome."

Even as she was giving it, the explanation seemed suspicious to her. Monsignor Pizza was now deep in conversation in Arabic with Busi and Mohammed Al Bakri. Salvatore Balistreri looked at her with eyes as deep and dark as Michele's.

Similar and yet so different.

"The senator's most obliging. But I don't think he likes journalists very much."

Linda realized that the words contained a warning. She wondered why. Knowing Emilio Busi's weakness for young women, was Salvatore Balistreri putting her on her guard against a night that could have complications?

But why? What does he care?

Then the other three men ended their conversation in Arabic and the dinner continued with the usual comments about the world's financial crisis. And yet Linda felt a hidden tension around the table, as if her presence there was preventing the conversation from getting down to the heart of something. At the end of the meal, Salvatore Balistreri stood behind Linda's chair and helped her rise from the table.

"Would you like a coffee?" he asked her.

Linda was taken aback. Then she followed him to the panoramic bar. They picked up two coffees and went outside on the deck. The sun had set some time ago, but the air was still warm and the lights on Elba were now glittering in the distance.

"Would you mind if I smoked a cigar, Signorina?"

She indicated that she did not. She was confused, but not ill at ease, and she was curious to get to know Michele Balistreri's father.

"You live in America, don't you, Signor Balistreri?"

It was hard to know what title to use in addressing him.

"Between America and Dubai," he replied.

It was clear he wanted no more questions on that particular subject.

He exhaled a little cigar smoke, taking care that none of it blew her way. He seemed pensive, as if her presence had triggered something inside him, partly annoying, partly happy.

Annoyed that I was at the table with them, happy that I'm now out here with him.

"Several years ago I read your articles on the Invisible Man. You really are *overly* courageous, Signorina Nardi."

It was the latter part of the last sentence that struck her.

A compliment and a warning.

Here lay the difference between father and son. Michele was incapable of ambiguity and wouldn't stand for mixed signals. In the wake of the elder Balistreri's comment, she found herself saying something that was seemingly unconnected to it.

"Your son's an excellent policeman, Signor Balistreri."

He looked surprised by what she said, as if he misstepped, but only for a second. Something passed across his face, perhaps thinking about a son he hadn't seen for more than twenty years. Again, the capacity for ambiguity.

Regret or resentment?

"I know," he said after a moment. "My wife predicted as much when he was still a child. And Italia was always right."

Then this handsome elderly gentleman, who looked so much like Clark Gable, despite his white hair and mustache, gave her his business card and took his leave of her with a simple *Arrivederci*.

. . . .

Emilio Busi was standing at the bar with Beatrice Armellini, Monsignor Pizza, and Mohammed Al Bakri. Busi took her aside a moment, his hand touching her bare arm.

She was expecting some questions about what she wanted with Monsignor Pizza, but Busi seemed upset by something, as if some complication had arisen.

"I have some business to attend to, Linda. I'll give you a call as soon as I'm free, keep your cell phone on . . ."

She felt relieved. Perhaps Emilio Busi wasn't really interested in spending the night with her. This was fine with her, seeing as she had now made contact with Monsignor Pizza.

She watched the Gruppo Italia chairman return to the bar and rejoin Pizza and Mohammed Al Bakri. Together they went over to an elevator, in front of which stood an attendant. He let them in and the doors closed in front of them.

After a while Linda went up to the elevator attendant.

"Can I use the elevator?" she asked.

"I'm sorry, madam, this elevator is private," the attendant replied.

Linda hung around the lounge for a while but, seeing her alone there, too many men came up to engage her in conversation. She took the stairs down to her cabin on the decks below. On each level she saw an attendant by the private elevator. Out of curiosity, she descended to the very lowest deck with cabins, just above the engine room.

The deck was deserted, except for yet one more attendant outside the private elevator in a half lit corner of the hallway. Then just as Linda was about to go up again, the elevator doors opened.

Out walked a refined and beautifully dressed young woman. It was the one Linda had seen a few days earlier in the Hotel Rixos lobby in Tripoli. She had a beautiful little girl in her arms. The young woman noticed Linda and came toward her. The little girl gave Linda a beaming smile, but her mother appeared to be nervous, her face looking strained. Nevertheless, she forced herself to smile.

"You're Linda Nardi, the journalist, aren't you?"

Linda was taken aback. Up until a few years ago she had often participated in the debates on television talk shows but now did so only rarely, in order to talk about the orphanages in Kenya and to appeal for funds.

"Why, yes, I had no idea I was so well known . . ." she smiled, trying to make light of it.

The young woman again tried to smile back. She wanted to be friendly, but it was obvious she was distraught. She had a foreign accent, but her Italian was excellent.

"I always read your articles, and I admire what you do in Kenya. Forgive me if I seem intrusive, but do you think we could have a few words?"

"Of course, whenever you like, Signorina . . . ?"

"My name's Melania, and this is Tanja. We could talk now, but Tanja has to go to sleep."

"Of course, do you have a number I can call?"

"We're getting off early tomorrow morning at Civitavecchia. I'm taking Tanja to stay with a friend of mine, Domnica, in Ostia. She works in a bar, the Stella Polare. You could reach me there whenever convenient . . . anytime during the day . . . I can offer you a coffee or whatever you like and . . ."

Linda was bewildered, but the little girl was yawning and the young woman seemed in a great hurry and not very keen to give out her number.

"All right . . ."

"Thank you," said Melania, interrupting her. "Now I have to dash. Tanja must get to bed."

For a moment, her face relaxed and she again looked like the beautiful young woman Linda had noticed in the Rixos lobby.

"Good night," said Melania and off she went before Linda could ask her anything more, hurrying off toward the last cabin at the end of the passageway.

Linda heard the sound of the key turning in the lock and went back up the staircase, feeling the eyes of the elevator attendant glued to her backside.

*Men, all the same.*

She went back to her cabin, but the ship was full of noises and her mind was full of thoughts. She was afraid that Emilio Busi might call at any moment.

*Come up to my suite.*

But the phone never rang and Linda fell into a fitful sleep.


# ROME

Balistreri was in a bad mood. The image of the girl's body surrounded by people taking photos with their cell phones had given him no peace for the whole night and day.

*But why should you care? What's it got to do with you?*

He was indignant, and understandably so, but decidedly too much so, according to his personal set of rules and the level of indifference he hoped he had reached toward the world.

On top of that, his knee was swollen from the strain and extremely painful, so much so he had had to renounce his daily walk and be taken to the office and home again in a police car.

A little before midnight he glanced at the newspapers, more to distract himself and settle his mind to sleep than any desire for news. He opened *Il Domani* and saw the lead article. It was an interview with the man who was perhaps the most powerful in the country, Senator Emilio Busi.

One of Dad's old friends. One of my old enemies, forgotten like all the rest.

He was struck by the headline.

Olympic Parks and a Bridge Across the Straits of Messina: Will they Really Help Italy?

Now, surprisingly, having always been so favorable, Emilio Busi was expressing doubts about the funding for the projects in this moment of deep economic crisis.

The man has no conscience. I know him very well. It must be in his interests somehow.

# FRIDAY, AUGUST 5, 2011

## AT SEA OFF CIVITAVECCHIA

Linda was woken at first light by the announcement that in one hour they would be docking in Civitavecchia. She dressed unhurriedly, then went up to the saloon deck from which to disembark. There was no sign of Emilio Busi and his friends. They were not the kind of people to disembark with ordinary mortals anyway. Probably they had already left by helicopter. She looked for Melania and Tanja, but couldn't find them. The Gruppo Italia car was waiting for her to take her back to Rome.

## ROME

Balistreri was woken by the telephone. He had only just fallen asleep. It was Corvu, slightly hesitant about a delicate situation.

"*Dottore,* sorry about the time, but they've found two bodies on a cruise ship just off Civitavecchia."

"Can't local police deal with it? Do they need Homicide?" he asked, hoping to get back to sleep again.

"It seems a young woman shot her two-year-old daughter then killed herself. The cabin was locked from the inside."

"Well then, the Civitavecchia police can shift themselves and get down there."

Corvu coughed.

Here goes, now for the bad news.

"There were some VIPs aboard. Such as Senator Emilio Busi."

"Then Civitavecchia can certainly handle it!" Balistreri exploded and hung up.

But there was no going back to sleep now. He got up and drank a cup of extra-strong coffee on an empty stomach against the advice of his gastroenterologist. Then he lit a cigarette (another no-no) and put on a Leonard Cohen CD. But it wasn't enough.

. . . .

Linda learned of the death of Melania and Tanja Druc from the eight o'clock news on the radio as soon as she arrived home. The information was still very basic. According to the police, the young woman from Moldova had first killed her little girl and then put the pistol to her temple. For the moment there were no doubts about the case for suicide, given that the cabin had been locked from the inside and the key had been found on the bedside table.

The item had come at the tail end of the news among the local items after the latest on the economic crisis, the index of public debt, and the all-around necessity for tightening the belt.

Linda tried to recover from the shock. She undressed and took an ice-cold shower, hoping to fight off the sense of guilt.

I should have understood how distraught she was.

She hated that side of herself, forever thinking she hadn't done everything possible. The faces of that little girl and the frightened woman wouldn't leave her alone.

I have to talk to someone. Get some advice. Help, even.

Giulia Piccolo was the right person. Despite their different personalities, with Giulia she had formed the most incredible and precious friendship she had ever had.

She called her on her cell phone and Giulia arrived a few minutes later on her Ducati Monster 900 Dark. She was wearing black jeans and a purple sweatshirt that matched the color of the streaks in her hair. She hadn't always gone around looking like this, only in the past five years since deciding not to follow Michele Balistreri into Homicide.

They sat down in the kitchen over a cup of tea. The sun was streaming in from the French windows on the small terrace overlooking St. Peter's cupola, and the atmosphere was of total domestic calm, but Giulia had noticed Linda's strained face and the dark shadows under her eyes.

"What's happened?" she asked her.

Linda told her almost everything about Melania, from the day she first saw her in the Hotel Rixos in Tripoli to the previous evening on the ship when she'd asked Linda if she could speak to her. But she mentioned nothing about Busi, Monsignor Pizza, and Salvatore Balistreri, not even indirectly.

"Are you sure it was the same person you saw in Libya?"

Linda had only seen her from a distance in Tripoli and in a poorly illuminated passageway onboard the ship, but as always she trusted her instinct.

"It was the same person. She didn't have the little girl with her in Tripoli, but it was her. I'm certain. I should have stayed with her, tried to understand what she wanted . . ."

Giulia shook her head, passing a hand through her purple highlights.

"It's not your fault at all, Linda. You were ready to listen to her."

Then Giulia considered the situation.

"What were you doing on the ship anyway?"

It was an appropriate question for a policewoman. Linda told her the other story about the kickbacks, slush funds, the IOR, and Monsignor Pizza's business card. She glossed over the precise means she used to extract the information from Gabriele Cascio and also over her encounters with John Kiptanu.

You wouldn't believe it anyway, Giulia.

"During the cruise Senator Busi introduced me to Monsignor Pizza," she concluded.

Giulia gave her a look of concern.

"Linda, Monsignor Pizza's one of the untouchables. As for the IOR . . ."

"I know, I know. But, as a policewoman, perhaps you can help me with this."

Giulia looked outside across the small terrace.

"Yeah, as a policewoman who's been suspended. I had an argument with two colleagues. An argument that got rather heated. They were hassling two girls they'd found kissing. I tried to reason with them, but when they told me to get lost, I kind of lost it instead . . ."

Linda made no comment. She could have said that violence isn't fought with more violence. But she knew very well this was only true up to a certain point. She had made an exception herself with the Invisible Man.

"Have you been fired?"

"No. Only suspended. Three months' enforced leave. Surprising, really."

"Surprising?"

Giulia bit her tongue and opted for a partial truth.

"You usually get the boot for those kinds of things."

She didn't tell Linda what she'd learned from Corvu, who'd gotten it from a cousin who was personal assistant to Colombo, head of the Flying Squad, that Michele Balistreri had intervened and saved her from being canned. She knew that in Linda's presence it was forbidden to mention Balistreri. Although it was an implicit rule between them, Giulia Piccolo was always of two minds about it. On the one hand, after the split between Linda and Balistreri, she'd taken her friend's side; on the other hand, deep inside her, she hoped the two would get back together again.

"So how can I help?"

Linda handed her the payment details that John Kiptanu had given her.

His gift to her. Together with the wilted flowers she had left in the hotel room where they had made love.

Piccolo looked at the sheets of paper. Then at Linda.

"Is this what you were telling me about? The account that swine in Nairobi was paying the kickbacks into?"

"Yes. We need to get into the IOR."

Giulia smiled and shook her head.

"Really? Is that all? Well, we could go together one night, like the good old days at Casilino 900. Look, it's much more difficult to get into the Vatican."

Linda also smiled at the memory of those crazy exploits that had bonded their friendship. Nothing to do with courage, only that stupid, insatiable desire for justice.

"No, I'll go there alone. You're already in enough trouble. I don't want you to risk your job."

Giulia sat in silence for a moment.

"Hang on, Linda, I think there's a way of getting in . . . without actually getting in."

"Getting in without getting in?"

Giulia broke out into laughter.

"Think about it, Linda. The Internet."

"Ah, of course."

"But I need to speak to an expert."

"You can really do this?"

"I'll call a friend of mine. But you'll have to be patient, I haven't heard from her for a while."

"And she'll do you a favor? And be completely discreet?"

There was a smirk on Giulia's face.

"I think I can persuade her. She used to enjoy my massages quite a bit."

Linda had nothing against Giulia's sexual orientation. It was totally alien to her, but not incomprehensible. She remained silent.

"Don't you worry about me, honey," said Giulia to calm her. "I'm the one that's worried about you. When was the last time you had a good time in the sack?"

Linda replied in total seriousness.

"Less than a week ago. A very handsome young black guy from a shantytown on the outskirts of Nairobi."

Giulia stared at her uncertainly for a moment, then burst out laughing.

"Yeah, 'course you did, Linda. Come up with a better one, will you? And perhaps more believable?"

They both laughed, hugged each other, and then Giulia left. Linda looked at her own face in the mirror. Giulia was right. She wasn't believable. Not in that role.

. . . .

Corvu saw Balistreri sprawled on his office sofa wrapped in a cloud of smoke, distractedly signing documents. Five years ago he had seen his boss's attitude as an obvious and almost in-your-face manifestation of alienation and indifference and had thought of it as an illness. He had even resented it, sometimes angrily; then, with the passing of time, had come to realize that the situation was different, perhaps worse. In other words, Balistreri no longer seemed interested in life. His perspective on time, that vision of the future that keeps us alive, had simply shut down.

It had become almost impossible to shake him out of it and Corvu only attempted it on rare occasions, but now he decided to try again.

"Commissario, this young lady was on that cruise as a stewardess. Now, what do you make of hiring a stewardess who has to bring a little girl along?"

Balistreri nodded, it was indeed odd. Except there could have been a thousand explanations and he had no intention of dealing with any of them.

"The Civitavecchia police have started an investigation. Let's leave it to them, Corvu."

"Well, I've never heard of anyone who worked as a stewardess who had to take a two- year-old girl along with her," Corvu went on, regardless.

"What were the names of the victims?" Balistreri asked, with a sigh of resignation.

"Melania Druc, thirty years old, from Moldova. And her daughter Tanja, aged two."

Corvu watched his boss for a reaction. At one time such a young victim would have at least have stirred up a little emotion in him. But now he went on smoking and signing papers without even reading them. Corvu tried again.

"Can I ask for the preliminary scientific police and forensic report? If it turns out there are doubts this was suicide and it becomes a homicide, then the case will come back to us."

"In that case, we'll see. But let's hope not. For the moment it's not our problem. Get a copy of the forensic if you wish, but not officially. I'm sure you can manage that."

Corvu scratched his head and remained standing in the room, not saying a word.

"Is there anything else, Corvu?"

"There were some important passengers onboard."

"I don't see why that should concern us."

"Among them was Senator Busi, Commissario. I'm certain I mentioned it."

Balistreri buried himself in his papers again.

"Another reason for not getting involved."

But Corvu caught a glimmer of interest. And he was a very stubborn young man.

"We've got the passenger list of all the official guests. But it's incomplete, I spoke to the Civitavecchia police . . ."

Balistreri looked up.

"You did what?"

Corvu turned slightly pale but kept his composure.

"Nothing formal. I've got a friend there."

"Yes, you have friends everywhere, we know. And so?"

"They say that Senator Busi came and went in a helicopter with several friends, who weren't listed among the guests."

Balistreri went back to signing the documents and switched on Leonard Cohen. It was the signal for Corvu, who made a swift departure.

Balistreri lit a cigarette. The shutters were drawn but let some daylight in, as well as the sounds of people and traffic from the street below.

# FRIDAY, AUGUST 5, 2011

ROME

After Giulia left, Linda was alone with her thoughts. She had discussed many things with her and as usual Giulia had listened to her and offered to help.

But she had laughed at the idea that Linda had a native Kenyan lover.

"'Course you did, Linda. Now come up with a better one . . . And perhaps more believable?"

If it was difficult to speak to Giulia about her experience with John, but she still wanted to share it with someone after the terrible things that had happened on that ship. She knew the person who would listen to her was the one she loved most and above anything else, the one who had been both mother and father to her when Linda was acting up as a terrible child.

She called Lena in California and heard her coughing before being able to speak.

"Are you okay, Mom?"

"A little out-of-season bronchitis. Nothing serious, dear. Where are you?"

"Rome. I've been in Kenya. Something happened there."

She told her mother everything that had happened with John Kiptanu, but kept quiet about the investigations into the deaths of Melania and Tanja Druc.

At the end, her mother's voice sounded as sweet as ever.

"I'm very happy for you, Linda."

"But what do you think, Mom?"

"That the more powerful men are, the less they love women, dear. And the converse is also true. Those who have the least to give are the ones who love the most."

Linda wanted to ask her: *Would my father agree with you?* But that made no sense, because her father *didn't exist.*

Then Lena had a fit of that ugly cough and they said good-bye.

Linda tried to distract herself, but couldn't get away from the image of Melania and Tanja Druc in that hallway on the ship. She had the feeling of having seen or heard something important, something she couldn't remember, couldn't quite focus on. But she knew the memory would surface one day.

· · · ·

Corvu came back into Balistreri's office looking worried but decisive.

"We spoke to the cruise line," he announced.

Balistreri didn't even look up from the papers he was reading.

"On what grounds?"

"Not everyone who works on that ship is up to date with their tax returns."

"And what has the Homicide Squad got to do with tax returns?"

His deputy gave a sly grin.

"I had a colleague in the Guardia di Finanza call."

Balistreri couldn't keep back a smile himself. Corvu's network of friends and relatives was an intricate web composed of a thousand threads. His deputy went on, satisfied.

"The Finanza asked to see the contracts of all the employees onboard. And obviously the cruise line pissed themselves."

"All right, Corvu. If you really must tell me, go right ahead. Why did the cruise line give Melania Druc a job as stewardess even though she had to bring a little girl onboard?"

"Because someone told them to. It came up on the database under her name. She had a special recommendation."

"Who recommended her?" asked Balistreri, trying to show a minimum of interest to placate this young policeman, who was so diligent and yet so stubborn.

"A well-known Catholic humanitarian organization. It's called Open Doors. It's been operating for more than fifteen years, it helps poor kids from all over the world get legal entry into Italy. It offers initial lodging and a place to work. Melania came to Italy by means of it when she was twenty-three."

Balistreri shrugged.

"There you are, Corvu, all quite normal, everything in order. It's perfectly logical for Open Doors to recommend Melania Druc to the shipping line. It was thanks to them she came to Italy."

Corvu shook his head, expressing his doubts.

"Commissario, she came in 2004. And seven years later Open Doors recommends her for a job when she has a two-year-old baby girl . . ."

"Perhaps they did it precisely because she was a young mother?"

Balistreri lit another cigarette. Since he had tried to rescue that girl his knee was killing him. He was thinking of her, not Melania and Tanja Druc. He was thinking about his clumsy attempt to save her that had lost them precious seconds, and then those photos taken by the bathers with cell phones . . . He had no intention of dealing with Corvu's doubts and a case that might involve Senator Emilio Busi.

He sent his deputy away and went to lie down, but the old sofa was unusually uncomfortable and the office, full of smoke and darkened, seemed suffocating. It was all the fault of Corvu and his questions, the damn kid.

Why had Open Doors recommended Melania Druc for that work so many years after she'd come to Italy? A very good and reasonable question.

"Oh, very well," he muttered, getting up and limping over to the computer. He typed "Open Doors" into Google and looked around the humanitarian organization's site with its mission statement, values, and projects. They even had an organization chart. His eyes came to rest on a particular name.

President: Monsignor Eugenio Pizza.

He stared incredulous at the computer. Emilio Busi was on the ship where Melania and the little girl had died. His old acquaintance and associate Monsignor Eugenio Pizza was president of the organization that had brought Melania Druc to Italy seven years earlier and had recommended her to the shipping line as a stewardess, despite her having to bring a two-year-old girl with her.

There are no such things as coincidences. Only the results of mistakes, rashness, and arrogance on the part of the guilty.

What came into his mind were the guests not on the official list, the ones who came and went in Emilio Busi's helicopter. He felt a burning sensation in his esophagus and a subtle disquiet that seemed to come from very far away.

He cursed Corvu and then called him. He tried to cover up his sudden interest under a surly indolence.

"Corvu, just so that we're not caught out unprepared, see what we have on this case. Get some info on Melania Druc, Open Doors, and its president, Monsignor Pizza. Nothing official, though. All right?"

The diminutive Sardinian supressed a smile and hurried off. Balistreri lowered the shutters even more on the outside world, lit a cigarette, poured himself a whiskey, and lay down on the sofa.

Something didn't add up.

A young woman with a little girl gets hired as a stewardess on a cruise ship. Already something odd there. Then what does she do? Goes on the ship in order to kill herself and her daughter?

His instinct told him was all was not as it appeared. Melania Druc had gone on that ship for a different reason. Almost certainly to meet someone. Except that something went wrong.

# FRIDAY, AUGUST 5, 2011

## ROME

Linda had fallen asleep on the sofa, exhausted. The ringing of her landline suddenly woke her. She'd slept the whole day and the sun was now setting. She dashed to the phone. It was Giulia.

"Linda, aren't you answering your cell phone?"

"Sorry, Giulia, I fell asleep . . ."

"Asleep? Is that what you do when you're home alone?"

"I'm tired, Giulia. Libya, Kenya, then Melania and Tanja . . ."

"Well, buck up, I've got great news. My hacker's done it!"

"Fantastic. She gets a special prize."

Giulia gave a sly chuckle.

"She's already received it. Very special. One of my custom massages, naturally."

"Okay, you can spare me the details. Tell me what you've found out."

"The account's in the name of Monsignor Eugenio Pizza."

Linda looked outside. She could see the wonderful cupola all lit up. And over there in a corner off St. Peter's Square was Torrione Niccolo V, the great round tower that was the Vatican Bank's headquarters.

She said good-bye to Giulia and made some herbal tea. She didn't want to go through Emilio Busi a second time. She had Pizza's Swiss cell phone number, the one on the visiting card she found in Gabriele Cascio's safe in Nairobi.

Perhaps I should give all this up and go back to my orphans in Kenya. And John . . .

Her thoughts weren't all that confused. There was a common denominator.

It's much easier to divide the world into the privileged and the destitute than divide them into the representatives of good and evil.

She picked up her cell phone and called the number she'd taken from the visiting card.

· · · ·

When he'd stubbed out his tenth Gitane, the daily limit fixed by his GP, Balistreri usually considered his day was practically over. But Corvu had furnished him with the further information he'd asked for and so he decided to read it before going home.

As usual, Corvu had been lightning fast. He'd done a good job, the result of a few hours at the computer and a chat with a friend of his in the Secret Service.

Balistreri started to read what Corvu had discovered about Don Eugenio.

Apart from occasional hiccups, the name of Monsignor Eugenio Pizza was linked solely to charitable works. But those hiccups were very interesting.

In 1982, Roberto Calvi, chairman of the Banco Ambrosiano, which was heavily in debt from its loans to the Vatican, was found hanged under Blackfriar's Bridge in London. Some said it was suicide, some said it was the hand of the Mafia. Among the many things never mentioned in public, according to the Secret Service contact, was the fact that one of the clergy officiating in the church that Calvi attended in Milan was a certain Don Eugenio.

Then in 1986, Michele Sindona, chairman of the Banca Privata Italiana and earlier the Franklin National Bank, died in prison from a poisoned coffee. The same source in the Secret Service revealed that

Don Eugenio had been his confessor in prison and that Sindona had made what turned out to be his last confession with him precisely on the morning of his death.

And in 1990, Archbishop Paul Marcinkus, founder of the IOR, the Institute for Religious Works, had left his job as head of the Vatican's finances. At the same time, Monsignor Pizza disappeared and no one heard any more of him for fifteen years. Every so often a little article appeared in an international newspaper based on someone's indiscretions, from which it was gleaned that Pizza had climbed up the clerical hierarchies to the level of archbishop, which role he executed in parts of the world that had significant financial importance. He had been the Pope's nuncio in Colombia and Washington, DC; that is, one country where the greater part of money laundering originated and the other which was most concerned with fighting it.

Then he was back in the Vatican with a seat in the Pope's Curia. But still little was said about him. Friends praised his highly active support for the dispossessed in the world's poorest regions. His enemies whispered about a certain casual assurance in financial circles, about a very powerful gay lobby in the Vatican and even told stories about a secret location for thought and prayer, but also sex and secret machinations.

In February 2006, Monsignor Eugenio Pizza was brazenly present at the funeral of Paul Marcinkus in Sun City, Arizona. But from 2005 there was a German pope who was very keen to shed some light on the obscure finances of the IOR and other internal questions about the Curia. And the Monsignor's presence at the funeral had not been appreciated.

And so Monsignor Pizza came to be transferred from Rome to the much more modest diocese of Lugano, which was his choice among the alternatives offered. It leaked out from the Vatican that, as with Marcinkus, Monsignor Eugenio Pizza was not be made a cardinal. And that he was by now over the age of seventy five which meant that according to canon law he was obliged to relinquish all clerical offices.

But Monsignor Pizza was still the highly active chairman of the humanitarian organization Open Doors, which gathered funds from all over the world from Gruppo Italia to Arab funds from Dubai and Libya. For years word had circulated about certain Sicilian friends of Monsignor, people who were not exactly squeaky clean and about various accounts in the IOR, used perhaps for laundering money of dubious provenance. But these were merely gossip, nothing concrete had been proven.

Balistreri absorbed it all quickly, without a great deal of interest.

*I know all this. I've known Don Eugenio for nearly half a century.*

Corvu had inserted in the dossier what little personal information they held on Melania Druc by Open Doors, the organization that had brought her to Italy in 2004 together with her friend Domnica Panu. Melania had been born in Tighina on February 1, 1981, the last of seven children in a very poor family, the father an unemployed alcoholic ex-miner, her mother a janitor in a school. In that difficult environment, Melania had nevertheless shown herself to be so academically gifted as to be able to obtain several grants, which had enabled to her to graduate with a degree in political science and communication with the highest grades and the publication of her thesis.

Then, with the lack of opportunity in her country, she had come to Italy with her friend and lived in the Open Doors hostel.

Melania left the hostel very soon and disappeared for seven years. There was no trace of her: not a credit card, social security number, cell phone, or contract for work or rental property.

Balistreri read that passage twice. Corvu was always like that, analyzing what was there, proofs and clues, while he used his instinct to insinuate himself in the interstices and filled in the gaps, what was not said.

It was as if Melania had melted into thin air. Impossible, even for a clandestine worker. Someone had hidden her, given her protection.

He sat on the sofa and studied the photocopies of her passport passed on by Open Doors. Melania Druc was a woman with delicate features, a beauty that was elegant without being provocative, and with two intelligent eyes.

Too refined to be a prostitute and too beautiful to work behind a bar.

There was something in Melania Druc's story that worried him. Something sounded false to him about the first idea that came to mind about her, that she was an escort. And then there were Emilio Busi and Don Eugenio. Names he had forgotten. Or had tried to forget.

He made a decision, trying to convince himself that he was only doing it for Corvu. He called Colombo.

"This case on the cruise ship in Civitavecchia stinks. Have you read?"

As usual, Colombo hadn't read a thing, but didn't want to admit it.

"Yes, yes, of course. I had some . . ."

"Right, well from this moment we're taking on the case, okay?"

"Okay. You better inform the public prosecutor and the Civitavec-chia police."

Half an hour later Corvu knocked on the door. He was beaming.

"So we're taking it on?"

Balistreri threw his hands into the air with resignation. It was better not to ask how his deputy had come to find out.

"Look, Corvu, this is just routine, enough to get us up to speed if the ballistics report and autopsy . . ."

"Of course, Commissario. We'll have them by tomorrow. Is there anything else I can do?"

"Nothing official. Use your many relatives and friends. I want to know why there's no trace of Melania Druc in Italy for the last seven years. I also want to know who arrived on the ship by helicopter with Senator Busi. And get me the official passenger list."

If Corvu noticed the difference between an everyday routine check and the amount of orders just given, he was very careful not to let it show. For him it was quite normal to work through the night.

Balistreri shut himself in his office with its worn furniture, its smoke, and the music of Leonard Cohen. The weekend was starting. The worst part of the week. He laid down on his worn-out leather sofa, closed his eyes, and tried to quiet his mind.

# SATURDAY, AUGUST 6, 2011

## ROME

When Linda Nardi had called Monsignor Eugenio Pizza the night before, he had been moderately surprised and extremely courteous. He hadn't asked her how she had come by his cell phone number and had arranged to meet her after seven o'clock Mass in San Pietro in Vincoli near the Coliseum.

It was already a clear day of warm sunshine when Linda walked up from the Coliseum toward the Oppian Hill. She passed by the Engineering department and came to the church façade. The little square in front of it was completely deserted and the only sound was the sparrows singing in the leafy trees. It was as if the world had been bewitched, rendered immobile and stupefied by the beauty of that magical place.

Inside the church was Michelangelo's *Moses*, one of the most extraordinary sculptures ever created, and also Monsignor Eugenio Pizza, for many a benefactor of humanity; for others a man who had been able to manipulate the Vatican finances behind the scenes for decades.

Linda went in once Mass was over and stopped at the end of the central nave. Monsignor Pizza was surrounded by several old female parishioners. That good-natured face, the blue eyes, and his soft smooth white hair gave him the appearance of an ages-old child as he dispensed his wisdom: a humble priest in a simple cassock at the service of the souls of the faithful and *one of them himself.* A priest known for his charitable organizations and for the funds he collected for charitable works to help the world's destitute.

When he's dead and gone, some Pope will make him a saint.

When the last old lady had disappeared, he went up to Linda, smiling and holding out his hand.

"Signorina Nardi, how nice to see you again, after such a short time, although I imagine it's work that brings you here. Some gossip about plots against our German Pope?"

Linda had no time to take in the slight provocation, and reacted instinctively.

"Investigative journalism isn't gossip, it seeks the truth."

Monsignor Pizza studied her and shook his head.

"And you think there's an indissoluble link between goodness and the truth?"

Linda pointed to the crucifix over the altar.

"I seem to think there's a commandment that says that very thing."

Monsignor Pizza nodded, while avoiding looking at the crucifix.

"An early version, if you'll allow me, written somewhere between the Stone Age and the Middle Ages."

"Then why not abolish the Commandments and Sacraments, Monsignor?"

"Because they give many people comfort, Signorina, just like wine and cigarettes. However the rules are a little rigid and shouldn't become an obstacle for the performance of good deeds."

"The Commandments are obstacles?"

The smile was that of an old instructor of religion to a young pupil.

A new version of the catechism for the modern era.

"Beneath the altar of this church lie some chains. Legend has it they're the chains with which St. Peter was bound, first in the Holy Land, then here in Rome. But if we're in chains, how can we perform good deeds?"

"So it's permissible to break the Commandments if you're convinced you're doing it for good? Such as stealing, for example?"

Monsignor Pizza winced slightly, as if he had detected a bad odor.

"I don't agree with the verb you use, Signorina. It's too harsh and crude."

"But Jesus Christ would be more in agreement with me than with you, Monsignor . . ."

Monsignor Pizza sighed, as if faced with a poor student.

"Jesus Christ . . . If we who represent him on this earth presented ourselves to the comon people as he did, immaculate, completely cleansed of every sin, perfect, well . . . everyone would feel excluded from a religion that was so implacable it would make them feel constantly guilty. Christianity would disappear off the face of the earth."

"So creating an understanding with evil is a marketing tool for modern Christianity?"

"I have just celebrated Mass, Signorina Nardi. I have preached about tending toward the good, not the perfection of sinlessness. The people listen to me because I'm a human being. If I were Jesus Christ, they wouldn't come back every Sunday. No one likes to have to face their own guilty conscience."

Monsignor Pizza looked at his watch.

"Unfortunately I have no more time for theological discussions, Signorina. What can I do for you?"

Linda decided that the only way forward with this man was the less prudent one. She took out the photocopies of the bank statements that John Kiptanu had given her a few days, or what seemed a century, ago and handed them to him. Monsignor Pizza stared at them in silence through his bifocals.

"Do you know whose account this is with the IOR, Monsignor?"

Slowly, very slowly, he gave her back the photocopies. His face was impassive. He appeared not worried in the least. The Institute for Religious Operations was his domain and certainly not open to any inspection by the Guardia di Finanza.

"I don't know how you came by these statements. I hope it was legally."

"Within the limits of legality that you've specified yourself, Monsignor. Ignoring one or two rules perhaps, but all for a good cause."

He smiled good-naturedly.

"I see. *Touché*. Will that be all?"

He was an intelligent man, cautious, well practiced, tempered by a thousand battles won in contests between St. Peter's Square and Piazza del Gesù, where the old Christian Democrats headquarters used to be. So he knew how to handle certain problems. And Linda knew that the only way to deal with men of this kind was the sudden surprise blow, but she couldn't think of one. This man was untouchable, as were his friends. But the recent cruise suggested a means of counterattack.

"There were two deaths aboard that cruise we were on, Monsignor. Did you know the woman and her daughter?"

He nodded slowly, as if considering for the first time that this journalist constituted a slight risk. Then he shrugged, as if he'd decided the matter was irrelevant. Standing below that crucifix, he looked at her with his pale blue eyes and smiled.

Ferocity in a sugar coating.

"I must now take my leave, Signorina Nardi."

Linda felt the words coming to her lips that the most basic common sense would have told her to avoid. But in her anger she couldn't hold back.

"Melania wanted to speak to me, did you know? She was extremely upset and made an appointment to meet me at her friend Domnica's."

A network of little lines suddenly appeared on the priest's soft features. Then he turned his back on her and walked away.

· · · ·

Balistreri arrived at the office, on foot, at seven. Corvu was already there in the next office, probably having spent the night there. This sudden activity was upsetting. The damned business of the cruise ship had caused Balistreri to sleep badly and he was irritated when he found his office windows left wide open on the Roman Forum's early-morning silence by the cleaning lady to air the smoke-laden room. Then, as was his habit every day, he pulled in the shutters, closed the windows, and switched on the lamp by the sofa.

He picked up the bundle of newspapers and started to leaf through them. A report of the double homicide/suicide in Civitavecchia was given two small columns in the local news. He also found a short article on Libya. The war there was in a stalemate, the battlefronts unchanged for three months. But it seemed the tight circle around Gaddafi was crumbling because of the war's enormous costs. There was also the question of the strange death of General Younis—Gaddafi's old friend who had betrayed him. Had it been the rebels or a man at the top of the Secret Service?

Balistreri was lying on the sofa to rest his painful knee and opened the first report from the Civitavecchia police on the homicide/suicide of Melania and Tanja Druc. It said the cabin had been locked from the inside. The key was found on the bedside table next to the one single bed on which the little girl was lying, a bullet hole in her right temple. Melania was sitting in the chair facing the desk, also with a bullet hole in her right temple, her body slightly inclined to the left, her right arm hanging loosely down and the pistol on the floor, fifteen inches away from her hand. There were technical terms difficult for the layman to understand. But Balistreri had read dozens of these reports in his thirty years with the police. Certainly, the gun was there beside her right hand and the woman hadn't been left-handed and this could confirm the idea of suicide. Moreover, the gunshot residue analysis had revealed traces of gunpowder on Melania's right hand. But there were also doubts. From the photo and the measurements, the weapon seemed a little too far away from the hand, according to his experience and also his intuition. The cabin floor had wall-to-wall carpet and the gun hadn't fallen from a height that would have made it bounce so far away from the point where the shot had been fired, given that Melania had fired—if she had fired—sitting on the chair in front of the desk.

And perhaps it would have been more obvious for a mother to shoot herself straightaway, as she stood there. Or else lying beside her daughter.

A picture of doubts was emerging. On the side of homicide/suicide was the question of the cabin door being locked from the inside and the key found on the bedside table. The door had been opened by a crewmember with a pass key when Melania and Tanja hadn't come up for disembarking.

But the gun's serial number had been filed away.

What the hell was a young Moldovan woman doing with a gun whose serial number had been filed away, the kind gangsters used?

He took the preliminary autopsy report. It said that Melania's stomach was empty. She hadn't eaten, although dinnertime had long passed. On the other hand, Tanja's stomach was full, she had eaten a fillet of sole two hours earlier.

She gives her something to eat, then kills her two hours later?

Impossible.

# SATURDAY, AUGUST 6, 2011

ROME

After her meeting with Monsignor Pizza, Linda walked down along the Roman Forums to the Coliseum. Mock centurions were charging five dollars to be photographed with the tourists. It was a job, and more dignified than stealing money from the public purse.

*To be given to the poor, Signorina. You don't understand.*

She looked up the number of the Stella Polare in Ostia and called. A woman answered with a foreign accent.

"Domnica?" asked Linda.

There was a moment's silence.

"Sorry, who is it wanting me?"

"I'm a journalist. My name's Linda Nardi and I'm writing a piece about your friend Melania Druc. Can I come over to Ostia and ask you a few questions?"

A longer silence.

"You pay for interview?" said Domnica at last.

Linda smiled. It was only fair.

Sure, like the Roman centurions, we all need to make a living.

"A hundred dollars for half an hour of your time, Domnica."

"All right. But come now. Bar empty, later many people coming."

# SATURDAY, AUGUST 6, 2011

## ROME

Linda took the Metro from Trastevere to Ostia and immediately found the bar. It was just nine a.m. and the beach was almost deserted, except for joggers, cyclists, and people taking dogs for a walk. Within two hours and the arrival of Rome's sunbathers, it would turn into one of the most crowded circles of hell.

She found Domnica Panu in the spacious bar of the Stella Polare beach facility. She was a blonde whose features were too mousey to be really attractive. She certainly had none of Melania Druc's charm, but she had a good body with the curves all in the right places, even if she was a little overweight. She had probably let herself go, albeit she was still young.

It was a good moment. There was only one other person serving at the bar and very few customers. They sat outside, looking directly at the sea. Linda put her recorder on the table and switched it on.

"Now, Domnica, I'm going to ask you a few questions. I'm recording your answers so I don't have to take notes. Then, if the paper approves, I'll publish an article on Melania and how the two of you came to Italy via Open Doors."

She didn't like lying, but Domnica was only interested in one thing, the money.

"You pay even if they don't publish?"

Linda put a fifty-dollar bill on the table.

"And another fifty after this interview, if you can give me some useful information for the article," she said.

"All right. You can start. I have only half hour. People come after nine thirty. I work here five years and always all in order."

The two Moldovan girls were very different. Melania Druc was exceptionally beautiful, intelligent, and elegant. And certainly not the type for that bar and the work there. Domnica Panu had a bland face and a body that was a little too provocative. And for sure, once they arrived in Italy, Melania had mixed in circles that would have been closed to Domnica.

"Did you know Melania since you were little girls?"

"We went school together. Always together, and Italy together."

"You came to Italy together, is that right?"

"Yes. In Tighina, cold and hunger. No hope there."

"How did you get to Italy?"

"We go to Chisinau. Office there of Open Doors. They ask if we cook and serve tables, so to work in Italian bars and restaurants. We say yes. They put us on bus for Rome."

"And when you got to Italy?"

"They put us in hostel near Rome. After two weeks come first job."

"Where was that?"

"In poker club."

"You went to work in a poker club?"

Linda had done various investigations into that field. Over time many activities had become legalized, but poker clubs at that time were absolutely illegal.

"Outside it say Billiards Hall, near Ciampino airport. After certain hour it shut and if you are friend you can stay and play poker."

"And what did you and Melania have to do?"

She shook her head with a sour look.

"I only waitress. Melania dealer. In Moldova she has degree in political science and communication. She is very good, very intelligent."

Linda nodded. The difference in appearance and education explained
a good deal. But there was no jealousy in Domnica. Rather, she spoke
about Melania with evident care and feeling. She had probably idolized
her. Capable, intelligent, beautiful.

"But you also left the club, Domnica. You said you'd worked here
in Ostia for five years."

The young woman let a tear fall and turned away to the sea.

"Yes. Work in poker club disgusting. After one year I have enough.
No more."

"Disgusting work?"

Domnica stopped. She stared at the recorder.

"You write my name and I lose work here."

"I won't give your name. Only the initials."

This imaginary article was almost becoming real.

"I am waitress. They say always be nice to customers but not prostitute, only company, drinks. No sex. Then they introduce another
person. Italian lady, very beautiful. She promises much more money
if I do sex with rich people, important customers. Not in poker club.
Other places, much more beautiful."

"What was her name?"

"I never know. Others call her *Fratello*."

"*Fratello*? Brother? But isn't she a woman?"

"Yes, but in poker club they call her that."

"And then?"

"This lady she organize parties. Men rich, famous. I see them on
television. Much much money they have. Parties in lovely houses, very
very lovely. And much cocaine . . ."

"Did they force you to have sex?"

The woman dried a tear.

"Not force me with violence. But everyone there easy like that,
clothes off, lap dance, cocaine. Men had masks like politicians,
actors, ancient Romans, cardinals. The girls like nurses, nuns,
sheep, pigs. At end, if you go away, then no money. Much money
only for sex."

Linda remained silent. Domnica stared at the ground, avoiding looking at her.

"Is cold in Tighina, Signora. Hunger there. They give money, much much money. Difficult say no, all say yes to sex. First only one man. Then two. They give money, cocaine. I frightened, very frightened."

"Why?"

"Cocaine too much. They play games, first only handcuffs, blindfold, vibrators. Then very dangerous. One night I naked with five, ten, I not know. They whip me, no stop, I am crying, I say stop now. Then they put rope around my neck and have thing, a pulley. I pee myself so frightened, and they all laugh. Day after I stop."

Linda looked at the sea, as smooth as a mirror. And the blue sky that was rapidly clouding over. Melania and Tanja were up there, somewhere.

This is the world we live in. Nothing new about it.

Domnica was in tears and Linda put a hand on her shoulder.

"Okay, no more, I have enough. Can you tell me about Melania? Was she involved in these parties?"

"No, she different level. She bring in customers, but no sex. She meet important man and then work no more in poker club. He maintain her."

"And he's the father of Tanja?"

"Yes."

"Do you know his name?"

"Melania she never tell me this, ever. Secret. I don't know where she live even."

"When was the last time you saw Melania?"

"On morning she leave with Tanja for Elba, on damned cruise ship. She came here with Tanja to say hello, after so many months."

"Was she happy?"

Domnica thought for a moment.

"At first Melania always happy. But last times no. That morning she very worried. I thought because little girl too young for cruise, I not know."

"But why did she come that morning? Just to say hello?"

Domnica looked at the sea, then shook her head.

"No, she say when she get back Rome I take Tanja with me for some days, because Melania not happy at home."

Linda remembered Melania Druc's agitation on the ship as she was coming out of the private elevator with little Tanja in her arms. Her friend was right, that was one frightened woman.

Tears were streaming down Domnica's face, mingling with the first drops of rain. Perhaps she was regretting not having stayed in her native country with Tighina's poor but honest people. To die from cold, perhaps, but not from men wanting to string her up, laughing as she peed herself.

"You really don't know who Melania was involved with? Tanja's father?"

They heard a thunderclap and it started to pour. Domnica shivered.

"Before she leave on cruise to Elba, she say he on ship."

Suddenly Linda felt a shiver down her spine. She thought about the men onboard, sitting around that table: the Libyan Mohammed Al Bakri, Monsignor Eugenio Pizza, Senator Emilio Busi, Salvatore Balistreri.

"But you have no idea of his name?"

Domnica avoided her eyes.

"Melania never say."

Linda stared directly at Domnica and switched off the recorder.

"And the real name of the woman they called *Brother*?"

A gust of wind suddenly chilled the air. Linda studied the horizon. A small dark line, then bolts of lightning. Domnica had come to a stop, as if in front of a doorway too dark to enter. She began to tremble.

"You not here for interview," she muttered.

Linda got up, holding out her card and two hundred-dollar bills. She had the feeling that Domnica was wondering whether to tell her something else. Domnica took the card but not the money.

"No, thank you, Signora. I know you come here for you care about Melania and Tanja. You here for justice, not interview. I don't want money for justice."

Linda embraced her, Domnica Panu's tears wetting her cheeks. But it was useless taking this any further right now. Linda said good-bye and quickly crossed the road along the front.

"Signora!"

Linda heard the cry when she was already across the road.

Domnica was on the pavement opposite, outside the bar, under the downpour of the summer storm. She had decided to tell Linda something more.

Linda started to make a move, but Domnica was ahead of her and had already stepped off the pavement and was crossing the small square toward her. The van came at over fifty miles an hour and hit her full on, hurling her another twenty-one yards forward. The driver made no attempt to stop and continued on his way in the rain.

· · · ·

After vomiting in the toilet Balistreri called Corvu into his office that was now swathed in a wreath of cigarette smoke.

"Who were the passengers in the helicopter with Busi?"

Corvu stared at him in surprise. In the face of his boss, a man tired and with little motivation, he could see a light that he hadn't seen since the days of the search for the Invisible Man.

"Couldn't manage it, *dottore* Balistreri. The helicopter took off from the roof of Gruppo Italia's tower block and returned there. I haven't been able to find out who was on the helicopter with Senator Busi. Not yet."

Balistreri was getting ever more impatient. And getting upset about his own impatience.

"And you've found no other traces of Melania Druc? How could she have vanished for seven years?"

Corvu was concerned by this sudden proactive mood, as well as upset by the reproaches, but happy about what appeared to be his old boss's resurrection.

"I haven't uncovered anything yet, but I'm working on it."

"Have you got at least the ship's passenger list, official guests and unofficial?"

"Only those officially registered."

Corvu was pale in handing over the list and Balistreri immediately knew more bad news was coming. He went through the list. It was in alphabetical order. Under *B* was Senator Emilio Busi. Under *N*, Linda Nardi.

Balistreri had always considered the use of four-letter words a sign of weakness. His mother had taught him so as a child. But the name of Linda Nardi and her being on that cruise was too much.

"Fuck," he mouthed.

He lit another Gitanes, trying to keep calm.

"Corvu, try to get a move on here. We need to find this friend of Melania she came to Italy with, she must know something else about her."

Corvu nodded.

"Domnica Panu. I wonder if she still works at that bar in Ostia."

The answer to that came up that very moment on the computer screen. It was the channel with updates of police investigations under way, which Balistreri kept on out of habit. It was a newsflash among the latest developments.

A hit-and-run driver has killed a woman outside the Stella Polare beach in Ostia. Her name was Domnica Panu.

Balistreri was dumbstruck, staring at the screen. He got to his feet, his stomach burning and his knee aching.

"Let's go to Ostia, Corvu. Get a car."

# SATURDAY, AUGUST 6, 2011

ROME

Giulia Piccolo arrived on her Ducati Monster half an hour after Linda Nardi's phone call. She found Linda sitting at a table outside the Stella Polare, her eyes staring wide at the pathetic sheet with which the traffic police had respectfully tried to cover Domnica's body.

The sun had come out again after the storm and all around them life was running by as it normally did: bathers under umbrellas, children with ice cream, the strident horns of drivers irritated by that sheet blocking half the road.

Linda gave her statement as an eyewitness. The van was white, possibly a Fiat Ducato, she hadn't seen the license plate. There was only one person inside, who'd made no attempt to brake.

Then Giulia took her home, gave her a sedative, and forced her to go to bed. She lay down beside her quietly until she saw that Linda was asleep.

. . . .

"Come on, Corvu, drive faster, will you?"

Despite hating to leave his office, Balistreri was in a hurry to get to the accident scene in Ostia with Corvu at the wheel. During the journey they didn't exchange a single word. Balistreri seemed in the grip of a sudden fever. Corvu was watching him with ever greater surprise.

Once at the Ostia police station they quickly read the traffic police report of the RTA. The van hadn't even braked, but rather accelerated and immediately driven off.

Then Balistreri went through the eyewitnesses's reports. There he found that name again, Linda Nardi.

Balistreri swallowed a swear word. He was a man who didn't believe in coincidences when they cropped up in an investigation. Nor in life either.

*We're the authors of our own destinies.*

That sentence didn't come only from Nietsche's reading. It came from his conversations with a young Arab boy who had saved his life twice and whom he had killed.

In the tense silence during the trip with Corvu back to Rome, his thoughts were giving rise to conflicting feelings. Only by discipline and force of will had he been able to suppress his imaginary conversations with that woman over the last five years. It had taken a long time before those conversations with Linda wore themselves out, along with any desire to see her again.

So as not to think of that night anymore. *The night I almost raped her.*

# SATURDAY, AUGUST 6, 2011

ROME

Linda woke toward the end of the afternoon and joined Giulia on the little terrace. She was still suffering from shock, with no energy to speak and handed the recorder to her friend, who listened in silence to the conversation that Linda had recorded that morning with Domnica. Her face hardened as she heard what Domnica had to say.

"More than Melania's lover, it's that woman who took those poor girls to those filthy rich swine that makes me sick. We know what men are like, but a woman doing that . . ."

"Do you know anything about this Open Doors organization that Domnica was talking about?"

"Never heard of it, but there are so many of them. Let's take a look online."

They easily found the Open Doors website and, like Balistreri, found themselves looking at a name. *President: Monsignor Eugenio Pizza.*

They stared at each other in amazement.

"A ridiculous coincidence," Linda whispered.

Giulia Piccolo thought about what her ex-boss Michele Balistreri used to say about coincidences. But she took care not to name him.

Then Linda's cell phone rang and she recognized the number on the display.

"Graziano . . ."

The little Sardinian's voice was jabbering in agitation, his consonants doubling as he spoke.

"Linda, that accident in Ostia, you were there, weren't you?"

"Yes, Graziano. I was on the other side of the street when . . ."

"He wants to see you, right away."

Linda remained silent. She could always refuse and Balistreri would be forced to bring her in officially with a warrant for questioning.

That would be worse. I'd have to respond to too many questions.

"Tell him I'm on my way."

. . . .

When Linda arrived at the Homicide offices, Corvu came out to meet her and accompanied her to the room at the end of the corridor. It was the first time she had seen the armchairs with the broken springs, the worn leather sofa, the ancient peeling desk full of papers, the closed shutters, the bluish smoke filling the air.

No one was there, but she immediately knew whose office it was. In some way what lay before her was what she'd understood that day she had expelled Michele Balistreri from her life.

A man who's no longer living. Dead before he gives up the ghost.

Seeing the empty room, Linda gave a sigh of relief. Perhaps Graziano Corvu would be interviewing her and she could avoid Michele Balistreri altogether.

Corvu was upset.

"Linda, what the hell were you doing . . ."

Balistreri came in at that moment.

"You can leave us, Corvu. And you can take a seat, *Dottoressa* Nardi."

The return to formality reminded her of their first face to face meeting in the church of Sant'Agnese in Agone in Piazza Navona, when she had told him about the terrible violence that men inflicted on Agnese and he had almost laughed in her face.

Corvu left the room without a word. Linda moved to the side of the room with more light.

"I'll remain standing, I'm only staying for a minute."

Balistreri lit a cigarette and sat down.

"Remain standing, if you wish. But this is a murder inquiry and we will take all the time that is necessary."

He looked at the computer, the papers on his desk, the glowing point of his cigarette. Linda felt anger rising up from her heart to her brain.

*Why? This is a man who no longer exists, he's one of the living dead . . .*

"Aren't you able to say my first name, Michele?"

An interminable moment passed in which he neither looked at her nor said anything. Linda feared he almost might attack her again, as he did that night five years ago.

Then he stubbed out the cigarette, got up, and went to open the windows. He turned around and finally looked her in the eyes.

*Five years ago I didn't want to believe you. I desired you without even knowing how to kiss you. I attacked you and didn't protect you, leaving you alone against the Invisible Man.*

As with Linda, he also felt angry thinking of his memories and pushed them aside as he spoke.

"You may not leave whenever you feel like it. So, please take a seat, Linda."

The words were harsh, but the use of her first name was a concession, if not a capitulation. For a moment she remained suspended between rebellion and acquiescing. Then she chose a middle pathway. Her body refused to move. She didn't try to leave but neither did she sit.

"What do you want to talk to me about?"

"A great deal, starting with the death of Domnica Panu this morning in Ostia."

"Is Homicide now dealing with car accidents?"

"Was it just a car accident?"

"Can you tell me why it might not be?"

"No. It's you who has to tell me what you were doing there this morning."

The quick back and forth and brute force against scorn were all that was left between them after five years. They both felt it, they both thought it.

Neither of us wants to be here right now.

Balistreri stared at those light transparent eyes where he had once thought he'd found everything he'd always missed: fidelity, sharing, even love. He stared at Linda as a shipwrecked sailor might contemplate an enchanting sea the moment he escaped his death there. And only once he was out of it did Balistreri realize the beauty he had left behind.

Linda was studying the man as well, his hair was too long and turning gray, his clothes rumpled, his cheeks sunken, and there were dark rings under his eyes. This was the man who'd declared his deep love for her with the words *You're mad.*

*You must have been a different person at one time, Michele.*

She sat down in the chair in front of the desk, looking Balistreri in the eye, as he had done to her, forcing herself to concentrate on the events of the day and to answer his questions.

"I was on the other side of the road along the front when she was hit. I gave my statement to the traffic police . . ."

"I know, I've read the report. But the woman at the cash register says that you and Domnica had spoken at length, right up to a minute before the accident."

"It was an interview, for an investigation I'm undertaking."

"What investigation?"

"Michele, there are laws protecting journalist's sources . . ."

"Linda, I am the law and this is an inquiry into a possible murder. Or rather, three murders."

Linda observed him, stunned.

"What are you talking about? What murders are these?"

He looked directly into her eyes.

"Those of Melania and Tanja Druc."

She stared at him, waiting for more. But Balistreri had no intention of explaining anything more to her. All at once Linda felt vulnerable and exhausted. The man in front of her was the one she had expelled from her life, after he'd attacked her. But perhaps he was the only one who could uncover the truth, no matter who tried to stop him, even a powerful man like Monsignor Pizza.

She pulled the recorder out of her bag, pressed the switch, and started to play the recording of her interview to Domnica Panu. Balistreri listened to the end of the interview without making any comment. He called an officer in and told him to make a copy of the tape right away. He gave the recorder back to her, knowing very well she'd already made a copy for herself.

"And don't even dream of using the contents of this pseudo interview for an article," he warned her.

She picked the recorder up. She wasn't taking any orders from him. On the contrary.

"We must find Melania's lover. Domnica says he was also on the ship. And that woman, *Brother*."

Balistereri stared at her.

*An exceptional woman, indomitable. Therefore dangerous.*

"You don't have to find anyone, Linda. We, the police, will see to that. Now tell me why you were on that ship where Melania and Tanja died."

Linda tried to collect her thoughts.

He's the worst kind of man, but an excellent cop. This is the right question to ask. One that opens up a very different front.

"I was there for my work."

He pressed her for an answer.

"What work?"

"My work as a journalist. I had to speak to someone."

"Who was that?"

"I'm a journalist, Michele. I have the right . . ."

"You have no rights here. I've already told you that this is an inquiry into three homicides. Who did you have to speak to?"

Linda breathed a long sigh and told half the truth and half a lie.

"With Senator Emilio Busi."

Balistreri suddenly lifted his gaze, his eyes had a different light above those dark rings.

"Busi's a friend of yours?"

Linda picked up on something behind the question.

Bitterness, anger, fear.

She felt a wave of tenderness that she immediately swept aside with her reply.

"It's none of your business if he's a friend or not, is it?"

"What did you have to speak to him about?"

"He was supposed to introduce me to Monsignor Pizza."

Balistreri gave a slight start, then became even more gloomy. He lit a cigarette.

"Why did you want to meet Monsignor Pizza?"

"I'm investigating the IOR."

Balistreri kept silent, waiting.

Linda observed him. After she'd mentioned the names of Emilio Busi and Eugenio Pizza, something in the hardness of his face had slipped away. He now seemed more concerned than angry and a mental picture came back to her, the distraught Michele Balistreri who ran to save her from the Invisible Man.

A last reflection of the man he had once been. Loyal, courageous, good.

She then told him everything. The conversation with Bashir Yared in Tripoli, the building site in Nairobi, the slush funds used for greasing palms, the Swiss group's memorandum of association, the IOR bank statements, the account held by Monsignor Eugenio Pizza. She left out her affair with John Kiptanu and the way she'd dealt with Gabriele Cascio.

*You wouldn't understand. Only judge and nothing more.*

"And you came to know all this via legal methods?" Balistreri asked her when she'd finished.

The same question that Monsignor Pizza had asked. Put by the priest it had been a provocation, from Michele it expressed his concern.

"A journalist can do things that the police aren't allowed to do. Those two investment companies that run the Swiss consortium, for example. You would have to send an international letter rogatory to find out who's behind them, they would oppose it and a whole year would go by. I can use other means."

"The same methods you used to obtain the memorandum of association and the bank statements?"

Linda looked him straight in the eye.

"I got them by adopting the manner you men want women to have: by behaving like a whore. And this morning I went to see Monsignor Pizza and threw them in his face."

Balistreri stubbed out his half finished cigarette.

"You did what? Linda, are you completely mad?"

She observed him, eyes gleaming.

"Do you know how Melania and Domnica entered Italy? Thanks to Open Doors, whose chairman happens to be Monsignor Pizza."

Balistreri knew this already but didn't want the conversation to go in that direction. He hesitated for a moment, on the verge of anger for what Linda had done and fear for what might happen to her.

*Because I know them very well. I know what they're capable of.*

"Did you tell him that you were going to see Domnica Panu?" he asked her.

He saw Linda thinking; she was trying to remember. Then vertical lines creased her forehead, her features shrinking in anger and pain.

"Not exactly," she whispered. "But I said something that could have made him suspect it. I wanted to scare him."

*And you succeeded, Linda. You have no idea who you're dealing with.*

"Let me get this straight. Busi introduced you to Monsignor Pizza on that cruise, right?"

Linda nodded and sighed. She was still uncertain on that issue.

"I had dinner with them and two other men."

Balistreri felt an uncomfortable feeling stirring within him, the burning sensation rising up his esophagus along with the thoughts spreading from heart to brain.

*Busi, Don Eugenio, the helicopter, the other guests. Okay, Michele. That's enough. Stop right here, right now.*

But it was impossible.

"And who were these other two?" he asked.

He could feel the uncertainty in his own voice, which was almost a plea.

*Tell me it isn't true.*

She looked up into his face and their eyes met. She was worried and apologetic.

*She's sorry for me, not herself.*

"With Senator Busi, there was Monsignor Eugenio Pizza, a Libyan named Mohammed Al Bakri, and . . . your father."

Balistreri was speechless.

Forty-one years had passed in vain, ghosts are forever.

He had to hurry, get his mind around it all as soon as he could.

"How did you come to know Domnica Panu?"

"By speaking to Melania on the cruise. She approached me. She wanted to tell me something but was clearly frightened. She told me to get in touch through this friend of hers, Domnica."

"You spoke to Melania on the ship?"

"There was a private elevator between decks that Busi and his guests used. I went down to the bottom deck to have a look around and Melania came out of it with her little girl . . . I recognized her immediately."

Balistreri frowned.

"You recognized her? You already knew her?"

"I'd seen her a few days before."

"Where?"

Linda sighed. Her memory wasn't clear and she wasn't exactly sure that it was the same person.

"In the Hotel Rixos, Tripoli. She didn't have the little girl with her then. She had an escort of Libyan special agents and was with a man. The one they were saying was responsible for the Zawiya massacre and the death of General Younis."

Balistreri again felt the slight anguish that had gripped him when he'd read Linda's first article about this.

"Young man or old?"

Linda tried to focus on the memory.

"He was thin, slender, olive complexion, curly gray hair, about sixty. A piece of his ear was missing."

Balistreri was shaken. This was too much. All his old enemies. All those he left alive. That missing part of an ear was inexorably dragging him back toward that old promise.

*In a month, a year, a hundred years, I'll find out the truth about my mother's death. And I'll settle what remains to be settled.*

It had taken him decades to bury that promise and to bury Mike Balistreri, the kid with too much past and no future. It had taken him decades to be able to live without living so that hate, anger, and remorse, could not touch him anymore.

But this is too much.

He accompanied Linda to the door.

"Leave this business to the police, Linda. And that's *not* a suggestion."

He said this in a tone that allowed no objections. In fact, she left without saying a word.

# SUNDAY, AUGUST 7, 2011

ROME

Balistreri hadn't slept a wink. He couldn't stay shut in his office smoking and waiting for life to end anymore. That choice had been taken away from him.

Arriving at headquarters, Balistreri found Corvu in his office. He had the red eyes of someone who had worked all night, and his crumpled clothes were the same he was wearing the day before.

"Found something useful, Corvu?"

He nodded. His face showed mixed feelings about his findings.

"Something, perhaps. Thanks to a friend in the Secret Service. Monsignor Pizza uses a Swiss SIM card with which he speaks only to three other foreign SIM card users: one in Switzerland, one in Dubai, and one in Libya."

Balistreri looked at him.

"You have found something else, right?"

He nodded again. Yes, he was not really happy about his findings.

"We've gathered a little more information about Open Doors."

It was the list of main financial sponsors of Open Doors: Gruppo Italia, President Emilio Busi, Libyan Charity Fund, President Mohammed Al Bakri, Dubai Charity Fund, President Salvatore Balistreri.

While the burning in Balistreri's stomach was spreading, his thoughts were stirring with ghosts from the past.

*Was it possible or impossible?*

He still had a choice. Pass this investigation back to the Civitavecchia police, who would probably close the deaths of Melania and Tanja Druc as homicide-suicide and the death of Domnica Panu as a car accident.

But on the night of his twentieh birthday, forty-one years ago, he had left a job unfinished and had made a promise.

*One day I'll settle with all of them.*

. . . .

Corvu had found the name of the religious house where Monsignor Pizza stayed when he was in Rome, and early in the morning Balistreri, and his limp, headed over there.

He crossed the Sant'Angelo bridge over the Tiber to the famous Castle and again saw an image of his life as a boat running smoothly over calm waters toward the sea. But now there was an unnatural current opposing him, putting a stop to that peaceful end. And it *was* unnatural, because instead of carrying him toward the river mouth and the sea it was dragging him back against the current toward its distant source in a harsh, wild, and violent country from which he'd escaped and then buried away in his memory.

He stepped into the narrow alleyways full of locals and tourists south of Borgo Pio behind the Castle, then came to the hostel in the vast square dominated by the sunlit cupola of St. Peter's. Nearby was the headquarters of the IOR, the Vatican Bank, and in the surrounding few square miles stood the world's greatest and most longstanding power.

The power of fear that replaced the power of reason. A power that's tolerated everything over the centuries in the name of faith. Even men like Monsignor Eugenio Pizza.

The porter at the hostel desk was a polite young priest.

"Monsignor Pizza's in his room, he's had breakfast, and I think he's now in prayer before going out."

"I'm an old friend. Do you think you could tell him I'm here?"

While the porter delivered his message over the phone—*There's a Signor Michele Balistreri here to see you, Monsignor*—he wondered how Don Eugenio would react.

*He's a very intelligent man, knows it's the Head of Homicide who wants to see him, and he'll have me come up.*

In fact, the young priest was smiling.

"The Monsignor's waiting for you in his room."

The hostel for the religious was clean, sober, and silent. Balistreri went up in the elevator to the second floor and Don Eugenio opened the door before he even could knock.

"Come in, Michele. Please sit down. I'm sorry there's not much space, it's a very small room."

The man facing him had the same smooth skin and rosy complexion of all those years ago. The same intelligent light blue eyes. The same excessive friendliness. But his untroubled front was betrayed by a look that Balistreri had come to know well during his thirty years as a cop.

*Perhaps it's my visit. Perhaps Linda's.*

The little room was simply furnished: wardrobe, desk, bed. A padded kneeler underneath a crucifix. Pizza's clerical dress was almost threadbare.

*A humble servant of God, espouser of charitable causes.*

But Balistreri was well acquainted with this man and knew how deceptive appearances can be. Here was an old man, his hair now white, with the face of a child and that same benevolent look. But he was also the same man who had attempted to molest Nico and was present on La Moneta that terrible day Italia died.

*All that stands between him and evil is a wall of thin air.*

"There's only one chair," he said, pointing to it as he went toward the bed.

Balistreri sat down. Those light blue eyes were following him and Balistreri again felt himself back with Nico at their school desks in front of the teacher.

"Out with it, Michele. Is this an official visit? Should I call my lawyer, perhaps?"

Balistreri caught the hint of anxiety in the typical sarcasm of his old religious teacher. Monsignor Pizza wasn't at ease, he was only keeping himself under control.

"Not yet, Monsignor. I've nothing to accuse you with. Today, that is. Only some questions."

"I'm all ears, Michele."

The same words that Don Eugenio had used in Tripoli when his father Salvatore had made him confess so he could take communion.

"Yesterday Linda Nardi came to see you. She asked you two questions. One about Melania Druc and one about an IOR account. But you never answered."

Don Eugenio seemed not the least concerned.

"Are you going to ask me the same questions, Michele? Is there an investigation under way?"

His tone was as calm as ever.

"There's no investigation. Even though Domnica Panu died just after Linda Nardi had spoken with you."

As an expert fighter, Don Eugenio took the blow but a slight shadow, like a very faint breath of air passed across his face.

A tiny ripple across a calm sea. The cold wind of fear.

Then Don Eugenio nodded, as if following his own thoughts.

"I don't remember Signorina Nardi mentioning that name. But what is it you want to ask me, Michele?"

"Who was at your table on that cruise the night Melania Druc and her daughter died?"

"And Linda Nardi hasn't told you? She was there, as I'm sure you know."

Balistreri ignored the provocation.

*I'm not longer Michelino and you're no longer my religion teacher.*

"Perhaps she did, but I'd prefer to hear it directly from you, Monsignor."

Don Eugenio sighed and nodded, as if he were still dealing with Michelino, his most unruly pupil. But it was also the sigh of someone having to reveal something he'd prefer not to disclose.

"There was myself, Senator Busi, Mohammed Al Bakri . . . and then your father, of course."

Don Eugenio studied him with his kindly eyes. Linda had already told him that his father was there, almost apologetically. But coming from Don Eugenio, the same words were pure poison. And this time the provocation found its target. Balistreri's voice betrayed his anger.

"My father's not even supposed to set foot in Italy!"

*Keep calm, Michele, this man's known you since you were a boy, he knows how to stop you from ruminating on the past, he only has to touch your wounds.*

"Really, Michele? I didn't know that he'd ever been expelled."

The light, soft voice and provocative tone were confusing him, just as his memories often did.

*I expelled him with that photograph of him with Gaddafi at Abano Terme just before the coup d'etat.*

Balistreri tried to control himself. But what was rising from his stomach to his brain was too strong to control.

"And why were you all together there?" he asked.

Don Eugenio smiled softly.

"We're all old friends, Michele, as you know. It was business, pleasure, the usual things. A quiet dinner."

Balistreri could contain himself no longer and committed one of those errors that he'd been teaching less experienced investigators to avoid.

"Which required the use of foreign SIM cards to communicate between yourselves, of course."

The monsignor remained silent, lost in his thoughts. But now there was something that really did resemble fear at the back of those light blue eyes. Then his gaze turned back to Balistreri. He was no longer smiling.

"But that's no business of yours, Michele. And there's nothing illegal about it."

"Except that a young woman and her daughter were killed on that cruise."

For a moment Don Eugenio's jaw dropped, but he soon was in command of himself. He made a light gesture with his open hands and spoke softly.

"That's not what I've heard, Michele. Rather it was a murder and a suicide. Perhaps the poor young woman was depressed . . ."

He had always hated that man, his tone, his hands. Right at that moment the memory Nico with his shorts pulled down in front of this priest came back. Balistreri got up, took the letter opener off the desk, and moved close to Don Eugenio, who sat back farther on the bed.

"There was no suicide, Monsignor. Melania Druc wasn't depressed, she was frightened. Linda Nardi told me so, because she'd spoken with her not long before she died. Both she and Domnica Panu had come to Italy via Open Doors. And Melania was on that ship thanks to a reference from Open Doors!"

Balistreri could see the fear in those light blue eyes. Monsignor Eugenio Pizza had now realized whom he was dealing with. And it wasn't Deputy Assistant Police Chief Michele Balistreri, respected Head of Homicide, but the young boy of all those years ago.

Mike and his friends in the MANK.

Balistreri moved the letter opener closer to the priest's terrified face.

"Domnica told Linda Nardi that Melania Druc's lover was onboard that ship and Linda had also seen Melania in Tripoli a few days before. She was with a sixty-year-old Libyan man that people were saying was behind the Zawiya massacre and the death of General Younis. Now listen, priest, you tell me the truth or I'll do to you today what Ahmed wanted to do to you all those years ago."

*You remember that knife?*

Don Eugenio was now terrified. But he wasn't looking at Balistreri, nor at the letter opener. It had to do with something worse.

He's struggling between two different fears. And the other is far stronger than the letter opener.

"I can't," he whispered feebly.

That "I can't," spoken by such a powerful man with a letter opener to his throat was both a confession and undeniable concealment of the truth.

The priest looked at Balistreri, his blue eyes full of fear.

"You managed to save yourself that day in Tripoli, Michele. Now you either forget this business, or this time you will die."

But what he said didn't sound like a threat from him. Balistreri felt Don Eugenio was giving him good advice.

Forget or die. A fear that comes from long ago.

He left the priest's room, leaving the letter opener on the table.

# SUNDAY, AUGUST 7, 2011

ROME

Linda Nardi's night had been neverending. The meeting with Michele Balistreri in police headquarters had only brought back ugly memories and negative feelings. One was that he wouldn't be able to open an investigation and confront such powerful men.

Besides, there was no concrete proof. Monsignor Pizza and Senator Busi were part of an untouchable circle and neither ELCON nor the IOR could be so much as touched by the methods of Italian justice, so concerned as it was with protecting civil liberties.

*But I'm not Italian justice.*

At seven in the morning she woke Giulia, who was sleeping on the sofa.

"We have to find out who's really behind that Swiss consortium and GB Investments in Luxembourg and that Charity Investments in Dubai."

Giulia lifted her head up.

"No, Linda, give it a rest. We've had three deaths, and Balistreri's right. Leave it to the police now."

"The police won't be able to discover who it is that controls ELCON's shareholders, they'd need a warrant signed by a judge, an international letter rogatory to Dubai and also one to Luxembourg. The two of us can do it much quicker."

Giulia was now wide awake and totally against Linda's plan.

"Listen to me, Linda. First let's find the woman that Domnica Panu told you about, the one they call *Fratello*."

"What use would that be, Giulia? Even if we did find her, we'd only be where we were before. Going nowhere fast."

Giulia sighed.

"So what do you want to do? I don't think my hacker friend's going to be much help this time."

"Come with me to Lugano tomorrow. There's an early morning flight."

# SUNDAY, AUGUST 7, 2011

ROME

Balistreri told Corvu about the conversation he'd just had with Monsignor Eugenio Pizza. But only what had to do with the present investigation. He avoided mentioning Libya, his father, and the man with the sliced ear. He'd have been forced to move on to other investigations and had no intention of doing that right now.

Corvu heard him out. At the end, he drew the obvious conclusion.

"After Linda's visit, perhaps the Monsignor told someone she was going to see Domnica Panu. It was probably Melania Druc's lover."

"I figured that out by myself, Corvu," Balistreri shot back rudely. "Only we don't know who he is."

Corvu smiled and handed him a photograph.

"Perhaps we do. My Secret Service friends have sent me this."

The shot showed Melania Druc leaving a luxury nightclub with dark windows and a small main door in a square in Rome's historic center.

"That car's part of the escort of Gruppo Italia's chairman, Senator Emilio Busi, which is why they were following it. As you know, the Secret Service keeps tabs on everyone, even itself."

Balistreri nodded. But it wasn't enough.

"Have you identified which apartment she was going into?"

Corvu shook his head.

"There are ten of them and not a single name on the entry phone."

"Check the deeds in the land registry to find out who owns them. Something's bound to come up, you'll see."

But Corvu had been working through the night.

"Already done that. The whole block's owned by Gruppo Italia and all the apartments are rented out at ridiculous rates. But not one of them to Melania Druc."

Balistreri knew that Corvu was doing exceptional work and he should have congratulated him. But his mood was dark and his thoughts were still upsetting him.

"The trouble is, Corvu, that none of this proves that Melania was Busi's lover nor that he had anything to do with the deaths of her and her little girl."

Corvu smiled and handed over to him what looked as a book.

"Civitavecchia's police sent over everything they found in the cabin. Melania Druc knew three languages. This is the Italian version of her final thesis."

Balistreri stared at the bound copy and sighed.

"And how the devil is Melania Druc's thesis going to help?"

"To know her better, *dottore*," Corvu replied.

Balistreri recalled Domnica Panu's words on Linda's recording.

Melania was educated, a degree in political science and communication. *But in my mind she's nothing more than a call girl.*

The thesis had a surprising title that immediately caught his attention: "Large Scale Public Works and the Criminal Underworld in Italy."

He quickly skimmed through. It was a serious study, the result of dedicated research. Public tenders falsified with expertise and skill, repeated contact between public officials and entrepreneurs, connections between entrepreneurs and the Mafia, the 'Ndrangheta, and the Camorra. Things that everyone talked about, but Melania Druc had gone to great lengths to collect official data of the last twenty years, and not only in Italy. Nothing original perhaps, but the thesis left no doubts about Melania.

This wasn't an escort girl who'd inveiled a wealthy man. Perhaps she was only a deluded idealist who thought she could cure evil with love.

He closed the thesis, but Corvu was still standing in front of him.

"Between the folder and the cover, *dottore* Balistreri."

Hidden in the fold of the last page was a photograph of Melania in front of St. Peter's with little Tanja in her arms. On the back of the photograph, which perhaps she never gave to the recipient because it was too compromising, was a handwritten dedication.

*To Emilio, with all our love from Melania and Tanja.*

Melania Druc had told Domnica Panu that Tanja's father was also on the ship. And Senator Emilio Busi had been on that ship. And he also appeared in the dedication.

Balistreri remembered the article in which for the first time Busi had voiced doubts over the possibility of constructing a bridge across the Straits of Messina.

Had Melania been trying to convince him? Perhaps yes, perhaps no.

His acid reflux was rising and burning his esophagus.

Four men who'll stop at nothing have a project. An idealistic and inflexible young woman tries to stop them. The young woman dies.

Those four men were on the cruise ship between Elba and Civitavecchia.

Those four men were on La Moneta the day Italia died. With them too was a boy who later had part of his ear severed. And Nadia Al Bakri's killers were also there. They were all there.

"Get Busi's number, Corvu."

"It's Sunday afternoon, *dottore* Balistreri."

"Get a cell phone. Move."

· · · ·

Corvu came back in a few minutes with the cell number of Busi's personal assistant, Beatrice Armellini. Balistreri introduced himself and she sounded like a cross between a television announcer and a rigid military chief.

"The president is in his office at Gruppo Italia. Very busy with meetings," she said in a polite but cold tone.

"On a Sunday afternoon?" objected Balistreri.

"Clearly you don't know the senator. He's always working."

*Oh yes, I know the senator very well. He's always working on his own projects.*

Only by mentioning what had happened on the cruise ship and by recourse to a veiled threat to bring the senator to the Flying Squad offices on a hot Sunday could Balistreri bring about a brief interview.

· · · ·

Balistreri walked through the heat of the late afternoon. Gruppo Italia's front offices were located in an eighteenth-century building behind Piazza Navona. Its façade was dominated by a grandiose main door below an architrave. In that mass of friezes, marble columns, and capitals, Emilio Busi ran an economic empire with the light but sure hand that enabled him to look nonchalantly and with detachment at the comings and goings of prime ministers, governments, and parliaments.

Emilio Busi wasn't one of the many politicians who wastes time over garnering a handful of votes, or who exploits their momentary power for personal gain and who sooner or later ends up on the scrap heap or in jail. Busi was at the center of political, economic, and media power, which he knew like the back of his hand and dominated with the astute cynical ease of a puppet master who amuses himself by leaving the leading roles to his puppets. He hadn't appeared on television for years and only occasionally granted an interview to a newspaper, as he had done a few days earlier with *Il Domani*.

A security guard opened the inside gate that led onto a huge rectangular courtyard bordered on three sides by arcades. In the middle were the remains of ancient statues and a fountain. A doorman in a dark blue uniform took Balistreri to reception, where ancient and modern were blended with great taste, then to the paneled elevator with a red seat. The doorman turned the key to the top floor and pressed the button.

Another doorman met him at the other end and pointed to a long corridor with walls and ceilings decorated by sixteenth- and seventeenth-century artists. At every turn there was another desk with a doorman to show him the way.

The last man took him across the council chamber, a room as large as a tennis court with a marble floor, a frescoed ceiling, and the walls covered in a series of paintings, tapestries, and mirrors that would not have disgraced the Louvre.

Lastly, the man showed him into a small waiting room, all wooden paneling, sofas upholstered in alcantara, and beautiful photographs of Rome on the walls.

The person with whom he had spoken on the telephone greeted him with a cold, professional smile.

"Beatrice Armellini, I'm the chairman's assistant."

She was a splendid woman of about thirty-five, as smart as the furnishings: her black hair rolled into a chignon, her spotless iron-gray suit a discreet but slightly teasing cover for an impressive figure that not even a nun's habit could have totally deadened. Glasses with gray frames completed this extremely refined picture.

Balistreri had the impression he'd seen her somewhere beforebut couldn't remember where.

"The senator's very busy, Commissario, he can only see you for a few minutes."

Balistreri followed Beatrice into the large beautifully furnished office. The window that took up almost an entire wall held a spectacular view of Piazza Navona's rooftops on one side and St. Peter's cupola on the other.

When they entered, Gruppo Italia's chairman was on his feet with his back to them, watching a news flash about Libya on a large plasma screen. He didn't turn around. NATO was dropping bombs on Tripoli.

Balistreri saw a transformation in Emilio Busi that wasn't there in Don Eugenio. He'd first known Emilio Busi as a young man, when he dressed in the most appalling mismatch of clothing and smoked hideous plain-tipped Nazionali cigarettes. His once unruly and uncombed hair was now very short and gray. His dress was in keeping with the place and his role in it. No more horrendous short-sleeved check shirts under a white vest, no high-waisted shapeless pants, no more short socks and worn-out moccasins. Busi now sported a Marinella tie,

Church's shoes, and a Rolex on his wrist. His cigarettes were no longer Nazionali but long slim Dunhills. Over the years he had become a very powerful man, with longstanding links to the Left, new links on the Right, and, via Monsignor Pizza, with the Vatican. There was no large-scale work financed from public coffers that didn't cross his desk.

*A man for whom olives were of no use at all.*

Only at the end of the news item did Busi turn off the sound and face Balistreri. Neither man smiled. Nor did they offer to shake hands.

"Commissario Balistreri. I didn't think we'd meet again. I imagine you're happy they're dropping bombs on Gaddafi."

It was a cruel sarcastic remark from a man who knew very well that the other man's mother had died a few hours before Gaddafi came to power.

And perhaps because of it.

Balistreri replied in the same vein.

"Everything has to end, sooner or later, Senator. Even the Communism that you admired so much . . ."

Busi made a brief gesture with a hand, as if to brush away an insect as annoying as the memory.

"Communism was a stupid idea, even if it was necessary for a certain time to get rid of Fascism. After 1989 it no longer served any purpose. Anyway, none of this has any importance. What did you want to see me about so urgently?"

"Melania and Tanja Druc," replied Balistreri curtly.

Busi gestured for him to sit in one of the luxurious armchairs. His face was inscrutable, a mixture of cynicism and toughness, but those two names had created a tension that deepened the furrows in his brow.

*Fear, remorse, pain?*

"Fire away, Balistreri. I will only reply to things I judge to be relevant."

Busi wasn't even bothering to put up a front. He didn't need to. He was in the circle of the untouchables. A circle inside which everyone knew everyone else and everyone helped each other out. The same schools, same gyms and clubs, same parties, and, in some cases, the same churches.

"Did you know Melania Druc?"

Busi shut up like a clam. But, unexpectedly, faced with a question to which he could have replied, "And who is she?" what Balistreri read in the senator's features wasn't reticence or fear. It was a mixture of anger and sadness.

He handed him Melania Druc's bachelor's thesis.

"I think you already know what it says."

Busi studied it for a few seconds, then handed it back. His wrinkled hand was that of an old man, and was shaking slightly. Balistreri produced the photograph of Melania and Tanja in front of St. Peter's. He handed that over and Busi studied it carefully.

"Please turn it over, Senator, it's addressed to you."

*To Emilio, with all our love from Melania and Tanja.*

The senator's lips trembled. But he immediately checked himself and gave the photograph back. Again, he said nothing. But that silence didn't deny a thing, it was only the silence of a man who for the first time in his life found himself without words.

"Senator, I'm opening an investigation into a homicide. And the first thing I'm going to do is ask for a comparison of the little girl's DNA and your own."

Busi shrugged, as if this were completely irrelevant.

"Commissario, if I oppose this, you won't even get an investigation started."

Balistreri ignored the threat. He knew that the photograph and its dedication had shaken Busi and he wanted to exploit the fact straightaway.

"Melania Druc died because she opposed the plans of someone who doesn't like to be stopped. Does that remind you of anyone, Senator?"

Busi remained silent for some time. When he eventually spoke, his voice was less certain than usual.

"The past usually helps us to understand the present, Commissario. But not in this case. You'd do well to accept the fact."

Balistreri tried to contain his anger.

"Senator, my mother died in 1969. It's long ago and out of my jurisdiction. But Melania and Tanja Druc *are* within my jurisdiction. If you had nothing to do with it, then tell me who did. One of the people you speak to when you use those foreign SIM cards, I imagine."

Busi lit a long slim cigarette with his Dunhill lighter.

"Balistreri, you should have grown up by now. Please stop chasing these ghosts from the past."

Balistreri looked him in the eyes.

"A few days ago Linda Nardi saw Melania at the Hotel Rixos in Tripoli. She was with a man who had a severed ear. Was he a ghost or real, Senator?"

Emilio Busi turned pale, now showing all of his years. A spider's web of lines scored his face and his ice-cold eyes closed in the effort to suppress something.

Regret, anger, fear, pain.

In the end, his lips moved in a whisper he would never have expressed in the past and never again in the future.

"Balistreri, you don't understand, you haven't understood for forty years. There are businessmen and then there are killers. Have you still not gotten over the desire to get yourself killed?"

The chairman of Gruppo Italia had recovered his icy calm. He pressed a button on his desk. His assistant came into the room immediately.

"Commissario Balistreri is leaving, Beatrice. Would you see him out?"

Balistreri got up. Busi had not given him any real answer, but after what Busi had said, he was now certain.

Everything started there. In the land of *ghibli*, olives, and oil.

Beatrice Armellini accompanied Balistreri to the main entrance. Her appearance wavered between that of a business manager, which is what her clothes, makeup, and hairstyle said, and that of a seductress, which is what those eyes behind the bookworm's glasses said.

It was a combination that the young Michele would once have found fascinating.

Once they used to hand over their underwear after a ride in the Duetto with the siren at full blast. But now he'd have to offer dinner, polite conversation, and court her. And who knows if even that would even suffice.

It was as if Beatrice Armellini had read his thoughts.

"Commissario Balistreri, I have to speak with you. But not here, if you follow . . ."

"Would you like to come to my office later on?"

She shook her head.

"That's not the right place, Commissario. For the very same reasons."

"Then you say where."

Beatrice Armellini took off her glasses and smiled. Once again, Balistreri had the impression of having seen that smile before.

"This needs privacy, Commissario. If you don't find the proposition out of place, I'd suggest a drink tomorrow at the Sky Suite. I have a dinner engagement earlier, we could meet there later on."

Balistreri had heard of the new establishment's reputation on top of the Janiculum. It was the most fashionable and pricey spot in Rome, a deluxe place where you could drink and dance on its panoramic terrace or stay the night in magnificent suites with views over the city.

A place that was certainly confidential.

Balistreri knew that it was rash to accept, but past and present were coming together in a way that was drawing him in irresistibly.

He nodded at Beatrice.

"I'll see you there tomorrow evening at ten."

Off he went on foot among the tourists. It was still very hot and although there was nothing more he could do for the day, he went back to the almost deserted offices of the Flying Squad. He arrived in his office, closed the door and the blinds, lit a Gitanes, allowed himself a glass of Lagavulin, put on Leonard Cohen's music, and laid down on the old sofa.

# MONDAY, AUGUST 8, 2011

## LUGANO

The early flight from Fiumicino took an hour. From Lugano's tiny airport, Linda and Giulia quickly arrived in Collina d'Oro by taxi. Everything there was perfect, clean, and calm. Low houses nestled in the greenery and below them stood the lake.

They had the taxi stop outside the address shown on ELCON's memorandum of association that Linda photocopied in Gabriele Cascio's office.

"Okay, Giulia, you stay here. If I don't come out in half an hour, you come in and get me out the Piccolo way."

"So we can end up eating chocolate in a Swiss prison?"

Linda gave her a little caress.

"It's a civilized country, they won't treat us badly."

The office was in a small single-story villa, very simple. There was no ELCON sign, only a plaque below the bell, which said CERTIFIED ACCOUNTING ASSOCIATES.

Linda rang the bell, and the door was opened by a middle-aged lady who must have been the secretary.

"Good morning. How may I help you?" she asked with studied politeness.

Linda immediately showed her the photocopy of the consortium's memorandum of association.

"I'm from GB Investments in Luxembourg. I need to speak with whoever deals with ELCON's accounts in Nairobi."

The lady looked perplexed, and so Linda added the magic words.

"It's a highly confidential matter."

The lady thought for a moment. She wasn't prepared for a decision like this.

"We only see people by appointment."

Linda adopted a serious tone.

"A grave matter has suddenly arisen in Italy."

At this point the lady decided to pass on the responsibility.

"Very well, take a seat. I'll call Signor Milani right away."

She showed Linda into a small lounge with a table and four chairs. Signor Milani arrived a few minutes later, a pleasant man of about forty and very self-confident.

All the better, it'll make it easier.

"What can I do for you, Signorina . . ."

"Nardi, Linda Nardi."

She showed him her passport before he could ask for it. Signor Milani examined it, comparing the photograph with her face, then lingered on her breasts.

He handed the document back and smiled at her. She returned the smile in a way that men could interpret as they wished.

"And so, Signorina Nardi, what is this about?"

Linda spoke in a low voice.

"The judiciary in Luxembourg have asked us for the names of the real owners of the company. It seems there's been a request by the Italian Guardia di Finanza."

Milani looked at her uncomprehendingly.

"I don't understand . . ."

Linda put on a conspiratorial air.

"We have our confidential sources, Signor Milani. For some time there's been an investigation into the IOR by the Guardia di Finanza.

And what's come out are several payments by ELCON to a certain monsignor."

Milani turned pale. Keeping the accounts, he couldn't be unaware of the payments.

"An international letter rogatory's been sent . . ." Linda added vaguely.

Milani was now sufficiently alarmed and confused.

"Signorina Nardi, I can't possibly discuss these matters with you without the authorization of GB Investments. You understand, we have to observe confidentiality, I don't know who you represent."

Linda gave him an encouraging smile, in all senses of the word. Then she tried her bluff, as a close friend had taught her in poker all those years ago.

The more impossible it sounds, the more credible it is.

"You can call Giacomo Busi directly. He's the one who sent me."

Milani was speechless. Linda knew she had hit the bull's-eye. Then she got confirmation.

"Give me five minutes to make a call."

Milani got up and left the room. Linda sneaked out immediately after him.

"I'm going out to have a cigarette," she told the secretary.

As soon as she was out, she got into the taxi where Giulia Piccolo was waiting for her.

"Airport, please!" she ordered the driver.

Giulia looked at her.

Linda smiled.

"Spot-on target."

"So would you mind telling me how you did it?" Giulia asked as they were waiting in the small Lugano airport for the return flight to Rome.

Linda was more thoughtful than cheerful. Her success was linked to an intuition that wasn't too difficult to fathom. And it reminded her of the arrogance of the men in power who govern Italy.

"The children of powerful men are often very stupid. They think they're above the law and become reckless. Such as using their own initials for the name of a company . . ."

"You mean 'GB' stands for Giacomo Busi? But how on earth did you figure that out?"

"It was Domnica Panu who told me that Busi was involved."

"But that's not true, Linda. You played me the recording of your interview with her and she never mentioned Busi at all."

"She said that Tanja's father was on the ship. And that Melania had kept his name a secret. It had to be someone really important, who also liked young women. That fits Emilio Busi . . ."

"Busi was the father of Tanja? At his age?"

Linda smiled.

"Grand old men of importance can always find novel ways of doing things, Giulia. From Viagra to those little suction pumps . . . Besides, Domnica mentioned many other things that made me think of Busi."

"Such as?"

"That woman *Fratello*, wasn't she a procuress who found clients for Domnica in return for a certain percentage? And she took Domnica to them."

"So what's Busi got to do with that?"

"Do you know how I came to meet him? During an inquiry into the presumed very informal methods used by Gruppo Italia to influence its potential clients."

Giulia looked at Linda as if she had wings and a wand. Then she smiled.

"You make me feel very stupid sometimes, Linda. So now what do we do?" she asked.

Linda's face clouded over. She was remembering that Clark Gable face with white hair and a mustache, the soft but firm manner with which he had both praised and warned her.

*You really are overly courageous.*

"We now know that Emilio Busi's behind GB Investments in Luxembourg and that the IOR account is in the name of Monsignor Pizza. That leaves Charity Investments in Dubai. There was also a man who lives in Dubai at the table on the ship with Busi and Pizza."

"You never mentioned that. Why not?" Giulia asked, slightly resentful.

"Because his name is Salvatore Balistreri, that's why!"

Giulia Piccolo turned pale. She brushed a hand through her high-lights, which were now green, and shook her head.

"Linda, there have been newspaper articles about the Balistreri family. Perhaps it was idle speculation or malicious gossip, though he was never accused of anything. But there's also objective proof against his four elder brothers in Palermo. They had a successful business in Sicily's earth-moving sector and owned land, betting parlors, and bars. One of them, the eldest, was put on trial accused of having links with the Mafia. . . . You know all that, right?"

Linda Nardi nodded slowly. She couldn't forget the grim face Michele Balistreri made whenever she mentioned his father.

The very Michele she had sent packing because he didn't want to shoot anyone anymore.

*Perhaps this is the last thing I can do before going back to John Kiptanu and my orphans in Kenya. So I can leave without feeling as if I'm running away.*

Out of her purse she took the business card that Salvatore Balistreri had given her out on deck between Elba and Civitavecchia. There was a cell phone number that began with the prefix 00971, that of Dubai.

"Don't do it," Giulia begged her.

Linda smiled at her.

"Giulia, I want to leave Italy for good. But if I leave this business halfway through, it would be like running away. I couldn't forget that."

She entered the number and after a few rings heard the warm voice that was a little throaty and a little gravely.

"Hello . . ." he said in English.

"It's Linda Nardi," she said simply.

There was a moment's silence.

*You can hang up and keep me out of all this. But if I've understood correctly, you won't.*

"So I did well to leave you my card, Signorina."

There was no irony in his voice. And no surprise or irritation either. Perhaps a touch of concern, that was all.

*You really are overly courageous.*

"I need to talk to you, Signor Balistreri, if you're still in Rome."

"I am in Rome, but I'm about to go to the airport. I have a flight to Geneva."

"I'm not in Rome but I am also about to get on a flight. I'll be in Rome in an hour. Could we meet at Fiumicino airport?"

"Of course. Where are you coming from?"

Linda had a moment's hesitation, then decided it was better to be cautious.

"From Turin. Where shall I meet you?"

"At Alitalia's VIP lounge in international departures. See you later."

## ROME

Balistreri hadn't slept at all. The thought of his father on that cruise ship meant that the exile he had imposed on him had been unilaterally canceled.

*All four of them were on that ship together when Melania and Tanja died. The same as that day on La Moneta when my mother died.*

The whole morning in the office he reexamined all the recent facts with Corvu. Starting from the day Linda Nardi saw Melania Druc in Tripoli with the man with the severed ear up to his visits to Don Eugenio and Emilio Busi. But he now felt he had to meet another man, the man he really didn't want to see for the rest of his life.

*But Dad and the man with the severed ear are the real connecting point between the past and today.*

So at lunchtime Balistreri called his brother's cell phone. As ever, whether he was in a meeting with a minister or having lunch with his wife and children, Alberto answered on the first ring.

"Michele!"

He hated asking him the question, but there was no avoiding it.

"Is Dad in Italy, Alberto?"

There was a moment's silence.

"He's been here for a few days, Michele. He had some urgent business to resolve, but he's leaving today."

"I think I need to talk to him."

Alberto again hesitated, but only for a moment.

"He's got a flight to Geneva at three o'clock. If you hurry you'll find him in Alitalia's VIP lounge in international departures."

Balistreri went on foot to the Metro to take the underground to Fiumicino. He had no idea yet what he was going to do. But he had to see his father.

## FIUMICINO

Linda and Giulia talked for the whole flight back from Lugano. Giulia was troubled and opposed to Linda's upcoming meeting with Salvatore Balistreri. As a good policewoman, she knew that what they were doing was not only illegal but also probably dangerous. But her friendship with Linda was more important than these considerations and when they landed at two in the afternoon she went with her to international departures.

Linda tried to allay Giulia's fears.

"No one's going to kill me here at the airport, especially not in Alitalia's VIP departure lounge. Go to my apartment, Giulia, and I'll meet up with you there."

Giulia reluctantly nodded her agreement and left. Linda walked quickly to the VIP lounge. When she entered, the lounge was quite crowded, but she spotted Salvatore Balistreri immediately, sitting in an armchair reading the *Financial Times*. He was beautifully dressed, as usual, in a midblue sports jacket with gray slacks, white shirt, and midnight blue tie.

As soon as he saw her, he got up to meet her and shook her hand with a smile. But this handsome elderly gentleman was not interested in her in the way that men usually were.

"I'm happy to see you again, Signorina Nardi."

*He seems to be sincere . . .*

Linda forced herself not to lose sight of the facts: this man was a friend of Monsignor Eugenio Pizza and Senator Emilio Busi, both of whom were involved in the IOR business, as was Salvatore Balistreri himself perhaps, considering ELCON's memorandum of association. And all three were on the cruise where Melania and Tanja Druc died. And he had questionable brothers in Sicily.

Linda accepted his offer of an iced tea from the bar, and they sat down in front of a window where you could see the airplanes lined up by the runways. He noticed she was very tense.

"You were different on the cruise. Has anything happened to you, Signorina?"

*Indeed, Signor Balistreri. Melania and Tanja Druc and Domnica Panu are dead. And I've found that your friends are behind the slush funds and IOR account. Which leaves your role in all of it.*

Linda reflected for a moment. Then she decided that there was no other way with this man than to tell him everything, or *almost* everything.

"Yesterday morning I went to Ostia to meet a certain person."

He just stared at her, waiting. Despite his cheerful, smiling manner and his politeness, this old man struck a fear in her that she'd never felt before.

*He knows I'm a dangerous journalist. Why is he so polite?*

"She was a friend of the young woman found dead with her daughter on the cruise," Linda went on.

Salvatore Balistreri didn't move a muscle or even frown. Only after a little while did he nod and lean over toward her.

"And why did you go to Ostia to see this woman?"

Linda looked out of the window. An airplane was taking off. She imagined herself getting on it, escaping from the horror, going back to Kenya, to her orphans and to John Kiptanu. But that was precisely what she didn't want to do: run away.

"To find out the truth . . ."

Her voice was faint.

This time he did frown, but not because he didn't understand, rather the opposite.

"You suffer a great deal, Signorina Nardi. I feel very sorry for you."

It was absurd, but despite coming from Salvatore Balistreri, who was probably a very shady businessman, perhaps a Mafioso or even worse, the words actually sounded sincere.

*He really is sorry. Perhaps he's sorry he's going to have to kill me.*

He bent forward and smiled at her.

"Come on, tell me why you were on that cruise. Was it to meet Monsignor Pizza?"

Looking into his impenetrable yet understanding eyes in that moment, Linda was convinced that there was no other way of fighting and winning against this man, to see if he was sincere or not, than to tell him the truth. Lying to him would only be pointless and perhaps even more dangerous. She decided to tackle him head-on, regardless of the consequences.

"It's an ugly business, Signor Balistreri. Would you like to hear about it?"

He poured her another iced tea.

"Of course, Signorina Nardi. I will listen very closely."

Linda told him the whole story, starting with the information she had from Bashir Yared about the IOR involvement in Kenya. Then she went on to Nairobi and Gabriele Cascio, the bank statements, and the account in Monsignor Eugenio Pizza's name. She also told him about the meeting she'd had with Monsignor Pizza in San Pietro in Vincoli just over twenty-four hours earlier, the conversation with Domnica Panu and her death, the trip to Lugano, and the discovery that Emilio Busi's son was behind GB Investments. The only thing she didn't mention was Michele Balistreri.

As she told him these things, she gradually felt lighter and less worried about what might happen to her.

Salvatore Balistreri heard her out in silence, his eyes closed, as if he were searching in his memory for the answers to her questions. At the end of her story, Linda stopped and Salvatore Balistreri opened his eyes again.

"Why did you call me, Signorina Nardi?"

The tone of his voice was warm and polite. Linda plucked up the necessary courage.

"To find out if you're the man behind Charity Investments, Dubai, the other partner in the Swiss Consortium."

He nodded and continued to stare at her. She thought there was a great deal behind those eyes. They were the same as Michele's, yet very different.

Such contrasts. Hard and soft. Determination and regret.

Salvatore Balistreri bent forward and looked her in the eyes. There wasn't a trace of resentment or threat in his look, nor in his voice.

"I'm no longer an Italian citizen, Signorina Nardi. I have an American passport and I live between the US and Dubai. If I were behind the Dubai Charity Investment Fund, it wouldn't be considered a crime, and no one could accuse me of anything. The information is of no consequence for me, nor of any use for you."

Linda nodded slowly. The man was right. Even if he had admitted, *Yes, I'm behind Charity Investments, Dubai,* he would have risked nothing in terms of criminal prosecution.

"And why did you go to see Domnica Panu?" he asked her.

"Because Melania Druc mentioned her. I spoke with her briefly on the cruise. She was worried, scared. Very different from the other time I saw her."

Salvatore Balistreri frowned.

"The other time?"

"A few days ago I saw her in the Hotel Rixos in Tripoli. She was with an important Libyan, a member of the Secret Service. A man of about sixty with a severed ear."

For the first time, Linda saw a shadow cross the old man's face. Then he sighed.

"I've already had occasion to tell you, Signorina Nardi. You are overly courageous."

"And so what should I do now, according to you, Signor Balistreri? Go to the police or forget all about it?"

He reflected on this for some time with his eyes closed so he could concentrate better, as if the question really were of considerable importance. Finally, he looked her in the eye.

"Neither, I think. As for forgetting all about it, I fear that's not in your character."

He said this with a smile. But Linda knew that that smile could mean anything.

"So what should I do?"

"You're a journalist, Signorina. Leave those poor victims to the police, and don't bother yourself with them anymore. You have solid proof enough for the other story, which is your real field. You can write a good article about that."

Linda shook her head.

"I don't think you visit Italy enough, Signor Balistreri. Not even *Il Domani* would publish any article that involved Senator Busi and Monsignor Pizza."

He nodded.

"I understand, but you undervalue certain men and think too highly of others. Write a piece based solely on the established facts and call *Il Domani*'s editor personally. He'll publish it. Otherwise, the *Financial Times* or *Le Monde* will. You'll see."

In that "You'll see" was the absolute certainty of a man who can accomplish anything. It was pointless asking how or why or who. Completely pointless.

"I thought Monsignor Pizza and Senator Busi were your friends . . ." Linda said.

He shook his head and continued to smile.

"Friends are another matter, Signorina. My brothers, my cousins, are the only people I call my friends. Anyone else is just an acquaintance. Or perhaps I should say, ex-acquaintances."

Linda was speechless. The last sentence, spoken completely calmly, had something final and terrible in it.

Salvatore Balistreri rose to his feet.

"I have a flight to catch. I have a meeting at the Geneva airport. Try to do as I say. By all means call me again, if it would help."

They stopped just outside the door to the lounge. He took her hands between his. They were the hands of an old man, well manicured but full of spots and thick veins under the wrinkled skin.

He looked at her directly and spoke clearly.

"I would hate for anything bad to happen to you, Signorina. Promise me you'll be careful?"

Linda stood stock still as she watched him disappear with those two contradictory phrases ringing in her head.

A threat posing as a concern. Or a concern posing as a threat?

. . . .

Once at Fiumicino, Michele Balistreri hid himself behind a notice board. From there he kept an eye on the Alitalia VIP lounge waiting for his father to exit toward the departure gates.

He had no idea what to say to him.

Are you behind that investment company in Dubai? Did you push my mother off that cliff?

He was well aware of the inappropriateness of both those unconnected questions.

Or perhaps they were linked by an extremely long invisible thread.

He wanted to leave, shut himself in his office full of smoke, and continue his calm voyage toward the mouth of that river and the sea. It was Mike, not him, who wanted to confront this man and who had those thoughts that Michele couldn't manage to dispel.

The VIP lounge door opened and his father came out with Linda Nardi. Balistreri couldn't believe his eyes. Those were two people he had never wanted to see together.

He watched his father clasp Linda's hands and whisper something to her. On his lips he could read: *"I would hate for anything bad to happen to you, Signorina. Promise me you'll be careful?"*

For Balistreri, who had known this man down to his very soul for so long, those words were very clear. As Don Eugenio and Emilio Busi had told him with different words, the concept was clear.

Forget or die.


## ROME

It was the middle of the afternoon when Linda arrived at her apartment. She immediately told Giulia about Salvatore Balistreri.

"You shouldn't have told him everything, Linda. He's a very dangerous man. He was threatening you."

"He didn't threaten me, Giulia."

"He said 'I would hate for anything bad to happen to you,' didn't he? Will you listen to me? He also said that his only real friends are his family in Palermo, and those are people that . . ."

"I don't think that Salvatore Balistreri would have me killed, Giulia. Not now, at least."

"Exactly. He had you promise that you wouldn't do anything more, otherwise . . ."

"That wasn't what he meant."

"All right, so how do you want to proceed?"

"I'll do what Salvatore Balistreri said. I'll write the article and then call *Il Domani*."

Giulia Piccolo ran her long strong fingers through her green high-lights. As a policewoman, she knew exactly what she should do.

Notify Michele Balistreri and the Homicide Squad.

Linda went to the computer and started to write. She mentioned Kenya, Gabriele Cascio, the slush funds used for kickbacks deposited in Monsignor Pizza's IOR account, and the fact that GB Investments was run by Giacomo Busi, son of Gruppo Italia's chairman, Senator Emilio Busi. Nothing about Melania, Tanja, or Domnica.

*I'm doing what you suggested I do, Signor Salvatore Balistreri.*

Then she called the office of *Il Domani*'s editor Albano. Linda had known Albano since she'd started at the paper as a trainee. He was an excellent journalist, but also a well-balanced and prudent man who would never put his newspaper at risk for the sake of an article. It wasn't even a given that he'd answer the call, given that—among other things—it was almost eleven o'clock at night, the busiest time before the paper was put to bed. However, his secretary put him on the line immediately.

"I was expecting your call, Linda. I'd have preferred you to get in touch directly, without someone giving me advance notice."

So no pressure there . . .

"I'm sorry," Linda said. "This isn't exactly my idea. But would you like to read the article?"

"We're putting the paper to bed right now. And we'd also have to show it to our legal department, Linda. Can you send it to me now, then I'll call you back?"

She sent him the piece and he called back in fifteen minutes, his voice deadly serious.

"We'll put it on the front page, Linda. But you know what you'll be facing, don't you?"

*I'll be put through the wringer, surely. But what you don't know is that this isn't the whole story: there are three murder victims as well.*

"Okay, thanks. And please don't worry about me."

Albano sighed and his voice became even more animated.

"It's an excellent piece of work, Linda. I'd publish it no matter what. Good luck."

Linda ended the call. Another seemingly interminable day was coming to an end. She and Giulia settled down on the sofa to watch a black-and-white movie from the 1950s.

It was a love story.

# MONDAY, AUGUST 8, 2011

## ROME

The Sky Suite Hotel's roof garden was crowded out. Many of the men were over fifty and many of the women under thirty-five. In the majority of cases, the couples were clandestine. A colorful nightlife that reeked of money, power, and sex and flaunted all three.

Balistreri missed Beatrice Armellini when she first came in and only became aware of her by the reaction she caused among those seated at the tables—lasciviousness in the men, jealousy in the women. The transformation in the woman he had met in Gruppo Italia's offices was extraordinary.

This is the real Beatrice.

Gone were the thick gray glasses, the chignon, the pale makeup, the severe clothes. The person entering the room was a woman close to forty who looked less than thirty, beautifully made up, her black hair loose on her tanned shoulders, now wearing contact lenses and a short, red sleeveless dress that both hugged and exposed her terrific figure. Again, Balistreri wondered where he had seen her before.

She came over smiling as he rose to greet her. Conscious of the stir she was creating, she did nothing to minimize it.

"Good evening, Commissario Balistreri. Oh, I feel so important. Imagine the Head of Homicide taking the trouble to meet me, especially in a place like this!"

"I imagine you're used to feeling important. Should we take a seat at the bar?"

"I'd prefer somewhere away from people's stares, Commissario. If you feel at ease with me, let's take a suite."

*"If you feel at ease with me." Once upon a time this kind of woman was my daily bread.*

She laughed at her own joke and Balistreri asked the maître d' for a suite.

"Do you have a reservation, sir?"

"No."

"Then I'm sorry, everything's already taken."

"Oh no," Beatrice muttered.

Balistreri took out his wallet, but the man assumed an apologetic look.

"It's not a question of tipping me, sir."

Balistreri smiled. This was a typical Italian reaction. But over the years he'd learned how to deal with Italians. His took out his police ID, which stated that he was in charge of Section III, Homicide Section of the Flying Squad and showed it to the man.

"Now please have a suite prepared."

The maître d' went pale.

"Of course, sir. I beg your pardon. Please come this way."

Balistreri smiled at Beatrice.

The maître d' accompanied them to a suite on the eleventh floor: living room thirty yards square, dining table already laid out on the terrace facing the city, flat-screen television, CD and DVD player, directionable halogen spotlights in the ceiling and floor, a master bedroom with an enormous four-poster bed, strategically placed mirrors, bathroom with Jacuzzi.

"The floor waiter will be with you in a moment," said the maître d'.

Then he bowed and left them alone.

## ROME

Linda and Giulia were exhausted. The trip to Lugano, the meeting with Salvatore Balistreri, the article for *Il Domani*. Fortunately, the old black-and-white love story on TV had a happy ending.

"If only love was really like that . . ." Giulia muttered. "But it's not women's fault. It's men who bring out the worst in us . . ."

"Not all of them," said Linda, thinking of John Kiptanu.

But Giulia was lost in other thoughts.

"The trouble is we're capable of lowering ourselves to men's level, like that woman who took Domnica to Gruppo Italia's clients. They called her *Brother*, as if she were a man . . ."

Suddenly a face popped into Linda's memory.

"Beatrice . . ." she whispered to herself.

"Who the hell is that?"

Linda went to the computer and Googled *beatrice armellini*. Wikipedia came up with the biography of the winner of Italy's *Big Brother*.

. . . .

Michele Balistreri and Beatrice Armellini were sitting on the terrace with an excellent bottle of white wine. Beatrice wanted to take her time, so Balistreri let her talk. The economic crisis, inept and corrupt politicians, the euro, and all the poor people who were losing their jobs.

Balistreri watched her as she put the glass to her lips, smiled, crossed her legs, and caressed her hair, recognizing the gestures of feminine seduction he'd learned from the days of Marlene Hunt.

He'd decided to wait, given it was Beatrice Armellini who had asked to speak to him. Indeed, after a couple of glasses of wine and a little chitchat, she decided to unbutton.

"You're looking into the deaths of Melania and Tanja Druc, aren't you?"

"Is that why you wanted to meet me here?"

Beatrice relaxed and smiled.

"For that and a little more. Assuming you're interested, of course."

"I'm interested in what you have to tell me, Signorina. Assuming you're not going to tell me any lies."

She licked a drop of wine off her lips with the tip of her tongue.

"And how would you deal with those lies, Commissario? Corporal punishment?"

Balistreri lit a cigarette. He had to put a stop to the way this was going. Beatrice was steering him onto the path where she felt more at ease. But he had neither the time nor the desire for the performance.

"Why has Senator Busi sent you to me, Signorina?"

She smiled again.

"For the questions he couldn't reply to. But also to propose a deal."

"I don't do deals."

Beatrice wasn't put off in the least.

"Let me tell you something, Commissario, then you can decide if you want to go forward."

Balistreri said nothing. He was trying to ignore the low-cut dress, the thighs, the eyes, all the provocative ways that Beatrice Armellini was trying to make him more malleable. It was a game at which she was an expert, and men had taught her that it worked and paid off.

"I've been Senator Busi's assistant for years, Commissario. And since he became chairman of Gruppo Italia, I've been in charge of the special entertainment program."

"And what does 'special' mean?"

Beatrice leaned gently toward him. It was obvious she wasn't wearing a bra.

"The word speaks for itself. Each time Gruppo Italia invites important guests to Rome, whether Italian or from abroad, I look after their stay here, right down to the last detail."

She stopped for a moment and smiled at him. That word *detail* was said precisely for him.

"What kind of detail?"

"Our important clients are almost always men and you know what you men want, don't you, Commissario?"

"Why don't you tell me in your own words, Signorina?"

Beatrice leaned over even more in his direction. She looked directly into his eyes, and now Balistreri couldn't help but let his gaze be drawn to the nipples on view.

"For men fifty and over it's no longer enough for a girl to give them oral stimulation. The man needs to feel as if he's really turning a woman on. And that he becomes erect by himself, not because she's done her best to arouse him for half an hour."

She laughed, putting the glass to her lips, well satisfied with her crystal-clear explanation. She looked at him, putting a hand on his arm.

"I hope I haven't shocked you, Michele?"

Balistreri made no reply and stared at the city many yards below the terrace, penthouse floors and church domes all lit up, the stream of cars along the Tiber.

*This is a game, Michele, and watch out, she can play it even better than you.*

Beatrice got to her feet, swaying gently on her heels, a cigarette in one hand, glass of wine in the other. Balistreri stared at her, suddenly struck. Now he remembered her perfectly well from that pose, perhaps even that same dress, on the front pages of the newspapers. The year that Bea won *Big Brother*. He recalled the conversation Linda had recorded with Domnica Panu.

*Others call her "Brother."*

"All right," said Balistreri, "if I'm sure that you and Senator Busi had nothing to do with the deaths of Melania, Tanja, and Domnica, I'm happy to leave you in peace. Now tell me who did kill them."

"The person being interrogated would like to ask for a pause, Commissario, and a little gift. A dance. If not, I won't be able to talk anymore."

She switched on some background music on the stereo, then took his hand, made him get up, and led him to the space between the table and the terrace balustrade. With the palm of his hand on her spine, Balistreri could feel the soft naked skin as they slowly danced. She lifted her head and their lips were only an inch away.

"Is there anything else you want from me, Michele?"

Years ago he would have flung her down on the tiles, lifted her dress, and ripped off her underwear, having been schooled by a great teacher, the best in the world.

Beatrice steered him to the balustrade. It was about thirty yards above ground level and Balistreri felt a little vertigo, while Beatrice sat easily on the yard-high balustrade, her back facing the night. As she crossed her legs, it was evident that her attire that evening didn't include underpants.

"The senator's told me several things about you when you were young. You were crazy, but women were also crazy for you. Can you still drive them crazy, Mike?"

That name echoed in Balistreri's brain.

*Mike.*

His gaze traveled from Beatrice to the space below the balustrade. Just like that damned cliff.

Beatrice lifted her dress and straddled the balustrade, one leg dangling outside, one leg inside to balance herself on the terrace floor, her naked buttocks on the concrete ridge.

"Sit up here with me, Mike, and I'll tell you the truth."

Balistreri looked over the edge and stepped back. He had twice jumped from that height on La Moneta, but below had been the sea, not asphalt and parked cars. And too many years had intervened.

She smiled at him, prepared for this. She knew how to ensnare him.

"You're not interested in today's truth, are you? Come up here with me and I'll tell you the truth you really want to know . . ."

Yesterday's truth. The only truth.

As if in a trance, Balistreri went up to the balustrade and cautiously lifted one leg over it, his knee crying out in pain, then sat himself down, one leg dangling in the void, one firmly inside on the terrace. He tried in every way not to look down.

Beatrice lifted her dress up to her waist and slowly unbuttoned his pants. Then she put her mouth close to his ear, kissed it, licked it, and whispered something barely audible.

*Do you remember that afternoon, Mike? You were in bed with Marlene, while your mother was breathing her last.*

Balistreri wasn't sure if she'd really said this or he'd only imagined it. But he had no time to consider it. Beatrice lifted herself up, sat on his lap and guided him into her.

The legs inside the terrace brushed the tiled floor, those outside swayed in empty space. She was close to him and they moved gently backward and forward, life on one side of them, an abyss on the other. She again put her lips to his ear.

"Your friend with the severed ear's been waiting many years for you, Michele. He will tell you the truth."

At that moment, Balistreri heard the hiss of the projectile. Beatrice Armellini's face exploded, and her blood, brains, and fragments of her skull spattered over him and were spread across the terrace.

• • • •

Linda and Giulia were still debating how to deal with Beatrice Armellini when Sky 24 announced the breaking news. A young woman had been killed by a rifle shot at the Sky Suite Hotel. Nothing was known about her identity, but it said that also present at the scene of the crime was the Head of Rome's Homicide Squad, Michele Balistreri.

The two women stared at each other a moment. It could have nothing to do with the matter at hand, but both felt their nerves shaken. Giulia grabbed her cell phone and pressed the speed dial for Graziano Corvu's number. He replied, struggling for breath.

"This isn't a good moment, Giulia. I'm rushing to a crime scene."

"Can you tell me the woman's name?"

"What woman?"

"The one killed at the Sky Suite."

"Are you crazy? I can't . . ."

"Was it Beatrice Armellini, by any chance, Busi's assistant?"

"How the fucking hell did you know that?" yelled Corvu impulsively. Giulia closed the phone.

"Well?" she asked Linda.

Linda was physically exhausted, but her mind was wide awake.

"Call your hacker friend and tell her to get into the Open Doors database. We want the names of all the girls. And their cell phones, if they have them. Then we'll get in touch with them, right away."

"Linda, it's almost two in the morning."

"Don't they all do their work at this hour? We have to find at least one girl, Giulia, and right now. Just one with the courage to speak out. My piece is coming out in *Il Domani* and all hell's going to break loose. We have to be ready."

Giulia Piccolo ran a hand through her green highlights. She remembered the day she and Linda went into the Casilino 900 camp to face the gang there.

"All right, I'll do it, but it's going to end in trouble. Big trouble . . ."

. . . .

Balistreri had called Corvu. In a few minutes, everyone was there. Forensics, Colombo, the duty public prosecutor, and Police Chief Floris. The hotel was both surrounded and invaded by police.

Sitting in the suite Balistreri gave them all the details up to the meeting with Beatrice Armellini and the balancing act on the balustrade. He kept Linda Nardi out of it and didn't mention Beatrice's last words to him. Neither were relevant.

They had to do with another crime, another time, another justice.

Naturally, there was a big stink. Balistreri's violations of investigative procedure would not be tolerated. An investigation in which leading members of the country's governing class were involved had been seriously compromised by the direct involvement of the commissario's father—as Balistreri himself had admitted—and by questioning methods that were absolutely against the rules.

But Chief Floris had long held him in regard. He was also one of the few who was honest and had balls.

"All right," he said, "I'll call the Interior Minister right now. If he's agreeable, we'll request an official interview with the senator tomorrow. But you, Balistreri, will not say a word to anyone. Is that clear?"

Balistreri pointed to the broadcast vans already outside the hotel.

"The media mustn't know the identity of the deceased here until we can see Senator Busi."

Balistreri's boss, Colombo, took him by the arm.

"Okay, but now stay out of this, Balistreri. You've already caused enough trouble."

Balistreri wasn't even listening to them anymore. He couldn't care less about rules and regulations, about his pension or the police. The only thing occupying his mind was that island, La Moneta. And Beatrice Armellini's last words.

*Your friend with the severed ear's been waiting many years for you, Michele. He will tell you the truth.*

The truth about the past and present were one and the same. One single truth.

. . . .

Senator Busi had just retired to bed but couldn't sleep. He received a phone call from a contact in the Secret Service who told him that *Il Domani* was going to press with a piece by Linda Nardi about him, Monsignor Pizza, Gruppo Italia, and the IOR. His contact didn't know the content in detail, but advised him to stop the publication, if he could.

Before calling *Il Domani*'s editor, Busi opened his safe and found the photograph that was almost six years old: it showed him and Melania together in a Bahamas hotel room, where he had taken her to be away from prying eyes. Her expression was radiant, looking at him contentedly. And he was smiling.

*Yes, I was happy that day. I was happy with her, with her and with Tanja.*

But the trouble had started from that time on. Melania had become even more combative, having found out more about the kind of contracts he dealt with and had no wish for the father of her child to finance public works in which people and businesses of dubious background had a hand. He had obviously resisted, having agreements with associates dating back forty years that couldn't easily be dissolved.

Then came the Arab Spring, in Libya as well. Initially, Busi had exercised all the pressure he could in Gaddafi's favor. He had done all he could to avoid NATO getting involved—or at least Italy taking part in it—but not even he with all his political clout had been able to convince the Americans, British, and French, who were all too ready to let bombs drop in the name of liberty of the Libyan people while looking at Libya's oil, to stand down.

With NATO's intervention, the risk of finding himself ultimately on the losing side—something Busi had always avoided—had become very real. It had been then that he decided to use Melania as an excuse and the means to distance himself from his associates.

He had sent her into the lion's den in Tripoli to tell Gaddafi's men that she had nothing against them, the problem was the links with Dubai and the Sicilians: she didn't want the father of her child to have anything to do with people like that. They had told her that if Busi stopped supporting them, he would be considered a traitor.

But he was every day more certain that NATO would win and that continuing to support Gaddafi and the projects that helped finance him would have him end up on the wrong side. So he had engineered that interview in *Il Domani,* where he'd started to express doubts about the financial backing of projects that served many purposes of his old associates. To them he had said that he'd been forced to do it, otherwise Melania Druc would have revealed their relationship and the fact that he was the father of her child.

So Mohammed Al Bakri had brought them together on that cruise and asked Busi to bring Melania along as well. He wanted to persuade her to wait until the end of the war. Busi had turned to Don Eugenio to have Open Doors recommend her so she could be onboard without being linked in any way to him. Melania had wanted to bring Tanja with her because there was no longer anyone she trusted in Rome.

During dinner Busi had explained in Arabic to his associates that Melania's blackmail could destroy him. In reality he was depending on Melania's determination in order to be able to jump ship in time from the losing side.

After dinner there was a heated confrontation in his suite between Melania and Mohammed Al Bakri. Salvatore Balistreri had declined to speak to Melania himself. He had said it was both dangerous and useless.

As Busi had foreseen, Melania had been steadfast. What he hadn't foreseen were the consequences. Melania and Tanja died that night. An unambiguous message for him, the would-be traitor. He should have understood that. They were people who would stop at nothing. As he had known for more than forty years.

And yet now he wasn't frightened, neither of them nor of Linda Nardi's article. There was only one crazy thought running through his head.

*Melania would have wanted to see Linda Nardi's article in a news-paper. And now I do too.*

That thought made him feel better. He decided to leave it to Linda's article to decide his fate and that of many others. He would not to call *Il Domani*'s editor in an attempt to stop publication.

Instead he called Monsignor Pizza on his cell phone. A few coded words were enough to get the message across. Soon afterward they were in Busi's car heading toward the nearest highway. No driver, this time. Just the two of them.

. . . .

They headed north. For a while neither of them said a word.

"Were Melania and the little girl murdered?" Don Eugenio asked when they were far from Rome.

At the wheel, Busi nodded.

"Michele Balistreri knows it's true too."

Don Eugenio leaned back in his seat.

"I didn't think it would end like this. And I have Domnica on my conscience, I should never have called Mohammed Al Bakri about Linda Nardi's intentions. The Lord will never forgive us."

# TUESDAY, AUGUST 9, 2011

## ROME

Thanks to some tranquilizers, Balistreri had been asleep when the telephone rang. It was a breathless Corvu.

"Read *Il Domani, dottore*. Right now."

Still drowzy with sleep, Balistreri thought he meant that something about Beatrice Armellini's murder had leaked, despite the precautions taken. He got dressed and went down to the newsstand.

The article, which took up nine columns, gave him an electric shock.

*Good-bye Italy. Good-bye Gruppo Italia.*

Seeing the name Linda Nardi instantly produced the usual acidic burn in his stomach.

Balistreri took the copy of the paper back to his apartment, lit his first cigarette of the day, and began to read. The article began with a detailed reconstruction of the assignment of a contract for a hospital in Nairobi to the Swiss consortium ELCON: false invoicing, GB Investments in Luxembourg and Charity Investments in Dubai. About GB Investments, an unknown company, the owner and administrator was

Giacomo Busi, the son of Senator Emilio Busi, chairman of the committee that had awarded the contract in the first place. Then the article followed the trail of ELCON funds from a small bank in Nairobi to an account in the Institute for Religious Works, otherwise known as the Vatican Bank in Rome. Sources confirmed that this account was held in the name of a Monsignor Eugenio Pizza.

Linda's conclusion was a brief comment. We want a country in which the young working class can win a public works contract and in which the young politicians and the wealthy are also among the workers. We want a country in which the ruling class is composed of the most able young people and not the offspring of that same ruling class. We do not want monies from the Italian people to end up in unknown foreign companies. We want a Catholic Church that has no need of a bank.

Balistreri switched off the computer and the television, flopped onto the sofa, stretched out his painful leg, and waited for whatever was to happen next.

Linda and young Mike would have gotten along well.

## LUGANO

In the little villa in Collina d'Oro facing the lake, lost in an unreal tranquility, Senator Busi and Monsignor Pizza calmly read Linda Nardi's article on the webpages of *Domani.it*. That article was a problem, but one that could be solved. All they had to do was give the system and public opinion enough time to let the dust settle on it in the time-honored Italian way. The real problem was Gaddafi and their former associates. Five months of war were nothing to the Colonel, nor was NATO bombing his people, who now couldn't sleep for fear of it, nor was the lack of electricity that caused food to rot in the August heat, nor having to fight on an empty stomach during the day because it was Ramadan. Gaddafi was a leader who had come to power without violence, thanks to the help of a good many interests and the weakness of those who had preceded him. For his tribal mentality, honor was a value that sanctioned any amount of atrocity.

"They'll be looking for us, Emilio. But we have friends and money everywhere. We can disappear," Don Eugenio suggested.

"But first I want to ruin Melania and Tanja's killers," Busi said.

Don Eugenio nodded slowly. He was tired, exhausted by that senseless race toward nothing that had consumed him for more than half a century.

"I'm with you, Emilio. And I have an idea of how we can bring that about before we leave."

More than regret, it was exhaustion that suddenly struck then, like what hits a marathon runner when he crosses the finishing line, because they both knew this was the end of a journey that had begun *on that day of 1969, in the land of sand, olives, and oil.*

## ROME

Reaction to the article on both sides of the Tiber, initially via the online press, television, and social media, was what Balistreri expected from those in power. They showed no concern for what the public might think: it was simply a unanimous chorus of outrage against the mudslinging press, bringing together politicians of various stripes, Vatican spokespersons, senior judges, and journalists: some defending Busi, others defending Monsignor Pizza. In reality everyone was defending everyone else, because they knew the story could drag not only those two into the mire, but also expose and put at risk Italy's largest and most flourishing business, that of corruption and privilege.

By means of a series of finely drawn distinctions, Linda Nardi would be slowly alienated, isolated, and then left exposed to reprisals from her enemies. It was a well-known method, tried and tested, particularly by certain parts of the political and business class. It had worked well against the lawyer Giorgio Ambrosoli, Carabinieri General Carlo Alberto Dalla Chiesa, and the anti-Mafia judges Giovanni Falcone and Paolo Borsellino, all of them assassinated for having tackled the Mafia head on after first being marginalized by those whose eyes and ears were shut to the evidence.

Balistreri felt a growing disquiet and called Colombo.

"So when is Senator Busi coming in for questioning?"

A morose grumble came from the other end of the line.

"The Interior Minister's at a conference in Palermo. When he returns, Floris will see him to get the necessary authorization. What the hell, Balistreri, your friend Nardi may be right, but she's crazy, you need to do these things calmly, not like this!"

Balistreri hung up on him.

People like that made him sick. First, so as not to appear reactionary, they made comments supporting the obvious criticisms, but then came the appeals for caution and, finally, the thousand cavils and subtle excuses offered so that nothing would ever really change. He was sick of a country where the political leaders were old men who talked with heartfelt concern about the future for young people, when it was they who had taken that very future away. He was sick of country where funds allocated for public education were swallowed up by illicit activities, where many jobs were the result of political patronage, and a country where a terrifying bureaucracy armed with countless purposefully complex and hair-splitting laws produced a caste of unproductive workers who had slowly squashed the life out of the healthy and productive part of their society. In short, he was sick of a country where the people of good will who wanted change were either rendered impotent or were killed off.

*But why are you still here, Michele?*

He knew the answer to that question very well. Italy was a perfect place for him to forget. To live a life without being alive.

· · · ·

Immediately after lunch Linda went into Sky's television studios for the talk show that followed the news.

Facing the cameras were several representatives of the political parties and the press. None of them attempted to greet her and many ostentatiously turned the other way as she came in. Only the host offered her a courteous handshake, but no smile. He had been forced to accept her on the show by the London central office, which Linda had contacted to offer her willingness to appear.

She sat down in the armchair indicated and the host introduced the first round of comment. It started with the usual dance around the need for defending civil liberties, defending the state, and the need for sober judgment. Without stating so openly, the senior voices appeared supportive, speaking with good-natured condescension about this article by a young freelance journalist, emphasizing especially the "young" and "freelance." In Italy, being young and without a permanent position meant being less credible than someone who had held such a position for half a century, often completely undeservedly.

And in subtly different ways, the fresh-faced MPs hinted in a grave manner about the risks of crowd pleasing, political nihilism, defeatism, and the serious damage done to Italy's image by investigations like the one Linda Nardi initiated.

They all spoke about the necessity for clarification and for change, but accompanied by countless assorted banalities and quibbles—the need to be tough while preserving civil liberties, the importance of protecting the offices of state from the errors their representatives made, the respect that was owed to the millions of good Catholic citizens, and the ever more questionable methods used by investigative journalism—all rounded off by the usual hackneyed warnings not to make a mountain out of a molehill nor throw the baby out with the dirty bath water.

Linda watched them all in silence, calm and composed, her mind wandering between her orphans in Africa and the faces of the invited guests.

Some of them were indeed more reform minded, advocating change. They edged toward some criticism of the system and ventured to say that, for all their parliamentary privilege and Vatican immunity, perhaps—but only perhaps—Senator Busi and Monsignor Pizza did deserve some blame and censure. But nothing more than that. What was not said and could not be said was obvious. A simple and powerful weapon was pointing against every one of them. Busi and Pizza had something on all of them: a contract awarded here, a job offered there, a daughter taken on by a ministry, an apartment owned by a public body rented for nearly nothing.

During this orchestrated dance, Linda Nardi sat silently in her seat, making no interruptions or contradictions, nor responding to any of the provocations. Initially the presenter, the other guests, and the audience thought she was having some kind of difficulty or was too embarrassed, then concluded she was simply an arrogant snob. But gradually that prolonged silence became more deafening than any reply.

When everyone had had their say, the host was forced to let Linda have hers. Taking out a sheet of paper, she began to read from it and did so without even looking at the camera. She wanted her message to be devoid of anything that could be interpreted as manipulation of the unfortunate general public by such means as body language, eye contact, and the rest, as taught by PR consultants and communications science for telling lies and wriggling out of corners.

"Since last night there have been new developments to the story that I wasn't able to include in the article. Decisive new developments."

She paused and looked around at the suddenly astonished faces. The disgust on some deepened, the fixed and mocking smiles on others became clownish caricatures.

Linda went back to reading.

"During the night we collected the testimonies of several foreign girls who came to Italy thanks to the nonprofit organization Open Doors headed by Monsignor Pizza and who were housed in properties owned by Senator Busi's Gruppo Italia."

The tightly controlled body language of the other guests began to crumble. Hands gripped arms, arms were folded across chests, feet tapped nervously on the floor. The manifest disintegration of the establishment on live television was a spectacle somewhere between burlesque and horror show.

Linda had asked for and received a hand-held mike. She held it in one hand and the sheet of paper in the other, which was trembling slightly. But it was clear to the millions watching that her trembling was bottled-up anger, whereas in the other guests it was fear.

"The job of these girls included *specialty* dinners with influential people involved with Gruppo Italia's affairs. The specialties weren't the dishes served up but the costumes the girls were forced to wear as animals, nuns, or nurses and Angela Merkel or Condoleezza Rice facemasks. The guests were a specialty too: influential men and, unfortunately, also women of the privileged cast. One of these girls is here in the studio right now."

The host and guests exploded in protest.

"You'd better take responsibility for what you're saying!"

"You should be ashamed!"

"You'll answer for this in court!"

"You'll never write for another newspaper!"

Linda made no response. She rose and handed the microphone to a young girl who looked under eighteen sitting among the audience next to a tall muscular woman with green highlights in her hair. The young girl had been well briefed by Linda and began speaking before anyone could stop her.

"My name is Annika, I came to Italy through Open Doors and was then chosen for the parties held for Gruppo Italia's clients. I took part in many parties in private houses, hotels, beach clubs, corporate and public offices. Basically, it was a question of lap dancing or games where the men put on wolf masks and we girls put on those of sheep, or they dressed up as hunters and we dressed up as pigs. Sometimes we were tied up, hung up, and whipped. I had sex with several participants each time I was ordered to and snorted coke with them. In return I received money, drugs, and a free apartment. Many of these men are well known. I've seen them in the papers and on television. I've given their names to Signorina Nardi."

All hell then broke loose. Several guests got up and left the studio. The director cut the sound, but left the camara on. In the confusion, a politician already well known for insulting various journalists went up to Linda in a threatening manner, but never reached her. Giulia Piccolo cut him off, placed a hand on his shoulder, and stopped him in his tracks with no trouble.

"Beat it, you swindling piece of shit. You and all the other assholes like you."

The man met her gaze, saw her muscles, and did a silent about turn. Giulia's words were lip read by an expert and posted on Facebook. The "Likes" soon totaled six million after her words were translated into twenty languages.

Sky's switchboard was rapidly overwhelmed by viewers protesting over the break in transmission. The network director received a call from London. He was told to resume transmission and let Linda have her say. All the foreign stations were frenetically trying to link up with Sky. Nothing like this had ever happened in the history of television.

In a glacial silence, Linda Nardi picked up where she left off. She still had the single sheet of paper in her hand.

"This is a preliminary list of the names of the people we already know are involved. I've sent them to the Public Prosecutor's office, which will look into the rest."

At this point Linda met the eyes of Giulia Piccolo, who was desperately signaling "no" to her.

*No, sister. Stop here. They'll kill you if you go on.*

Then she read the last words in a voice that was the most violent whisper ever heard on television.

"The person who recruited these girls was Beatrice Armellini, Senator Busi's personal assistant. She was killed by a sniper's bullet last night here in the center of Rome. Two of her girls, Melania Druc and Domnica Panu, have also been killed in suspicious circumstances in the last few days. Melania's little daughter, Tanja, also died on the cruise ship she was on between the island of Elba and Civitavecchia. Also onboard were Senator Emilio Busi, Monsignor Eugenio Pizza, and other very important individuals whom the police will seek to identify."

Linda put the microphone down and left the television studio, followed by Giulia Piccolo and the young girl who had testified. The show was over.

## LUGANO

In the little villa in Collina d'Oro, Senator Emilio Busi and Monsignor Eugenio Pizza were watching Linda's appearance live on Sky.

When it was over they exchanged looks. They had just witnessed their own downfall and they knew it. And yet they felt lighter, resolved, and almost relieved. Linda's appearance had made their futures irrelevant and removed any lasting doubt. They had spoken at length earlier, but this talk show had made everything more simple and inevitable.

By phone and online they could give all the necessary banking instructions, country by country. Transfer of funds, blocks of funds. The accounts were almost all in their personal names, including those in the Vatican Bank. Mohammed Al Bakri was the only other person who could observe those operations, but he could not intervene. This had been the agreement for over forty years. And it had worked perfectly well until the start of that damned war in Libya.

Monsignor Pizza switched on the computer.

"We only need a hundredth of that money to live on happily for the rest of our lives, Emilio. The rest we can transfer to Catholic organizations who deal with the world's poor."

Busi nodded.

"That's what Melania would have wanted. Let's do it, then let's book the first flight out to the Caribbean. We'll be safe there, they'll never be able to extradite us."

They sat side-by-side at the computer and connected to the Internet. As they shifted enormous sums of money from one part of the world to another, from secret accounts in tax havens to those of humanitarian organizations, they gradually felt younger.

They directed the fruits of evil to works of charity with a lightness of spirit they had entirely forgotten: that of the young boy who wanted to become a priest to serve God and that of the young boy who wanted to become a Carabiniere to serve justice.

In between the two spirits, young and old, a lifetime had passed. This conclusion could not change what they had been, but for once it was not the result of convenience but the genuine emotions of remorse and vindication that they themselves had always found to be a weakness and irrational.

## ROME

After the Sky talk show, Linda and Giulia took refuge in Linda's apartment. They reexamined the whole of Open Doors's database, in particular the lists of girls who had come in recent years. Dozens of names. Many of them had gone to work for Gruppo Italia as cleaners or barmaids, the more educated as secretaries.

"That wretched Beatrice, she deserved what she got . . ." said Giulia, scanning through the list.

"I heard that you spoke to Corvu again, Giulia. What was Balistreri doing with that woman in the Sky Suite Hotel?"

Giulia looked at her in surprise. She had finally mentioned him, emphasizing the words *Sky Suite Hotel* and *that woman* with evident disapproval.

"Corvu told me that they've taken him off the case . . ." said Giulia.

"Why?"

Giulia shook her head.

"I'd prefer not to say, Linda."

"Why is that?"

Giulia decided that in the end it was better to tell her the truth, so she could wipe that unpleasant and arrogant old misogynist from her mind forever. He was incapable of loving a woman anyway.

"When Beatrice Armellini was shot, she and Balistreri were sitting astride the terrace balcony, thirty yards above the street, fucking."

Linda looked out of the window toward St. Peter's Square. It was full of noise and people. She then shut herself in her room and threw herself onto the bed fully dressed.

She found herself empty, worn out, without even the energy to move even her little finger, but her mind continued to thrash about like the tail of lizard detached from its body. She was incapable of stopping her thoughts.

Balistreri and Beatrice on that balustrade.

After a while, she fell into a fitful sleep.

· · · ·

As she was half asleep and half awake, many images mingled together.

Balistreri and Beatrice clutching each other on the terrace. Herself and John Kiptanu in Nairobi. Melania at the Rixos in Tripoli. Melania and Tanja coming out of the private elevator on that cruise ship.

All of a sudden, she was awake. She hadn't slept more than an hour. It was still only five in the afternoon. But something in her sleep had disturbed her. She forced herself to remember.

*Melania.*

She tried to focus on the thought. In the Rixos, Melania had been surrounded by Libyan security men, following one of Gaddafi's men, the one responsible for repression, the Zawiya massacre, as the terrified Bashir Yared had told her. A man with a piece of his ear cut off. Her mind had preserved these images, like certain photographs seen once and then put away.

Melania in Tripoli at the Hotel Rixos in the company of that man with the severed ear. Melania on the ship with her little girl, coming out of the elevator on the deck where her cabin was, a security guard standing by. She'd been asked if the woman she'd seen in Tripoli and the one on the ship had been the same and she'd said yes. And they were. But no one had asked her the other question.

*Was it the same man? My memory's only very indistinct, but yes, it was the same man. The security guard near the elevator had the same severed ear. I caught a glimpse of it in the dim light. I must trust my memory.*

At that moment her cell phone rang. It was early morning in San Francisco and Lena must have just gotten up.

"Linda, dear, I switched on the computer and found the whole world's talking about you!"

Her cough was worse. Linda gathered two feelings behind what her mother had said: one was pride and the other was concern. Both understandable.

But Lena only knew a part of the story. Senator Busi and Monsignor Eugenio Pizza were certainly not as dangerous as the man with the severed ear.

"Would you like me to tell you the whole story, Mamma? It's very long."

She told her everything, from that first meeting with Melania and the man with the severed ear in the Rixos to that on the cruise with Senator Busi, Monsignor Pizza, Mohammed Al Bakri, Salvatore Balistreri, and once again, as she now remembered, the man with the severed ear. And then all the rest, right up to that very moment.

Lena listened without interrupting, except for fits of coughing. In the end, she did speak.

"I'm coming to Rome, dear."

Linda was shocked. There was something decisive and urgent in that sudden decision. And yet Lena, who was always so generous and open with her explanations, was giving nothing away. Linda heard her mother coughing as she checked for an available flight.

"There's a night flight to London that leaves this evening, then from there I can get one to Rome. I'll be with you tomorrow afternoon. In the meantime, don't do anything that might be dangerous Linda."

Words similar to what Salvatore Balistreri had told her.

*I would hate for anything bad to happen to you.*

She found it difficult to make any objection. Lena said good-bye and ended the call. Linda remained flat-out on the bed, happy and exhausted. It didn't occur to her to tell Michele Balistreri that the man beside Melania Druc in the Hotel Rixos was the same man by the elevator on that ship.


## ROME

Balistreri's heartburn flared up after Linda Nardi's appearance on Sky. And he was furious. She had not stuck to his order to keep away from this story and in a very short time had found out who was behind GB Investments in Luxembourg. And with that last sentence of hers she'd openly challenged the police—namely, him—and also some very dangerous people.

*Also onboard were Senator Emilio Busi, Monsignor Eugenio Pizza, and other very important individuals whom the police will seek to identify.*

But those other very important people weren't like the senator and the monsignor. Busi had told him so immediately after he'd mentioned the man with the severed ear.

There's a great deal of difference between businessmen and killers.

Balistreri was in an ever more anxious state. He got up and hobbled over to the telephone and dialed Colombo's cell phone.

"Have you found the senator and the monsignor yet?"

"Not yet, Balistreri."

"Well, you either find them alive right now, or later they'll be dead. This is about Libya. They haven't helped those they should have, and those people don't joke around with anyone who betrays them."

He heard a sigh, then the barely contained anger in Colombo's voice.

"We've warned you already Balistreri. Forget this whole business. Including Libya."

Balistreri put the phone down and went to lie on the sofa. He couldn't forget Libya, not anymore. He had left the two women he'd loved there. Italia was dead, and he'd never wanted to know anything more about Laura Hunt.

He felt totally overwhelmed by the succession of events.

He knew the key to everything lay there in the tangle of the past, present, and future. But there were too many threads; he couldn't find a place to start.

*Now, that isn't really true, Michele.*

Beatrice Armellini had told him where to start. Your old friend is waiting for you . . . he will to tell you the truth.

Balistreri thought about that absurd moment of intimacy, suspended between life and death. She certainly hadn't done it out of passion. She was almost an actress. After all, hadn't she won *Big Brother*? But then why do it without an audience . . .

But there had been one spectator to the show.

She was acting for whoever was watching, except she thought she was being observed through a pair of binoculars, not a telescopic sight on a rifle.

Beatrice Armellini was acting the part that her real boss, not Senator Busi, had ordered her to play. But why?

The answer came floating up, like a piece cork from the depths of the sea.

*To take you back where you don't want to go. It was the killer who sent her to you. He didn't shoot too late! He waited until she'd passed on the message.*

All his experience as a policeman and his rationality as an adult, all the efforts he'd made over the years to forget, to let the roots of evil dry up and wither inside him, all were telling him the same thing.

*Call Colombo and Corvu. Wait till they find Busi and Don Eugenio and question them.*

But that was Michele Balistreri, the adult who was rational and wise; an experienced policeman who was near retirement. But by means of Beatrice Armellini the man with the severed ear had sent his message to Mike Balistreri.

*He's waiting for you after all these years and he'll tell you the truth. A challenge down to the last drop of blood. Just like the old times, Mike.*

Those words weren't an invitation. They were a challenge. But he'd become a coward. Or simply a very tired old man.

*On August 15, 1970, I was Mike, not Michele. No one can ever make me go back to Tripoli. Not even you.*

# WEDNESDAY, AUGUST 10, 2011

## LUGANO

It was almost dawn. Don Eugenio Pizza and Senator Emilio Busi were sleeping in the living room. They had collapsed after having emptied all the accounts and made the last indispensable phone call.

At a certain point Don Eugenio opened his eyes. A faint light was coming from the kitchen. It was the light above the range hood. And yet he was certain he had switched it off. Unsteadily, he got to his feet. He was overcome with tension and tiredness.

He woke Busi and pointed to the light. Together, they went cautiously toward the kitchen.

The light above the range hood was switched on and the door that opened onto the lawn that led to the lake was open. They could see the dark waters and the streetlamps that illuminated the Riva Paradiso. The sky was showing the first light of dawn and the moon was slipping gently away.

The man sitting at the kitchen table was staring at them with a Walther PPK in his hand. Neither man needed to ask *What are you doing here?*

They had known this man for many years. They knew very well why he was there and what he was capable of doing. He would put an end to their lives as he had done with so many others.

## ROME

Giulia was sleeping on the sofa, but Linda hadn't slept a wink. She had remained lying on the bed with the television on and the sound off. But the images running through her mind were completely different.

*Melania and Tanja, Domnica, the man with the severed ear, my mother coming to Rome. What should I do?*

At nine o'clock the faces of Busi and Pizza came onto the screen. Linda immediately switched on the sound and heard the news about the discovery of the two bodies in Lugano.

Giulia was still asleep in the living room. Linda ran to wake her. Together they heard the latest from Switzerland.

Giulia Piccolo's face was drained of color.

"This is it, Linda, no more. We have to tell the police. And you need to go somewhere safe."

"Why?"

"Because you know too much. Remember which one of us happens to be a policewoman?"

"Where should I go?"

"As far away from here as you can. What about your mother's in California?"

Linda smiled.

"My mother's already on a plane for Rome. She'll be here this afternoon."

"No, Linda. You're not safe here. You should go to California. Please listen to me. As soon as your mother gets here, both of you go back to San Francisco. I'll come with you. I already have a US visa and you have an American passport. We'll go this evening."

Linda shook her head. After the deaths of Senator Busi and Monsignor Pizza, she no longer had any doubts.

*I can go away, but I can't run away.*

"We'll go and pick my mother up, Giulia. We'll speak to her and then decide. But first I have to tell you something. And I'll need your help."

. . . .

At nine in the morning, Balistreri's cell phone began to ring. Slowly, the ring tone began to penetrate the artificial sleep induced by the many sleeping pills he had taken the night before. At every ring his foggy head became clearer, but his mind resisted. Eventually, he picked up the phone.

Corvu gave him the news but made no comment.

Two hours earlier, the bodies of Senator Emilio Busi and Monsignor Eugenio Pizza had been found at Busi's son's house in Lugano by the young woman who cleaned every morning. This was what was being made known to the public.

Then there was the confidential information supplied by the Swiss police. The two bodies were found facedown on the kitchen floor, each shot with a single bullet to the back of the head. Among their personal belongings were two cell phones with Swiss SIM cards.

"The numbers correspond to the ones we know," said Corvu.

Balistreri remained silent. Then, while his deputy was asking him what he wanted to do, Balistreri ended the call, switched off his cell phone and unplugged the landline.

He lit a cigarette and lay down on the sofa. He could picture those two old cronies kneeling next to each other with the barrel of the pistol an inch from the back of the head, conscious that their lives were about to end right there. He felt no pity for them.

More than forty years ago four men came together to bring about a certain end. My mother was against it and died. Today we have the same four men again. Except the pact they had has come apart, like the MANK back then.

Almost all the news on the radio was dedicated to the mysterious deaths of Senator Emilio Busi and Monsignor Eugenio Pizza. With extreme caution it was suggested there might be a *possible* link with Linda Nardi's investigation.

He got up off the sofa to go out and replenish his whiskey and cigarettes. On the floor, sitting by the front door, was an envelope. It was
brown and with no stamp on it. Inside was a sheet of white paper and a
smaller white envelope. The sheet of paper had an address typed on it.

Via dei Pini 1952, Rome
Sender: PO Box 150870, Tripoli, Libya

Balistreri could see the city outside beyond the windows. This piece
of paper came not from the living city out there, but from somewhere
far in space and time, written on an old typewriter in another time.

Balistreri opened the white enveloped and stared at it for a long
time. The color photograph had been taken with a powerful telephoto
lens from the stern of a boat in the open sea. Farid Al Bakri's face con-
torted with pain and terror, tied to the game chair of a fishing boat,
his own severed penis stuck in his mouth, a stream of blood, and two
shark fins circling him. On the back, handwritten, a few words in
Arabic and a date.

For Nadia. March 1983.

Now he could fully apprehend the deeper meaning of the piece of
paper and that picture, together. An older code of chivalry. That of the
MANK and of the brotherhood of sand and blood. The man with
the severed ear had taken his girl and his money and he had taken his
brother's life.

*We left this pending for so long, Karim.*

But now something had changed. After more than forty years, the
regime that had been born out of injustice was now in collapse, with
the traitorous Italians to blame, and time was running out.

*And Karim wants justice for Ahmed. In exchange, he's offering me the
truth.*

Obviously he could decline. He could refuse to go to via dei Pini
1952 where he would most likely die. But the picture made damn
clear what would happen. And Karim had always been a deep Muslim
believer.

The Koran. An eye for an eye, a great grief for a great grief.

He was absolutely certain Karim knew all about his life, and Linda Nardi would be the means by which Karim would expell his grief.

He grabbed his cell phone and called her. The ring tone went on for some time, then he heard Linda's voice.

"What do you want, Michele?"

"Where are you?"

*Silence. None of your business, Balistreri.*

"Linda, that man's here in Rome. You're in danger."

Silence.

*And what will you do about it, Balistreri? Leave me to fend for myself as you did with the Invisible Man?*

"I'm with Giulia. She'll protect me," said Linda finally.

Then Balistreri heard a sigh, like a last feeble remnant of something between them.

"That man in the Rixos, the one with the severed ear . . . I've thought about it, he's the same as the security guard near the elevator on the cruise ship, when I saw Melania and Tanja . . ."

The call ended. Balistreri tried calling back, but there was no reply to the ring tone. There was no longer any doubt in his mind.

Either I accept his invitation or Linda Nardi dies.

He called Corvu, who answered at the first ring.

"Corvu, put Linda Nardi under police protection. Have someone follow her immediately, twenty-four seven. A little while ago she was with Giulia. Not a word to anyone. I'm putting you in charge of this."

At any other time, Corvu would have objected strongly, having no liking for anything that smacked of American police methods. But he caught the same desperation in Balistreri's voice as he had five years earlier, when they were coming back by helicopter from a false trail and leaving Linda to face the Invisible Man alone.

• • • •

Corvu called back five minutes later.

"I've put two plainclothes men outside Linda's building. I also called Giulia Piccolo. She didn't want to tell me exactly, but she said they're getting their bags ready."

"They're leaving?" Balistreri asked, in alarm.

"They're going to America. They've got two seats for Los Angeles at nine o'clock tonight. Then from Los Angeles there's a connection to San Francisco."

"Oh, they'll be going to her mother's," Balistreri said, a little relieved.

"Yes, but we can't follow them all the way to America. Fortunately Giulia's going with her."

Balistreri was hesitant for a moment. He was powerless to stop them. Perhaps Linda was safer in America, at least until he had gone to the address he'd been directed to.

"Speak to Piccolo, tell her to be on the lookout. Have them followed right up to boarding, make sure they take off safe and sound."

Balistreri ended the call. He wondered if the precautions would be sufficient.

*If I refuse to go, I can't protect Linda forever.*

He also wondered if he was overly dramatizing things. But on the rational rather than the emotional plane, it was clear that Melania had been killed along with Tanja as revenge, Domnica killed like a dog, and Beatrice first used and then also eliminated.

*There's nothing else I can do other than go where Karim's asking me to go. I can only hope that Linda boards her plane safely.*

· · · ·

It was just before eight in the evening when Corvu called.

"Linda and Giulia are at the airport. They've checked in and now they're going through security. I made it clear to follow them right up to boarding and make sure they take off safely. Don't worry."

"All right. Call me when they're boarding."

He hung up, went to the desk, and looked in the bottom drawer. There was the Beretta that had not been fired since that night five years earlier when he'd been shot in the side and his knee had been fractured. He looked at it for a while and left it there.

It wouldn't be of any use.

He was forced to take his old Fiat Ritmo and punched the address into the GPS: via dei Pini 1952, Ciampino, Roma.

Obviously he knew what a real policeman should have done: notify his colleagues and go with them to Via dei Pini. But the killer, who had slipped the address under his door, wouldn't like that.

*That invitation is for me alone. Otherwise Linda will die.*

## CIAMPINO

He drove to the beltway and from the city to the Via Appia. After the turn off for Ciampino airport, he turned onto a dark road, Via dei Pini. He traveled several miles through the countryside wrapped in darkness, lit only by the moon. He had no fear for himself: he never had, but even less so in this case. His only fear was for Linda Nardi.

The narrow road ended in an unpaved path leading to a large green gate bearing the number 1952. It was very secluded, the ideal place for a killer on the loose away from his home base. One hundred yards from the gate he glimpsed a huge dimly lit farmhouse, with a large-engined Kawasaki parked in front.

Balistreri looked at his watch. It was 9:05. He called Corvu, who answered at the first ring.

"Have they left?"

"The plane for Los Angeles took off a few minutes ago with Linda and Giulia onboard."

"You're sure now? You had them followed right onto the plane?"

"Of course. The officer followed them right up to the last moment of boarding."

"No one came back down the jetway?"

"No one. The officer had confirmation from the flight attendant via the intercom that Linda and Giulia were onboard. And his colleagues didn't move until the plane doors were closed. For the next fifteen hours Linda and Giulia will be flying to California. There's no need to worry."

But Balistreri wasn't happy. Something was telling him that it wasn't that simple.

"Corvu, are you sure someone else wasn't following them? Someone else who got on the same plane?"

A brief silence.

"Well, actually, I can't be sure, I'm going off what the officers following her have told me."

"Okay, then. Check the passenger list. And get copies of all the footage of the airport's CCTV cameras where Linda and Giulia can be seen."

"All right, will do. But where are you? Are you at home?"

Balistreri ended the call and took the battery out of the cell phone. It was 9:10.

He looked at the gate and felt a warning twinge in his knee. But he ignored the pain and climbed over.

. . . .

He had almost reached the farmhouse when he felt a gun pressed against his neck.

"Welcome, Commissario Balistreri. Place yourself against the wall with your arms and legs spread out."

The man spoke in English with an Arab accent. He checked to see Balistreri had no weapon on him and took away the cell phone and the battery. Then he had him go into the farmhouse and enter a large room with simple furnishings.

"Turn around, very slowly."

Balistreri turned around. The man with the gun was a black African, probably a member of the Libyan Special Forces. He was four inches taller, forty pounds heavier, and younger by even more years. And he was holding a gun, which he showed every sign of knowing how to use.

"You've come here alone, unarmed, and have taken the battery out of your cell phone so that your colleagues can't trace you. Aren't you afraid of dying?"

Balistreri ignored the question.

"I'm here simply to see your boss. After all this time I think he wants to see me in the flesh before killing me."

"Well, I'll ask him that. Meanwhile, start walking."

Under the threat of the gun, Balistreri walked down a long, almost dark hallway up to an open iron door followed by three steps down.

"In you go," ordered the man with the gun.

Balistreri walked down the three steps and found himself in a cellar lit by a single bulb, with two chairs in the center.

"You see those handcuffs, Balistreri? Put them on your wrists and lock them, that's a good man. That's it, excellent. Now hand me the key and sit down there. You won't have long to wait; he'll be here soon. It'll give you some time to say your prayers."

Balistreri heard the heavy door close. Then the key turning in the lock. He thought about the person who was about to arrive, but felt no fear. That person would never shoot him in cold blood, handcuffed as he was.

That would be too much, even for Karim Al Bakri. Or too little.

• • • •

After ten minutes he heard the sound of the Kawasaki leaving.

Then he heard the cellar door open and hesitant feet come down the three steps.

The footsteps of an old man.

Although he was the same age as Balistreri's father, Mohammed Al Bakri looked a lot older. His face was deeply lined, with only a few white hairs on his head and a good many dark blotches; he was very bent and wore very thick dark glasses.

"Stay seated, Signor Michele. And keep still, otherwise I won't hesitate to shoot."

He spoke in Italian, with the same respectful title he used to use when he was his father's right-hand man. He was struggling for breath a little and his bony hands were shaking a great deal, but in the right one he held a Smith & Wesson.

*He's shaking, half blind, but from three yards away he can easily kill me with a gun like that.*

Mohammed Al Bakri was very different from Karim. He could shoot him in cold blood, no problem. And, in the meantime, Karim could kill Linda.

The words that came from his mouth sounded pointless, stupid in the moment.

"I'll do whatever you like, Mohammed. Just don't hurt anymore innocent women. Karim has killed all those women and Busi and Don Eugenio as well. He should stop here."

Mohammed Al Bakri took off his dark glasses. His eyes were red and misted with cataracts.

"Collateral damage of no consequence, or else traitors to Colonel Gaddafi. But I'm not here to talk about my son who's alive, Signor Michele. I'm here to talk about the other one."

*The other one, the one you killed. Ahmed.*

Mohammed stared at him.

"Karim doesn't want me to avenge that wrong here tonight. He still talks about that old brotherhood and the stupid things you did as boys together. He wants you to go to Tripoli to settle matters. He doesn't understand that you're a coward like all Italians and would never ever go there."

"I'll go there, Mohammed. If you can promise me that no harm will come to Linda Nardi."

Mohammed Al Bakri spat on the ground and looked at him with such deep hatred that Balistreri no longer had any doubts.

*I'm going to die here, tonight. And then they'll kill Linda.*

"You are unable to protect even those you love, signor Michele. After your mother went up to that cliff, a real son would have gone after her and offered some comfort. But no, you went off to Tripoli with that American *gahba* . . ."

Balistreri couldn't utter a word. He felt an intense pain in his stomach and his chest.

"Who killed my mother, Mohammed? Was it you or my father?"

Mohammed replied with a sneer.

"While the boys were on the beach, myself, Busi, the priest, and your father were in discussion in the living room for an hour, then Busi and the priest went off. Your father was very agitated, so I went up to the cliff to persuade your mother not to do anything stupid. I got there at three."

*The truth you no longer wanted to hear, Michele. The truth you'd sworn to seek forever.*

Mohammed paused, either to remember better or to catch his breath.

"Your mother wasn't there. And yet we'd all seen her go off just before you went with Marlene Hunt, so it was strange."

"Did you look down to the rocks?" Balistreri asked instinctively.

Mohammed Al Bakri nodded thoughtfully.

"I went partway down the slope, until I saw her body on the rocks."

Balistreri couldn't contain himself.

"You lying bastard!"

He motioned to get up and Mohammed pointed the gun at him.

"Do you want to die right now, Signor Michele?"

Balistreri tried to keep himself in check, but with his terrible rage was the desire to kill Mohammed Al Bakri by kicking his face in.

"And you kept quiet about this, Mohammed? My mother could still have been alive . . ."

Mohammed shook his head, the lines in his face looking even deeper.

"She'd fallen from a height of twenty yards. Her body was all covered in blood . . ."

"You couldn't have seen any blood . . ."

"I saw it, it was on her bathing suit, everywhere . . ."

"You're lying, Mohammed. When they picked her out of the sea, she was wearing her kaftan over her bathing suit."

His father's old employee snorted. He was tired and fed up with this story. He had only told him these things to torture him more.

Mohammed moved toward the stairs.

"That's enough now. I'm going to speak to Karim. I'll remind him that in Muslim families the father rules, and then I'll come back down here and shoot you."

The old man walked up the three steps with difficulty, then Balistreri heard the click of the lock and the turning of the key.

Three minutes of absolute silence went by. Balistreri concentrated. The possibilities were very limited in such a restricted situation for a man in handcuffs facing another man who, no matter how sickly, had a Smith & Wesson in his hands and knew how to use it.

In that moment there was a gunshot. For a minute he was unsure what to do, then in the distance he again heard the sound of a motorbike departing.

Then he made a move. There were various tools in the cellar, including a pickax. He grasped it in his cuffed hands, went up the three steps and began to hit the door. It wasn't particularly strong and he took only a few minutes to break it down.

He dashed out into the hallway, but found no one there. Mohammed Al Bakri's body was in the middle of the entrance hall, lying face up on the parquet, next to a small table, on which were his cell phone and battery. Mohammed had been killed with a single shot to the chest. There was no sign of a gun. The killer must have taken it away with him. Balistreri felt inside Mohammed's pockets and found a small key—the key to his handcuffs.

Balistreri knew what was waiting for him. Expulsion from the police force, perhaps the accusation of obstructing an investigation. But he couldn't care less. A single thought was torturing him.

*Karim's going to kill Linda.*

He put the battery back in the cell phone, switched it on, called Corvu and rang the alarm bells.

· · · ·

They were all there within half an hour, just as before at the Sky Suite Hotel. Police Chief Floris, Colombo and Public Prosecutor Madonna. All were furious.

"Sheer folly, Balistreri. You're a madman, we told you to stay out of this business and so what do you do? You meet the chief suspect and confront him alone. This is Italy, not the Wild West," said the public prosecutor aggressively.

"And not Libya either," Colombo observed.

Madonna stared right at him.

"You didn't happen to shoot him yourself, did you, Balistreri?"

Balistreri didn't care what they thought. All he wanted to do as soon as possible was check that Linda Nardi and Giulia Piccolo had arrived safe and sound in the United States.

"If I'd come here with the intention of killing him, I think I'd have been a little more careful . . . afterall, I am—or was—Head of Homicide!"

"It's not that you got here all nice and calm and then changed your mind?" Colombo asked.

"There's no gun, Colombo . . ."

"You could have gotten rid of it."

"Then swipe me, if you like. You'll find no traces of gunpowder on my hands."

Madonna shook his head.

"You could have used gloves."

Balistreri shrugged.

"So find them then, these gloves. They must be somewhere around here."

Madonna turned to the police chief.

"I spoke to the chief public prosecutor. Until we have proof positive of Balistreri's innocence, we can't rule him out as a suspect."

Floris was clearly unhappy.

"All right, then test him for gunpowder and look for a weapon and some damned gloves. Until then, you're suspended, Balistreri. And stay away from this investigation, for your own good."

Balistreri turned his back on them and went off to his car, accompanied by Corvu, who spoke to him in a hushed tone.

"Tell me where you hid the gun and gloves. I'll make sure they disappear."

Balistreri put an arm around his shoulders.

"I didn't kill him, Graziano. And I don't want you to get into any trouble. Now, tell me instead about Linda and Giulia. Are you sure no one could have followed them onto the plane to San Francisco?"

Corvu hated not being able to give him that assurance.

"Our men were following Linda and Giulia and obviously focused on them, not on anyone who could have been following *them*. They were certain that the women were onboard at the moment of take off. They were absolutely sure. Meanwhile, I checked the passenger list and there are no suspicious names there."

"Well, send it to me at home, will you? Have you also checked the CCTV footage?"

"The technical staff are preparing a DVD with all the footage where Linda and Giulia appear from the airport entrance to boarding."

"Good. Well, study it carefully. Check everything, people who look strange, people who crop up in two different places, any meetings, no matter how brief. See if anyone was following them. And call me at home. I won't move an inch from there."

# THURSDAY, AUGUST 11, 2011

ROME

Balistreri spent a sleepless night with his unrelenting memories and his one fixed idea. Linda and Giulia would still be in the air for hours and he could do nothing for them.

Linda was sitting by the window, Piccolo by her side to protect her. But it wouldn't be enough.

He was still dwelling on that idea when his cell phone rang. It was seven in the morning. Corvu's voice sounded tired but cheerful.

"Forensics have found neither a weapon nor gloves. They have nothing against you. In the Ciampino farmhouse they found the rifle that killed Beatrice and in the garage the van that ran down Domnica Panu. The murder weapon has disappeared, but Ballistics says the same gun killed Emilio Busi, Eugenio Pizza, and Mohammed Al Bakri."

"I don't really care, Corvu. Did you check the CCTV footage from the airport?"

Obviously, Corvu had worked on it all night.

"We've examined all the places where Linda and Giulia appear. There's absolutely nothing out of the ordinary. No one was following them, neither at the check-in or after."

"Get the DVD sent here. When do Linda and Giulia arrive?"

"They land in Los Angeles at three in the morning there, midday here, and they have a connection for San Francisco at seven a.m. They'll be at Linda's mother's house at about nine a.m. local time."

"What time's that here?" Balistreri asked impatiently.

"About six in the evening. More than ten hours from now. Please don't worry, nothing's going to happen . . ."

Balistreri ended the call. He refused to look at the clues, at Melania and Tanja, Domnica, Beatrice. It was pointless, that case had been resolved. He knew who the killer was. He also knew where to find him. But he had to wait until Linda and Giulia arrived safely at Linda's mother's house. He poured himself a double whiskey, put a Leonard Cohen CD on the stereo at a low volume, and lay down on the sofa.

*I can only wait.*

· · · ·

At six in the evening, he was awoken by the door bell. Staggering, he went to open the door. It was the courier with the DVD Corvu had promised him.

Balistreri took a cold shower and drank a whole pot of black coffee. He then put the DVD in the player and sat down in front of the screen.

*It's a way of passing the time until they land.*

He studied the footage carefully, searching for known or suspicious faces. He watched it three times, but saw nothing. Corvu was right. Apparently no one had followed Linda and Giulia either in the airport or on the plane.

Then, eaten up with anxiety, he made a decision. Linda must have landed by now. He dialed the landline of Lena Nardi in San Francisco, which Corvu had found for him.

The telephone on the other side of the world rang for a long time. Then a woman's voice answered.

"Hello?" followed by two repeated coughs.

Michele Balistreri was taken aback. He'd hoped Linda would have answered the phone.

"I'm sorry, Mrs. Nardi, I need to speak with Linda. It's Michele Balistreri."

He heard nothing for some time, and at one point he thought Lena Nardi had hung up.

"Ma'am . . ." he whispered.

"What do you want?"

The voice was now unquestionably Linda's. And her very simple question made it clear that his call wasn't welcome. And neither was he.

"Nothing, I'm sorry. I wanted to make sure."

"That I was here?"

"That you're okay."

*That you're alive.*

"I'm here. And I'm okay."

"And Giulia's there with you?"

Linda passed the phone to her, without saying good-bye. Giulia Piccolo's voice had a touch of hostility.

"Oh, *Dottore* Balistreri, are you worried about us?"

"Stop joking, Piccolo. I want you to buy a gun. It's easy to do there. And don't let Linda out of your sight."

Her voice became ice cold.

"I'm not on duty, *Dottore* Balistreri. And I'm not under your authority."

The line went dead.

Balistreri lay back down on the sofa. His knee was giving him a devil of a time, but that wasn't the problem.

The endless running away was over. The past was becoming the present, the future becoming the past. He had been running away from that wretched day his whole life. And in exchange for a peace that had simply been a long endless pause, he had broken his promise to discover the truth about his mother's death. He was back to staring straight at his worst memory.

# FRIDAY, AUGUST 12, 2011

## SAN FRANCISCO, CALIFORNIA

The young Libyan agent approached her in the early morning at San Francisco airport, where Linda had just said good-bye to Giulia Piccolo, who was on an early flight back to Italy.

"I am coming from the man you are looking for, Miss Nardi."

She had stared silently at him, and the man smiled gently.

"He can get you safely to Tripoli, where he can offer you an exclusive interview. And then send you safely home."

Linda shook her head.

"I do not interview murderers," she said coldly.

The man nodded and handed her an envelope.

"Please look at this now, so you can make a better decision."

She opened the envelope. It took only a minute for her to change her mind.

"Okay, when?" she asked.

The Libyan smiled again.

"I will drive you home so you can get your passport, pack a small bag, and invent some excuse with your mother. You have to be on the flight to Tunis three hours from now. We'll take you from there to Tripoli. Thanks to the time difference you'll be in Tripoli by dinnertime. Shall we get going?"

# SATURDAY, AUGUST 13, 2011

Two days had passed by since the killing of Senator Emilio Busi, Monsignor Eugenio Pizza, and Mohammed Al Bakri. Balistreri had left his home only to go to the corner shop to buy the newspapers, cigarettes, whiskey, and some frozen food. Nothing significant came up on the death of the senator and the monsignor in Switzerland, while the Italian political scene was in turmoil. Corvu had informed him that no gun or gloves had been found on the death scene of Mohammed Al Bakri, and that he was therefore cleared of any possible accusation. But Balistreri didn't care about any of this. He just wanted to be sure that Linda was safe in San Francisco.

He walked slowly on his aching knee to the corner bar, had a good espresso, then he bought the newspapers, went back into his apartment, and laid down on the couch.

He opened *Il Domani* and stared, paralyzed, at the title on the front page.

Dictators or Terrorism?

And the subtitle.

*Exclusive Interview with One of Gaddafi's Key Men.*

The byline was Linda Nardi. *From Tripoli, Libya.*
He quickly read only the first few lines, just to make sure this was
real and not a nightmare.

I am here in Tripoli with one of the men leading the resistance to the
rebels. He authorized only a few questions he would answer now,
limited to the events that are taking place in Libya. Others, pertain-
ing to events that recently took place in Italy and Switzerland, he
refused to answer now. Perhaps tomorrow.
    "Is it true that you ordered the killing of General Younis?"
    "Yes. Younis was a traitor of Colonel Gaddafi. This is the way we
deal with traitors over here, since the very start. The first one I dealt
with was found on August 15, 1970, during the tuna fishing. I had
killed him myself."
    "Did you order and attend to the massacre of rebels and civilians
in Zawiya?"
    "Yes. You in the West pretend to be horrified by this, but you don't
understand. Colonel Gaddafi, just like Saddam Hussein did, really
protects your own economic interests and your own safety. If Gaddafi
falls, Libya will become a nightmare for the West."
    "You don't believe in democracy?"
    "In Arab countries democracy is impossible. You Westeners can
only choose between dictators and terrorism. You can choose between
terror here or terrorists at your doorstep."

Balistreri dropped the newspaper. He could easily recognize each of
those concepts, a mixture between the cold killer instincts of Ahmed and
the hate for the West of Karim. But still he wouldn't have cared anymore,
except that Linda Nardi was now there, in the most dangerous place of
all. And he knew that those words from the man with the severed ear
were not really addressed to the million of people in the West, but only
to one of them.

*Come back here Mike, or . . .*

The picture of Farid Al Bakri among the sharks made clear what could happen to Linda Nardi if he refused to go back to the last place on earth he wanted to go.

He didn't waste a second. He walked to the nearest post office and dictated the short cable addressed to PO BOX 150870, Tripoli, Libya.

*I am ready.*

# SUNDAY, AUGUST 14, 2011

Balistreri hadn't even had his early morning espresso when his cell phone rang. The person on the line spoke Italian with an Arab accent. He was told to pack and be ready in half an hour.

At nine a black Mercedes picked him up. The driver drove fast toward Leonardo da Vinci airport.

"It's impossible to fly you directly to Tripoli, Mr. Balistreri. Because of the no-fly zone. We'll use the few real friends we have left. You'll fly from Rome to Moscow International at Sheremetevo. From there we'll drive you to Vnukovo 2 airport, just south of Moscow. You'll catch a Russian diplomatic flight that the NATO butchers will not dare touch. You'll be in Tripoli by late tonight."

## DIPLOMATIC FLIGHT, MOSCOW TO TRIPOLI

During the flight from Moscow to Tripoli I fell into a fitful state between waking and sleeping, more like the delirium of someone with a very high temperature. Every kind of memory—thought, doubt, and certainty—rose to the surface, disappeared, and then returned with details I'd completely forgotten. Or had wanted to forget.

The gunfight between Rock Hudson and Kirk Douglas, the bodies of the young woman and child in the cesspit, Granddad's sadness beside Jet's kennel, Ahmed slitting that infected dog's throat, Nico lisping while Don Eugenio felt him up, Ahmed's knife at Don Eugenio's throat, Emilio Busi telling my mother and grandfather "the future lies under the sand, not above it," the blood brotherhood, Cairo, the three soldiers with their throats cut, the MANK organization, the first kiss with Laura and my hands on the hem of Marlene's briefs, Nadia's corpse in the olive-pressing shed, my mother's hand raised in farewell on La Moneta, Marlene's naked body and my blood, Salim with his throat cut by Ahmed after he'd severed Karim's ear, General Jalloun asking us to assassinate Gaddafi, racing motorbikes with Ahmed along the jetty, Jalloun's body among the tuna and my father's last warning look, Gaddafi in my telescopic sights and the whistling sound that sent it all sky high, Karim furtively leaving Laura's house, me ripping her clothes off and her hands on my shoulders as I force myself on her, the MANK's strongboxes lying empty under the sea, Ahmed firing at me with an unloaded pistol and me firing back at him, then running over his body with the motorboat, and, finally, Nico Gerace. And still, it wasn't over.

If I look back now on the arc of my life, after forty years everything slowly disappears from sight, but in the mists of memory what I can always make out is La Moneta. My physical body has survived its shipwreck and reached a shore somewhere, but my spirit's stayed there, facing the rocks around that island, facing the lights of the Tripoli coastline that grew more distant as I was running away from what I was: Mike Balistreri.

As the plane was taking me back to where I'd grown up, something inside me was beginning to rebel against those thoughts. The memory of that last day in Tripoli seemed unreal, unbelievable even, as if it had been someone else whose life had been cut in two.

*There are always two sides to every truth.*

This thought came to me in increasing waves as the plane was flying over the Mediterranean and nearing the African coast. They weren't even thoughts as such, more a growing feeling that this physical flight toward the past wasn't a journey toward a truth or an enemy, but toward *the person I really was.*

Young Mike was a criminal, a murderer of friends, and a rapist. But also an idealist with an inflated sense of loyalty. Easy to manipulate. So, had I been the real author of my own destiny? Or just a puppet in someone's hands? Someone tapped me on the shoulder to fasten my seat belt. We were landing at Mitiga airport, once Wheelus Field. As the airplane slowed down, I could hear the noise of the wheels from the undercarriage, the brakes, the engines whistling. And everything seemed to be happening in slow motion to me as well in an unreal insulated silence. When I put my head out the door and walked down the steps into the hot night, I remembered the thoughts I had as a boy seeing Neil Armstrong put his foot on the moon.

*I'll stay here only a short while. Or perhaps forever.*

What I saw was a place unknown to my eyes, but very familiar to my spirit. What was humble then, was today false and pretentious. But what I could smell—that mixture of eucalyptus, earth, and manure—and what I could hear in the quiet depths of the African night—leaves, crickets, frogs—and what I was feeling—the soft slowness of Africa—was much stronger than any external change. This had been my home, the home I'd run away from in order to bury myself in the untroubled routine of the present.

And in order to do that I'd had to condemn a part of me to death.

Suddenly I felt relieved, light, and ready. And very certain.

Michele Balistreri can die only here, where Mike was born.

· · · ·

A black armored Volvo was waiting for me at the bottom of the boarding steps. The driver was a Libyan in a uniform I couldn't recognize. More likely he was a secret agent than a chauffeur.

The unfamiliar and deserted Tripoli of 2011 began to roll past the window. We drove along an almost completely empty modern road through the outskirts: no cars, only a few bicycles. Gas was evidently in short supply. These were the days of Ramadan, snipers, and bombs. And also curfew. NATO fighter-bombers could attack at any moment. But the fear of dying was the last thing on my mind.

This unexpected and unwanted return was for a noble cause.

To save the life of Linda Nardi, a life worth saving, in exchange for my own.

The driver interrupted this tumult of thoughts.

"We will be at the Hotel Rixos shortly, Signor Balistreri. There's a room ready for you. Please do not leave it, and wait to be called there."

We arrived at midnight. The hotel was surrounded by an iron enclosure similar to a bamboo fence that marked out the grounds. In front of the modern two-story building the activity was orderly: Western cars, some SUVs, and a good many security guards, but no more than at a grand hotel in Riad or Dubai. In all, a normal flow of people seeing the daylight fast of Ramadan was over. From one of the lounges came Asian-sounding music.

But in the end, this apparent normality was nothing more than a show for the few remaining journalists, the last desperate tail end of propaganda from a regime that was on its knees. The show of calm that dictators put on, such as Gaddafi's game of chess with the Kalmuck president, which more often than not shortly precedes their downfall.

I entered the Ottoman-style lobby, walking past the glass cube and the two pools and came reception, followed a footstep behind by my driver/minder. The conversations around me were either whispered or too loud. People shot furtive glances in my direction, wondering who the devil the poor cretin was who'd come to Tripoli when almost all journalists had left by then and the staff evidently had nothing to do because there were no guests in the lobby, only the secret police.

Wool pulled firmly over the eyes, just as when we Italians were here. Indeed, especially when we were here. Wool over the eyes like the dinner dances on terraces overlooking the sea in clubs called the Beach and the Underwater; like the card games held in Don Eugenio's parish for the people who mattered; like Sunday Mass in the cathedral, where everyone noted who was with whom and who was absent, followed by the swish of the young boys and girls walking past in their Sunday best.

What had changed now was only who was pulling the wool.

No one took my passport to register it. I was immediately given a key and accompanied by my pseudo-chauffeur to a room on the first floor.

"Just wait in here," he told me and said good-bye.

The window looked out onto an inner courtyard wall. No view and no possibility of escape. Inside everything was functioning normally: electricity, hot and cold water, shower, flushing toilet. The sheets were freshly laundered, pressed, and perfumed. In the middle of the bed lay a package of dates. What had I expected? What had I hoped for? Burned-out cars and rubble on the streets, beetles and spiders in the rooms? Did I need those to remove any doubt from my mind that this regime, Gaddafi, my father, Mohammed, Busi, Don Eugenio, weren't fundamentally evil?

All of a sudden, in the darkness of this alien room, I was struck by the dreadful suspicion that it wasn't true at all.

Perhaps Gaddafi did have good reasons, perhaps my father and his associates were only shrewd businessmen, simple precursors of the eighties, perhaps Nietzsche was a doddering old fool and my mother a haughty idealist incapable of living with the world as it was. Perhaps the man with the severed ear was right in his interview with Linda.

*You in the West can only choose between terror in these countries or terrorism at your doorstep.* And perhaps I hadn't been betrayed by Ahmed, Karim, or Laura.

Ahmed had twice saved my life, first in that Cairo alley and second when I slipped down the cliff face on La Moneta. He'd come with me on the suicide mission against Gaddafi. And perhaps he'd saved my life a third time by organizing my escape from Tripoli on August 15, 1970. Karim had been close to Laura after I'd devastated her by sleeping with Marlene, and perhaps the Karim I saw leaving her house on August 15 was still only a friend. Perhaps Laura Hunt did love me and that same evening, instead of committing an act of violation, it was an act of love. The thoughts continued to surface, like the flashbacks on the plane. No longer shadows from the past but a foretaste of what was to come.

*Nothing happened as you thought it did. There are always two sides to every truth.*

# MONDAY, AUGUST 15, 2011

I lay down on the bed, trying to focus on Linda Nardi.

She's still alive.

I was sure of only one thing. Karim Al Bakri, *the man with the severed ear,* would kill her before my very eyes. Or else he'd be satisfied simply to take my life.

The life of his brother's killer for the life of Linda. An eye for an eye.

I remained like that, looking at the ceiling, fully dressed and ready to go.

At two there was a knock on the door. I hurriedly splashed water on my face and followed the driver to the Volvo. The temperature outside was over a hundred degrees.

Just like that night. August 15, 1970.

We skirted past horrendous modern apartment buildings modeled on Khrushchev's *khrushchevka,* low-rise low-cost workers' housing that Gaddafi had wanted to emulate from the Soviet regime. We traveled along what, as a child, I knew as the Adrian Pelt coastal road. Who knew what the hell it was called now? It was certainly no longer the old graceful promenade lined with palms, only a horrendous highway.

Then we came to the Castle in the Green Square. A vast parking garage had been erected in the middle of the square. It was now deserted except for two truck-loads of soldiers wearing the same uniform as my driver. The two monumental columns facing the sea were still there, one with its caravel, but in place of the Roman wolf on the other there was now a mounted Berber warrior.

We drove right past the apartment building where I was to shoot at Gaddafi standing on the battlements. Only a little while ago, Gaddafi's fierce scowl had addressed a crowd of supporters and threatened the insurgents there.

Then we took the road for the coast again, passing by hotels that were new to me, the Corinthia and the Sheraton. And finally out onto another modern road that led to Gargaresh and the beaches. But there was no longer any sign of the old beach clubs, the Lido, the Sulfur Baths, the Beach, and the Underwater. Only an endless line of little shops. All closed.

Finally, the car turned off toward the coast. At the end of a short descent was a small private harbor with several guards. They signaled me to get into a motorboat together with two armed soldiers and the pilot.

As the boat set off, I recognized the route immediately. I'd followed it countless times as a kid. We were going precisely where I didn't want to go.

Where everything began and where everything will come to an end.

## LA MONETA ISLAND

When I saw the jetty lit up in the distance, I immediately realized something.

This is the only place in Tripoli where nothing's changed.

The wooden jetty was the same, the lamps beside it the same. The beach was identical to that of my youth; the umbrellas and deckchairs were the same make and color. The villa was as white as ever and perfectly maintained, as were the guest house and house for the domestic staff.

An armed guard was waiting for me on the jetty and led me to the door of what in another life had been my house, or rather, my father's house.

He opened the door and I entered a museum of memories: perhaps a dreadful torture the new owner wanted to inflict on me. Nothing inside had been touched. Everything was the same, perfectly preserved: furniture, ornaments, lights, pictures on the wall. I passed the mirror in the hall toward the back of the house and saw a figure reflected there. But I no longer knew who it was . . .

*Michele or Mike?*

The guard pointed to the last room, my father's study. The door was open and from it came the weak light of a desk lamp. I remembered that lamp, Dad always kept it lit on his desk, day and night. It was like going back toward the biggest mistake in one's life, to the moment before you make it, but without being able to make a different choice. And in that very moment, before spepping through that door, I was certain: Nothing had happened as I thought. Mike wasn't the puppet master, but rather the puppet.

But instead of feeling pain, rancor, anger, I felt the world had lightened, and I stepped into that room without any fear at all.

. . . .

The man with the severed ear was sitting in an armchair in the corner. Another armchair was facing him. They were my father's old armchairs. The one he used to sit in and the one he offered his guests. His was the one with its back facing the wall, obviously. And that was the one the man waiting for me was sitting in. He was the new owner, the new boss. There were deep furrows in the hollow cheeks under his prominent cheekbones, his hair was still thick, but now gray. Only the severed ear hadn't aged.

"Ciao, Mike," he said, without getting up, "Happy birthday. Take a seat."

He spoke in English as we did as boys when we didn't want people to know what we were saying. I'd even forgotten about my birthday, but there was no sarcasm in my old childhood friend's greeting.

I sat down opposite him. He was in civilian clothes, a blue shirt and gray slacks. He seemed older than me. It was his eyes that aged him.

The eyes of someone who'd massacred many innocent people.

"Make yourself comfortable, Mike. So, you've finally come back!"

I still hadn't said a word. I was observing him, the scourge of the rebels, the exterminator of innocents, the murderer of Melania, Tanja, Domnica, and all the others. And Mike's old friend.

Everything I'd believed for decades, all those thoughts as heavy as millstones had no importance anymore. There was only one thing that mattered, the present.

"You know why I've come back. Because you called me here by killing innocent people and by finally bringing Linda Nardi here."

He nodded.

"I wanted to be sure I had your attention, Mike."

"Is Linda still here?" I asked him.

He nodded.

"Yes, she's here. You really had many excellent reasons for never coming back. And yet you've finally done it, only for this woman. In that you haven't changed much, Mike."

All he wanted was to talk about the past and all I wanted to talk about was the future. "I came back also to pay off an old debt with you. All I want is for Linda Nardi to go back to Italy. You can then do with me what you want."

He seemed upset. It was as if my statement, my immediate confession and unconditional surrender, without putting up a fight, weren't at all what he wanted.

He doesn't want to kill a compliant and reasonable old man. He wants to kill Mike.

"Is that all, Mike? Nothing more? Is there nothing we need to explain to each other?"

"You get Linda Nardi on a plane for Rome. Then we can talk for as long as you like."

He shook his head, amazed at my stupidity.

"You think it's that simple, Mike? A flight to Rome through a no-fly zone? And Colonel Gaddafi doesn't trust Libyans anymore, only his mercenaries."

"But you're his right-hand man, aren't you? Doesn't he trust you?"

"For a good many years indeed I was, but since my father's friends reclaimed the Colonel's funds, I'm regarded with suspicion. If I still enjoy any benefit of the doubt, it's only because I eliminated those two turncoats in Lugano."

"Wasn't your father with the turncoats?"

"No, Mike. He fought for the Colonel to the bitter end. I killed women and children here and in Italy, the very last ones were those two cowards, Busi and Don Eugenio. And I did it for my father, not for Gaddafi. Because they had betrayed him, after so many years."

"But then you killed your father as well. Was that because he wanted to kill me there and then, while you wanted me here in Tripoli?"

He shook his head.

"You never could understand Muslims, could you, Mike? We can disagree with our fathers, but we'd never betray them. Nor do we kill them."

He was sincere, with no reason to lie to me.

"So who did kill your father? Do you know?"

He stared at me.

"I'm still the head of Libya's Secret Service, Mike. Of course I know."

"So tell me."

A thought crossed his mind, then he shrugged.

"What does it matter? You came here for Linda Nardi, didn't you?"

"And where is she?"

"I had her arrested and secretly brought here to La Moneta by men I could trust before I was put under surveillance. I saved her life. The guards think she's a concubine of mine."

"Good. So let her escape and then we can deal with the past."

He looked at me as if I hadn't understood a thing.

"I'm surrounded here and watched over by the Colonel's body-guards. Apparently for my own protection, but in reality so they can keep an eye on me. We're free here on the island, but under direct surveillance. It's as if I'm under house arrest."

"So where does that leave me? Am I your prisoner?"

"The men out there belong to Colonel Gaddafi's personal body-guard. I'd no other way of getting you into Libya than by selling you to them. The kid who wanted to kill Gaddafi on August 15, 1970. You're their prisoner, not mine."

I said nothing. He got up and went to the window and looked out across the sea.

"They still have a little faith left in me. But not enough to save your life. At dawn they'll shoot you here on the beach. The Colonel's personal order."

He stayed where he was in silence, looking at the sea. Then he turned to look at me and an unexpected smile crossed his face. He suddenly seemed lighthearted and cheerful.

"So we don't have that much time, Mike. We'll have to make a move during the bombardment that's coming in just before dawn. While the Coast Guard boats take refuge in port to avoid the NATO bombs."

I stared at him, dumbstruck.

"But, how . . . ?"

"I've been in charge of Libya's Secret Service for years, Mike. I've got many friends in NATO as well. An inflatable's moored off the other side of the island, below the cliff there. And an Italian cruiser will be there in an hour. One of my men will take Linda out to the cruiser in the inflatable."

He opened the closet, my father's old closet, and took out a Kalashnikov. Then he smiled again.

"Linda Nardi's in the guest house. There are two militiamen on the jetty, two on the two doors of the villa, two over at the guest house. They're all armed, but it won't be a problem if some old expert would help me."

I looked at him and shook my head.

"I don't shoot people anymore."

Again that intense crazy smile.

"I know, Mike. You've become what Laura Hunt wanted you to be. A sensible old bourgeois. But you're simply the diversion. You're under arrest and I'll have to handcuff you. And that's how you'll help me."

He put the cuffs on me and pocketed the key.

"I'll hand you over to the militiaman guarding the exit around the back of the house. He knows the Colonel wants you alive for the firing squad. I'm going across to the guest house to get Linda."

"One of the men on the jetty's got a walkie-talkie," I said.

"Doesn't matter. We should have half an hour's advantage and pretty soon they'll have other things to think about on the ground when the NATO planes come in."

I looked him in the eye for the first time since I'd entered the room and he recited the magic formula that was supposed to take me back forty years or more.

"If you want to save Linda, there's only one way. Just like old times, Mike. One last time."

He dragged me to the door at the back and handed me over to the militiaman who was drowsing in a chair in the heat of the night, a Walther PPK in his holster. He said something to the man in Arabic and then turned to me, speaking in Italian.

"I told him that you'll be here in handcuffs for a while. And that he should shoot you if you try to escape. Just get yourself *close enough,* all right?"

*Close enough, Mike. You remember how to do it?*

He walked away calmly, as if going for a stroll along the beach. There was one militiaman on guard outside the guest house fifty yards away and the second one must have been inside watching over Linda.

I heard the guard greeting him deferentially at the door, then the man with the severed ear placed the Kalashnikov against the wall and went inside.

## LINDA NARDI

When the man with the severed ear entered the room, the militiaman guarding me got up, almost obsequiously, but still took the gun from his holster.

"Signorina Linda, Michele Balistreri's here. And he's come to save you," said the man with the severed ear, speaking in Italian.

During this entire crazy trip I kept telling myself that I was coming here solely to kill the monster who'd shot Melania and Tanja Druc, run over Domnica Panu in a van, shattered Beatrice Armellini's skull with a bullet, and massacred rebels, as well as old men, women, and children in Libya.

*But it's not true, Linda. You came here to see if Michele Balistreri would come after you and try to save your life.*

I now felt terrible remorse for this madness.

"He'll be shot at dawn. But you can save yourself, Signorina, if you do everything I tell you."

"I don't take orders from a child killer."

He maintained his calm.

"Balistreri came here only for you, to save your life. Please let him die a happy man!"

He didn't wait for a reply and addressed the other guard in English, holding out a pair of handcuffs.

"Put those on the lady."

The militiaman hesitated a moment. Then he put the gun back in his holster, took hold of the handcuffs, and bent toward my wrists. But he had no time to handcuff me. The saw blade of a knife slit his throat from ear to ear.

As the blood spurted in my face, over my T-shirt and jeans, I heard a sound like a sink being unblocked, a terrible gurgling noise as life left his body. The man with the severed ear took the guard's gun from its holster and gave it to me.

"Now, Signorina, either you really try to help me or we'll all die. And Michele will be the first."

The gun found my hands and our eyes met for a second.

"I'm sure you know how to shoot. This is our only chance."

He then knocked three times on the guest house door, the signal that he wanted to exit. The militiaman outside opened it and the man with the severed ear shot him in the head before he was even past the door.

## MICHELE BALISTRERI

I was ready even before I heard the gunshot. As soon as the guest house door was opened I distributed the weight on my feet and launched a kick at the militiaman's chin at the same time as the shot was fired. The man had no time to get out of his seat.

As the spasm of pain shot from my knee to my brain, I almost passed out, but I saw the man with the severed ear come out with Linda. He grabbed the Kalashnikov left against the wall and pointed agitatedly in the direction that the militiaman guarding the villa would come from. Then he ran off, going around the villa to go down to the jetty.

But he'd overlooked another possibility. The militiaman emerged behind me from inside the house and gave me a kick in the back that sent me sprawling on the wooden decking. A moment later I felt the barrel of a gun at my neck.

## LINDA NARDI

Perhaps I've always been like this. Perhaps it's my true nature, the dreadful rebellious girl that only Lena's tireless dedication had gradually been able to calm down.

*I'm not going to let him die for my sake.*

The man with the severed ear was right. We only had one chance. I knew what to do and how to do it. Five years ago Angelo Dioguardi had taught me how to play poker and Michele Balistreri had taken me to a shooting range to teach me how to use a gun. So I took aim.

*Use both hands, aim at the target.*

The first bullet hit the militiaman exactly in the center of his back, fracturing his spinal column. I ran to Balistreri, who was staggering to his feet. He said nothing, but took the gun from my hands into his. He was still handcuffed.

The man with the severed ear was behind the corner of the house nearest the jetty, the Kalashnikov in his hands. A militiaman standing on the jetty was firing at him, while another was speaking furiously into the walkie-talkie.

Michele fired a shot randomly in their direction. The man on the jetty was taken aback a moment, then turned toward us. It was all we needed. The burst from the Kalashnikov sent him sailing into the sea. The last of the militiamen dropped his walkie-talkie and started running for the motorboat.

"Shoot him, Mike!" shouted the man with the severed ear. His ammunition was spent, he'd thrown the Kalashnikov down and was racing toward the jetty.

## MICHELE BALISTRERI

Linda stared at me.

"Shoot him, Michele!"

I'd only shoot someone if I was forced to.

With those words I'd risked her being killed by the Invisible Man. Mike would never have allowed that.

I stretched out my arms and aimed at the man's legs. A Walther PPK is an accurate weapon, but the distance was huge. However, I was still a good shot.

The man went down, hit in the left calf. He started to drag himself along the jetty to the motorboat, but the man with the severed ear caught up with him. With one hand he grasped the man by the hair, lifted his head and slit his throat. He picked up the man's gun, tucked it in his belt, and set off calmly toward us.

"Give me the gun," said Linda.

"We're not here for this, Linda. You should go back to Italy now and I'll see to him."

"Michele, that man killed Melania and her daughter and all those others. In Libya he's massacred old men, women, and children."

The man with the severed ear had reached us. There was a look of irony in his eyes, almost one of amusement.

"Mike isn't here for that, Signorina Linda. He's here to save you, if you want to be saved."

He took the gun from my hands and slipped it into his belt. Then he took out a key and released me from the cuffs, pointing to the path behind the villa that led to the other side of the island.

"You remember the way, Mike? We have to get moving. Soon bombs will be raining down on here."

He turned and started running toward the path to the cliff.

"Let's go then," I said to Linda.

Our eyes met for a moment. She was an extraordinary woman, calm, intuitive, rational, sweet, compassionate.

But capable of killing, if need be.

If there'd still been a glimmer of Mike in me five years earlier, we could have understood each other and continued to live happily together. Instead we'd damaged each other more than we could have imagined.

The ice-cold anger I saw in her eyes frightened me more than our unending battle.

"That man is a cold-blooded killer, Michele."

I tugged her violently, but she wouldn't come. Exasperated, I slapped her. She looked at me for a long moment. We both remembered another slap from five years earlier. And we remembered what I'd said.

*I should have fucked you like an ordinary whore.*

There was something in her eyes, a look of pain or regret, which I couldn't bear or understand. I expected a slap back or an insult. Instead, her face slowly softened and she calmed down, as if that slap had brought her to a different decision. Then she set off at a run along the path.

Neither of us spoke. While I was running along that path in the night I was thinking about another time I ran to the cliff in the dark on August 31, 1969.

When we came out onto the open space, the man with the severed ear was already there beside the old tree lit by the full moon. He pointed to the cliff edge with the Walther PPK in his hand.

"You'll have to jump from here, Signorina Linda."

The dark sea glinted twenty yards below. I'd already leaped twice from that cliff, but I didn't want Linda to run the risk.

"Is the water high enough?" I asked him.

"For another fifteen minutes, Mike, then Signorina Linda would no longer be able to jump. One of my men is below with an inflatable. He'll take her out to the Italian cruiser, which will take her back to Italy."

The man with the severed ear studied us. He was calm, measured.

"I let NATO know that Gaddafi has a stockpile of weapons on the island. In half an hour La Moneta won't exist anymore. Now, please jump, Signorina Linda."

She was staring at the rocks rising out of the sea. I thought she was terrified at the idea of jumping. But instead she whispered something.

*So this is where it happened . . .*

For a moment I thought I was dreaming, or simply imagining it. Linda turned toward me, tears streaming from her eyes.

She's not crying for herself, out of fear. Nor for Michele Balistreri, but for young Mike.

Linda dried her tears with the back of her hand. She turned directly to the man with the severed ear.

"I don't care what happens to you, you'll soon be rotting in hell anyway. But Michele's going to jump with me."

He pointed the gun at her.

"Mike's staying here. We have some business to finish alone, he and I. Now you either jump or die. You have ten seconds. One, two . . ."

He started to count in Arabic. I knew for certain that he would shoot her.

"Linda, I have to stay here. All that matters to me is that you stay alive. Please."

The words were broken, uncoordinated; my expression must have been desperate.

Suddenly Linda smiled at me. I'd dreamed for years that she might do that again. Her hand lightly brushed against mine. Only for a moment. Then she ran to the edge of the cliff and leaped into the air.

• • • •

The man with the severed ear was holding the pistol in his left hand, the pale scar I glimpsed in my father's study was on his right wrist.

The surgeon had done a good job with the ear.

*Nothing has happened as you thought. There are always two sides to every truth.*

I should have understood back then when he sent me the photographs of his sister's killer fed to the sharks with his pecker in his mouth. Karim would never have been able to kill him in that way.

Nor would he have been able to handle a Kalashnikov and slaughter women and children.

Ahmed Al Bakri lit a long slim cigarette.

"So, we have fifteen minutes, Mike, before the water's too low and the bombs lay waste to this wretched island. There's another inflatable and it'll be there for another twenty minutes. Let's get some matters straight."

Ahmed sat down, leaning against the tree trunk. He took a drag on the cigarette and slowly blew out the smoke, a slow moment that seemed to last a few minutes that then stretched out to more than forty years. I sat down facing him. The exterminator of innocent people. My best friend.

*The other side of Mike Balistreri. The dark side Laura had feared.*

"On August 15, 1970, you were out of it, and it was easy to fool you. Everything was planned and you never noticed a thing."

I was the only puppet among all those holding the strings. Each scene had been constructed especially for me.

The trip to Misurata, the tuna kill, Jalloun's body, the failed attempt on Gaddafi's life, taking Laura by force, the birthday party with my friends.

"When we got back to your house in Garden City, you were very upset, Mike. You unloaded my gun and Nico's too. But I checked."

"And you put blanks in mine."

He nodded, looking pleased with himself.

"I always told you, Mike, destiny is in our own hands. That night out at sea you were too tired, too upset to notice the difference between blank shots and real ones and between a sinking corpse and a man submerging with air tanks. After you left I came to the surface. Karim was in the area, like I told him, and I turned on my flashlight and he came to pick me up."

"Laura was in on all this with you and Karim?"

He nodded his head, unhappy.

"I had told Laura you'd agreed to shoot Gaddafi. All she cared was that you didn't get shot yourself. And for that, it wasn't enough to get you to run away. We had to make sure that you never ever came back."

*So you had me violate my girlfriend and kill Nico.*

"Laura and I had agreed on a plan to save your life, Mike. Karim had you see him on purpose as he was leaving her house. Then he went out to the reef and took the money."

It was all so simple, so obvious. And there was only one explanation for Ahmed's severed ear.

"When did Karim die?"

"After you shot me, I went to Cairo. No one knew I was still alive, not even my father. Only Karim. In 1973 the war with Israel started up again and Karim was blown up by a mine. His body was unrecognizable and I decided to have my ear cut and assume his identity. So I stayed in Cairo and wrote regularly to Mohammed, who thought I was Karim, but I never went back to Tripoli. Only when the plot to assassinate Sadat was successful did I return and was treated like a hero. After all that time not even my father with his poor eyesight could distinguish me from Karim. I slowly rose through Gaddafi's ranks, thanks to Mohammed. And I was able to reopen some old investigations, here and in Italy. I found out you had arrived in Italy without Nico. And I got hold of some information General Jalloun had kept for himself."

"And that's how you got to Farid?"

"Yes. Farid and Salim knew the black woman found in the cesspit. They had tortured her and her baby and then threw them in the cesspit. Nadia had seen the boys with the woman and baby. She made the mistake of asking Farid about it. And those two bastards killed her with Nico's help."

"Don't you find that incredible plan too complicated for them?"

He nodded.

"Sure. It was not their own plan. When I dealt with Farid, he told me the story. The black woman was a chambermaid at Wheelus and had stolen some secret document from William Hunt and had asked him for money. So he ordered Farid and Salim to eliminate her, that's where all their money came from. And when Nadia found out Hunt made the plan for them to kill her, too."

"Where is Hunt now?"

Ahmed smiled.

"What do you think, Mike? Don't you know me?"

Up to that moment all we had heard was the calm sea as a peaceful background to our thoughts. Now in the absolute quiet of the sultry night, we heard a faint distant whistling, almost imperceptible, but growing closer.

NATO fighter-bombers. Ready for action.

Ahmed was suddenly impatient. He was right, we only had a few minutes and he had the right to his version of the events.

"But we're not here to rehearse those narratives, Mike. You wanted Linda Nardi safely away and now you have it. Now I want to know why you wanted to kill me."

Of course, this was always the real question, the reason why Ahmed had Beatrice Armellini whisper those words to me—*an old friend of yours*—a moment before he blew her head off. That whistling sound was getting louder, coming from my world to drop bombs on his. It was signaling the few remaining minutes we had for explaining away forty years.

"You know why, Ahmed. If you hadn't come to an agreement with our fathers I would have killed Gaddafi and today we wouldn't be here waiting for those bombs to fall."

All of a sudden his mood changed. I'd touched on the only point that still interested him in life and now his face was serious, intent. He showed me his right wrist with the white scar still visible.

"It's for this scar that I had you brought back here, Mike. Is yours still as visible as mine?"

He was right. His could plainly be seen, whereas mine was a faint line on my left wrist.

"They already knew, Mike, they had their sources. Your father wasn't worried about Gaddafi's death, but he was about yours. Mohammed threatened us, saying we either helped them or you'd be dead. Karim told Laura and we decided we'd have to force you and then help you to flee the country. And Laura did her part."

"Where's Laura now?"

The question slipped out and Ahmed gazed out to sea beyond the cliff edge.

"On the other side of the world, Mike. We all loved you, no one betrayed you."

He got up and I rose with him. Now the whistling sound of the warplanes was much stronger. He offered me a gun.

"I killed you off back then, Mike. I took away everything you had, your country, your money, your girlfriend. It was for a good reason, but if you think differently, this time the gun is loaded."

"And do you have a gun that's loaded?"

He shook his head, upset that I so slow in understanding. Or that I didn't believe him.

"I'd never would have shot you, nor will I now. We're united by a blood brotherhood and for me that still stands."

I stood there staring at this man, once the boy I had grown up with.

A born killer, exterminator of innocent people.

But one day Mike Balistreri had created a pact of blood and sand with that boy. Whatever he'd become, whatever he'd done, it wasn't going to be Mike Balistreri to end the life of Ahmed Al Bakri. The insurgents or God or Allah could see to that, not me.

I let the gun drop.

"I shot at you once, Ahmed. There's no point in doing it again today."

All of a sudden the fighter-bombers appeared on the horizon in the first light of dawn. They shot high over our heads, and after a few seconds the first bombs began to fall on Tripoli. Huge explosions raised columns of smoke and flame. Ahmed pointed to the cliff edge.

"You have to jump, Mike. The Coast Guard has other things to worry about now, and very soon there'll be no more high tide and the planes will come over here and raze this island back into the sea."

There was just one more thing. I looked him in the eye.

"Did you kill my mother?"

He suddenly seemed both tired and at peace. It was as if everything else was simple now that we'd clarified the fact we'd never betrayed each other; and that I wouldn't shoot him now that I knew who he was; and that the blood brotherhood between us still existed.

He pointed to the old tree where my mother used to read, as if the chair and the Nietzsche book were still there.

"I got to the cliff top here about four thirty. I wanted to tell your mother that you couldn't have a relationship with Laura anymore because you were a murderer, like me."

I stared at him, taken aback.

"You came to the cliff top here that afternoon?"

He nodded, as if his lying to me then and telling me the truth now had no importance.

"Your mother wasn't up here reading. So I went to see if she was swimming. But she wasn't there anymore. Her book was still on the chair, and inside it I found that torn photograph of Gaddafi."

"What do you mean *she wasn't there anymore*? Mohammed told me that at three o'clock that afternoon my mother's body was in a bathing suit lying twisted on the rocks below. And yet at half past four you couldn't see her, is that right?"

He looked straight at me, ever more reluctantly. Then one of the planes turned around over Tripoli's skies and came toward La Moneta. This seemed to persuade him.

"There was the inflatable from Wheelus Field, Mike. General Jalloun told us it was spotted at a quarter to four and at four it had disappeared."

"William Hunt?"

Ahmed nodded.

"Your mother knew from Nadia about his connection with the black woman in the cesspit and had discovered how Nadia was killed. She gave him forty-eight hours to disappear."

I shook my head.

"William Hunt wasn't on the island that day. He was in Benghazi and that's for certain. He couldn't have pushed my mother off."

. . . .

I was watching the bombers closing in on La Moneta, but they didn't matter. The truth that *Michele Balistreri* hadn't tried to discover; indeed, had buried and forgotten, was now an obsession for his alter ego, *Mike*. I knew that Ahmed wasn't lying to me, but I still couldn't understand.

He remained silent, shaking his head. He'd no wish to go any further with this. The fighter-bomber passed fifty yards over our heads with a deafening roar. A few seconds later, the explosion on the far side of the villa was so powerful it sent us reeling.

"Ahmed, either you tell me the truth or I'm staying right here."

He nodded, resigned.

"It was someone else. William Hunt had an accomplice."

A second plane passed over our heads and another bomb exploded even closer to us.

"Tell me the name."

He signaled me no. And it was a final no.

"The truth has sides to it we don't want to see. You came here for Linda, for the future, not for the past."

He was telling me the truth. And holding back a decisive part of that truth in order to save my life yet again.

"You have to jump off this cliff. Now or never, Mike."

He was right. It was now time to leave forever this country I'd loved with my heart but never my head.

Like a great love for the wrong woman.

For a moment I pictured those two young boys again, Mike and Ahmed, so different and yet so similar when they were boys. I felt no pity for the man in front of me, the exterminator of innocent people. But he was also the adolescent who'd saved my life and with whom I'd created a brotherhood of blood.

. . . .

A huge explosion shook the ground a hundred yards from us. The regime was crashing down, and so was La Moneta. It really was time for us to leave.

"Ahmed, finish what they didn't let us do forty years ago. If you can."

Finally Ahmed smiled, as he did in the old days.

"I will, Mike. Now forget Libya, and go back home to your country."

I took a run up and leaped off just as another huge powerful explosion shook the cliffs. It was the end of La Moneta.

An inflatable with a terrified Libyan took me to the cruiser in ten minutes while La Moneta and Tripoli went up in columns of smoke and flame.

There was a lifeboat already lowered from the davits. I climbed onboard and was lifted up. They told me immediately that Linda was safely onboard.

On the bridge I looked around trying to spot her, but evidently she was already below. I didn't look for her, nor did she look for me. I knew I had to respect that absence and that silence.

From the ship, I immediately sent an e-mail to Floris, Colombo, and Madonna giving them a version of the facts that was almost true.

The killer of Melania and Tanja Druc, Domnica Panu, Beatrice Armellini, Senator Busi, Monsignor Eugenio Pizza, and *also* Mohammed Al Bakri was a Libyan secret agent in Gaddafi's service. The murder of Melania and Tanja Druc was revenge against Emilio Busi for no longer protecting the Colonel's interests. All the rest followed as a consequence of that presumed betrayal. Linda Nardi had gone to Libya to get an interview and had been able to escape with me, whereas the Libyan secret agent died in the La Moneta bombing. The e-mail concluded with my irrevocable resignation from the Italian police.

# TUESDAY, AUGUST 16, 2011

## PALERMO

We docked at dawn and I was among the last to disembark. I looked for Linda on the quay, but they said she'd disembarked early and had already left. However I did find Police Chief Floris with Colombo, Corvu, and Giulia Piccolo. Floris was the first to come up to me. I was thinking of an excuse to tell him when he smiled and grasped me by the hand.

"Thank God you're not my son, Balistreri. I would have died of a heart attack many times over."

Colombo also shook my hand.

"Thank you for saving Linda Nardi. And for having found the killer. We've compared the DNA found in Melania Druc's cabin, in the van that knocked Domnica Panu down, in Monsignor Pizza's house in Lugarno, and in the house where Mohammed Al Bakri died. We don't know whose it is, but it's the same in each case. You're an excellent policeman, Michele. The best we have. And there's no way you are resigning."

Corvu looked at me uncertainly. In all our years together we'd never exchanged more than a handshake, or the occasional pat on his back from me in exceptional circumstances. Now the boy was sniffling and ultimately couldn't resist clasping me in a quick silent embrace.

Giulia Piccolo, the soft-hearted giant with muscles of steel, stood back a couple of steps. Then she came up and we looked each other in the eye.

She, too, held out her hand.

"Thanks for saving Linda's life," she whispered.

I smiled.

"Come here, Giulia."

It was the first time I'd used her first name in years. She smiled and came closer. I took hold of those hands, their nails painted green like the highlights in her hair, those hands that were so strong yet so soft.

"Commissario, you're better than . . ." Giulia whispered, before she seized up and choked on the words, but the tears on her face spoke more clearly than any words.

Giulia Piccolo's tears, Corvu's embrace, Linda's brief caress before she leapt off the cliff edge were the only things left in my life that had any meaning.

Both Floris and Colombo asked me to revoke my resignation, but I refused. It was neither obstinacy nor spite. It was simply that that part of my life had ended where it began forty years earlier. I was no longer a policeman and I mentioned nothing about the death of my mother.

A cruel death. Buried and then forgotten by men without honor. And then forgotten by me, who had sworn he'd never forget.

## ROME

Corvu and Piccolo took me home. They didn't ask me anything, not even if I wanted their company. They both knew me well enough.

I stocked up on whiskey and cigarettes and stretched out on the sofa. But now Mike was there in that apartment as well. And he was looking at the ancient ruin of Michele Balistreri, who was again trying to bury himself under a haze of alcohol, cigarette smoke, and Leonard Cohen.

And, against Michele's wishes, Mike was starting to think things over again, going over what he'd known then and what he'd come to know in the last few hours; the things that had been kept from him all those years. He was going over the other side of the truth.

The side I didn't want to see. Not then, not now.

My mother left the villa at half past one, she'd waved to us and set off walking to the cliff. Just afterward, I'd gone to Tripoli with Marlene Hunt, Farid, and Salim.

Mohammed Al Bakri was there at three o'clock and had seen my mother already dead on the rocks below.

Ahmed Al Bakri went there at four thirty and the body was no longer there.

In between William Hunt went to the rocks in an inflatable between three forty-five and four. He'd thrown her into the water to get rid of the body.

It was an accomplice of William Hunt who had pushed Italia onto the rocks. But his wife was not there, she was in Tripoli with me. So there was only one more left. A business accomplice. The man who could sell ice to the Eskimos.

. . . .

The sun had set over the city when I called my brother on his cell phone.

"You at home?"

"Yes, Mike, we're eating. D'you want to come over and join us?"

"No, thanks. I need to talk to you. Alone."

Alberto had no idea I'd just returned from Tripoli. Nothing had come out in the media yet and the police chief had promised my name would be kept out.

"Has something happened, Mike?"

It was a question to which there was no reply.

"I need to talk to you. Now."

He gave in.

"All right, the boys are going out in a while and it's my wife's bridge night. See you in a bit."

. . . .

When I went to Alberto's, I usually preferred to cross Rome underground using the Metro, away from the tourists and the partiers out for the night. But that evening, for the first time in years, I decided to take a taxi. I looked out of the window at the happy people, the teeming restaurants, the illuminated Roman Forum and Coliseum. This was life; this was the world.

As I was getting out of the taxi, Alberto was at the door waiting for me. He met me with a smile, the same smile he'd met me with, and looked after me with, since I was a child, even when he'd had to haul me out of the abyss I fell into as a young man. He had aged well, much better than I had—another way he took after my father.

I wandered around the living room while he poured a couple of whiskies. The black-and-white photograph was still there in its wooden frame on a table.

The Adrian Pelt coastal road. Two boys wearing shorts, and socks up to their knees. Beside them, their parents. Salvatore looking down at the ground, Italia up at the sky.

We sat down in the two armchairs facing each other, as we usually did.

"The news said that the rebels are only a few miles from Tripoli, Mike. Perhaps it won't be long now . . ."

"I know, Alberto. But I'm not interested in the present. That's not why I'm here."

He nodded, sadly resigned to the fact.

"You want to talk about that day, don't you?"

His voice was tired, exhausted. The voice of someone who knows that a long illness is at last coming to its final conclusion.

"Yes. Alberto, about that afternoon, after Italia left the villa and I went off with Marlene Hunt. It was nearly two o'clock. What happened immediately after that?"

He exhaled heavily and nodded.

"I already told you at the time, Mike. The young people stayed on the beach for a couple of hours. Then I went into the house to study."

I asked him the same question I put to him back then.

"And the adults?"

And he gave me the same reply.

"I saw them all again about five fifteen, coming out onto the beach, a few at a time."

Back then he'd been evasive, not answering the real question I hadn't managed to ask. But now I had thirty years of experience as a detective.

"What about before, Alberto, while you boys were on the beach?"

Alberto looked at me. We'd always been like this: close and distant, the same and yet different.

"They were in the living room, we could see them through the window . . ."

"Ahmed had mentioned that too. But according to him there was no one there in the living room after two thirty . . ."

Alberto poured himself another whiskey. This was already over the top for my teetotalling brother.

"Can you tell me where Dad and the others were?"

Alberto got up. All my life my brother had only put me off when I brought up this detail. But I never judged him, only tried to understand why.

He was silent for a while. Then he went over to the black-and-white photograph.

"I didn't see them come out onto the beach."

"The villa had a back door, Alberto, that led straight out to the path. You couldn't see Mom from the beach. But you went into the house about four. Was Dad there?"

Silence. Alberto placed a hand on the picture frame, as if by holding on to it he could re-create that moment of happiness.

Our handsome united family, just as Dad wanted.

He looked at me and the desperate expression on his face frightened me. He was my rational and very calm older brother. I'd never seen him look like this before.

"When I went back into the house at about four, I saw Laura near the back door."

He closed his eyes, as if watching these scenes again were his only true nightmare. And then in a whisper he said what he'd kept inside himself all these years.

*For fear of Mike.*

"The back door opened from the outside and Dad came in."

For years I'd imagined that moment. I'd imagined the hate I'd feel, the rage, the desire for revenge. But instead of quickening, my pulse slowed down, as if my heart no longer had the strength to beat. I'd come to the point that should have been the finishing line, but instead it turned out to be a point of no return. I'd arrived at this point without wanting to go there again, but I'd been dragged back to La Moneta by Linda Nardi and Ahmed Al Bakri. That journey had revived the adolescent in me who'd sworn to find out the truth.

I thought again about Mohammed Al Bakri, my father's old friend and right-hand man, lying in a pool of blood in that farmhouse. Ahmed had sworn to me that he hadn't killed him. And he was right.

It was William Hunt's old accomplice.

At my grandfather's funeral I heard Hunt say, *We must talk, Salvo.*

Back then I thought he meant about the affair between my father and Marlene. But I was still very young. Now I was a seasoned policeman.

"Where is he now?" I asked him.

Alberto sighed.

"I heard from him today. He's in America."

A shooting pain rose from my stomach to my chest.

*Linda, Linda.*

· · · ·

I took a taxi and was home in less than twenty minutes. I dashed up the stairs with my knee aching and throbbing and rummaged through the disordered papers on my desk.

Finally I found the sheet of paper on which I had jotted the number Corvu had provided several days earlier.

I misdialed twice, then heard the phone ringing in San Francisco. It rang for some time.

"Hello?"

It was the one voice I hoped not to hear. Not there, in America.

"Linda, it's Michele. What are you doing in California?"

She was silent, then her voice came distantly from the other side of the world.

"My mother is dying."

Then she hung up.

I knew nothing would be achieved by calling back and telling her to be careful. My father's words uttered a few days or a century ago exploded in my brain.

*I would hate for anything bad to happen to you, Signorina. Promise me you'll be careful?*

With my hands still trembling I managed to get onto the Internet. I was lucky. Ryanair's last flight to London was at eleven and from there I could catch the night flight to San Francisco. I booked everything online and called Corvu on his cell phone.

Ten minutes later a squad car with its siren on full blast was taking me to Ciampino airport.

# WEDNESDAY, AUGUST 17, 2011

## SAN FRANCISCO

The airplane landed at nine a.m., local time. I went quickly through customs and found the driver of the limousine that Corvu had hired for me from Rome. Waiting with a cardboard sign for MR. BALISTRERI was a short man with Asian features and an efficient look about him. He shook my hand and offered to carry my backpack. Once we were in the car I gave him Lena Nardi's address and he quickly pulled out of the airport.

We took 280 into the city, coming off at the piers before the Oakland Bay Bridge and turning north up to Fisherman's Wharf, with its bars and shops full of tourists. As we turned west toward the Golden Gate Bridge I could see the island of Alcatraz and the bay full of sailboats. We passed by Presidio National Park, crossed the Golden Gate, and arrived in Sausalito. Looking back across the bay we could see the San Francisco skyline.

We passed by the little tourist port and turned onto a quiet, empty street with white two- story houses fronted with gardens on either side. I had the driver pull over.

I got out and looked for the house number. On the mailbox was a single name: LENA NARDI.

I went back to the limousine and told the driver we'd be waiting here. From the car window, I kept an eye on Lena Nardi's driveway.

This was the second time I'd rushed to save Linda's life. The first time, while trying to tear her away from the hands of an exterminator of innocents on an island turned into a nightmare of falling bombs, I never felt any fear. But now, in this peaceful atmosphere, I was really worried.

*Why, Michele? Why would your father want to have Linda killed over of a crime committed over forty years ago, before she was even born?*

There was no rational reason for my fear. And the lack of a reason made it worse.

· · · ·

The hours passed and the sun began to set over the bay. It was almost seven in the evening when I saw two men arrive at the house in a black hearse. The men from the funeral home knocked on the door, then from the hearse they took in a coffin of light-colored wood. They stayed for an hour, and when they came out I went up to them.

"Hi, I'm a neighbor. Has Mrs. Nardi died?"

They gave a solemn nod.

"Yeah, two hours ago."

"And the service?"

"Tomorrow morning at ten at Saint Mary cemetery."

· · · ·

My driver was being handsomely paid, and so raised no objections to staying there for the night. While he slept, I kept an eye on the driveway. I knew that Linda was there keeping a vigil over her mother's body. And I was keeping a vigil over her.

I wasn't there only out of hatred alone, to avenge Italia. I was also there out of love. To protect the future, which, to me, meant Linda.

*Are you sure, Michele? Are you sure the past and the future are not two separate things? Or are they the same, and you'll have to choose between them?*

The question began to take hold like the first short tremors of a fever. It was a warm night, with a soft breeze coming off the bay. That street with its small white houses was the most peaceful place on earth. I got out of the car to have a smoke and walked up to the house, stopping at the mailbox.

All I could hear were the cries of seagulls and the wash of waves in the little harbor. Again I read that innocent name: LENA NARDI. I remembered her voice when she answered my call a few days earlier.

"Hello?"

"It's Michele Balistreri," I'd said.

Then silence.

I walked slowly back to the limousine. Very slowly, as the other face of the truth came into focus.

# THURSDAY, AUGUST 18, 2011

## SAUSALITO

The men from the funeral home pulled up at seven in the morning and quickly loaded Lena Nardi's coffin into the back of the hearse. Linda emerged at nine. Alone. She was dressed in black, wearing sunglasses. She never even saw our car with its tinted windows as she stepped into her own car.

I told the driver to follow her at a distance. In fifty minutes we were at the cemetery. I stayed in the vehicle. There was no one on the green lawn circled by white mausoleums, only the hearse parked by the little chapel. The coffin was taken inside. One at at time, a dozen or so elderly ladies arrived. They must have been Lena Nardi's friends and neighbors. Going up to Linda, they embraced her one by one.

Linda looked worn out, but the atmosphere was totally peaceful. The calm hills, sun in a blue sky, green lawn, white mausoleums, old ladies chatting.

No one dies of a bullet in surroundings like these.

Five minutes before the start of the service a black chauffeur-driven Mercedes pulled up and parked outside the cemetery. My father got out and walked slowly to the little church. He was dressed to the nines, as always. A dark suit, his white hair freshly cut, the air of a wise and protective old man.

He went up to Linda and embraced her. It was brief but unbearable; obscene, absurd, and yet inevitable. Dad was a man who believed that ethics functioned by means of compensation, so that spreading a certain amount of good around meant compensation for any evil committed.

This has always been the unbridgeable gap between us.

I wasn't sure if he'd seen me or not. Perhaps he had, perhaps not. Perhaps in this case, at least, he made the right choice, one which—all things considered—he'd already done when I was still a child and still his son, which was *to pretend not to see me at all.*

After half an hour everyone left the church and Lena Nardi's coffin was carried into a small white mausoleum nearby. The elderly ladies said good-bye to Linda and left the grave site.

Linda and my father went into the mausoleum together. They stayed there several minutes, then came out and together got into the Mercedes.

He wouldn't do anything to her. Not himself, not here.

I went up to my driver.

"Follow them. If they go to her house, then you can wait outside. If anyone else comes or they leave, then call me on my cell phone."

. . . .

The cemetery was at peace again. I walked over to the mausoleum. I gently opened the door.

The interior was in shadow, cool and silent. Its rectangular shape was lit by three red candles placed in front of the three plaques, one set into each wall.

The sense of restfulness was all embracing. It was like finding oneself in an Eyptian tomb or a catacomb, as if the dead surrounding me had lain there for thousands of years and me with them.

I went up to the first plaque. A photograph showed the face of a young man in civilian clothes, probably chosen by his wife, *a photograph of her husband before he became a soldier, secret agent, and killer.*

William J. Hunt, Dallas, Texas, February 4 1925—Mogadishu, Somalia, April 16, 1983.

Ahmed had told me as much.

*I already took care of him many years ago, Mike. Your mother knew about him from Nadia and gave him forty-eight hours to disappear.*

I'd also had further checks made on the information after having spoken with Ahmed. I went back to my old friends in the Secret Service. William Hunt was one of the most expert operatives in the CIA. He'd been killed by a hit man outside the American Embassy in Mogadishu. The guards were only able to give a general description of the man, because he was wearing a hoodie that covered almost all of his face.

And his severed ear.

*How much time do I have?* That's what William Hunt had asked my mother that afternoon on La Moneta. *Two days, no more.*

That was enough for William Hunt. The planning and execution of evil was an art he'd learned in killing Koreans and refined in hatching countless plots for the US government. That night, he left the party on La Moneta and went to Benghazi. And when my mother flew off that cliff edge, he had the perfect alibi. He simply wasn't there.

It was his accomplice who threw her over the edge. All William Hunt had to do was come along with an inflatable to pick up the body and deposit it at sea. No one would see it and the coup d'etat would be blocked.

I turned to the most recent plaque, the one put into place earlier that day.

Marlene Nardi Hunt, Los Angeles, California, March 1, 1935—Sausalito, California, August 17, 2011.

Linda Nardi had often spoke of Lena. An absolutely extraordinary mother who'd looked after her with love and dedication and rescued her rebellious daughter from many predicaments. Nardi must have been Marlene's maiden name before she married William.

Marlene Hunt had become Lena Nardi and must have turned her life around the moment I dragged her into the mud in front of her Laura. That mud on her body and soul had produced what no reasoning, psychology, advice, or threat could ever have effected. It transformed a capricious, dissatisfied, and self-centered person into a strong, honest woman totally dedicated to her daughter.

The photograph on Marlene's plaque showed Lena as an unwell seventy-six-year-old. As with William's photograph, she must have chosen it herself to wipe away any last trace of the extraordinary beauty that should have made her a fortune but had only led to her ruin. Neither old age nor illness had been able to extinguish the extraordinary light in the eyes that were now staring at me from the photograph.

She knew that Mike would be here one day to look at her.

She'd known since the moment, several days ago, when I telephoned to find out where Linda was and had introduced myself as *Michele Balistreri.*

I turned slowly to the central wall that separated William and Marlene. I already knew what I would find there even before I entered the chapel. Ahmed Al Bakri had told me two days earlier on La Moneta, when I'd asked about her.

It was for that reason I'd initially avoided looking at the third plaque. But now I had to look.

．．．．

The oldest plaque there was for the youngest person to die.

Laura Nardi Hunt, San Francisco, California, April 25, 1952—
San Francisco, California, April 29, 1971.

Ahmed had wanted neither to lie to me nor to cause me pain.

*On the other side of the world, Mike. We all loved you, no one betrayed you.*

In my deepest thoughts, I'd always known she was dead. I'd thought about her countless times over the years. And I'd never managed to visualize her concretely with a husband and children, at home or at work, whether it was in Tripoli, California, or anywhere else. All I could do was remember her with me, and then nothing else, as if both of our futures had ended together on August 15, 1970.

She'd died eight months later, and Ahmed had known it. He could have let me know, but once more he wanted to protect his friend from a truth that would have brought his downfall. Ahmed had saved my life yet another time. The Mike of 1971 would have discovered an *unacceptable truth* and gotten killed.

There were two photographs on Laura Hunt's plaque. They were both there for me and for me alone.

The other side of the truth.

My anger had led me to this place of peace. It was the anger of a child, Michelino, who'd fought a titanic battle in every way against a father who *couldn't accept him as he was*, and going as far as to make that father an icon of evil, of all the evils in the world and making him a killer forever.

But, together with his accomplices, Dad had only murdered Italy, not Italia, my mother. The other side of that truth, the real truth, was a far worse nightmare. Ahmed had mentioned it to me before I leapt off the cliff.

The truth has sides to it we don't want to see. Forget the past if you want a future.

Part of that truth was staring me in the face, unrecognized, that evening five years ago when I couldn't bring myself to kiss Linda Nardi and also that dreadful night when I stopped myself in time before violating her.

Now I had no choice but to see the truth in the two photographs on Laura Hunt's plaque.

One for Mike, the other for Michele.

The first was the one a fearful adolescent, who felt betrayed and full of anger, had left on his bedroom wall in Tripoli. Laura, looking ravishingly beautiful in an evening gown, walking down the Spanish Steps in Piazza di Spagna, imitating her mother.

*The shot of how I'll never be.*

The second was an extraordinary photograph in black-and-white taken in a hospital room a short time before she died. Laura was propped up on pillows, her pale complexion contrasting with the dark shadows under her eyes, but those extraordinary eyes were lit by the sunlight coming in from the window.

That beautiful young woman was dying yet she was happy, smiling at the very tiny newborn girl in her arms who was looking up at her mother with one half of her face in the sun, the other in the shade.

I didn't need that image, nor the dates, to tell me who the baby was. Even though I'd celebrated Linda's birthday with her years ago, I'd never put it together. She'd been conceived on August 15, 1970, and was born on April 28, 1971, a little prematurely. Probably because Laura was dying.

Now I knew where I'd seen Linda Nardi's eyes before: they'd taken their shape from their grandmother, Marlene, their color from their mother, Laura, and their expression from their grandmother, Italia.

And from her father, Mike, she had that shadow that cut her face in half.

And the courage to walk across hell.

All that hate, all that pain, all that wanting to know the truth were buried in that tomb surrounded by the most complete peace, where good and evil were at rest together.

I looked at Marlene Hunt's eyes again. I knew she was pleading with me.

*Forgive me, Mike. The fault was mine, and mine alone. But forgive yourself and her too.*

. . . .

The mausoleum door opened and then closed behind me. He said nothing, but stood by my side. Now that I could really see him, Dad was just an old man of eighty-six. He'd lost weight since I'd caught sight of him in Rome a few days before. His stance was a little more bowed, his steps less sure, his arms trembling slightly. His eyes were more sunken and appeared tired under his tinted lenses.

The two of us stood in silence, each with his own thoughts. I knew he was waiting for me to say something, anything at all, but nothing was coming from my heart to my lips.

I know it's been a long time, Dad. But nothing's distant enough between a father and son, everything is close, as if it happened yesterday.

Close and yet very distant. What both united and separated us was blood, his and my mother's.

Forgive, forget.

My mother would have said so, had she been able to.

But I can't, Dad. You can forgive a moment of madness, you can forget the past, but not the present.

Without saying a word, I turned my back on him and walked out, pulling the door closed behind me. Outside there was splendid sunshine, the cemetery's green lawn, the little church, the white mausoleums, the green hills topped with towering trees and rows of stone monuments. I went back to my car and told the driver to take me to the airport.

# THURSDAY, OCTOBER 20, 2011

## OSTIA, BEACH OF ROME

Tripoli had fallen to the rebels two months ago and the media was now hypothesizing about whether Gaddafi had left the country or not.

I thought how much Ahmed and Mike would have laughed at the idea. The West had exploited the dictator for more than forty years, but it continued to not see the difference between a desert Bedouin brought up in a tent and an employee brought up in the West. The Colonel was neither a Saddam Hussein nor a Slobodan Milosevic, he would never surrender.

He's like Ahmed Al Bakri and Mike Balistreri. Westerners would never understand his motives.

It wasn't a question of good or evil. Gaddafi certainly was evil, but he'd never run away. And Ahmed was right, he was our choice between terror in Libya or terrorism at our doors.

Each day of the two months following my trip to California had seemed unending, waiting for that meeting, wondering how it might come about, and I even hadn't managed to think of the first words I would to say to her. Everything seemed either false or too serious or ridiculous. And so for two months I'd resisted getting in touch with Linda. And, for that matter, she hadn't reached out to me, either. But then I had no illusions about that.

I'm the father who abandoned her.

As usual, I was in Ostia sitting at a table in a bar looking out at the sea. The weather was glorious, the tail end of a seemingly endless summer. Only people like me without a job or family could enjoy being there: taking walks, reading the papers, sunbathing, and at sunset going off to the pier to fish.

Why this routine? Because the endless repetition of nothing was all that was left for me. I went there every day and waited for another day to end.

I was eating, my fork in midair, while the bar's television announced that Colonel Gaddafi had been killed in Sirte. Watching the bloody scenes of what had evidently been a massacre, I wondered what I actually felt.

*Are you happy now that someone's done what they stopped you from doing all those years ago?*

I realized with some surprise that those images gave me no particular satisfaction, only a mixed sense of justice and repulsion, which any civilized adult would have felt about the death of a dictator, a death that had been nothing more than a massacre.

My cell phone started ringing, but I didn't answer the calls nor the messages of congratulation, as if I'd won something. Then came a message from a number I didn't recognize, with a photograph attached. The text was very simple: As promised.

I pressed the key to open the photo. The television in the bar was broadcasting scenes of Gaddafi's last minutes, but this shot—slightly out of focus and shaky—had been taken from a different angle, obviously from a cell phone. A group of young men was dragging along the obviously wounded Colonel.

It took me some time to pick out the small revolver in the middle of the crowd. It was pointed at Gaddafi's head. Then I saw the hand holding it, followed by the arm, shoulder, and the neck, then a face in profile I could just make out. Below the baseball cap, an ear could be seen. The picture wasn't clear, but I knew that I was looking at a severed ear.

. . . .

Alberto called me that evening.

"Dad saw the pictures of Gaddafi's death, then he put himself to bed and went to sleep. He's still sleeping. We're at his house in Palermo."

He said nothing more for a minute. It seemed like a long time. I knew from Alberto about Dad's recent problems with his heart and never in his life had my father slept in the afternoon, he thought it a stupid waste of time.

In the end, I made an effort.

"All right, Alberto, I'm coming," I said.

# FRIDAY, OCTOBER 21, 2011

## ISOLA DELLE FEMMINE

On the edge of the town, a track led to a gate that was identical with the villa where we lived at Sidi El Masri outside Tripoli, with the linked *S* and *I* of my parents' initials. The two villas beyond the gate were identical to the ones where I grew up. Two villas were surrounded by eucalyptus and behind them the beach, the jetty, the sea, and an exact replica of the white villa on La Moneta.

Dad had asked Alberto not to bother with a large funeral, simply to cremate him and scatter the ashes on the bay there. When Alberto and I arrived with the urn, Linda was waiting for us on the windblown beach, which was glowing gold in the sun.

No one said a thing. Alberto opened the urn and my father's ashes were scattered by the wind, mingling with the waters and the sands. Then he went indoors and left us alone together.

*Me and my daughter.*

Around us there was only wind, water, sky, and sand. She was staring at me with those eyes inherited from three extraordinary and very different women: her grandmothers, Italia and Marlene, and her mother Laura. The wonderful creature I had in front of me was Laura Hunt's present to Mike Balistreri.

There were two lounge chairs by the water's edge. We sat down. The sun was beginning to set and a kitesurfer was shooting past a hundred yards away.

"Michele, there's something I have to tell you."

I wanted to tell her that it wasn't necessary. I knew everything about my daughter, because I'd loved her with a different kind of love before I knew she was my daughter and had twice stopped myself from acting on it; once on the verge of paradise, the second on the verge of hell. And now I knew that what had stopped me wasn't an act of will, but Laura Hunt's spirit, wherever she was.

We know things about each other that fathers and daughters never know about each other, because we knew each other on the shores of another love in another life. She knows that her father is capable of violating a woman. And I know my daughter's capable of killing a man.

But there was no way of stopping the daughter of Mike and Laura, of telling her *Let's not talk about it, there's not point in rehashing old truths.*

In August, once back in Rome, after having seen Marlene Hunt's eyes staring at me from the funerary plaque after her service, I'd made a good many examinations of the DVD of Linda and Giulia leaving together for San Francisco under police surveillance. It was the evening I went to the farmhouse where Mohammed Al Bakri was later killed.

I'd also done this earlier, looking for faces that stood out as possible killers pursuing Linda and Giulia. And I'd found none, because there were none.

But in that DVD were both Mohammed Al Bakri's killer and my mother's murderer.

The kitesurfer performed an elegant twist and turned toward the open sea and the disk of the sun as it was setting over the horizon.

"I have to tell you, Michele. I have to say this and you have to decide."

# TUESDAY, AUGUST 9, 2011

## CIAMPINO

At twenty to eight, Linda Nardi came out of the bathroom in Fiumicino airport. She met Giulia Piccolo's friend Francesca, who was waiting for her outside the terminal with the Ducati Monster 900.

She thanked Francesca and got onto the bike. She drove at top speed down the highway toward Rome and then took the intersection onto the Appia Nuova and Ciampino.

After the airport exit, she turned down onto Via dei Pini toward the address that Emilio Busi and Eugenio Pizza had given her before they were killed. In the darkness lit only by the moon, she rode the few miles through the countryside. The narrow road became an unpaved track and ended at a large green gate with the number 1952 on it.

Just before the gate was a Fiat Ritmo, parked to the side. She knew that car from the trips to Ostia with Michele Balistreri five years ago. When she heard the sound of a motorbike in the yard, she quickly hid Giulia's Ducati behind Balistreri's Ritmo. The Kawasaki rider shot past without seeing her.

*If Balistreri's here, then the man with the severed ear must be here as well.*

She climbed over the gate and crept silently into the farmhouse. She immediately heard the voice. It was that of an old man speaking on the phone in Arabic and he sounded visibly upset. But Linda could make out nothing of what he was saying except the word *Balistreri*.

She peeked down the dimly lit hall. An old man was talking into a satellite phone. She recognized Mohammed Al Bakri from the night of the cruise.

His back was to her. On a small table lay a Smith & Wesson that Linda slipped into the pocket of her gray sweatshirt.

The old man ended the call, turned around, and saw her.

"Signorina Nardi, from that night on the cruise, I knew that in the end we would have to kill you as well."

"Like Melania Druc and her baby girl?"

He raised his shoulders and coughed.

"Yes, like them all. My son saw to it. I thought I'd only have to see to the end of Michele Balistreri this evening, even though my son's against it. But clearly I'll have the pleasure of doing away with you as well."

Mohammed Al Bakri was born and brought up in a culture in which women were at best obedient concubines. He felt sure of himself and took a step forward. Linda Nardi shot him without hesitation.

She put the gun and satellite phone in her pocket and rushed back to Giulia Piccolo's bike, stopping only to throw the gun and phone into a well. She reached Ciampino airport a few minutes later, just in time to catch the last flight to London and from there the night flight to San Francisco.

# FRIDAY, OCTOBER 21, 2011

## ISOLA DELLE FEMMINE

Balistreri listened in silence to what Linda had to say while he watched the comings and goings of the kitesurfer.

"Mohammed wouldn't have killed me, even if you hadn't come. His son had forbidden it."

"You're not surprised. How did you know?"

"When I came back from California I checked the DVD of the Fiumicino airport CCTV footage and the other reports from Ciampino airport that I'd asked Corvu to get. It was all there."

Right in front of my eyes, the truth I didn't want to see.

**August 9, 2011—Fiumicino Airport, Rome**
Time 19:17
Linda Nardi and Giulia Piccolo enter the International Departures hall. Linda has a single trolley and a bag, almost looks at the CCTV camera. They line up at the check-in, then go through baggage check

and passport control. Linda goes to the bathroom and comes out at 19:38. Giulia waited for her outside.

Time 19:40
A young woman in a baseball cap with no logo, sunglasses, gray tracksuit, and white sneakers comes out of the bathroom after Linda Nardi. The young woman quickly leaves the International Departures hall.

Time 20:35
Linda and Giulia are sitting down and reading in a corner of the waiting room, then they get up, walk to the jetway, hand in their embarkation cards, and show their passports. They are aboard at 20:45.

**August 9, 2011—Ciampino Airport, Rome**
Time 22:21
The same young woman who left Leonardo da Vinci airport at 19:40 wearing a baseball cap with no logo, sunglasses, gray tracksuit, and white sneakers, enters the International Departures hall and goes straight to baggage check, because she did an online check-in, and at 22:50 gets on the 23:00 Ryanair flight for London.

The kitesurfer was twisting and turning, shooting along and going ever farther out. Balistreri kept his eyes on him.

"Corvu even had you tailed, poor guy. Passengers L. Nardi and G. Piccolo appeared on the manifest and also disembarked in Los Angeles. But there's only the initial on the embarkation card. And at Ciampino you also used your initial, L. Nardi. You took the same flights that I did to get to Marlene's funeral, the last flight of the day from Rome to London, then the nonstop to San Francisco."

Linda nodded.

"Lena and Giulia left from Leonardo da Vinci at nine, while I left Ciampino at eleven. They got to San Francisco an hour before me."

"And you got there in time for my phone call, when Marlene answered and passed me on to you and Giulia."

Linda sighed.

"Lena had come to Rome to help me, because I told her about the man with the severed ear that I saw with Melania Druc in Tripoli, and she was frightened."

"Naturally, she knew who he was."

Except she thought it was Karim.

"She told me everything, who my real mother was, my grandfathers, and that the man with the severed ear was a childhood friend of my father's. But she didn't tell me who my father was. I learned that in San Francisco from the man Ahmed Al Bakri sent to persuade me to go to Tripoli."

"Persuade you?"

Linda also kept her eyes on the sea.

"He wrote to me. Told me who you were, who I was. And that I should trust my father, that you would come to get me."

*To trust her father, Mike.*

"Are you going to arrest me?" Linda asked.

I should have spoken to her like a father. Told her that Michele wouldn't have acted as she did, but I understood her. And told her that Mike would have acted as she did, but wouldn't have understood her, as he'd never understood her exceptional mother.

The kitesurfer did a splendid turn westward, where the rays of the setting sun were shining over the sea and the sky was beginning to turn red.

"There's no proof," I said. "I've destroyed the DVDs and I'm not a policeman anymore. And you couldn't have acted any differently."

"Lena acted my part out brilliantly. She could have been a great actress."

She was smiling as she stared at the earth's curvature where sea and sky met. The sun's red-gold semicircle was starting to sink down and color the sea the same red as the surfer's kite.

I started to feel something that I'd never had time to feel for Laura, her wonderful mother, and that was a sense of responsibility. It's that feeling—sometimes unfair but insuppressible—that leads you to want to spare your children from suffering. But it was difficult. Very difficult.

I turned toward her and looked her in the eye.

"Yes, a great actress."

*She already was, Linda. Many years ago in another time and another world. She was still Marlene, but playing another person.*

I closed my eyes against the sun, as I did on that day many years ago.

She had looked at us fleetingly from behind those large dark glasses, her hair tied up in the usual scarf, and wearing the long linen kaftan that left only her pale white arms bare. A book was protruding from one of her pockets, most probably Nietzsche. She raised an arm halfway up without smiling, a sort of interrupted wave. Then she stopped, as if she'd already done everything possible, turned, and went off at a brisk pace.

Now I knew that those arms were only so white thanks to the cream that Marlene would wash off only minutes later in the shower, and that the wave wasn't a farewell gesture from a mother about to commit suicide. It was a small act of consolation that Marlene Hunt was giving to Mike, the young man she would shortly take to bed to give herself an alibi, and whose mother she'd just killed. She'd pushed her off the cliff that morning and had put on her clothes, scarf, and sunglasses. She'd even fooled Alberto, who'd seen her from a distance, thanks also to her accomplices Farid and Salim, whom she could always blackmail into doing what she wanted. Then, right under my nose, at Wheelus, she'd given the bag with my mother's clothes to William Hunt, who'd just come back from Benghazi. He'd shot over to La Moneta in the inflatable, dressed the body again, because the disappearance of her clothes would have given rise to suspicions, and then dumped her into the sea so that no one would find her until the next day, when the coup d'etat had already taken place. Marlene Hunt had been William Hunt's accomplice. Marlene and no one else.

And I'd given her the alibi that saved her life. The worst side of the truth.

I'd seen Marlene Hunt's eyes in the funerary photograph on the plaque.

*Forgive me for killing your mother, forgive yourself for that afternoon with me, forgive your daughter for killing Mohammed. And please give her no more pain. Ever.*

Marlene killed my mother because she envied her a life she couldn't have herself and to save her husband from a Libyan firing squad. But that version of Marlene Hunt existed only in Mike Balistreri's time, a time when everything was more smothered in the *ghibli*'s sand and colored more red with blood.

*Shall I tell Linda or not?*

Linda held out a brown envelope.

"That man gave it to me in San Francisco to convince me to go to Tripoli. He told me to give it to you, one day."

I took the envelope, tore it open carefully. I immediately recognized the handwriting.

*San Francisco, April 20, 1971*

*Mike,*

*I wanted to write to you after that night when you ran away from Tripoli. And I did write to you in my head every night without being able to put a word of it down on paper. You and I both know that you can be physically close to people every day, but still far apart—like our parents. Or else far apart, and yet emotionally close, like the two of us . . .*

*Today is the day that my thoughts need to be set down on paper, because life has mysterious and wonderful ways that in time help us to understand our lives and each other.*

*One thing always united us: the desire to be different. Me from my mother, you from your father. We loved them as children, but they were everything we didn't want to be. What united us was the certainty that there was no dark side dark enough to separate us.*

*We were wrong, Mike, and you've seen that yourself. You only had to lie to me once for me to stop believing you. If our judgments are absolute ones, then our mistakes are unpardonable. And life is impossible for us.*

*That afternoon on La Moneta when Italia went out to the cliff, we were both wrong. You should have gone to your father and I to my mother to ask them what was going on.*

*Instead, we did the opposite.*

*As soon as you and my mother left with Farid and Salim, I made a decision. I went into the villa and sat outside the living room, where your father was alone for nearly two hours. Then I spoke with him for an hour. I won't tell you what was said. But immediately after that conversation, I went up to the cliff to talk to Italia.*

*Her book was open on the ground beside the chair, but your mother had already disappeared.*

*My parents would never send you this letter, so I'll give it to Karim, who is here. He is only a friend to me, but a very good friend. I trust that he'll find a way to get it to you.*

*Good-bye, my love, take care of our child.*

Linda looked at me with a questioning air.

"A note from your mother, with advice I intend to follow. But it's private, if you don't mind."

Love is stronger than evil. Always. And the future is more important than the past.

The kitesurfer performed another risky maneuver and ended up in the water. Instinctively I was about to get up, but Linda put a hand on my arm.

"He can manage without your help."

She smiled and her hand brushed mine. I felt empty but not tired; melancholic but not sad. I was happy sitting next to my daughter, just like Michelino that day in 1958 when I was sitting between Laura and Italia, Linda's mother and grandmother, with Domenico Modugno singing "Volare": *that dream does not come back ever again.*

A few seconds later the kitesurfer was again gliding across the water toward the shore, while the sun's last sliver glimmered in the autumn twilight and around us the first lights were coming on.

# ACKNOWLEDGMENTS

M y thanks firstly to my editors, Marco Di Marco and Jacopo De Michelis, who have shown even more patience than usual.

For help with reconstructing places and settings, I would like to thank the following: ex-Consul Guido De Sanctis for Tripoli in 2011, where he was stationed during the bombs and the shooting; journalist Pietro Suber for the adventurous sea trip between Benghazi and Misurata; Salah Omar for Cairo in 1967, a city of the living and the dead; and Moses Juma for present-day Nairobi. Thanks also to Professor Maurizio Bellacosa for assistance with legal aspects and to Carabinieri Colonel Luigi Ripani, head of Forensic Investigations (RIS) in Rome for assistance with investigative procedure.

And lastly, two friends who know they made an enormous contribution. They wish to remain anonymous and certainly neither of them needs the publicity.

## ABOUT THE TYPE

Typeset in Adobe Garamond at 11.5/15 pt.

Adobe Garamond is named for the famed sixteenth-century French printer Claude Garamond. Robert Slimbach created this serif face for Adobe based on Garamond's designs, as well as the designs of Garamond's assistant, Robert Granjon.

Typeset and book design by Scribe Inc.,
Philadelphia, Pennsylvania.